KISS
HER
GOODBYE

Also by Lisa Gardner

Novels

The Perfect Husband
The Other Daughter
The Third Victim
The Next Accident
The Survivors Club
The Killing Hour
Alone
Gone
Hide
Say Goodbye
The Neighbor
Live to Tell
Love You More
Catch Me
Touch & Go
Fear Nothing
Crash & Burn
Find Her
Right Behind You
Look for Me
Never Tell
When You See Me
Before She Disappeared
One Step Too Far
Still See You Everywhere

Short Works

The 7th Month
3 Truths and a Lie
The 4th Man
The Guy Who Died Twice

KISS
HER
GOODBYE

LISA
GARDNER

C

CENTURY

CENTURY

UK | USA | Canada | Ireland | Australia
India | New Zealand | South Africa

Century is part of the Penguin Random House group of companies
whose addresses can be found at global.penguinrandomhouse.com

Penguin Random House UK,
One Embassy Gardens, 8 Viaduct Gardens, London SW11 7BW

penguin.co.uk
global.penguinrandomhouse.com

Penguin
Random House
UK

First published in the US by Grand Central Publishing 2025
First published in the UK by Century 2025
001

Printed and bound in Great Britain by Clays Ltd, Elcograf S.p.A.

The authorised representative in the EEA is Penguin Random House Ireland,
Morrison Chambers, 32 Nassau Street, Dublin D02 YH68

A CIP catalogue record for this book is available from the British Library

ISBN: 978–1–529–91711–6 (hardback)
ISBN: 978–1–529–91712–3 (trade paperback)

MIX
Paper | Supporting
responsible forestry
FSC
www.fsc.org   FSC® C018179

Penguin Random House is committed to a sustainable future
for our business, our readers and our planet. This book is made
from Forest Stewardship Council® certified paper.

*In honor of the over one million men and women
of the U.S.-led coalition forces in Afghanistan and their
local Afghan partners, who fought together for a better
future and a safer world. May their efforts not be forgotten.*

KISS
HER
GOODBYE

PROLOGUE

WHEN I WAS A GIRL, I dreamed.

Running through my father's orchard in pursuit of my brother, ten years older and newly returned from school. Shrieking his name when he refuses to slow down, churning my stubby legs harder.

"Farshid, Farshid, Farshid!"

The sound of his laughter floating ahead of me, till suddenly I round a leafy tree heavy with bright red pomegranates and there he is, planted squarely in the middle of the path to sweep me up and swing me around. I giggle. He twirls faster. I laugh and beg him to stop, which only makes him gain speed, till both of us topple to the ground.

We lie in the late fall grass, the sky impossibly blue overhead. In the distance the snow-capped mountains beckon like teeth, while to the other side the flat plains sweep on and on in an endless apron of white-frosted earth. My country is beautiful, but I don't understand any of this yet. I just consider it home.

Collapsed on the ground, my brother tousles my dark hair, then demands to know what sort of trouble his favorite little *shekambu* has been causing.

"I'm not always hungry!"

"Of course you are." He pats my tubby little belly while I scowl at him.

"And I'm not greedy! At least I wouldn't be if I could go to school!"

"You are too young."

"How do you know?"

"Because schools have rules, everyone knows that."

"I don't know that. See, you must take me to school so that I can study these things."

"You want to go to school to learn why you can't go to school?"

"Exactly!"

"Soon, *shekambu*, soon. Next year you can have lessons on anything you want. Just remember that when the sun is calling and you're stuck with a pile of boring texts."

I wrinkle my nose, because I know already there's no such thing as boring texts. There are only wonderful and more wonderful novels to read. I've already learned this from my father, a literature professor in Kabul who practically lives with his nose stuck between pages, and my mother, who spends each night flipping through glossy fashion magazines before retiring to her sewing machine to tackle her next inspiration.

I have my own stack of brightly colored children's books. I diligently peruse them when my parents are watching, then steal from their piles when they are not. I love words. All words. I love ideas. All ideas. I love worlds. All worlds.

I love this world, and my larger-than-life big brother and brilliant *baba jan* and gorgeous *maadar jan* and crowds of aunts, *uncles, cousins who talk too loudly and lecture too much and swirl through our lives as busily and prettily as petals in the wind. We live part of the year in a walled compound in the hustle and bustle of Kabul and the other months in my father's favorite place on earth, his country estate in Herat, where roses bloom and the orchards bear fruit and there are so many places for a little shekambu and her brother to run wild and free.*

Two halves of one whole, my mādar calls us. And this sunny afternoon, lying side by side in the shade of a bushy pomegranate tree, that feels exactly right.

When I was a girl, I dreamed.

During the school year, my father trims his sharply pointed beard and buttons up his vest before heading to the university each morning. Half out the door, a distracted, befuddled mess, he will pause, turn back around.

He and my mother share a look. My brother and I have studied it many times. It is their look. We don't understand it, but on some level, we know it's good and we're happy they have it.

Then my father heads off to teach, while my mother prepares more tea for her and me to enjoy. Her long black hair is carefully coiffed and pinned at the nape of her neck. Her brown skin is flawless, her dark brows perfect arches framing her lustrous gray eyes. My mother is beautiful. Everyone says so, even my aunts, though they fuss over her choice in clothes and make faces that communicate both stern disapproval and powerful longing.

My mother loves fashion. She reads, she studies, she designs. Late into the night, I can hear her sewing machine whirring away.

In a matter of days, she'll produce the next stylish outfit, an ode to decades past and cities far away such as Paris, London, New York.

My mother never just goes to the market. It's an adventure of high art, where she'll riffle through piles of beads, rows of shoes, and boxes of hats in order to perfectly punctuate her chosen ensemble.

"Chin up," she states each time we prepare to depart, her in a perfect hat, me in a coordinating hajib. We exit my family's compound to enter a sea of bustling humanity, where waves of Western blue jeans and dull-colored tunics part before my mother's sapphire wrap dress or saffron-colored jumpsuit. Like my aunties, the other shoppers eye my mother with expressions that are a mix of awe and disapproval. Some gazes, under the thickly furrowed brows of darkly dressed men, follow her too long and too intently. Their stares are filled with a kind of heat I don't understand and already don't like. But when my mother catches them, she stops and skewers them with a look of her own, till one by one, they glance away.

My mother has many duties at the market. Picking out perfect cucumbers and ripe tomatoes for the evening's chopped salad. Inspecting the fresh herbs for just the right bundle of mint. But there are other activities, too. A pause here, a whisper there. A discreet passing of one palm across another. Like children everywhere, I know when to fade into the background.

Later my mother will smile at me and nod approvingly.

And I know we share something special, just like her and my father with their parting glance. So I never speak of these moments, not even with Farshid, who rolls his eyes and groans over how much time women spend in the market.

One day, I want to be just like my maadar jan. I will never be as beautiful but maybe, just maybe, I can be as clever.

When I was a girl, I dreamed.

The whispers start when I turn twelve.

Always behind closed doors. First my father and my mother. Then my aunts and uncles flitting about. Everyone talking, talking, talking. But no one saying anything.

My brother, returning home from his university studies. Additional murmurs behind my parents' bedroom doors, where my mother spends more and more of her days.

Pale when she comes out. Exhausted when she returns.

My auntie, Fahima, a hawkish older woman with a relentless attention to detail, starts meeting me each day after school. Stand taller. Don't read that. Don't look at him. Don't touch that. Don't, don't, don't, don't.

Her fashion tastes run to flowing trousers and plain billowing blouses with a simple dark hijab covering her hair.

I want my mother. I miss her warm smile and outrageous outfits and fierce stare. But my mādar appears only long enough to disappear. A sudden shadow of her former self, patting my cheek, stroking my hair, telling me I'm pretty today—which we both know is a lie—before retiring once again to rest.

Whispers.

In our house, the city, my country, where Blackhawk choppers now circle overhead and concrete barricades expand daily, along with checkpoint after checkpoint, until a walk to the local market feels as arduous as a border crossing. The American soldiers are leaving. Our own forces will now protect us, though safe doesn't feel so safe anymore.

Within a matter of months, my father summons me to the hallway outside my parents' room. My brother is present but doesn't meet my eye.

"Your mother wants to speak to you," my father states, his voice thick. He points to the cracked door, indicating I should go in. But my feet won't move. For once in my life, I don't want to know. Whatever awaits on the other side, there won't be any books that will be able to fix this.

I gaze at my brother pleadingly, but he keeps his attention fixed on the floor.

"Two halves of one whole," I try.

"Not this time, Sabera. Not this time."

My father pushes the door open. Slowly, I force myself to step inside.

"Janem."

My mother utters the term of endearment as half whisper, half sigh. I follow her hushed voice through the shadowed space till I'm just able to make out her face in a room where the drapes are tightly drawn and the bed piled high with blankets.

"Janem," she murmurs again. The covers shift. She reaches out a hand so skeletal it's painful to see. Her fingertips, light as feathers, dance across my forearm. She finds my wrist, clasps it lightly.

"Don't," I tell her. But I don't mean for her to stop holding me. I mean for her not to say what she's going to say. I mean for her not to leave me.

I drop to my knees, placing my forehead against the mattress, clasping her hand to my cheek. If I don't let go, she will have to stay. The future will not happen. My mādar will always be mine.

She speaks, a dry rustle of words spinning around me. That she loves me. That I'm beautiful and strong and she's very proud. That I am her daughter in every way possible, and she will always be with me, that voice in the back of my head, that feeling of warmth in my chest.

I can't answer. I bathe her fingers in my tears. I clasp her bony hand tighter, as if that will make a difference.

Then she says what I've always feared. She states the words that expose our little secret, a deathbed confession involving the one piece of our relationship I've always known is mine and mine alone. And I hate this, too. It makes what will happen next too real, this passing of the guard as secret keeper from her to me.

"You know." Her words are soft. A statement of fact. "You have seen."

I bite my lip, sullen and resentful. If I refuse to speak of the market, acknowledge everything that happens, then she will have to stay. I'm certain of it.

She seems to understand, stroking my cheek soothingly.

"Do you understand it all?" she asks me. "You've always been the cleverest girl. Watching from the sidelines. Your brother suspects, but you, janem, you peer beneath the surface, connecting what shouldn't connect, identifying a whole where others see only parts. You remind me of me, when I was a child."

"Mādar—"

"Shh, while I can still speak, this is what you must know: You cannot trust your uncles. Your father is too gentle. They will bend him to their will, and he will not understand the danger until it's too late. Never trust men who fatten their bellies off other people's pain. And never, ever, believe any man knows what's best for you. Even when they come from a place of love." A pause. "Especially when they come from a place of love.

"You and only you will clean out my sewing room."

I nod helplessly.

"You will be troubled, and I'm sorry. You will feel you're too young for such a burden, but you're strong and powerful, janem. You will find your way."

Her fingers squeeze mine. She raises her head to gaze at me with a fierceness I didn't know she had left.

"You will tell no one. Do you understand? Not even Farshid. You can peer into other people's souls, my sweet. But never let them see yours."

I open my mouth. I want to say no, to selfishly refuse such a giant and terrifying ask.

But it's too late. My mother's head falls back against the pillows, the exhaustion like an extra blanket weighing her down.

She slips her hand from mine, draws a thin line through the tears on my cheek. "Should the worst happen, people will want to take everything, but in the end, they will be allowed nothing. Remember this, my sweet. Remember."

I break down, sobbing, begging, demanding that she stay. She pats my back once, twice, three times. Then she gently pushes me away.

Her gray eyes stare straight into mine. Clear, purposeful.

She states: "Chin up."

And that's it. My father appears with my brother. More aunts and uncles and cousins. Until with a last exhale, my mother passes, her hand tucked into my father's, while my brother and I kneel with our heads against her feet. My father's wail is the first to crack the silence. Then we are all sobbing and moaning: Oh my God, I am dying, I can't live without you, why have you left us, oh God, please please I'm sorry I wasn't a better husband, sister, daughter, son.

We collapse over her body and howl our pain to the heavens.
She is gone from us. Gone from me.
When I was a girl, I dreamed.

Later, I clean out my mother's sewing room. I don't understand everything I find. But I realize enough.

More choppers roar across the minaret-studded skyline, and blast walls are built higher while roadside bombings become so common we barely flinch at the sound, just round our shoulders and scurry home.

My classmates exchange horrible tales of things going on in the outlying towns. A growing resurgence of Taliban fighters executing policemen, annihilating entire villages. Females dousing themselves in gasoline and setting themselves on fire to escape forced marriages. Even more women, schoolteachers, reporters, doctors, disappearing in the middle of the night.

And yet still we flit from coffee shop to coffee shop, post photos to our Facebook page, chat away on our cell phones. Because this is Kabul. The insurgents would never dare to attack here.

My brother, Farshid, disappears for longer and longer periods of time, returning home covered in dust and staggering in exhaustion. He cloisters himself in my father's study with the rest of the men, where low whispers and harsh exclamations reverberate down the hall.

They are arguing next steps. My mother's right—my father's too gentle for his brothers' avarice. They have worked too hard, built too much, to leave all their worldly goods behind. They will defend if they have to, bribe their way through the rest. There's still plenty of time to determine best options, they rashly insist.

Never mind that they have made enemies of nearly everyone, including our neighbors. And while my father might be more kindly regarded, he's also well known for his outspoken views on women's rights. The current government finds him annoying; in the eyes of the Taliban, he's downright dangerous.

In war, there are winners and losers. If Kabul falls, my family won't be on the winning side.

One day, I discover Farshid striding through the courtyard with an armful of rifles, his expression so grim it hurts. There's so much I want to tell him, but I remain bound by my mother's words.

"Farshid," I try.

"Not now, Sabera."

"If there's anything I can do to help ..."

"Go to school, Sabera. Study, learn, grow that stubborn mind of yours that enjoys torturing me so much. You do your job. I'll do mine. I will keep you safe, Sabera," he states darkly. "Trust me."

"I will keep you safe, too, Farshid. Two halves of one whole, yes?"

He smiles softly. "Two halves of one whole," he agrees. And for a moment, we are kids again, running through my father's orchard, and all is right with the world.

When I was a girl, I dreamed.

And now, with the Blackhawks thundering overhead, and the packed streets of Kabul exploding with the frantic cries of desperate people, I take the gun from my brother's lifeless hands. He has fallen outside the wall of our compound, his face a mask of blood and dust. I already know what I'll find inside will be even worse.

And yet, it still won't be the most terrible sight I've seen today, as I've raced frantically from the university to my father's house.

One man. I can still feel his eyes upon me from down the crowded street. His hand reaching out. His final aching look. And then…a single crack of a rifle. All it takes to end a life. Destroy a future. Orphan a child.

There's no time now. Maybe never will be again.

More screaming, families frantically forcing their way down streets that are no longer passable by car, lugging small children on their backs while dragging their most treasured possessions behind. Gunshots in the distance cause another terrified surge forward. Pockets of resistance being overrun. Petty grievances being settled. A young boy falls, an older relative scoops him up. The panicked mass of humanity churns ahead.

I enter my family's compound. My father is sprawled across the front steps. These are not gunshot wounds. I can't bear to think of it as I close his eyes, rock back on my heels, moaning.

"Oh God, why have you taken my daddy from me? I am dying, I can't live without you. I'm so sorry. I should've been a better daughter. I'm sorry, I'm sorry, I'm sorry."

But my ablutions change nothing. He's gone, while outside the chaos looms closer.

I continue on, finding one of my uncles in the front parlor, while down the hall my aunt Fahima is on her knees, wailing over her husband's body. When I try to approach, she hits me so hard, I stumble backward. I leave her to her grief, as I search room by room, rifle clenched tightly in my hands. The fight was heavy and fierce. There are bodies of men I've never met and already hate, though they're now gone from this earth.

The thunder of more choppers overhead, followed by the sound of explosions.

I end in my parents' room. I touch the edge of the bed where my mother died. I feel her hand in mine. I remember the taste of my tears upon my lips. The words she spoke to me.

"Should the worst happen, people will want to take everything, but in the end, they will be allowed nothing."

I understand now. I understand everything, including what there's still left to lose.

I take a quick moment to sort through my mother's jewelry box, then rummage through my father's study. I select a single necklace from my mother. A single book from my father. I don't expect to keep them, but they will serve their purpose along the way.

Then, I square my shoulders, raise my brother's rifle, and face the front door.

"Chin up," I murmur.

I run for it.

When I was a girl, I dreamed.

When I became a woman, I woke up.

CHAPTER 1

M Y FRIEND'S NAME IS SABERA. She's been gone for three weeks. You will find her. Here, try this."

My hostess, Aliah, picks up a pretty blue bowl and holds it out. The coffee table in front of me is covered with similar dishes, all in deep jewel tones with scrolling gold patterns that shimmer beneath the overhead lights. The overall effect is less an offering of treats than a scattering of gems. It's made me hesitant to touch anything.

Aliah's two-bedroom apartment in downtown Tucson may be a relatively modest affair, but her hospitality is clearly world-class.

I dip my fingers into the proffered bowl, tentatively extracting a few pieces of dried fruit. They resemble shriveled white blackberries, which is to say I have no idea what they are. So far, that's par for the course. I've spent the past ten minutes watching Aliah perform some kind of elaborate ceremony that resulted in the best cup of tea I've ever had—saffron, she informs me, which tastes just as good as it smells.

To accompany the tea is a dizzying array of nuts, dried fruits, crunchy chickpeas, and bright candies, all placed elegantly around a magnificent centerpiece of fresh whole fruit.

I sample the first wizened berry in my hand. Sweet, tart. I like it, follow it with more. Aliah nods in approval.

"Toot khoshk. White mulberries. They're my favorite. Here."

She hands me a shiny green pear. "Eat, eat. It's good for you."

I bite into the fruit, juice dribbling down my chin, while Aliah takes my plate and dishes up little piles of almonds, raisins, and hard-coated candies, then hands it back. She's very serious about this eating business, especially as there are just the two of us present, and she's laid out enough snacks to feed an entire elementary school.

As new case meetings go, this one is off to an auspicious start. Of course, I met my last client at a maximum-security prison where she was serving time on Death Row. Not too hard to beat that.

Aliah had found me through a friend of a friend, which was pretty good considering I don't have many friends. I was enjoying a long-overdue hiatus that had brought me all the way to Seattle when I got her call. Maybe I shouldn't have answered the phone. Maybe it's the true measure of my obsession that even happy and well rested for the first time in years, I clicked answer. Or maybe it's the full degree of my self-destructive streak that led me to say yes to her, and no to him, even though it hurt us both.

I'm not one to look back. At least, for the past twenty-four hours that's what I've been telling myself.

And now I'm at a charming tea party in Arizona.

My specialty is working missing persons cold cases. I can't tell you exactly why I take on this particular mission versus that one. Given there are hundreds of thousands of people who've disappeared at any given time, I might as well be throwing darts at a board. Money is not a factor—I don't charge for my services as I'm not a trained professional, just a woman with an obsessive hobby. Geography is also a moot point—I don't have a home, family, or real job, meaning I can go anywhere at any time.

Some people might find my lifestyle concerning. What kind of idiot dedicates herself to finding people she's never met in cities she's never frequented at the behest of complete strangers she'll never see again? I've spent the past ten years trying to answer that question. If only I knew.

In Aliah's case, the timeline sparked my interest. Her friend, a fellow Afghan, vanished three weeks ago. Definitely not my usual cold case terrain. In fact, not enough time had passed to motivate the police to search overly hard or alarm the husband enough to launch his own efforts.

The combination of searching for a missing refugee—exactly the kind of at-risk population that's often overlooked—as well as possibly discovering someone still alive proved compelling enough to bring me here. That doesn't mean, however, that I'm completely on board yet. In my line of work—okay, in my kind of hobby—it pays to be skeptical. People lie. Endangered people who live in marginalized communities often have a tendency to lie even more, with good reason.

"Look," I attempt now, setting down my pear, sampling another one of the ridiculously good dried mulberries, "you say your friend has disappeared, but you seem to be the only one who's worried about her. Why are you so certain she hasn't run off with another man, taken a mental health break, whatever? Didn't you say she'd just immigrated to the US? That's got to be a little traumatic."

"Of course, Sabera's overwhelmed. In the beginning, we all

are. But she has a daughter. No mother leaves her child, especially not after fighting so hard to get here."

"What do you mean by fight?"

"There are thirty million refugees in the world. Do you know how many are actually granted placement, a chance at a fresh start?"

"Not many?"

"Barely one percent. Sabera and her husband are the lucky few, and they know it."

I nod. "Fair enough. But fortunate or not, their stress level has gotta be real."

"She would not leave her daughter," Aliah insists. "Zahra is only four. She needs her mother, especially now that they're in a new country."

"What about Sabera's husband? The guy who's not even looking for her yet?"

"It's not a love match," Aliah confirms, her scowl returning.

"How long have they been married?"

"Four years."

Married four years with a four-year-old kid. I can't help but arch a brow. Aliah merely shrugs. "My understanding is that Isaad was a friend of her father's. They had just gotten married when Kabul fell. Isaad was able to get Sabera out of the country. Her family was not so lucky."

"What happened to them?"

"They're dead."

"All of them?" I can't quite keep the shock from my voice.

Aliah gives me a look. "Sabera is a refugee," she repeats. "Not a tourist."

"Walk me through this," I say at last. "When did Sabera and her family arrive in Tucson? Where are they staying? When did you last see her, that kind of thing."

"They arrived ten weeks ago from Abu Dhabi."

"Why Abu Dhabi?"

"After Kabul fell, they bounced from a temporary refugee camp in Islamabad to a larger one in Abu Dhabi, where they awaited official status. It's a process."

"And you went through something like this?" I ask Aliah, who appears closer to fifty than twenty.

"I went through something like this twenty-five years ago, the first time Kabul fell to the Taliban."

Her tone is hard. I don't blame her. "So how did you get to know Sabera?"

"There are local agencies that greet all arriving refugees and help them settle into their new lives. I'm a volunteer with one such agency here in Tucson. In particular, I try to assist with fellow Afghans. In this case, I prepared the Ahmadi family's apartment for their arrival—stocked it with tea, basic spices, halal meats, yogurt, that sort of thing. Enough to see them through the first week, while they're having to learn everything all at once."

"Are they also in this complex?" I gesture outside to the U-shaped collection of yellow-painted stucco buildings bordered by pretty blooming flowers and odd-shaped cacti.

"Oh, no." Aliah shakes her head. "There's money for assistance, but it only lasts a few months. Most refugees start out in a far different level of housing. I got my first apartment because the last tenant was murdered in it."

My eyes widen. "And the police are still certain nothing bad happened to your friend? I mean, given what you're saying about where she was living…"

"The police aren't certain of anything. They would have to genuinely consider Sabera's disappearance to reach such a conclusion, and so far, they can't be bothered."

"Why?"

"All refugees must immediately get a job. Money is important, yes?"

I nod.

"The resettlement agencies help with job placement, too. They have connections with employers who are open to hiring more refugees—for example, they have had success with Afghan housekeepers in the past, so are willing to hire more. Plus it's convenient to have their workforce living close together and speaking the same language. Means a large resort or construction company can send a single shuttle to round up all its workers in the morning."

I nod again, having witnessed such things in other cities.

"Sabera got a job in housekeeping at a big hotel. After the first week, the police went there to ask questions. Her fellow chambermaids reported that Sabera told them she was leaving her husband. She wanted a divorce. For the officers, that was good enough."

"But you don't believe it."

A slight shrug. "It happens. Trauma, hardship, stress is very hard on marriages. Couples get here, where suddenly everything is new, they are new...It happens. But there's no good reason for Sabera to leave her daughter behind."

"Or she's waiting to come back for her daughter when she has a place to stay. Could she afford an apartment on her own, given what you're saying about limited funds?"

"It would be very difficult. Certainly, if that was her plan, she'd need to continue to work."

"Except she hasn't returned to work?"

"No."

"Or her family?"

"No."

I'm beginning to see Aliah's point. "What does her husband say?"

Aliah's lips thin into a hard line of disapproval. "He says he's sure she'll be back shortly."

"She'll be back shortly? Like what, she went out for a walk? And the cops accept this?"

Another sniff of disdain, which is answer enough.

"Has she reached out to you?" I ask.

"No."

"Would she? If she needed help, had decided to leave her husband, would she contact you?"

A slight pause. "I would hope so. I'm divorced. She knows that."

Back to answers that aren't really answers. I tilt my head, study my hostess again. She's an attractive woman with wavy black hair cut short to frame her face. There are crinkles next to her dark eyes, lines furrowing her brow. But the effect enhances her beauty, gives an overall sense of strong will and determination. She's seen some things, lived some experiences, survived some hardships. She's not about to break now.

Would that be comforting for a young female immigrant such as Sabera, or overwhelming?

I gotta believe the police had to be a tiny bit interested if Sabera hadn't even returned to work. Unless her fellow chambermaids had provided additional details Aliah either doesn't know or doesn't want to share.

"How good is Sabera's English?" I change tack.

"Excellent. Her mother's people are from London. Sabera grew up speaking English as well as Dari and Pashto, which are the two most prominent languages in Afghanistan. She's also a skilled linguist, fluent in many languages, not to mention dialects."

"In other words, language is not an issue."

"No. Nor is the culture shock as significant for her as it is for others. Her father taught at the university in Kabul, while her mother was a noted fashion designer. The household was very Westernized. Certainly, her parents were progressive enough to support Sabera pursuing her own studies. Though of course..."

"She grew up in a professional, affluent family." I fill in the blanks. "Meaning it can't be the easiest thing to now be living in a run-down apartment while working as a housekeeper."

"This is not the end; it is the beginning," Aliah recites.

"Of?"

"Your new life in America. I was a nurse back in Afghanistan. When I first came here, I wasn't allowed in the medical field. I washed dishes in the back of a restaurant for pennies on the dollar. People think all refugees can do is drive taxis or scrub toilets. No, it's generally the only thing we're *allowed* to do. Do you know how many doctors, lawyers, engineers, and pilots have come over from Afghanistan in the past few years? And yet our professional degrees and licenses are not accepted here." She shrugs. "We must adapt. It's not easy, but it's the only option. And Sabera was committed to making life in this country work. For her daughter, if for nothing else."

"Where was Sabera last seen?"

"Leaving work. She'd stayed late, missed the employee shuttle, so she was headed to the bus stop."

"Did she get on?"

"You would have to ask the police that."

I nod, thinking. "And she has a cell phone? Everyone does now."

"Yes, with prepaid minutes."

"Ahh, a woman after my own heart. No one's tried pinging her GPS?"

"Again, you would have to ask the police."

"Or her husband?"

"Sure." Aliah's skepticism is palpable.

I pause, looking around me at this bountiful spread in a lovely, well-tended apartment with its stunning mix of richly colored tapestries and a comfy sofa set. If Aliah had started out scrubbing pots when she'd first arrived in this country, then she had adapted well indeed.

I haven't made up my mind yet, but I have a final question, often the most telling. "Why?" I ask, keeping my gaze upon my hostess's face.

"Why what?"

"Why do you want to find her? The police aren't interested, her husband isn't concerned, but you care enough to reach out to a perfect stranger to help your friend. Why?"

"You find people who can't be found," Aliah states.

"I find people no one else is looking for." I don't know why it's important for me to make that distinction, but it is.

"Exactly." Aliah nods. "And no one else is looking. Do you know what it's like to be an outsider? To watch your entire country disappear? To see your sisters, mothers, daughters be erased? As if they never even existed? That's now life in Afghanistan. For the second time. It shouldn't be life here. Sabera deserves better. And so does her daughter."

I stare into Aliah's dark, somber eyes. "Okay."

"You will look for Sabera? I'll pay you. Just tell me how much."

"That's not how this works. Let me be clear up front—I work for the missing, in this case for Sabera. That's the way I always do it. Family, friends, even the ones who invite me in." I gesture at her. "Once I start asking questions, not everyone likes me so much anymore. That could grow to include you."

Aliah tilts her chin defiantly. "I'm not afraid."

"Excellent." I set down my tea mug, rise to standing. "What do you think happened? Off the top of your head, what happened to your friend?"

"I…" A frown, that slight hesitation again. "I think maybe her husband. I can't be sure, but then again, isn't it always the husband?"

"Often seems that way." But what makes her answer most interesting is the raw bravado behind it. It's not clear to me that she believes what she's saying as much as she *wants* to believe what she's saying. Basically, I've no sooner said yes than my initial contact is dissembling.

A smart person would walk away now. A sane person would get a real job, maybe even an apartment, and if not a healthy and stable relationship, at least a cat.

And yet I don't even hesitate. I hold out my phone and request Sabera's mobile number, apartment address, recent photo, and name of her employer. Aliah gratefully provides those details, then adds the name of the family's caseworker and housing coordinator from the resettlement agency.

Just like that, I'm back to work.

My name is Frankie Elkin, and finding missing people is what I do. When the police have given up, when the public no longer remembers, when the media has never bothered to care, I start looking. For no money, no recognition, and most of the time, no help.

My mission has taken me all over the country, from inner-city neighborhoods to the wilds of Wyoming to even a brief stint in paradise. I've been cursed at, shot at, and nearly killed. I've watched people die. I've assisted with some of those deaths.

Clearly, I'm not a woman who learns from her mistakes.

Recently, I took a long-deserved hiatus to recover from a particularly horrific case, spending the time with a truly amazing guy. It was so good, it was even great. Yet still, when my phone rang…

From the very beginning, he whispered against my neck, *I knew you weren't the staying kind.*

Because that's also who I am. A woman with an inherent separateness I'll never be able to shake. So that no matter how hard I try, I will always be the outsider looking in. Some people understand real life. Then there's me.

A person who searches for the missing.

And who will always be the first to disappear.

CHAPTER 2

FIRST ORDER OF BUSINESS WHEN beginning a case: figure out employment and lodging in whatever city is about to become my temporary new home. Walking down the sidewalk from Aliah's apartment with all my worldly possessions—a brown leather messenger bag and a small rolling suitcase—I squint against the blazing desert sun and do my best to get my bearings.

In the less than twenty-four hours I've been in Tucson, I've already figured out a few things. One, that whole "at least it's dry heat" is a load of hooey. Mid-October, the mercury is still topping ninety, and I'm already sweating profusely after walking only three blocks. Even if it's slightly better than the tropical rain forest environment of my last venture, searing versus sweltering is hardly a consolation.

Two, it's sprawling. The city itself seems to stretch on forever. Long, expansive avenues; short, squat buildings; endlessly unfurling sidewalks lined with palm trees, mesquite, and palo verde. The green contrasts nicely with one of the other main features of Tucson—it's brown. Brown adobe houses with brown scorched-earth yards encircled by brown towering mountains. If I were more poetic, maybe I'd note the pinkish-red highlights or soft gray undertones, but I'm too tired and thirsty to care.

My final sad observation: the homeless epidemic has spread here as well, given the number of unkempt individuals planted in the middle of the broad avenues, begging for money at traffic lights. Most appear on the younger side, with the gaunt, haunted look of addicts.

I don't judge—I've spent enough years in AA to know better than to take my own sobriety for granted. Speaking for myself, I fight my demons on a daily, if not hourly, basis.

Which brings me back to the matter of finding a job. Ironically, my one employable skill is bartending. Maybe not the best choice for a recovering alcoholic, but being around booze isn't a major trigger for me. Getting up each morning is.

I make my way to a strip mall anchored by a massive grocery store. I'm grateful to step into air-conditioning, even if it has me shivering in a matter of seconds. I'm even more grateful to discover a local rag with a classified section.

I pause long enough to shrug on my worn green army jacket and purchase a bottle of water. Then I get to work.

Aliah hadn't been kidding; the rents I see listed are high and higher. I'm not exactly flush with cash. Taking into account that most reputable places would require first month and last month rent plus a security deposit, and I'm officially priced out of this market.

I switch to studying employment options. Good news, looks like every bar, restaurant, and hotel is desperate for workers. Which should be to my advantage, except doing some basic math on what I'd make in a month still leaves me in the red when it comes to housing. Yet another reoccurring variable I encounter across more and more of the country.

Fortunately, being a nomad of some experience, I know a few tricks—search for gigs that include housing. None jump out in the want ads, but no matter. I fire up my prepaid cell phone and spend some precious minutes visiting two websites that specialize in such exchanges—labor for rent.

One immediately jumps out at me. House/pet-sitting duties for one month, lodging included. With nothing to lose, I hit dial.

"Hello?" The voice on the other end is male, sounds younger than I would've expected, and is definitely frazzled.

"I'm calling about—"

"Yes! Can you start today? Excellent, you're hired!"

This level of enthusiasm is a little off-putting. "Um, just so we're clear, I don't have much pet-sitting experience unless a feral cat or flower-loving crab count."

"Do you have a pulse?"

"I'm pretty sure—"

"Great, I'm sending the driver."

"There's a driver?"

"And a swimming pool. An entire estate, actually. You'll love it. Definitely, absolutely, yes, you will *love* it!"

The man/kid sounds so desperate, I feel compelled to at least humor him.

"My location for the driver—"

"No worries, I already have it."

"How?" Belatedly I stare at my cell phone. "You can do that?"

"Driver will be there in twenty!" the kid says, and ends the call before I can utter another word.

Apparently, I now have an employment and housing opportunity all rolled into one. I'm already willing to bet I'm not tending something as simple as a cute puppy or fluffy kitty. But really, given some of my past rooming situations, how bad can this be?

"WHAT THE HELL is that?"

"Petunia. Isn't she beautiful?"

My mouth opens, my lips move. No words come out. Though I now totally understand Boy Wonder's hiring enthusiasm, or maybe it's more like panic.

Driver came. Built like a bruiser and dressed in a Blues Brothers black suit to go with the sleek black sedan and luxurious black interior. I got my own personal climate zone, while the sedan purred its way out of the concrete-and-stucco city into the cactus-and brush-covered foothills. We wound our way up to a massive wrought-iron gate that seamlessly gave way to a long, curved driveway leading to a fountain and what appeared to be a luxury hotel but I quickly realized was a single-family home/estate.

Owned by a kid who didn't look a day older than fifteen, but apparently is actually twenty-seven.

The driver, who clearly wasn't paid to speak, led me through a two-story marble foyer to a kitchen that was roughly the size of a gymnasium and decorated in a distinctly Mediterranean style. It also sounded like a summer meadow. Crickets, I realized, chirping away from various nooks and crannies.

Which may or may not have something to do with the room's main occupant. The driver, I notice, remained rooted in the doorway.

"Have you ever had an iguana?" the kid, scruffy beard, ripped jeans, and worn gray T-shirt declaring *Don't have a cow, man,* asks me hopefully.

"Uh...no."

"They're amazing pets! Some consider them to be the bunnies of the lizard world. I wouldn't recommend a male. They can be pretty territorial and aggressive, which you know, given their ripping claws and razor-sharp teeth, can lead to problems. But Petunia here has been hand-reared by humans since birth. She's a giant love."

Petunia, all four to five green feet of her, is currently slumbering in a bright sunbeam pouring through the sliders. At the sound of her name, she cracks open one golden eye while the spikes running down her back briefly flare, then settle. Like she's pleased by the attention. Or preparing to attack.

"Now, for care and feeding," the man child continues.

"I'm sorry, your name again?"

"Uh, I'm Bart." He gestures to his T-shirt as if that should've been a clue. I got the reference, didn't realize it was a statement.

"And you are?"

He blinks dark brown eyes behind wire-framed glasses. "The homeowner." His voice has grown sharper.

I can't help myself. I gesture around me. "As in..."

"Yeah, mine, mine, all mine. Including Petunia. Look, you know anything about gaming systems?"

I shake my head.

"Well, I do. So yeah, mine, mine, and all mine. Speaking of which, I gotta vamos sooner versus later. Major gaming conference, world tour, already two days late given what happened to my last caretaker—"

"Petunia didn't eat the pet sitter, did she?"

"Nah, fucking idiot got bitten by a hot."

"I have no idea what that means."

"Venomous snake," Bart fills in at my blank expression. "His own, no less. I mean seriously, if he can't handle his own snakes, why would I want him handling mine?"

"Wait a sec—"

"So Petunia here. Super simple. She eats once a day, basically a salad of rough chopped fresh veggies sprinkled with a special calcium plus vitamin D powder. I have the next two days prepped, which should get you off and running. Fresh water is very important, as well as her mister. Ahh, just to be clear, don't walk around with a banana peel or apple core or, really, any kind of fruit or veggie refuse in your hand. Iguanas are primarily herbivores, but sometimes they're herbivores with really bad aim. Hand, peel. Peel, hand. Just don't do it, okay?"

Bart is already on the go. He walks past Petunia in bare feet. I edge behind her with as much distance between myself and her long, pointed tail as possible. I wonder if mango-scented sunscreen counts the same as holding a scrap of mango. If so…

There's nothing about this conversation I find comforting.

At the end of the kitchen, a glass corridor opens up, leading to another wing of the mansion. The hallway is carpeted in a tightly woven cream-colored rug, while off to the right side is a small room roughly the size of a den. Except this room features a terrarium theme of lush plants, zigzagging tree limbs, and definitely a tropical misting system. The lower part of one wall appears to be swinging slightly. Some kind of flap, I realize. As in a pet door for an iguana?

"I let Petunia out for most of the day to roam the kitchen and family room. It's important for iguanas to have enrichment and socialization, especially one as domesticated as Petunia."

I hear a noise behind me, turn around. Sure enough, Petunia is standing right there, stretched up tall on her front legs, staring at me with those crazy golden eyes while a large, nearly human-looking tongue lolls out, licks her lips.

I twitch but hold my ground. Never let them see your fear. Isn't that the number one rule when encountering wildlife, including other humans?

"Petunia will wander in and out of her room as she needs. She prefers a humid environment, and I can hardly turn the entire house into a rain forest—especially, you know, given that I'm living in a desert—so this works for her. The flap allows her to go outside when she wants, which helps her get enough UV light. And of course, she has a small pool."

Petunia is still staring at me. "Of course," I manage.

"In the evening, she likes to sit on your lap while you watch TV."

"What?"

"She doesn't always realize her own size," Bart concedes. "Really, she rests her front half on your legs, which is your hint to rub her shoulders."

"Wh-wh—" I can't get the rest of the word out.

"Don't touch the spikes running down her spine. I'd think that much would be obvious? But yeah, rub her shoulders like you'd do with any life-form. She doesn't exactly purr, but you can tell you're doing it right when she, like, totally zens out. Her skin's a little bit rough, a little bit silky. Hard to explain. Up close you can appreciate all her colors, blues, greens, blacks. Even by green iguana standards, she's a beaut."

I don't bother with a reply. I'm pretty sure I've entered a parallel universe, or drifted into a particularly realistic and disturbing nightmare. Which explains Bart's next statement.

"Now, for the snakes."

He turns, marches to the end of the corridor, where there's a single closed door. "First rule of thumb, *never* let Petunia in the snake room." Then for added emphasis, he turns to the lizard in question. "Petunia, stay. You get the rest of the house, pretty girl. But this room is *off-limits*."

Maybe Petunia blinks in acknowledgment. Maybe I drank a magic potion while in the black sedan. Anything is possible.

"All right, your next responsibilities." Bart pops open the distinctly heavy door and marches inside the darkened space. "Meet my babies. And by that, I mean literally. Look, baby ball pythons!"

CHAPTER 3

D O MOTHER PYTHONS THINK THEIR babies are adorable? Isn't there some rule about that? I don't know, because I don't think any snake is adorable. I think snakes should be avoided at all costs. Spiders, fine, if I really have to. Snakes, hard no. Don't approach, don't go near, certainly don't touch.

How the hell did I get in this room?

It's a shadowy space, with the only source of natural light filtering down from narrow windows ringing up top. Against the lower half of two walls sit impressively sized individual terrariums, each sporting heat lamps in one corner.

Good news, occupant of the largest terrarium isn't immediately visible. Less good news, occupants of smaller, split terrarium, very visible. All twelve of them.

"You know anything about ball pythons?"

I don't answer, as I'm too busy swallowing back a primal scream.

"Super docile. Love nothing better than to curl up in the palm of your hand. You know, hence the name. Wanna hold one?"

Furious shake of my head.

"You like snakes at all?" Bart peers at me intently.

I don't care about employment or lodging anymore. Another furious shake of my head.

"No matter, you'll do fine."

Third shake of my head.

Bart continues as if he hadn't seen: "Okay, so again, pretty simple. First rule of snakes, larger they are, easier the care and feeding. Marge over there only eats twice a month. Whereas these gorgeous little minions"—Bart bends down, gazes adoringly at the collection of curled and slithering shapes in mottled shades of light brown and deep black—"these little dudes will require some genuine tending, but nothing any person of basic competence can't handle."

"I'm not competent," I attempt weakly.

"You got here, didn't you? That's competent enough. So: feeder crickets." He's off and running. How every three to five days I should be feeding live crickets to baby pythons. Always after dark. Wear the red headlamp. Use tweezer tongs to offer crickets first to snakes on the move. Ignore those curled up or in hide boxes. Hold cricket still till baby can pluck from tweezers (or I can rip legs off of crickets so they can't hop away. What the fuck?).

Fetch new cricket, he continues breezily. Will know which snakes have eaten by noticeable bulge in their stomachs. Oh, and don't worry about cricket escapees, impossible not to lose a few, hence the meadow-like ambiance throughout the rest of the house.

Once all babies have been fed, leave alone for next few days to digest their meal. When they become noticeably active again, time to eat. Oh, and refresh water and clean cage. Okay, now for Marge, a five-foot-long albino Burmese python, whose yellow head rests atop her massively coiled body.

Marge eats a medium-sized rat every two weeks. Will find them vacuum-sealed in the freezer. Cut open package, dump frozen rodent in mug of hot water. Warm to around a hundred degrees. Using larger tongs, remove now thawed rat from cup, slowly lower into terrarium, and wave gently in front of Marge to get her attention. She will snatch dinner from tongs, and just like that, be all set for the next few weeks.

See, easy peasy. Oh, don't forget to change out the water that sits in the bottom of the terrarium in a giant stainless-steel water bowl. If I'm really squeamish, here's a pair of welder's gloves to use, but really, Marge's a love. All snakes are loves. Just giant docile beauties with gorgeous markings and ill-deserved reputations.

At this point, Bart's talking faster and faster with most sentences ending with an emphatic "Easy peasy!" as if he knows at any moment I'm going to run screaming from the room.

When Marge lifts her head to peer at me through the glass while flicking out her tongue, it doesn't help.

"I can't do this," I finally gasp. "Nope. Not gonna happen. Gotta go. Now. Dear God. Where the hell is the door?"

Bart plants himself in front of me, grabs my shoulders.

"You got this," he declares. "You are a strong, capable person. I have total faith you can feed salad to a lizard once a day, and some miscellaneous crickets and rodents to other reptiles twice a week."

"You don't even know me—"

"You're wearing wrinkled clothes, traveling with a single suitcase, and calling for jobs that provide lodging. Clearly, you just got into town, and you need a place to stay. Given what I can judge by your appearance and already know about Tucson rents, you're not affording anything in this market anytime soon."

"I don't like snakes."

"Why? You ever touch one, hold one, been attacked by one? What you're feeling is nothing but some overactive neurons firing away in your brain in response to a basic primal fear."

"Exactly!"

"You don't want to be ruled by fear, do you?"

"At the moment, doesn't feel like I have much choice in the matter."

"Sure you do! Four weeks. That's all I'm asking. Which is only two feedings for Marge, plus eight or so cricket sessions for the little dudes. Come on, surely you can handle a handful of brief interactions in return for a month of luxurious living. An entire guesthouse at your disposal. Access to the pool, car service with Daryl…"

"His name's Daryl? He doesn't look like a Daryl."

"I know! I tried calling him D, but he doesn't like that."

"Why doesn't he feed your snakes?"

"Daryl doesn't like snakes."

"I don't like snakes!"

"Yeah, but I'm already paying him to drive, and apparently there's only so much money the man needs."

"Don't you have friends—"

"My friends are gamers. You know what gamers do?"

I shake my head.

"Game, twenty-four seven. They can't remember to feed themselves most of the time. No way I'm entrusting them with Petunia, let alone my babies."

"You shouldn't entrust me with your babies. I might rob you blind."

"Nah, you're not the type."

"How do you know?"

"Daryl has a radar for these things. If he thought you were off, he wouldn't have brought you home."

"What is he, like your guard dog?"

"I tried calling him D-dog as well," Bart says seriously. "But he didn't go for that, either. Look, you're gonna be fine. Wear the gloves first few times if you have to. Once you have some experience, you'll see there's nothing to worry about. Snakes are shy. They just want to hang out, do their thing. And they're gorgeous, with distinct markings and individual personalities. Watch a little more, judge a little less. By the end of this month, you'll have conquered one of your biggest terrors and gained a whole new appreciation for these amazing creatures. And had free lodging in one tripped-out pad to boot. I'm telling you, you got this—"

I open my mouth.

"Great," Bart states. "Knew you'd see it my way. So, like, I already have a pilot firing up my jet on the runway. Got questions about anything, ask Daryl. See you in a month. Oh, by the way, Marge needs to be fed like tomorrow night. Date's marked on the corner of the aquarium."

He whirls toward the snake room door.

"Wait!"

I need to say so many things. Should ask so many things. What comes out isn't what I expect. "Why is it so important Petunia stay out of this room?"

"Oh. Marge would try to eat her."

"Isn't Marge locked in the terrarium?"

"Another fun fact about snake-rearing: never trust the terrarium lids."

Then Bart is bolting out the door. After a last look at massively coiled, pale-colored Marge, I scramble after him.

CHAPTER 4

I FOLLOW DARYL THROUGH THE COMPOUND, rolling my suitcase and too stupefied to speak. The residence seems to go on
forever, a giant U or square or what the hell, an infinity symbol for
all I can figure out. Lots of stone fireplaces, dark-stained beams,
yawning ceilings, and pouring sunlight. The air-conditioning costs
alone must be astronomical.

"You a herper?" Daryl asks abruptly.

I focus my attention on the enormous driver, moving sound-
lessly ahead of me across the tiled floor. Boxer, I'm guessing, given
how light he is on his feet. The rest of him is harder for me to com-
pute. His swarthy complexion could belong to any number of eth-
nicities, while his dark, silver-streaked hair places his age anywhere
over forty. His voice, on the other hand, deep and whiskey-soaked,
sounds straight out of a jazz club. Which would match the stubby
ponytail at the nape of his neck and diamond stud in one ear.

"What's a herper?" I manage.

"Someone who loves snakes."

"Then definitely not. Are you sure your employer is sane?"

"Kid's crazy," Daryl concedes, "but decent. I've worked for worse."

"How'd you meet him?"

"Answered an ad."

"And how long have you been with him?"

"Five years."

"Seriously? He's owned this place since he was like, twenty-one?"

"Exactly."

Daryl exits through French doors to the outside courtyard, where there's a massive, kidney-shaped pool, featuring a slide and volleyball net. Also, an inflatable unicorn. I have no idea.

The impressive landscaping offers several large palo verde trees for shade and a striking collection of barrel cacti, saguaros, and aloe plants set among red rocks and gray stone. I can just make out a screened-in area to my right with a shimmer of water. Petunia's private patio with designated swimming hole. But of course.

Daryl leads me to an adobe structure featuring more French doors. The pool house, I'm thinking. But instead:

"Here you go." He ushers me into a cool interior featuring a dark wood ceiling fan whirring above a massive California king bed. Spanish-style headboard and bedside tables. An antique dresser across the way, topped by a giant flat-screen TV. Stone fireplace to the right. Door leading to a master bath to the left.

If the snakes hadn't already robbed me of words, this would've done it.

Daryl walks me through a brief tour, including the expansive walk-in closet, a minibar featuring a half-fridge and Italian coffee maker, and a master bath complete with a double sink and steam shower built for six. Thick towels and high-end toiletry products round out the extravagance.

Maybe this place really is a luxury resort. Except I've never stayed in any hotel this nice.

Daryl is already crossing to a panel set in the wall next to the French doors. It features a speaker and a column of buttons.

"Whole compound is connected," he states, his deep baritone resonating across the room. "Button one, the kitchen. Jenny's there most days, eight to six. Sundays off."

"Jenny?"

"Cook, housekeeper. Genni, G-E-N-N-I."

I nod my head to acknowledge the unique spelling.

"Buttons two through four are for the kid. Don't worry about them."

"Okay."

"Button five, me. Need anything, anytime, you ring, I'll answer." There's nothing lascivious in his tone, just basic reassurance. Which I truly appreciate at the moment.

"You live here, too?"

He nods.

"Another bungalow on the compound?"

"Mine's a little bigger." First crack of a smile across his broad face. "Seniority."

"What do you do when Bart's away?" I ask curiously. "Since, you know, you bailed on the care and feeding of snakes."

Smile grows. "Anything I want."

"Not a bad gig."

"Kid's generous. Take care of him—and his pets—he'll take care of you."

"You know anything about the gaming world?"

"Nope."

"But you trust him."

"Yep."

"You also serve as hired muscle?" I ask.

"Never come up."

"But you could if necessary. Boxer, I'm guessing?"

Daryl gives me an unexpected wink. "Ballroom dancer."

Well, now my day of surprises is complete. What the hell. In for a penny, in for a pound. I unsling my messenger bag, let it rest on top of my luggage. "Guess I'll give this a try."

Daryl nods as if my decision was never in doubt. Maybe when it comes to the workings of Boy Wonder, Bart, it never is.

"But any snake that escapes is a you problem," I warn him.

"Nope." He pauses. "We'll put Genni in charge."

"Deal." I stick out my hand. After a belated moment, he shakes it, his expression serious.

"Genni will provide meals," he explains. "When you need to go somewhere, ring for me."

"You'll drive me anywhere at any time?"

He pauses long enough to give me a considering look. I don't think there are very many things Daryl misses, and even fewer people he can't assess. "What kind of places are you thinking?"

My turn to smile. "Well, now that you've brought it up..."

"THIS IS NOT a good idea."

"You'll learn soon enough, most of mine aren't."

"You know anything about Tucson?" Daryl asks from behind the steering wheel. After a quick shower, change of clothes, and apple snagged from the fridge, I'd met him out front, destination address in hand. I tried to ride shotgun. He'd pointedly opened the rear door for me.

"First time here," I concede. I have my phone open and am studying the picture Aliah gave me of her and her missing friend, Sabera. The two are positioned with their arms around each other's shoulders, heads touching. Aliah is recognizable with her short, tousled hair. Sabera, on the other hand, sports more traditional long black locks. The pose is intimate, speaking of a deep friendship between the older woman and her younger charge, but there's something about Sabera that tugs at me. She isn't classically beautiful; her face is a bit wide, her brow heavy. But her eyes—a deep gray—grab you. They speak of limitless secrets and sorrowful knowledge.

I can already tell she's one of those people who will never truly be known, not even by those who love her.

I think, if someone took a picture of me, I would look much the same.

"Grant and Alvernon is what you'd call the not-so-good side of town," Daryl is saying.

"That makes sense." And matches the scenery. The clusters of bright, shiny strip malls and big box stores lining each side of the crumbly six-lane avenue are rapidly giving way to boarded-up buildings, vacant lots, and pawnshops. Always a sign in my business that I'm getting close.

Daryl slows, peers to the right where there's a squat, bile-green apartment building with a cracked asphalt parking lot and sagging second-story deck. One of the rain spouts has come loose and is falling away from the beat-up exterior, which fits with the eviction notice I already spy plastered against the lower corner unit windows. I'm guessing that's our destination.

Daryl pulls into the parking lot. Beneath the shade of a broad tree dotting the front corner, six people turn to stare. Two adults, two teens, two smaller children. Maybe all one family, maybe two families hanging out together. I peg them to be refugees. Syrian, Pakistani, Afghan. The possibilities are endless. They're currently eyeing the luxury sedan with the carefully guarded gazes of people who've come to expect the worst.

Up ahead to the left, I see another apartment with yellow crime scene tape strung out front. Hmm, now I have two possibilities to check out.

Daryl parks the car, engine still idling. He twists around and gives me a disappointed expression. "You quittin'? Just like that?"

"No, meeting someone. Though now that you mention it, never hurts to consider other options."

"This is no place for a single female."

And yet a family with small children, like the ones still regarding us with hunched shoulders, the woman clutching the youngest closer?

"What do you think rent goes for in a place like this?" I ask him.

"Five, six hundred a month."

"Better than what I was seeing in the paper," I murmur.

"No first and last month rent required. Just first month plus security deposit. Big difference."

"You ever live in a place like this?" I ask curiously, given he seems so knowledgeable.

"Somewhere similar."

"When?"

"Six years ago. When I first got out of prison." He eyes me expectantly.

I merely shrug. "I've never been to prison, but I have been to jail. Little problem with alcohol."

"Drugs."

"Been sober eleven years."

"Eight."

"I gotta keep moving."

"I gotta keep dancing."

I nod again, his words making perfect sense. I also better understand his loyalty to Bart. Few would hire a convict recently released from prison. Fewer still would entrust him with their six-figure luxury sedan.

The door to the eviction-notice unit opens. A woman appears, young, white, and with a mess of curly blond hair gathered high in a ponytail. She's dressed in jeans and a pink T-shirt, with a blue bandana tied around her neck and yellow dishwashing gloves on both hands.

She glances over at the idling car, does a double take at the obvious wealth. I pop open the door and step out.

"Ashley Cantrell?" I call out.

She raises a gloved hand in tentative acknowledgment. I smile broadly, then duck my head back in the sedan long enough to declare, "I'm gonna need an hour. Maybe two if there's still a lot of cleaning to be done."

"Not a good idea," Daryl states.

"Most of mine aren't," I remind him.

"Get yourself killed," he warns, "and Petunia will be pissed off."

I shudder slightly at the reminder. "Don't worry, I doubt the housing coordinator of a resettlement agency is much of a threat."

"Sure you know what you're doing?"

"Never."

Then I shut the car door and prepare to meet the first of many people I hope can tell me all about Sabera Ahmadi. Mother, wife, refugee. Three weeks later, I wonder which of these roles cost her the most.

I can't help myself; I check my cell. No texts, no voice mails, no contact.

I put my phone away and get back to work.

CHAPTER 5

Earlier this afternoon, while waiting for the mystery driver of the mysterious job opportunity to pick me up, I'd reviewed all the contact information Aliah had provided for Sabera's known associates. Generally, I start my inquiries by speaking with the family. But in this case, my conversation with Aliah had revealed to me how little I knew of the refugee experience, so I decided to start broader, gain an understanding of Sabera's current challenges and stress, then visit with her husband.

I'd begun with calling her designated caseworker, which had gone straight to voice mail. Then a volunteer coordinator, also no luck. But the housing manager, Ashley, had answered, sounding rushed. The moment I mentioned Sabera's name, she was already bailing. I should reach out to this person, that person, another person, anyone other than her.

Which is often a sign she's exactly the person with whom I should be speaking.

Not being a dumb bunny, I bulldozed ahead in a state of

cheerful exuberance. Of course, you're busy. No matter. I'll come to you. Better yet, let me help you out with whatever you're doing; we can chat while we clean.

I didn't get the impression Ashley was thrilled with this option, but like most people who were raised to be polite, she couldn't figure a way out of it. Score one for me.

But I meant what I said. I'm a decent scrubber, and in my experience, some of the most revealing conversations happen when two people are doing their best not to think about what is that black stuff growing in the corner.

Now I cross to Ashley, who has big brown eyes and a sprinkle of freckles across her nose. Cute in the proverbial girl-next-door look. And already trying to save the world at the ripe old age of twenty-something. Poor thing.

"Frankie Elkin," I introduce myself. "We spoke by phone."

Ashley nods. She looks even more stressed than she sounded by phone. "I'm sorry, I really don't have time," she rattles out. "Just got a call that another family is due to arrive day after tomorrow, and it was all I could do to line up one three-bedroom apartment let alone an additional two-bedroom unit. Not to mention the furniture I need to scavenge. Mattresses. Shoot. I have a pair of bunk beds in storage but not the twin mattresses."

"This is the three-bedroom unit?" I point to the one she just exited. "Have you finished cleaning it?"

"Still have the kitchen to do. I need more paper towels. And bleach. Lots of bleach."

She's standing near a battered Subaru that had seen better days around a hundred thousand miles ago. The rear window bears the emblem of a Jesus fish, which tracks. I move to pop the hatch, withdrawing a two-pack of generic paper towels and gallon jug of pure bleach. Ashley doesn't argue anymore, shoulders slumped, face drawn. The girl is clearly teetering on the brink of exhaustion. Which is the problem with trying to save the world; it's much too big for one person to handle.

"I'll help with the kitchen," I announce. "We'll get this unit squared away, then focus on the second. You know the landlord here?"

"Yes."

I point to the crime scene tape across the way. "I'm guessing there's a recent opening."

Ashley's lips finally crack into a smile. At least she's not without a sense of humor. "When I first started placing families here," she murmurs, "this complex was a hotbed of drug activity. Strung-out addicts sprawled outside all times of day and night. Broken-down cars and trash littering the parking lot, puddles of urine on the sidewalk. When I brought the family here, the mother broke down sobbing while the father begged me to take them anywhere else. Their children, they kept saying. Surely there had to be someplace else. Except there wasn't—Tucson is in the middle of a major housing crunch, and the meager three-month stipend these refugees receive...That was my first lesson in being a housing coordinator. That even when you're doing your best, you mostly feel helpless. Which is still better than the days you feel hopeless."

"Today is a hopeless day?"

"At the moment. But give me a few hours. I'll get over it." She summons a determined smile. There's a set to her chin I can't help but admire.

"How long have you been doing this?"

"Fourteen months. Which makes me the current record holder."

"That kind of high burn?"

"I haven't seen my own cat in two weeks."

"But you're sticking it out?"

"I have to." Her gaze takes on a manic gleam. "I'm finally winning."

"Winning what?"

"This!" She waves her free hand around the general area. "Look around. See any addicts lined up for a fix? Or human feces on the walls?"

"There is the matter of the crime scene tape."

"Last dealer. Had a beef with his supplier. Or so I'm told. But the rest of the complex…almost all refugees now. And you know what refugees have in common? They're seeking safety for themselves and their children. And they don't take having a roof over their heads for granted. The landlord was reluctant to take the first family. Now he's ready to take them all. They work, they pay their rent, and they stay out of trouble. If only he had more tenants like that."

I study Ashley for a moment. "And Sabera Ahmadi and her husband? Are they like that?"

Her face shutters, her expression immediately becoming more cautious. Because she doesn't like them, or doesn't like talking about them? More things I need to know.

"You said on the phone you were searching for Sabera," she states carefully, "but you're clearly not the police. So who are you?"

I consider her question, trying to put it in terms Ashley might understand. "Think of me as like a Good Samaritan. Except I seek so that others can find. One of your volunteers reached out. She doesn't believe Sabera is the type to simply run off and leave her four-year-old daughter, especially without a word to anyone else."

Ashley doesn't give any hint of her thoughts on that subject. Instead, she offers up a simple half shrug. "I think people can have different definitions of what starting over means. Many of these women are coming from societies where they had no choices. Now, suddenly, they have limitless ones. They get a job outside the home to help pay rent, then realize they like it. They throw on blue jeans to better blend in, then figure out they can walk faster, move less constrictively. They see other women speaking up, attending colleges, driving cars...Change can have a domino effect. Once you start, there's no telling where you'll end up."

"Including abandoning your own kid?" My turn to be skeptical.

"Because no mother in her right mind would ever leave her child? The amount of trauma these people have suffered, from emotional loss to physical violence..."

Ashley regards me intently. "Sometimes, parents abandon their families for selfish reasons. But sometimes, they genuinely believe their children would be better off without them. Personally, I can't pretend to know Sabera's thoughts on that subject, any more than I can pretend to know what she's gone through. My imagination isn't horrific enough."

I take a minute to absorb what Ashley's saying. I get it, while registering the whole point is that I'll never get it, and to think otherwise would be a mistake. Then again, when it comes to experiencing violence, fear, loss, maybe Sabera and I have something in common. I don't like nights anymore. And sleep hasn't been my friend in a very long time.

Ashley is watching me. I don't know what emotions are playing out across my face, but eventually she sighs, reaches for the bottle of bleach. "I gotta get back to work. Sorry I couldn't be of more assistance."

"No worries." I ignore her outstretched arm and head for the open apartment door, cleaning supplies firmly in hand.

After a startled moment, Ashley falls in step behind me.

"Seriously, you don't have to help. The kitchen alone involves mold, cockroaches, and what I'm pretty sure is blood spatter."

"Sounds like just another Friday night in my world."

"Who are you again?"

"My name is Frankie Elkin, and I never back away from a challenge. So, come on, let's get this done."

CHAPTER 6

"WHAT GOT YOU INTO WORKING with refugees?" I ask five minutes later, contemplating the brown flecks covering the wall in front of me. I've cleaned up after enough bar fights to know Ashley's instincts had been correct—it's definitely blood. And not exactly the kind of spray you'd get from nicking your finger while cutting up carrots. Interesting.

I pick up a bottle of bleach solution and start spritzing.

"My youth group at church. We volunteered to help several years ago. The resettlement agencies were getting one to two families a month back then, which meant they could spend more time on the housing. We'd spruce up the rentals with fresh paint, assemble furniture, make simple repairs. Some of the families had spent years living in makeshift tents constructed from tarps and wooden pallets. Freezing in the winter, baking in the summer. The look on their faces when they'd first walk in..." Ashley glances up from where she's furiously scrubbing cabinet shelving. "The women always cried. Except in those days, it was happy tears."

"Not so much anymore."

"When I took this job fourteen months ago, the rate of placements had already ticked up to three to four families a month. Now it's eight to fifteen. There aren't even that many rentals available on the market. Let alone, instead of having two weeks' notice, I sometimes get as little as twenty-four hours. It's crazy. I mean, I've forged relationships with some landlords who are now willing to help, but then again, more and more apartment complexes are owned by out-of-state real estate corporations. They'll deny families housing and blatantly declare they don't work with programs, even though that's illegal. So I stick small children in units where the previous owners were drug dealers. I mean sure, why not?" She scrubs more furiously. That is going to be one darn clean cabinet.

"Who's sending the families?" I ask. "I mean, why so many on such short notice?"

A snort of derision. "Welcome to the global refugee crisis. Wars, famine, natural disasters. You read the morning news and think, oh that's sad. I read the morning news and think, now where am I going to put them?"

Hence her level of exhaustion. "How do the families end up in Tucson? Do they get to pick?"

"Oh, no, it's all a bunch of administrative red tape, global, federal, local. Okay, so you, Frankie Whomever, are declared an international refugee by the UN."

"Thank you?"

"Hey, this is an official legal status that can take years and over half a dozen attempts to earn, all the while having to live in fear of sudden deportation back to your home country, where your government may or may not kill you." Her tone is serious. She starts scouring the countertop. "But go you, Frankie—you got the golden ticket."

I remember what Aliah said about Sabera and her husband knowing they were the lucky ones. "Okay."

"Nations around the world pledge to take in so many refugees each year. Our government just promised to take in a hundred and twenty-five thousand this fiscal year, which is a significant leap from last year and still not even a rounding error in how many people need sanctuary."

I nod to show I'm paying attention, then brush a cockroach off the wall. Honestly, I just cleaned there.

"In the US, the Office of Refugee Resettlement works with designated resettlement agencies to get the families into the US and handles all the basics. Background checks, medical exams, in-person interviews. Lots of shots. You have no idea how many people I see whose entire concept of the American medical system is a military doc armed with a needle."

"Military doc?"

"Entry point is generally a military base where the families will spend their first six to eight months."

"Six to eight *months*?"

"Nobody ever accused the government of moving quickly."

"Touché."

"From there, the larger resettlement agency will start doling out families. Each state has already agreed to take X many bodies. Some bureaucrat with a red pen—well, more like outdated modeling software—arbitrarily sticks in random information, gets back a random location. Tucson! Welcome, Ahmadi family of three, to your new town."

"What if they don't want to go to Tucson or, say, have family elsewhere?"

Ashley shrugs. Countertop done, she moves on to the lower

drawers. The top one opens with a sharp screeching sound. Three cockroaches pour out. Without missing a beat, Ashley grabs a rag from the countertop, rolls it tight, then snaps it out, one, two, three. The cockroaches fall dazed to the ground. She raises her foot and stomps them dead.

"Do you make house calls?" I murmur. "And what are your thoughts on snakes?"

"What?"

"Never mind. Family learns they're headed to Tucson, but don't want to go there."

"For the Afghans, there are significant communities in San Francisco and northern Virginia, so many would prefer to relocate there. But you go rogue, you lose your three months of federal aid. And given those cities have high costs of living, not to mention you think it's hard to find an apartment here..." Ashley gives me a look. I get her point.

"So Sabera, her husband, and daughter start researching Tucson." I almost get it now.

"Please, half the time they're told their destination as they're boarding the plane."

"Seriously?"

" 'For we live by faith, not by sight,' " she informs me.

I hear her, which brings me to another point. "Your resettlement agency is obviously faith-based. Does this create issues?"

"Actually, it's the one thing that gives me hope. I might be the first Christian some of these families have ever met, while my friends from the Jewish Family and Children's Services agency— also an excellent agency—are the first Jews. But person to person, no one cares. We're neighbors helping neighbors, and that's what matters. If only the rest of the world got that memo."

Makes sense to me. "So the Ahmadi family arrives in Tucson," I prod.

Ashley nods while tending to the kitchen drawer. "Step one, meet the family at the airport. This is something I like to do personally if I can. The families are always dazed and confused—no idea where they are, no clue what's going to happen next. The kids are exhausted, clinging to their parents, who are standing there with nothing but the clothes on their backs. And yet, they always have this set to their shoulders, a smile plastered on their faces. They might not know where they are, but they already know it's better than where they've been."

"Sabera and her family?"

"She was holding their daughter, Zahra—a petite little thing with huge gray eyes and the world's most serious expression. Honestly, I took one look at the girl and would've gotten them a penthouse suite if possible. Zahra's like the poster child for displaced children everywhere." Ashley scowls. "Which is a terrible thing for someone like me to say."

"Kabul fell in 2021. Sabera's family has been in a refugee camp the entire time since then?"

"Most likely several different camps. There's a whole global system most refugees process through."

"So Sabera gave birth while in one of the camps?"

"Much less than ideal," Ashley assures me. "Pregnant women, women with infants are particularly vulnerable in such places. Way too many people, not enough resources to go around, violence a daily occurrence. First rule of refugees, they will almost never *ever* speak of their time in the camps."

Which returns us to Ashley's original point—it would be foolish to think anyone knows what Sabera has gone, is going, through. And Aliah's conviction that her friend would never leave her child is also premature.

"What was your first impression of Sabera and her family?" I ask Ashley now.

She shrugs, moving down to the next drawer. "She was quiet, let Isaad do the talking. I assumed that indicated a more traditional marriage, which surprised me, because according to their file, they were both in academia. He taught mathematics at Kabul University. She worked in the department. Aliah, who was the volunteer assigned to the family—"

"She's the one who reached out to me."

"She's amazing!" Ashley's voice picks up. "She'd already remembered a booster seat for Zahra, and had one delivered to my car—you don't know how many times we forget things like that. But Aliah's a pro and a great role model for the younger females. I mean twenty-five years later, look at her now!"

"Absolutely." I've finally finished scouring the wall running perpendicular to the kitchen cabinets. It turns out the original color is almost as dingy as the previously grimy version, so I'm left with a mostly moral victory. At least the blood is gone. Until I glance up at the ceiling.

Definitely not from an injury while cutting up produce. I raise the bottle of bleach spray and get to it.

"What did Sabera and her husband think of the apartment?"

"Oh, the look on their faces when I pulled into the complex's parking lot..." Ashley sighs heavily. "Isaad asked a lot of questions about their three-month allowance, which is exactly how long families are given to be financially independent once they are settled in a city."

"Three months?" I can't keep the disbelief from my voice.

"Exactly. First task is to assess their English skills, then enroll them in the proper English as a second language class. Good news for the Ahmadis—I could already tell Isaad's English was good enough, while Sabera's was absolutely perfect. She even enunciates with a crisp British accent, which I assumed was from private school education, but later learned her mother was originally from London."

I take a break from dabbing the ceiling to regard Ashley. "How did Sabera seem with her daughter? Did she engage..." I hesitate, picking my words carefully. "Or hold herself separate?"

"You encounter many traumatized people?" Ashley asks me levelly. "I mean suffering from serious PTSD. Kids, parents, individuals subject to years of stress, terror, uncertainty?"

I don't shy away from her gaze. "Yes."

"Sabera did the right things, said the right things. If her daughter grabbed her hand, she held it. If her husband asked a question, she answered it. But at the same time, she remained removed. There, but not there. For the record, it's not the first time I've seen such behavior."

I nod, recalling the Sabera I'd studied in Aliah's photo. Present, but separate. Like Ashley, I'm familiar with such behavior. Including from myself.

I switch gears. "Do you like him? The husband, Isaad?"

"I don't know him. I've interacted with him maybe three or four times, mostly about tactical issues. Their air conditioner wasn't working properly. I walked him through how to contact his landlord, draft an email requesting repair work, that kind of thing."

"Did he seem uncomfortable talking to a female?" I ask.

She shrugs. "We're given guidance on various cultures and religions. I know there's no physical contact between men and women—don't greet with a handshake or tap the husband on the shoulder, that kind of thing. But Isaad seemed more comfortable in my presence than many."

I'm still watching her. "But did you *like* him?" I know I'm repeating myself, but I also think Ashley isn't truly answering my question.

Her slight hesitation again. "Have you met him?"

"No."

"But you will?"

"I hope to speak to him sooner rather than later."

She nods. "You do that. My understanding is that he's regarded as a brilliant mind in his field. Certainly, he can be very charming when he wants something. And...not so charming, when feeling denied. Which, given his change in life circumstance..."

I think I get it. I also hear the sound of a car pulling up outside, the purr of a clearly well-tuned engine. I don't have to look outside to know Daryl has returned.

"Your chariot awaits," Ashley murmurs. And for a moment, her shoulders slump, her expression once again taking on its strained look.

"I can stay longer."

That faint smile. "It will never be long enough." She cocks her head sideways. "Though, somehow, I think you understand that better than most."

"I can return tomorrow afternoon. Bring extra supplies. Maybe some extra muscle." I'm already thinking of Daryl, whom I'm willing to bet is a giant softy. But even as I say the words, I see the doubt on Ashley's face. My mission often feels overwhelming, but I'm only ever trying to help one person. She is literally trying to assist a community of thirty million. Her poor cat indeed.

I finish up the ceiling, set down my spray bottle and sponge. There's no easy way to walk away, but we've both picked the loads we're determined to carry. Sometimes, the best thing to offer a fellow warrior is faith in their fortitude.

"I've left messages for Sabera's caseworker," I say, "and the volunteer coordinator at your resettlement agency."

"Who are much too busy to call you back," Ashley provides.

"Even about her? A woman missing three weeks? None of you are worried about her?"

"Worried? Haven't you heard anything I've said?" Ashley's turn to set down her cleaning supplies. "I'm worried about *all* of them. Every single person I've placed in every single apartment. I don't have enough hours, days, or headspace for the amount of worry I carry in my heart."

"I understand."

"Do you?" Her tone is hard now, her gaze piercing. I imagine weaker humans quaking before that look. But I can hold my own.

"I'm here to help," I state. "To find Sabera Ahmadi and bring her home to her family, or at least discover the kind of answers that will offer some comfort. And I'm staying till I get this job done."

"I won't pretend to understand you, Frankie Whomever, but I will pray for you." Ashley bites her lower lip, stares at some point just past my ear. I sense some kind of internal battle...

"We're not supposed to talk about the families," she states abruptly. "That's one of the issues you're encountering, why Staci and Carlos won't call you back."

I wait.

"Privacy matters. These people aren't going to just grant us their trust; we must earn it."

I don't say a word.

"Sabera and her husband are Muslims. Among other things, most practicing Muslims don't drink." That pause again. I keep my face blank, my body language neutral.

"The last time I saw Sabera...I would swear she smelled of alcohol. She noticed, mumbled something about having to deal with spilled wine in one of the rooms she was cleaning. I know sometimes people leave booze behind in the hotel rooms. Once, she gifted me a bottle of champagne. But...her words were too slow, her movements awkward. She was impaired in some manner, I'm certain of it. And Isaad knew it, too. The expression on his face—he was not happy with her."

Ashley looks at me. "I don't pretend to know what Sabera has gone through," she repeats. "But from the little I've witnessed... There are things she has seen, things she knows, we should both be grateful to never have in our heads."

Ashley picks her sponge back up, opens the next kitchen drawer. And after a final moment, I exit the apartment.

CHAPTER 7

A RE WE CLOSE TO THIS address?" I ask Daryl as I climb into the back of the sedan. He's covered the black leather seat with a checkered red wool blanket. Smartass. Then I look down at my T-shirt, which is now covered in flecks of grime and white splotches of bleach. Maybe he has a point.

Daryl takes my phone and studies the information Aliah has supplied on Sabera and her husband's apartment. He grunts, which I take to mean yes, hands back my mobile.

It's after five P.M., but still hot enough you'd never know. The family, I notice, has disappeared from underneath the tree abutting the parking lot. A young white male, however, now stands in front of the murder unit, peering intently at the door. He's tall, thin, and wearing a long-sleeved flannel shirt in the searing heat. I'm already guessing it's to cover the track marks on his arms.

Daryl doesn't give the man a second glance, just peers over his shoulder and expertly reverses the sedan out of the parking lot. He has the car's radio tuned to the news, which is listing a drug-related shooting, a near-fatal stabbing, and just to round out the trifecta of violence, two men attacked and killed with a hammer. I'm grateful when he shuts it off.

"I'm still alive," I speak up cheerfully after a bit. Maybe to break the silence. Maybe to irritate my driver. Even I can never tell.

Daryl merely shakes his head, keeps his gaze fixed on the road. We make it a few more blocks and then he takes a right, followed by a left, followed by another right. I know we've arrived at the target location when we hit a run-down apartment building that's missing entire chunks of stucco and has red roof tiles dangling down like bloody teeth. To add insult to injury, a razor wire–topped fence separates the mud-brown complex from a clearly brand-new, shiny, white storage facility next door.

Last time I encountered such a formidable chain-link wall, I was visiting a female penitentiary in Texas that housed death row inmates. Versus, say, the two children I now see attempting to roller skate around the cracked and cratered pavement, while a tired woman in a voluminous white blouse and simple gray head covering watches from the door of one of the units.

She glances up at the sound of the car engine, a flash of alarm crossing her face. She claps her hands, saying something to the boy and girl that I can't hear. Both kids, clad in jeans and T-shirts, scramble toward her, the younger girl, maybe sixish, trying to change direction too quickly and promptly wiping out.

The woman yells something else, but the older boy is already turning back for his sister, while Daryl hits the brakes, slowing the vehicle to a gentle stop. He looks at me via the rearview mirror.

"If I get out, it will scare them further," he states.

I see his point. A dark sedan driven by a hulking male? I scrabble with the door handle, grateful for my small size and disheveled appearance. How threatening can a scrawny female in a grungy T-shirt appear?

The little girl is crying as I exit the vehicle, her brother kneeling beside her and working the straps of the ancient metal skates buckled around her sneakers. He has thick black hair and carefully guarded eyes as he watches me approach.

"Excuse me," I say brightly. "I'm a friend of Aliah's. She sent me here to meet with someone."

At the mention of Aliah's name, the tense line of the woman's shoulders relents slightly. Ashley had said Aliah was one of their go-to volunteers. I'm banking on these residents having met her as well, and that the reference to a mutual friend will help ease their fears.

The boy glances from me to his mom, back to me again. His sister's sobs have slowed to a wet hiccupping sound. She doesn't appear seriously hurt, just the minor scrapes and scratches that define most childhoods.

"My name is Frankie Elkin," I volunteer in the same super cheerful tone. I'm friend, not foe. Talk to me!

I'm not convinced the woman is buying it, but she hasn't grabbed both her children and bolted. I'll take the win.

"I'm looking for the Ahmadis. Isaad and Sabera. Can you point me to their apartment?"

Now the woman does move. She walks directly toward me, her left hand shifting by her side. I catch the gesture. She's waving her children inside. The boy helps his little sister to her feet, her skates held in his hand. He's still wearing his, but has no problem navigating both himself and his sister to the open doorway. He lingers just outside, still staring at me.

Eight years old but ready to come to his mother's defense. I wonder what he's seen to have instilled such a level of hypervigilance at such a young age. I'm not like Ashley. My imagination is horrific enough.

"Who are you?" The woman's accent sounds Middle Eastern, but I don't have enough experience to be certain.

"Frankie Elkin—"

"Who are you?"

I pause, getting her point. She doesn't care about my name. She wants to know my business here. Which is a good question. What is my business here?

Most people have been lied to enough in their lives. It's my general policy not to add to the carnage.

I go with: "Aliah is worried about Sabera. She asked me to check on her."

The woman's expression doesn't ease, her attention flicking from the luxury vehicle back to me. I may need to ask Daryl to find something less conspicuous.

A man has appeared in the doorway, his white collared shirt wrinkled, hair mussed, as if he just woke up. Or had possibly been dragged out of bed by his two frightened children. He steps outside, taking up position next to his wife.

"Isaad is not here," he states. His English is clearer, but his regard no less suspicious.

"He's out? At work?"

"He's not here."

There's a definitiveness to those words that is starting to worry me.

"The Ahmadis live here, right? This is where Aliah told me to find them."

"He is gone."

"Maybe I should come back tomorrow?" I'm trying to understand the nature of Isaad's, and presumably his daughter Zahra's, absence. As in ran out to grab dinner, or packed up and departed for good?

The neighbor merely shrugs. Clearly, he has no intention of giving anything away. Though his gaze has now darted to the same door twice, which is useful enough.

I make a show of nodding in acknowledgment and turning back toward Daryl's idling vehicle. From this angle I can see the front window of the unit in question. It's covered in cheap plastic blinds. I pause for a moment, my hand on the car door, waiting to catch some sign of life, say two slats being pushed apart so Isaad can peer out.

Nothing. I sigh and declare defeat just in time to hear from behind me, "Excuse me."

I twist around to discover the original family has gone inside, but now a young woman has materialized in the doorway of another apartment, holding a drooling toddler on her hip. She has high cheekbones set in a stunning face, with the kind of thick lashes women spend a fortune on mascara to achieve. She appears to be mid-twenties, and given the hard line of her compressed lips, a woman who means business.

"You are looking for Isaad and Sabera?"

I nod.

"You are not government. You are not military. You are not police. Not with that vehicle." She cocks her head to study me further. "Who sent you?"

"Aliah," I answer honestly. "She's worried about her friend." In a fit of inspiration, I remember the photo of Aliah and Sabera

I have on my phone. I cross to the young woman, holding out the image as proof of my good intentions.

The woman studies it. She's about the same age as Sabera, I realize. And also has a small child. Maybe they're friends?

I stay silent, will the woman to come to me. Finally, she pulls her gaze from the photo and studies me instead.

"Isaad received a package yesterday morning. He asked me to watch Zahra for a bit, possibly overnight. Then he left."

"Did he say where he was going?"

"No."

"But he hasn't returned yet?"

"I expect he will show up sometime this evening. Isaad is Isaad. He is brilliant with all numbers, except those on a clock."

This is interesting. "Have you watched Zahra before?"

The woman shrugs, shifting the drooling toddler on her hip. "Childcare is expensive and Zahra is close in age to my oldest. So yes, we help each other when we can."

"I'm Frankie Elkin," I volunteer. "Your name?"

"Nageenah." She tilts her head toward her hip ornament. "Hasan." Who looks to be a little over a year, as he gnaws furiously on his knuckles.

"According to Aliah," I venture, "Sabera has been missing for around three weeks. Have you heard from her at all?"

Nageenah shakes her head.

"She hasn't dropped in even briefly to grab clothing, personal possessions?"

Another shake of her head.

"Don't you find that odd?" I press. "That she would suddenly take off and leave her daughter behind?"

"She is a good mother. She would do what is best for her child."

Interesting answer. What had Ashley the housing coordinator

said about depression, PTSD leading some parents to think their children would be better off without them?

"How did she seem the last time you saw her?" I try.

A delicate shrug. "She was tired. Zahra had had a cold, keeping them up all night."

"Is Isaad an attentive father?"

"Isaad is Isaad."

I really gotta meet this man. For now, I switch gears. "You're from Afghanistan? Your English is excellent."

"My father is Tajik; they have more liberal views on education and women's roles in society. He ensured all four of his daughters attended university, even if many thought it foolish."

I regard her curiously. "What did you do in Afghanistan?"

"I worked in the government, for the Ministry of Women's Affairs. We focused on legislation to improve women's rights. We created the first anti-harassment laws. I was very proud of that."

Her tone is matter-of-fact, her expression unchanging. But I can feel the hard edge of her grief. All that work, dedication, hope. All that love for a country that disappeared nearly overnight. I'm impressed she remains standing on her own two feet. I would be curled in a ball, still screaming at the injustice of it all.

"Did you know Sabera when you lived in Kabul?" I ask now. "I understand she attended college there as well."

"No, but Kabul is a major city. It would be like asking you if you saw my cousin that one time you went to New York. I met Sabera when her family arrived here two months ago. It's nice to have another young family as neighbors. I helped connect her to the Afghan society, recommended the best local restaurants, things such as this. The mountains here are good; they make Tucson feel more like home. But it's very hot here and...Kabul is Kabul, a city that has existed for over three thousand years..."

She regards me with her piercing gaze, the toddler on her hip still chewing on his fist. "It is my experience that most Americans think of Afghanistan as a backward country with backward people. You don't want to hear about corner coffee houses, or that most of us talked on cell phones and worked in cubicles that look exactly like the ones you have here. You don't want to know that I went to my office at eight A.M. one Sunday morning to catch up on paperwork, and by eight P.M. the Taliban entered the city, and my country as I knew it was gone."

Her voice cracks slightly at the end. She glares at me, as if daring me to acknowledge her pain. I'm starting to understand the housing coordinator's point more and more. I may know death. I may know grief. But I've never known the kind of anguish that comes from losing *everything*.

"Do you still have family there?" I ask at last.

"My sisters made it to Islamabad. My parents remain in Kabul. We can WhatsApp for now. My family are Tajik, though, and the Talibans are Pashtuns; they don't care for Tajiks. They are starting to seize property, possessions. Each time we talk, my parents' faces are thinner, their clothing shabbier."

"There's no one to help you? What about the resettlement agencies?"

"There are forms for reunification, but there are rarely results."

I don't know what to say. Eventually, Nageenah fills the silence.

"Isaad got a package," she repeats. "But not from UPS or FedEx—there was no delivery truck. Just a man in a black shirt, black pants. He handed Isaad a box. Isaad opened it, inspected the contents, then signed on the delivery man's tablet. Ten minutes later, Isaad knocked on my door with Zahra in hand and asked me to watch her for the night."

I frown, consider what she's saying. "Sounds like a private courier. Delivering something Isaad expected. Needed? What size was the package? Envelope, container, chest?"

"Say, a box no larger than a shoebox."

I frown, still contemplating. Sabera has been gone for three weeks, though her husband doesn't seem worried. Yesterday he received a package from a private courier and then took off without his daughter. I run the information through my head several times, still have no idea what it means.

"Do you think Sabera was doing okay?" I ask at last. "With marriage, motherhood? I don't know. Any of it. All of it."

Nageenah regards me with her level brown stare. So does baby Hasan, who's finally pulled his fist out of his mouth.

"Speaking for most of us," she says at last, "this is a lonely life. We're used to being surrounded by our grandparents, parents, aunts, uncles, cousins. Everyone, everywhere, all the time. Here, what you Americans consider family...It is not enough. We don't just miss our home. We miss *home*."

A noise comes from behind Nageenah, the clatter of toys, a childish squeal of indignation. It's her cue to return to her other childcare duties, which apparently now include Zahra.

I give Nageenah my number, asking her to call if she thinks of or sees anything else.

Then she slips away while I return to my chauffeured sedan.

Daryl glances up as I clamber into the back seat. His gaze is questioning, but he doesn't speak. I recognize the strategy, utilizing the silence to trigger a confession.

I sigh, look out the window where the sun is finally starting to descend. On cue, my stomach growls.

"Does Petunia have a set dinner time?" I ask.

"Seven. Genni serves dinner. Bart gives Petunia her salad."

"How cozy. Well then, guess I gotta pay for these wheels with some quality pet care. All right. Home, James."

Daryl doesn't seem amused by the reference. But then, as he puts the car in reverse, I meet his gaze in the mirror. "So, Daryl, would you like to know what I'm up to? Because, boy, do I have a story for you."

CHAPTER 8

YOU ARE PLAYING WITH THOSE rocks as if you've discovered a great treasure," I tease him.

"Of course. I'm a geologist. Rocks are always a great treasure."

I roll my eyes, mostly because I know he's telling the truth. The sun is shining brightly overhead, the sky a deep shade of blue, and the warm temperature perfect for a day at the lake. Around us are the excited cheers of kids playing football on the shoreline, while the air is heavy with the scent of grilled meat from dozens of barbecues. Most of our classmates are already splashing through the water, laughing at various antics.

But we have wandered away to carve out a sliver of privacy, respectfully close enough for public scrutiny, while being just enough alone.

"Did you know," he says now, gazing at me with dark eyes that send a shiver down my spine, "that Afghanistan has mineral deposits estimated to be worth nearly a trillion dollars? It's one of the reasons so many foreign powers fight over us. They *might make a good speech about freedom and liberty, but mostly, money is money, and the new global currency is rare earth elements. Everyone needs them. And we have them in abundance.*

"Except of course, we don't have." His tone turns to one of disgust. "Because that would require long-term investment in infrastructure and political security, and what government minister wants that when he can line his pockets instead?"

"Maybe it will give the Americans incentive not to abandon us completely," I try. "They must want these resources, too."

"You would think."

But I hear the doubt in his voice. Feel it, too. In a matter of months, all American troops will be withdrawn. And judging by the stories we hear from the countryside...

With a single swipe of his hand, he sends the pile of pebbles tumbling.

"What is your treasure?" he asks me.

I don't have to think about it. "Words."

"Not numbers?"

"No. Books, stories, poems."

He gives me a sideways glance. "And yet, you study with Professor Ahmadi."

I shrug. "He's a brilliant mathematician."

"He's an old man with a younger man's appetites." He makes a fake coughing sound. "Dokhtar Baaz."

I understand his less than complimentary label. Professor Ahmadi has a reputation for hiring only pretty young assistants. Not that he's such a handsome man, but genius can be attractive in its own way.

I flash a smile. "Jealous?"

"Always. Forever." But his expression is serious. "You should be careful."

"He's an excellent teacher," I state firmly. "And a friend of my father's."

"An old man with a younger man's appetites," he repeats.

"Jealous," I chide him.

"Always and forever."

Later, we go diving into the crisp lake, our loose clothing at first plastering to our limbs, then spreading atop the water like a silvery halo against the dark depths. The foreigners play in the shallows, wearing swim trunks and tiny bikinis that expose their overly pale skin. The baby-rocking aunties and pipe-smoking grandpas shoot frowns of disapproval, but for the younger crowd there are only exchanged grins at the outsiders' ignorance. We understand the fierceness of the bright sun shimmering overhead. There's no such thing as gentle beauty in our country. The sun burns, the mountains bite, the wind batters.

And we would have it no other way.

We swim deeper into the lake, until we are bobbing shapes in the distance, bodies modestly covered, my head respectfully wrapped. While beneath the lapping waters, a brush of toes against ankles, fingers dancing down backs, palms sliding around waists.

"Jigarem," he murmurs the endearment as his hands slip beneath the hem of my shirt, stroke a long line up my ribs.

He touches, I sigh.

He retreats, I protest.

We drift atop the water, playing, not playing, playing, not playing, till our skin is pruned and we know it's time to return to shore. At the last moment, I tighten my hand around his. I feel *like a child again, kneeling at my mother's bedside, desperate for her to stay. This day is so perfect. And I already know with a terrible sense of dread, we will never have such magic again.*

"What kind of fool falls in love when the world is burning?" I murmur.

He regards me seriously. "What kind of fool doesn't?"

If you are reading this, Zahra, my precious girl, then the worst has happened and I, too, have left my daughter much too soon.

Forgive me.

I love you. Forever and always.

And now, sweet child:

Chin up.

CHAPTER 9

GENNI IS MAGNIFICENT. SIX FOOT four inches of exquisitely groomed drag queen glory, currently standing in the kitchen in a flaring black 1950s vintage dress, topped by a frilly white apron and choker strand of pearls. To complete the ensemble: a Lucille Ball–style wig and two red gingham oven mitts. Even the crickets are chirping their applause.

Now Genni stabs the oven mitts in our direction.

"You. Are. Late."

The glare is for Daryl, thank heavens. I notice Petunia has taken up position way back, one claw in the kitchen, where she's possibly anticipating dinner, the rest of her as far away from Genni as she can get.

The kitchen smells unbelievable. Like a fantasy of homecooked perfection, except I have no idea what that might be, having been raised on a steady diet of frozen pizzas haphazardly warmed by my alcoholic father.

Genni turns toward me in a whirl of black-and-white flounces. "Genni, she, her," Genni declares, with just the right note of drama to justify Daryl's spelling of the name.

"Frankie," I manage.

Genni remains expectant.

"She, her," I provide. "Though, to be fair..." I take in my less than impressive appearance. And not just my stained T-shirt and unisex olive-green cargo pants. I wear my long brown hair habitually scraped back into a ponytail, and I haven't attempted makeup for years. In contrast, Genni's face is a flawless study of arched brows, thick lashes, and ruby-red lips.

"You are Bart's latest?" she wants to know.

I glance over at Daryl for support. He's already taken a seat at the round kitchen table, unfolding a black linen napkin and smoothing it over his lap.

"Bart's known for his Island of Misfit Toys," Daryl supplies. Then to Genni: "Frankie's the designated lizard-slash-snake sitter for the month. Go easy on her. She's not a herper."

Genni regards me more thoughtfully. "Just passing through or looking for a fresh start?"

"Not the staying kind." As if to prove me wrong, my fingers find the outline of my cell phone in my pants pocket. I refuse to take it out, check for any missed calls. I will not be that weak.

"How long have you been in Tucson?" I ask Genni.

"Twelve years, darling. The heat's a real bitch, but it'll grow on you. Now: feed the lizard, then meat loaf for the humans!"

Sounds like an amazing idea, if only I knew how to dish up salad for an iguana.

First up, I gamely inspect the ginormous stainless-steel fridge, which appears to hold every kind of energy drink ever made, including a few that I'm pretty sure have been outlawed in most states. In a lower bin, I discover a stash of three labeled containers. "Petunia, Dinner 1" seems like a good bet.

I remove the lid to discover a salad. Really. Truly. Rough-cut lettuce, carrots, cucumbers, broccoli, peppers, green beans, and squash, sprinkled with a white vitamin powder. Frankly, it looks better than most salads I've eaten lately. I glance around the immense kitchen for anything that might say, "Feed Petunia Here." I don't spot so much as a dog bowl.

Genni sighs heavily. "Her private suite…"

"The enclosure. Got it. Umm…" Petunia is currently planted in the middle of the carpeted corridor leading to the reptile wing of the house. More important, her gaze is now locked on the container in my hands, her tail flicking side to side.

I glance at Genni.

"I don't do cold-blooded," she states.

Now, why hadn't I thought of saying that? Clutching the container in hand, I venture closer. Petunia doesn't move. I'm now right in front of her, holding out the salad like a peace offering. She still doesn't flinch. I take the first little step to pass her. Then, when she doesn't latch on to my ankle, I bolt to her private room, where I spy a stainless-steel bowl and throw the salad in it. Just in time for Petunia to come scurrying past me in a blur of green limbs and swishing tail. She heads straight for dinner. I take the hint and scamper back to the kitchen, where Genni is pulling a perfectly shaped loaf of ground meat from the oven, topped with a stripe of red sauce and surrounded by a medley of roasted potatoes.

"Dinner is served."

———

AFTERWARD, I OFFER to do the dishes, as much by habit as by training. But Genni is adamant—domestic chores are her gig; I should save myself for the snakes. Which, according to the care instructions that magically appear on my phone, should be fed tomorrow night. All of them. Oh goodie. The next text reminds me not to forget Petunia's nightly massage and TV time.

Sure. I'll get right on that.

Daryl excuses himself the moment he's done eating. Given the number of times he's glanced at his watch, I'm guessing some kind of pressing engagement. Ballroom dancing? Booty call? Daryl isn't one to volunteer such details.

Following Bart's directions, I return to Petunia's room. It takes me a moment to spy her tucked under a collection of leafy branches in a corner, one golden eye peering out.

"Um, wanna watch TV?" Then, as I genuinely consider the matter: "Do you have a favorite show? Wait, I'm being stupid. It's *The Simpsons*, isn't it? Yeah, never mind, shoulda known. Okay, I don't know you, you don't know me, so I think we can both agree this is awkward. But your loving and devoted human seems to think we're perfect for each other. So, um, I'm going to head to the family room. Assuming I can find it. Then I'll turn on the TV. And then, well, suit yourself, okay? You show up, you show up. If not, no harm, no foul. I'll still sleep well tonight."

Petunia continues to regard me with one unblinking golden eye.

I sigh heavily, turn on my heel, and return to the kitchen, where Genni is harmonizing with the crickets as if they're one big happy family/chorus group. I do my best to remember Daryl's brief tour of the house and find myself in a yawning room dominated by a TV larger than most automobiles and positioned in front of a U-shaped sofa big enough to hold a football team. This must be the place.

On cue, my phone buzzes. Remote is on the charger on the table. Hit power button up top.

I nod, identify the black charger on the sofa table and then...Wait a minute, how did he know? Cameras. Has to be. Whiz kid gamer has his house wired. And is watching me right now, because he's actually not stupid enough to trust a perfect stranger with the care and feeding of his pets. I look around, till I spy the lens tucked halfway up the stone fireplace.

I give it a little wave. Then stick out my tongue.

Nice, Bart texts me.

Little shit. With a sigh, I work the remote. The flat-screen TV graciously offers me a collection of favorite shows. Sure enough, *The Simpsons* tops the list. I hit play just in time for the distinctive sound of clicking claws and rustling tail. Petunia has entered the room. She scrabbles inelegantly across the tile floor, smooths out when she hits the tightly woven area rug. Which probably explains why there are so many carpet remnants around the place.

I take a seat. Stare at bright animated characters bouncing around a screen so huge baby Maggie is bigger than my entire head.

And then...

I glance at my phone. I wish for contact from someone I told not to contact me. I wish for time to move backward. I wish I didn't still remember the smell of his skin, the feel of his arms, the whisper of his voice. "Do what you gotta do, Frankie. I would never want you to be anyone less than who you truly are."

Because that's what happens when you let someone in. When you let them get to know you *that* well. They learn who you are. And they learn who you are not.

Even when you wish it were different.

More rustling. Petunia appears at the far end of the sofa, now perched on top of the arm.

She makes no move to advance. I make no move to draw closer.

Eventually, I sense a small shift in her posture as she settles in.

On the TV, Lisa Simpson plays her saxophone.

Petunia watches from one side of the couch, and I stare from the other. Two life-forms, alone together, which feels like the only way I know how to live anymore.

Later, she follows me back to her private room, where I lock her in for the night, per instructions. Then, because I just can't help myself, I venture to the snake room, easing open the door, peering in the darkened interior. No immediate sign of movement, sounds of alarm. I pull on the headlamp with its night-friendly red beam.

I make out slender, twelve-inch baby pythons slithering along the sides of one enclosure, some sliding over others, some dotting the bottom in tight little balls.

On the farthest wall, pale yellow Marge is a stack of thick coils, her narrow head now lifting up from the pile. She stares at me expectantly, tongue forking.

Nothing but an illogical fear, Bart said. No problem conquering your greatest terror, he promised.

I replace the headlamp on the hook, then carefully shut and lock the door, testing the handle several times for certainty.

I bolt for the safety of the guesthouse.

I DON'T DREAM of snakes. At this stage of my life, my nightmares are much more specific. The first love of my life, holding his bleeding abdomen, a look of surprise on his face. Except then it's some young man I barely know, and we're in a back alley, his head on my lap as he gasps desperately for air, his dark gaze still angry, still defiant, still determined to live.

Until it isn't.

Now I'm running through the rain with Bigfoot hot on my heels. Or maybe it's a coconut crab with giant, snapping claws. I clamber up the steps of a darkened cabin, seeking shelter. Except there's the severed head, with its sightless eyes and still-screaming mouth.

I don't look away. I know this head too well. I know what will happen next, as I place my finger against those bloody lips and stare deep into milky-white eyes.

"Shhh," I remind the dead man. Always remind the dead man. "You must be quiet. She's still out there. She's..."

The snapping of a twig directly behind me. Myself, twisting around in the howling storm.

Catching the silvery gleam of the machete as it arcs up, up, up.

She's laughing. Now. Then. Now again.

The machete falls.

But it is someone else who screams in agony.

I BOLT AWAKE just in time to catch a faint musical chime building to a larger, louder crescendo. My phone, ringing. I fumble around the top of the nightstand for the squawking device, registering the first hint of daylight beyond my window. No more raging storms. No more dying men or murderous females.

Thank God for morning.

I snatch up my cell, suddenly hopeful.

But the number isn't from Washington. According to my caller ID, it's Aliah.

And it's way too early for a social call.

I hit connect in time to hear her rushing demand: "Turn on the TV. Right now. The local news, you need to see this!"

"What?" I drag myself out of bed, feeling like I've drowned in a massive sea of mattress. It takes me a minute to find the remote, hit power.

"It's Sabera," Aliah rattles out. "She's on TV!"

"The police found her?"

"No! They're showing a video of her. The two men killed with a hammer..."

I have a vague memory of hearing about that yesterday.

"They have footage of a woman walking away, her face covered by a headscarf. I know that scarf; I gave it to her as a welcome present. The woman in the video is Sabera. And she's exiting a murder scene!"

CHAPTER 10

DRINK THIS." ALIAH SETS A tall glass of frothy white milk in front of me. "Stir first. The cucumber and mint settles to the bottom. You will like it."

She sets a second glass in front of Daryl, who immediately perks up. "Doogh?" he asks.

"You know Afghan food?"

"I love Afghan food."

"You just love food," I mutter, having witnessed a similar display of lust over Genni's meat loaf last night. I'm not very happy with Daryl right now.

He raises his glass and takes a considering sip. "Salty, with just the right touch of sweet. Excellent."

I take a swig of my own drink and nearly start choking as a mouthful of brackish yogurt hits the back of my throat, followed by a crushed mint leaf and diced cucumber. "What the... That's like drinking feta cheese!" I manage to gasp out.

Aliah calmly thumps me on the back. "It is not for everyone.

For you"—she nods at Daryl—"I will bring you mantou, the best you ever tasted. Ten minutes."

She disappears through the swinging door to the rear of the small deli/grocery store, leaving Daryl and me sitting at a table near the window. To our right are several aisles bearing bags of fragrant spices, boxes of bright-colored candies, and containers of every kind of nut, chickpea, and dried fruit imaginable. I recognize the white mulberries from my visit to Aliah's apartment. Daryl, on the other hand, nods thoughtfully at every other item, then stacks several selections near the register for our departure.

I'm still mad at him.

Aliah owns the Afghan deli. Apparently, her help doesn't arrive till noon, so she requested that I meet her here around eleven. Which I thought was perfect. Gave me plenty of time to visit the crime scene and check out the supposedly abandoned warehouse where the two murder victims were found. I also planned on identifying the location of the camera that caught Sabera on video, then continue walking in the direction she had headed. Made total sense to me. When looking for a missing person, always good to start with their last-known location.

Daryl, however, refused to take me. Too dangerous, he said.

I cajoled, threatened, then flat-out badgered the man. In the end, I got a curt promise: "I'm not taking you to a crime scene. But I will bring the crime scene to you."

I still have no idea what that means, and the fact he's barely spoken to me since has only added to my irritation.

"How do you know so much about Afghan food?" I demand to know now.

A single-shoulder shrug. "Tucson is known for its culinary scene. Been recognized by UNESCO as a City of Gastronomy. The air force base helps—deploys thousands overseas. They discover new and exciting food while abroad, then bring those tastes home."

"I'm still angry with you," I inform him.

A second shrug. "And I'm still right."

We are saved from further arguing as a gorgeous Latina in form-fitting jeans, a deep-red peasant blouse, and chunky turquoise jewelry comes storming through the entrance. Her glossy brown curls are piled high enough to justify their own zip code, while her giant silver earrings could easily double as lethal weapons. She immediately homes in on Daryl, stalking toward our table and planting herself in Daryl's line of sight.

"What. The. Fuck," she states.

Daryl picks up his doogh. Takes a long milky sip. I settle in to enjoy the show.

"Are you getting yourself in trouble again, Daryl? Because I might not be your parole officer anymore, but that doesn't mean I won't haul your sorry ass in. Asking questions about a double homicide? Seriously—"

"I see your brother called you."

"Of course he called me! Daryl, what went down in that warehouse is not good news. If you know something pertinent—"

"I never know anything pertinent."

"Daryl D. Daniels!"

That's his full name? Daryl D. Daniels? Now I'm fully invested in the drama.

"What aren't you telling me, Daryl?" On cue, her gaze slides over to me. "And who are you?"

"Umm, Frankie Elkin?"

"Is that a question or a statement? What, you don't know your own name?"

Damn, she's good.

"Leave her alone," Daryl orders. "Chase her off and *I* gotta feed the snakes."

"Oh." Mystery woman's eyes light up. "She's Bart's latest misfit?"

"Exactly."

"When not running in fear from hungry snakes," I provide, "I locate missing people. For the fun of it."

"What? Wait. *Who* are you again?"

I'm saved by Aliah, who returns with a steaming platter of something that smells amazing. She nonchalantly slides the dish onto the table, while giving the new woman a quick up and down.

"You are Daryl's friend? The one who can tell us all about the murders?"

"Seriously, Daryl? I'm gonna kill you for this. Absolutely, positively, wring your oxen-sized neck. But first"—the woman's gaze lands on the freshly arrived food—"is that mantou? Somebody, bring me a spoon!"

THE MANTOU STUFF turns out to be amazing. Perfectly cooked pockets of pastry stuffed with ground beef, then covered in a red chickpea sauce, then drizzled with garlic yogurt. An ode to comfort food everywhere.

Aliah beams with happiness as the three of us demolish the platter.

"Roberta," Daryl finally manages. "Meet Aliah. She owns the place."

"Thank you, thank you, thank you," Roberta informs our hostess.

There's one dumpling left on the plate. Roberta gives Daryl a pointed look before snagging it for herself. He shrugs, sits back, dabs delicately at his mouth with his napkin.

"So...you're a parole officer?" I start out, remembering her announcing that much. "Daryl's former parole officer?"

"Yeah. First five years after his release, this dumb lug reported to me. Drug testing, working, socializing. His successful re-entry to society all came down to me, me, and me."

Daryl smiles. "Roberta's selling herself short. It was all about her."

"And now?" I venture, still trying to understand the dynamic between these two.

"We dance."

I do a little a double take, return my attention to Roberta. She certainly has the grace of a dancer, but her following his lead...I don't see it.

She sighs heavily. "I know, but it's true. Big boy here didn't just stay on the straight and narrow; he actually, like, chilled out. Even started to act happy. For most parolees that's not how life works, so I asked for the secret to his success. His answer: ballroom dancing. What the fuck, right? I had to see it to believe it. Next thing I knew, I was mamboing away."

Aliah perks up, her gaze going between them with clear approval.

"No!" Roberta cuts our hostess off at the pass. "It's not like that. Daryl was my parolee. Now he's my dance partner. But I go home to my main man every night. He tolerates Daryl, mostly because there's no way in hell he's gonna shake, rattle, and roll. Last time I mentioned rumba, he thought I was talking about a vacuum cleaner." She rolls her eyes. "Luca has his gifts, but rhythm isn't one of them."

She leans forward. "Seriously, Daryl. Why are you interested in two guys whose skulls were shattered by a hammer?"

Daryl doesn't say anything so much as nod in Aliah's direction. Roberta immediately swings her attention toward the older woman.

"What do you know? You see something, hear something? Tell me."

Aliah recoils. There's something in her gaze, a bit hunted, a bit haunted.

"What do you know?" I speak up, if only to rescue Aliah. "You're a parole officer, not a homicide detective."

"The homicide detective would be my brother. Whom Daryl called first. Except Marc isn't that stupid. It's an active investigation. No way he's speaking out of school."

"But you're here." I tilt my head, regard her more seriously. "Because while a detective couldn't comment on an active investigation, there's nothing stopping you..."

"What do you know?" Roberta repeats impatiently, willing to take me on if Aliah won't play.

"Primary crime scene? Or body dump?" I'm pleased that I sound like I know what I'm talking about, because I genuinely do my best to avoid crime scenes. Though lately, that system hasn't been working for me, and now I know things such as the look in a man's eyes right before a bullet obliterates his brain.

My hands are shaking slightly. I place them on my lap under the table.

Roberta is still frowning at me with impatience.

"Dance," Daryl speaks up softly, his attention on her. "Take the lead. Get the rhythm started. Let them join."

Roberta huffs a little. Finally: "Primary crime scene. Messy one at that."

"The two men?" Aliah asks hesitantly. "You know who they are?"

"Prints weren't in the system."

"A description? What do they look like?"

Roberta arches a brow. "Honey, they look like men who had their skulls annihilated by a hammer. The crime scene specialists are still collecting all the teeth."

Aliah winces. I fist my hands under the table.

"It sounds like a scene of incredible violence," I say softly. "Overkill?"

"Or sending a message. That area of town...It's a known location for all sorts of nastiness. What did you say you did again?"

"Find missing people," I murmur, then: "Is there a particular gang or group that's known to operate in this area? Such as the Russians or Mexican drug cartels, or..."

"Honey, have you looked at a map lately? Tucson sits close enough to the border to have more ICE agents than local LEOs. We don't just have internationally known factions, we have internationally known factions of factions. Come now, I showed you mine. Time to show me yours."

Aliah does the honors. "I don't know what happened," she begins. "But the video of the woman walking away. The police said they would like to interview her. Let me just say, I have a friend who owns a hijab exactly like the one in the video—dark blue with tiny turquoise-and-white flowers."

Roberta stares at her. "Seriously? You had Daryl call in a personal favor over a matching *scarf*?"

Now Aliah is insulted. "My friend is missing. Has been missing for three weeks! And your police hasn't made any effort to find her, not even pinging her phone—"

"You know it's her, you can absolutely positively identify her from blurry footage that doesn't even show her face?" Roberta arches a brow.

"I know that fabric!"

"Really, and how well do you know your friend?"

Aliah rears back with a gasp. I hold up a hand.

"All right, all right. Enough already. Aliah knows what she's talking about. And you know she knows what she's talking about, or you wouldn't be here." I regard Roberta for a minute. "Your brother the homicide detective can't talk about a crime scene, but he provided you with details to act in his stead. Because he loves Daryl, your parolee-turned-dance-partner, that much?"

Daryl shrugs as if to agree he's not that worthy.

"He sent you. He approved you giving up certain information because…" I glance around me. "Kabul Corner. Daryl said to meet here, and the second your brother heard you were going to an Afghan restaurant, that caught his attention. Homicide may not know who the men are, but they know where they're from. Afghanistan, yes? That's the connection."

Aliah appears suitably impressed. Roberta merely scowls at me. Her gaze returns to Aliah.

"Tell me about your friend. Where did she work? What was she involved in?"

"Sabera worked as a chambermaid at a resort. She was involved in trying to help herself and her family adapt to an entirely new country in a matter of weeks."

"Do you think drugs?" I cut to the chase. "The two dead men, are they drug dealers or criminal syndicate members or something equally dangerous and terrifying?"

"I wasn't lying before," Roberta allows. "No one knows who they are."

"If they got into the country—"

"Oh, please, like there aren't a million ways to get in this country."

"Sabera is a mother!" Aliah pounds the table, clearly having had enough. "She is not some villain. And she went through rounds and rounds of screening and interviewing and questioning. We all do. She's not some closet criminal."

"Really, because according to you, she's disappeared. No one knows where she is."

"Because she's a victim."

"Or she's caught up in something bigger than you know."

Now Aliah positively glares at Roberta. "You have never met my friend. You have no right—"

Aliah's tirade is interrupted by a loud chime from her phone. She glances at the screen, frowns. "I must take this. Also"—she rakes Roberta up and down with a look of disdain—"I will never cook for you again." Aliah stalks away with her phone glued to her ear.

"I see you haven't lost your charm," Daryl murmurs after Aliah has disappeared into the kitchen.

"This is serious. Stay away, Daryl. Whatever the hell happened in that warehouse, you want no part of it. Marc showed me photos. Just a few, but it was enough. That is some sick stuff."

"Which was possibly witnessed by a missing woman whose safety is already in question," I point out.

Roberta glares at me.

I couldn't care less. "Sabera disappeared three weeks ago. Last seen exiting her housekeeping job too late at night to catch her bus. Her husband doesn't seem to care, the police aren't interested. But the next possible sighting of her is at a brutal double homicide. That's gotta be worth investigating, and surely your brother's wondering the same, or he never would've sent you."

Roberta harumphs, but her shoulders come down. She opens her mouth as if to finally say something interesting, when Aliah bursts through the swinging doors, her eyes too wide, her face too pale. "We must go. Now." She focuses on Daryl. "Please take us. Your presence would be much appreciated."

Daryl is already rising to standing, while Roberta and I blink in confusion.

"What happened?" I ask, as it's clearly nothing good.

"That was Nageenah, the Ahmadis' neighbor. A strange man just pulled into their complex and tried to grab another family's daughter. Her older brother was able to hold him off while she ran for their parents. The man escaped, but this is the thing—he kept calling the girl Zahra. 'Zahra, come here. Zahra, it's okay. Zahra, I will take you to your mother.'

"The man wasn't looking for any child. He was trying to abduct Sabera's."

CHAPTER 11

Daryl does the driving, heavy on the gas, light on the brakes. Roberta follows close behind. It's still a solid ten minutes, which Aliah spends trying to reach Isaad Ahmadi. Failing that, she calls Sabera's cell phone, only to disconnect moments later, muttering in frustration.

"The mailbox is full. I can't even leave a message."

Given Sabera's been out of touch for three weeks, that doesn't surprise me. It does imply that others are still trying to reach her. Including her husband, Isaad? Or the man trying to snatch her daughter? Or the two men brained to death in a warehouse?

I don't want to think about that. My current nightmares are bad enough.

By the time we arrive, it appears half of the tenants are milling about the parking lot in various states of agitation. The men look up sharply as Daryl careens to a halt, several adopting defensive stances, hands fisted by their sides. These are people who don't expect assistance, only new levels of threat.

Daryl doesn't even have the vehicle in park before Aliah is bolting out the door and heading straight for the parents of the roller-skating children. I'm assuming it was their little girl the man approached and her big brother who took on a grown adult twice his size. Certainly, that tracks with what I observed yesterday.

Many in the assembled group relax a fraction at the older woman's approach. Others, from a melting pot of countries, cue off their neighbor's ease, releasing clenched fists.

Until Daryl steps out of the car, at which point a murmur of alarm flares through the crowd, just in time for Roberta to come barreling into the space behind him; then a black-and-white patrol car squeals to a halt at the curb.

Given the reputation of policing in so many parts of the world, mothers quickly start ushering their children away. Aliah doesn't bother to explain. She has attention only for the Afghan couple, while across the way, I spot Nageenah standing in the doorway of her unit, diaper-clad baby once more perched on her hip. She's clearly anxious, but with two other children tucked inside, she can't abandon her post.

While Aliah starts talking rapidly to the parents in their own language, I cross to Nageenah.

"Are you okay?"

She nods. Her gaze is fixed on the patrol car, tracking the uniform exiting the vehicle. When the officer turns out to be a young Black female, Nageenah slowly exhales.

"I did not see anything," she murmurs, hitching her drooling son higher on her hip. "I was in the living room with the children. It faces the rear of the property. I knew nothing until I heard Pazir yelling and then a car thumping over the sidewalk. I had no idea. What if the man had come here? What if he still wants Zahra?"

Her agitation ratchets up another notch.

"Have you heard from Zahra's father?" I ask. "Do you know when he's returning?"

"No. I texted earlier, but never received a reply. I tried calling again. Nothing."

"And Zahra? Your other boy? Are they okay?"

"Their morning has been wooden blocks and workbooks. The rest of this, they have no idea."

Just then two little faces appear in the hallway behind her, a dark-eyed boy in a red dinosaur T-shirt and a dark-haired girl with impossibly huge gray eyes. She peers at me solemnly, while the boy tugs on the hem of his mother's shirt. The baby glances down, squeals something at his brother. The boy responds by pinching the baby's big toe.

"Taimur!" Nageenah reprimands sharply.

Taimur grins, but releases his brother's foot. In return, the baby waves a slobbery fist at him. More squealing ensues.

I squat down till I'm eye level with Zahra. She's not said a word, just stands a few feet back, right shoulder tucked against the wall. I have vague memories of babysitting as a teenager, but primarily so I could steal the parents' booze. I would refill the bottles with water, which might have covered my tracks if I hadn't ended most evenings passed out drunk. Needless to say, there wasn't a huge demand for my services, and to this day, I know next to nothing about kids.

Now I study Sabera's daughter, while she studies me back. What is it Ashley the housing coordinator had said? Zahra could be the poster child for refugee children with her stunning features and solemn expression. She isn't just beautiful, she's haunting, like an old soul peering at the world through a child's eyes.

I want to tell her everything will be all right. I will find her mother, I will bring her home, I will save her family.

But I already think she knows better. I'm the one with the questions, while this little girl has all the answers; she's simply waiting for the rest of the world to catch up.

Aliah arrives behind me. I glance over my shoulder to see that Roberta and the uniformed officer are now talking to the other parents. I'm assuming asking for a description of the subject, taking down basic information. By now, I can predict their responses, the same the world over—I don't remember, I didn't see, it all happened so fast.

Personally, I have only one question for Pazir and his family. I'm curious who will ask it first.

"Are you all right?" Aliah arrives at the unit, attention focused on Nageenah. The baby is now kicking away at her hip, trying to play with his big brother. Aliah plucks the younger boy out of his mother's arms and folds his drooling form into her own. The baby babbles in delight. Nageenah sighs in relief. So that's how it's done.

A slight tug of my hair.

Zahra. Standing directly in the doorway now, so close her nose is nearly touching mine.

God, those eyes. The mysteries of the universe, the heartbreak of eons past, the sadness of homeless, countryless children everywhere.

"My name is Frankie," I murmur.

She stares at me. Stares, stares, stares until I can feel each of my sins, all of my secrets slowly being stripped bare. I let her take my full measure. The losses I have felt, the pain I've inflicted, the sad little girl who still lives deep inside me, longing for her father to sober up, wishing for her mother to come home.

The damaged woman I've become, unable to stay too long or connect too deeply because the sheer anxiety of such intimacy makes me want to drink.

Zahra nods as if that makes sense to her. Maybe it does.

Then she states in perfectly clear English: "A lock to a key for a key that has no lock."

She leans closer, whispers in my ear: "You must find it."

Then she turns and vanishes back down the hall, Nageenah's older son scampering to catch up.

I glance up to find both Aliah and Nageenah regarding me.

"There is a word," Nageenah says, "for an extremely talented young child?"

"Prodigy?"

"Yes, that's it. Isaad is brilliant with numbers. Sabera has skills with language. Zahra...she never forgets. Words on a page, dates on a calendar. Whatever she sees, she carries in her head." A slight hesitation. "Her life will not be an easy one."

I consider what I've learned about the fall of Kabul and life in refugee camps, then contemplate what that might mean for a four-year-old who remembers everything.

"How absolutely horrible," I murmur at last.

Neither woman disagrees.

CHAPTER 12

ANOTHER VEHICLE PULLS UP OUTSIDE the apartment complex. At this point, every tenant has dispersed save the father, Pazir, who remains standing before Roberta and the uniformed officer with his hand on his son's shoulder.

The boy's expression remains wary. He lets his father do the talking, maybe out of respect, maybe out of fear.

When a male detective materializes at the scene, I can practically hear Pazir's sigh of relief, not to mention Roberta's huff of agitation. The curt greeting the man gives Daryl confirms my suspicions. Apparently, we are now worthy of Roberta's cop brother's personal attention.

Aliah hands back the baby and strides forcefully toward the action. Whether to protect her countrymen, assist with translation, berate an official member of law enforcement who three weeks later has finally bothered to show up, is anyone's guess.

"I have nothing more to say," Pazir is rattling off to the

detective. "My son kept his sister safe." The "which is more than you people did" is fully implied.

"I understand that, Mr.... ?"

"Noori."

"Mr. Noori. Clearly your son is a brave young man. Now I just need one more small act of courage. You and your son come with me to headquarters, where we can take an official statement and set you up with a specialist who will turn your verbal description of the subject into a picture we can circulate among law enforcement. Sooner we catch this guy, sooner both of you can feel safe."

"They already provided a description." Aliah nods her head in the direction of the uniformed officer. "Ask her."

"With no disrespect, Officer Kade is not an expert in this area. Now—"

"Brown hair," the boy speaks up abruptly. "Light eyes. He reminded me of the guards." He glances up at his father.

"At the camp?"

"Yes."

Pazir presses his lips into a thin line. "Then the man is military or maybe special police."

I perk up at this piece of information, while Aliah looks like she wants to hurt someone.

The detective—Marc?—leans down to be closer to the boy.

"How tall?"

Shrug. "Same as most."

I take that to mean average height. Given Detective Marc's nod, I'm assuming he agrees.

"What was he wearing?"

"Gray pants with many pockets. White shirt with a collar and many buttons."

"How was he built?" The detective points to himself. "Like me, or maybe like him?" He points to Daryl's bulked-up form.

The boy hesitates, murmurs something to his father.

Aliah does the honors: "Thin, but strong thin. Wiry, I believe is the word?"

Detective Marc nods. "His hair, short or long?"

"Short, very short." The boy slides his hand along the top of his head. Buzz cut, consistent with the military appearance.

"His eyes. Close or far apart?"

The boy shrugs.

"Could you see any special markings, tattoos, freckles, maybe a scar?"

Another shrug.

"He is…just a man," the boy says finally. "He used nice words, but his eyes didn't match. I have seen such things before."

Pazir's hand tightens on his son's shoulder.

Marc nods, straightens. "You're a brave boy. Your sister, your family, are very lucky to have you. Last couple of questions, okay? His vehicle. Do you know what kind of car?"

"White. Big, like a truck, but fully enclosed. An SUV?"

Detective Marc glances at the father. "Any chance you caught the license plate?"

Pazir shakes his head. "I ran out when I heard my son call. But the man was already jumping into his vehicle. He wanted to cause trouble, I am certain. But he did not want to be caught."

The detective nods, glancing around the parking lot. Looking for cameras, I'm willing to guess, but no such luck at this address.

"You said he spoke," he asks the boy now. "What did he say?"

"He called my sister Zahra. He said he was a friend of her

mother's. That he would take her to her. But my sister is not Zahra. The man should know that."

"Do you know who Zahra is?" Detective Marc asks. "Does she live here, too?"

"I will assist with that," Aliah interrupts curtly. "You must finish. Pazir is an Uber driver. It's important he get to work."

The detective gives her a look but seems to decide not to press it. "Final question: Would you know the voice if you heard it again?"

The boy immediately nods. "Yes."

"Because it's distinct?" I interject, as this is what I want to know. Sabera and her family have just arrived from Afghanistan, the two murdered men are also from there, meaning... "Did he sound like he's from your home or neighboring country?"

"Oh, no, he is not one of us." Again, a look at his father, followed by a quick exchange of whispered words.

His father frowns, then focuses on Detective Marc. "The man spoke English the way our neighbor, Sabera, speaks English."

"The missing woman?" Detective Marc glances at Aliah. She glares back.

"Yes, but not quite. Same but different."

"And how does Sabera speak?"

"British," Aliah supplies. "Her mother grew up in London. Sabera learned English from her, including the accent."

"Except not," I muse. "Same but different. Australian?" It's all I can think of off the top of my head.

The boy shrugs; this is clearly beyond his pay grade.

"We will go now," Pazir states.

Detective Marc nods, hands over a business card, then does a neat little pivot to regard me more fully.

"And who are you again?"

"I'm the woman already looking for Sabera. Feel free to catch up."

"*Excuse me?*"

"Yeah, yeah, yeah, whine to someone who cares. At the moment, you need to come meet Zahra. Because both of her parents have now vanished, and there's no way this is over yet."

CHAPTER 13

NAGEENAH APPEARS WARY WHEN WE all reappear on her doorstep. Aliah speaks to her rapidly in their shared tongue; then, with a slight nod, Nageenah allows us to enter. I notice the detective nods at her respectfully but doesn't try to shake her hand. Daryl, however, reaches out reflexively, only to have Roberta quickly yank down his arm. He grimaces at his cultural faux pas, then tucks his hand behind his back as if to keep from repeating the mistake.

Nageenah leads us past the kitchen to the living area at the rear of the apartment. The baby is now sitting on the floor, chewing on a wooden block, while his older brother zooms a toy car across the sofa. I don't immediately spy Zahra; then her head pops up from behind the sofa. She takes in the gaggle of grown-ups, then slips back down into her hiding place. I don't blame her. At least the patrol officer has moved on, but six adults is about five too many for a space this small. I also have no idea how we're going to talk about anything meaningful with three children present, including one who apparently remembers everything.

Aliah exchanges low words with Nageenah, then heads into the kitchen to put on a kettle of water.

The three-year-old is eyeing Detective Marc with a look of wonder, his gaze fixed on the gold shield dangling from the man's neck. The baby is less subtle. He drops his block, waddles over to the detective, and grabs his pant leg.

Nageenah utters a word of reprimand, but the detective merely smiles, unloops the chain from around his neck, and hands over the desired item, only for the three-year-old to jump up, grab the new toy from his younger brother, and bolt out of the room.

Immediate wailing, flailing of tiny fists. Before Nageenah can respond, however, Daryl hefts up the toddler into his arms. In some act of dance partner telepathy, he and Roberta appear to arrive at a mutual conclusion.

"Hey, little man, wanna tango?" A quick two-step and the baby's drooling mouth is converted into a silent O, as Daryl cha-cha-chas both of them out of the room. Not to be outdone, Roberta peeks behind the sofa.

"Zahra, I presume? Would you like to learn how to dance? We don't want the boys to have all the fun."

Zahra's head reappears. She regards the curly-haired brunette solemnly, then slides her hand into Roberta's. With a wink, Roberta plucks her charge from behind the sofa, then twirls her down the hall, leaving the adults to speak in private. Well played.

Detective Marc takes a seat on the sofa while Aliah returns bearing a tray filled with fragrant cups of green tea.

"All right," the detective acknowledges. "You have my apology and now my attention. So, the missing woman, Sabera Ahmadi? And that's her daughter, Zahra? Start from the beginning and tell me everything."

———

ALIAH CATCHES HIM up on Sabera's disappearance three weeks ago, vanishing after work, and not seen again until this morning's news broadcast showing video clips of a mystery woman walking away from the scene of a double murder. Aliah is convinced the woman is Sabera based on her headscarf, while Detective Marc, like his sister, appears skeptical to accept any ID based solely on textiles. For her part, Nageenah describes the courier who visited Isaad yesterday, after which Isaad handed over his daughter to Nageenah and is now also MIA.

"But you're saying Isaad isn't always reliable? He's often late?" Detective Marc asks.

Nageenah shrugs. "He is a brilliant man, but like many who see what no one else can see—"

"He's arrogant and selfish," Aliah provides more bluntly.

"You don't like him," I speak up, not really a question as the answer is written all over Aliah's face. "Why? You said he and Sabera were not a love match. What are they, then?" Then in the next second: "Wait, you also commented Isaad was a friend of her father's. How old is this man?"

"Fifties? Sixty?" Aliah gives a harrumph of disapproval. "Certainly, closer to my age than hers."

If memory serves, Sabera is twenty-three. So, yep, that's definitely an age gap.

"It is not that uncommon," Nageenah counters. "A good husband is expected to be a provider, which requires a certain level of age and experience. At least it wasn't a forced marriage like so many others."

"So you like him?" I ask Nageenah.

She hesitates. Finally: "Isaad fills a room. Sabera withdraws accordingly. He is older, dominating. She is one person when she is alone. A different woman when she's with him."

There are some things that require no cultural explanation. I follow up with the next logical question: "You ever witness Sabera appearing bruised, injured, perhaps suffering from a rash of accidents?"

Nageenah shakes her head. "In my position in the ministry, I spent much time learning exactly how defenseless a wife, daughter, sister can be. Isaad...he's not an easy man, but I don't believe he hurts his family."

I purposefully avert my gaze from Aliah before launching my next question. "Have you ever observed Sabera acting like...not quite herself. Maybe stumbling a little, slurring her words. Incapacitated?"

"Wait, what are you implying?" Aliah is already sounding outraged. "Are you asking if Sabera was drinking?"

I keep my attention fixed on Nageenah, whose eyes have widened slightly.

"Sabera is Muslim. She would never—" Aliah's voice cuts off, Detective Marc raising a silencing hand. I can already tell he's as interested in this answer as I am.

Nageenah doesn't say anything.

"Couple of times?" I supply softly. "Or at least one episode, where you had to wonder?"

Nageenah bows her head. Then, a single faint nod.

"No!" Aliah protests.

I finally shoot her a glance. "Remember our deal. I will ask any question. I will consider all answers—even the ones *you don't like*."

Aliah has the good grace to flush. She slumps back on the sofa, appearing less angry, more distressed. Then her own mind connects the dots: "You've heard of this behavior before. That's why you made the inquiry. Someone else thinks Sabera is drinking. I didn't . . . I never saw anything myself."

"Sounds like there's a lot of strain on the home front," Detective Marc murmurs, focusing our attention. "Domineering older husband, stressed out young wife. Is it possible Sabera was planning on leaving him?"

"Leave Isaad, maybe. But leave Zahra? Never." Aliah's conviction is absolute. "Nor would she have to give up her child to end her marriage. She could have talked to me about how to go about such a thing. I promise you, she's never said a word."

Detective Marc turns his attention to Nageenah. "What do you think?"

Nageenah is more circumspect. "Right now, divorce would not be practical. For most families, both the husband and wife must work outside the home in order to pay bills, and still, each month is a struggle. On her own, where would Sabera go? How would she take care of her child? These are questions she would ask herself. And without the answers . . ."

"Could she have met someone?" Detective Marc pushes. "Another man who could put a roof over her head?"

Nageenah shrugs as if to say she has no idea. Aliah once more cuts to the chase. "When? She worked, and when not working, she watched her daughter. When would she have the time to meet this fictional someone?"

"That's not true."

Aliah turns to Nageenah with a frown. "Now what?" Because apparently all bad news is Nageenah's fault. The younger woman eyes the older one coolly, before stating:

"A couple of afternoons a week, I watched Zahra for her. Few hours here, a few hours there. Sabera said it was so she could buy food, take care of household chores, but I never saw her return with any groceries or store items. She left on the bus and would return three hours later, always empty-handed."

"That doesn't mean she had a lover!"

"It doesn't. But there was more to Sabera's life than work and home. What that was, I don't know."

"You saw her returning," I ask abruptly. "Could you gauge her mood? Did she seem perkier, more carefree, hell, relaxed?" Because having just spent time enjoying the company of a very sexy man, the relaxed part stands out to me. Until, of course, the weeks became months and my natural-born terror reared its ugly head.

You're afraid of being happy, he told me. And I totally agreed with him.

"I don't know." Nageenah furrows her brow. "She seemed... like herself. Serious. Tired. Worried. But who isn't?"

"What would her husband do if he found out she had a lover?" Detective Marc again. "Does he strike you as the jealous type? A man capable of violence?"

Nageenah lowers her gaze to the floor, while Aliah does the honors.

"In Kabul, Isaad was a man of great respect. But living here...He's just another refugee. He's not used to such things. And he is a man with a temper. I once saw him throw a pomegranate against the wall with such force it splattered."

I can't help myself. "Why throw a pomegranate?"

"Because there's nothing in this world as good as a Kandahar pomegranate," Nageenah states seriously. "And sometimes, it's not the big differences between Kabul and here that are too hard to take—you expect them. But little things, say, a piece of fruit that looks and smells like home, but tastes wrong...Some days, that feels like enough to break you."

"Or causes a grown man to have a temper tantrum," I mutter. "Do you think Isaad still wants to be married? Like you said, his life has also undergone a great change."

"He is respectful," Nageenah begins, while Aliah snorts.

"He is controlling. The fruit may be different here, but getting to feel powerful by bossing around a vulnerable young woman...I am sure that never gets old. And certainly isn't something he'd want to give up anytime soon."

"I have seen him look at her with genuine warmth," Nageenah counters. "Isaad is moody to be sure, but I think he has affection for his wife. It's just...When he grows frustrated, he can be quite intimidating. I don't blame her for finding that difficult."

"How is Isaad as a father?" Detective Marc switches gears. "Does he seem interested in his daughter?"

"He dotes on Zahra," Nageenah answers immediately, voice firm. "He takes care of her at night while Sabera works, has even learned how to cook, clean. These are big steps for a man of his years. And I've watched him play with Zahra. He creates little games, puzzles for her to solve. She is very clever, and he delights in that."

"She is his favorite student?" I fill in dryly.

Nageenah gives me a look. "Maybe. But most likely, none of her schoolteachers will ever be able to keep up with her, so it's good she has such a parent at home."

"How smart is she?" Detective Marc wants to know.

"She's been reading since she was two. Can already do all sorts of math in her head. And she has a very good memory. Extraordinarily so."

"Did she see the man who tried to abduct the other child?" Detective Marc perks up. "Because if her memory is that good..."

"None of us saw anything. There's no view of the parking lot from this room."

"White male," Detective Marc rattles off. "Wiry build. Speaks with a British-like accent. Sound like anyone you've seen around here before?"

Nageenah shakes her head. "What if he comes back, tries again?"

"I can ask for more patrol cars in the area."

"I have two other children. I love Zahra, but I can't put their lives in danger. What if...what if?" Her gaze goes to Aliah, who sighs heavily.

"I will take Zahra. She knows me, and even if that man has Sabera and Isaad's address, there's no reason for him have to mine. Once Isaad returns, he can find us."

"You're still certain Isaad's coming back?" I ask.

Even Aliah seems startled by my doubt. "Of course. Family is everything."

I wish I shared her optimism. And I really wished I knew what was in that box, that made him hand over his daughter and vanish in the wind. "The private courier." I turn to Nageenah. "Can you remember anything about him? Logo on a shirt, identifying ball cap, color of car?"

Nageenah shakes her head. "He drove a black vehicle. Something rugged. That's all I remember."

"A lock to a key for a key that has no lock," I ponder out loud. "Does that sound familiar to anyone?"

I receive three blank stares.

"Where did you hear that?" Detective Marc.

"Zahra said it to me. According to her, I must find it."

"A four-year-old recited that?"

"With an exceptional memory." I nod toward Nageenah. "Meaning Zahra has read or heard that before. A book? A poem? A note?"

Still three blank stares.

"Well." I rise to standing. "I know what I'm doing next. When you finally identify the two victims in the warehouse, you'll let me know?"

"I sure as hell will not," Detective Marc assures me.

"Come on now, there's no use fighting my charms. You'll need to run the names by Aliah and Nageenah to see if they recognize them from the Afghan community. Once you do that, they'll share the information with me. Might as well start by dialing direct and save us all a bunch of time."

He scowls. "Who are you again?"

I consider the matter seriously. "I'm a person who's terrified of snakes yet due to feed a bunch of pythons dinner later tonight. I'm a woman waiting for a call from a man I instructed not to call me. But mostly...mostly right now, I'm a recovering alcoholic who desperately wants to crack open an ice-cold beer. Because I'm tired and frustrated. And it's too damn hot outside. And oh, yeah, it's a day that ends in Y.

"In other words, I'm someone who needs to get back to work in ways I don't expect the rest of you to understand."

I pause, study the good detective. "How much trouble do you think Sabera Ahmadi is in?"

Detective Marc hesitates.

Death by hammer times two, never a good thing. Attempted child abduction, also quite terrible.

"Don't be a stranger, Detective," I murmur. Then I head out of the room to find Daryl.

CHAPTER 14

MY MOTHER ADVISED THAT TO *keep myself safe, I should peer into other people's souls but never let them see mine.*

My father said in the case of danger, I should find a man. Specifically, his dear friend Professor Ahmadi, who would always take care of me.

I think of these instructions now as I weave my way frantically through the streets of Kabul, dodging milling families, umbrella-topped food carts, and a pile of blocked vehicles honking furiously at one another. Some people draw back from the strange sight of a traditionally garbed female in a dark head covering running around with a long gun. Most are too consumed by their own panic to notice.

I dash behind a line of market stalls in various states of packing. Race through another narrow alley, then another. I careen into the wider cross street in time to discover a black-turbaned Taliban fighter standing on the other side of the jammed street.

From across the way, he takes me in, a lone female, and smiles. His gaze falls upon my rifle. His smile grows.

I don't know what to do. Raise my weapon threateningly? Flee back the way I'd come?

Except there's a press of people behind me as well. Everyone trying to pour into the main avenues. Everyone desperate to escape.

A man pulling a four-wheeled wagon piled high with stacks of swaying trunks halts between me and the leering militant. I don't wait. I turn and run, bouncing off surging bodies and tripping over abandoned belongings as I fight my way upstream. The university, from which I had fled just hours ago, now seems my only hope.

When I finally glance to my left, I don't see the Taliban fighter anymore. But I still catch glimpses of black turbans pushing through the streets, emerging from various storefronts and side alleys. The crowd's growing fright is palpable.

The smell of exhaust fumes and sweat-covered bodies. The feel of steel and concrete blast walls, pressing against a swelling tide of humanity. The congestion of red-and-black-umbrellaed four-wheeled market stalls, once set up to feed milling shoppers, now desperate to escape.

I veer right when a second scowling man appears in front of me, swerve left when a third snatches at my arm. It feels like swimming upstream, which makes me think of the last day at the lake, the feel of his fingers entwined in mine . . .

By the time I stagger through the university gates, I'm gasping in a gut-churning combination of grief, fear, and exhaustion. All I want is sanctuary. What I discover, however, is a scene only slightly less chaotic than the city streets. People dashing here, dashing there, while others appear to be nearly spinning in place. And the noise—an undercurrent of anxious mutterings that seem to come from everywhere and swell to a crashing crescendo. What's happening, where to go? Rumors fly that the Taliban have entered from the west and south and are capturing all government institutions, including schools. And yet the idea that an institution as prestigious as this university might fall still feels preposterous. Of course, the Taliban, marching straight into Kabul…

No one knows what to do, because none of us possessed this level of imagination. And yet now, here we are.

Pressing my back against the wall, I work my way quickly to Professor Ahmadi's office. Inside, I find him sorting through his oldest and most precious notebooks, whose ragged pages are filled with lecture notes he has carefully curated over the years, official textbooks being hard to come by. Even more amazing, he has an entire red binder filled with meticulously developed theorems and proofs, in hope of the day he'll have a wider audience. Now, one by one, he's piling such treasures into open boxes.

He stills the moment he sees me. His dark eyes, set deep beneath heavy, gray-shot brows, fall to the rifle clutched in my trembling hand.

"It is that bad, then? Your father?"

I can't say the words. The professor nods once, saving me from the heartache.

"And your brother?"

I shake my head.

He grunts. "I tried to warn your father. His brothers were doing him no favors. Side with them, pay the price."

I open my mouth, but all that emerges is a half-choked sob, the beginning note of an animal's wounded scream.

Ahmadi sets down the red-covered journal in his hand,

considers me straight on. An older man, he wears his intelligence like a fierce cloak wrapped around his tall frame and hawkish nose. I've seen women swoon over him. And I've heard whispers about the others, female students upon whom he set his gaze, then dismissed once they succumbed. Dokhtar Baaz, they whispered behind his back, a lecherous old man. I don't think they were wrong.

I've worked for him for nearly a year, an exalted position for someone of my junior standing. But I'm not stupid. I observe how his gaze spends more time roaming the lines of my body than reviewing the long and torturous equations he has me copying onto the chalkboard.

Lately his focus has grown even more attentive, the first to notice my drift into bulkier, more traditional dress. Then later, seeming to actually notice how my hastily scrawled numbers are scratched across the blackboard with surprising speed and fluidity. I've had to force myself to slow down, to glance repeatedly at his annotations, as if in need of the information.

Now he considers me. Then, as a direct order: "Tell me."

I want to make the announcement matter-of-factly, if not defiantly. Instead, my cheeks flush hotly, and I'm acutely aware of my shame.

I miss my mother. It's foolish, but now more than ever, I long for the comfort of her embrace. I want to confess to her all my stupidity and naïve female failings. I want her to tell me everything will be all right, and even if she's lying, at least for a moment, I will be able to set down my burden.

Now I try to utter three simple words. My mouth opens, closes. No declaration emerges. I blush harder, try again. I still can't make my throat work. My father might be progressive, but even he would be appalled by what I've done.

For an instant, terribly, selfishly, heartbreakingly, I am grateful he's dead and will never know of my disgrace. Which makes me hang my head in shame all over again.

Professor Ahmadi, finally taking pity on me: "Who's the father?" He asks the question brusquely. I'm grateful for the lack of berating.

"Does it matter?" I whisper.

"I would say, given the circumstances, it matters very much."

I shake my head. "He's gone. I'm alone. That is all that's relevant."

"Is he American?" Ahmadi asks sharply.

"No."

"But you could say he is. An American combatant, recently recalled from Bagram?"

"I . . . I guess."

"Then this is what we shall do: we will head to the base together. You'll be the expectant sweetheart of a US soldier. I'll be your father. They will fly us both out of here."

I give him a puzzled look. I highly doubt it will be that simple. And yet, having dictated his plan, Professor Ahmadi has already resumed packing.

"Is that all you're taking?" He nods his chin in the direction of my only visible possession, the rifle dangling at my side.

I remember what my mother said. About what we would want. About what we would be allowed.

"I have everything I need," I say at last, drifting a hand over my slightly rounded belly. And when he assumes that I'm talking about my unborn child, I don't bother to correct him.

———

In the end, it is not so simple. Professor Ahmadi loads his car with all his boxes of books and bags of valuables, everything he's convinced he can't live without. The moment we depart the university gates, however, we are immediately stalled in the same heavy congestion I encountered earlier. No amount of honking or swearing makes a difference, and it quickly becomes clear we'll never make it to Bagram, which is a full hour north of the city. Instead, we set our sights on the Hamid Karzai International Airport, spending an agonizing four hours covering what should've taken thirty minutes.

Even then, by the final few miles, the crush of humanity has grown too dense to be passable by car. We park in the middle of the road, the professor picking one suitcase, topping it with his most precious box, before slinging a black duffel over his shoulder. He hands me a second. We set out unsteadily, quickly overwhelmed by the sheer chaos. Women sobbing and wailing in the oppressive heat. Grown men wading through drainage canals filled with knee-deep sewage.

The closer we get, the worse it becomes, the press of humanity congealing into an impassable wall pressing against a second even more imposing physical structure, this one topped by coils of razor wire and manned by grim-faced US Marines armed with assault rifles. Children are being passed forward through the crowd. Someone has even climbed halfway up, frantically trying to hand over a baby as if gaining access to the stream of departing US cargo planes is the only hope of survival.

I watch in a mix of horror and fascination. The Americans have abandoned us. The Americans will save us. It makes no sense and yet still isn't as crazy as the three-thousand-year-old capital, my city, my family's home, collapsing in less than twenty-four hours.

There are faces in the crowd I recognize and who recognize me. We all studiously avoid eye contact, though at this point, it hardly matters.

In war, there are winners and losers. Here are the losers, hundreds of thousands of Afghans who dared fight for a better future, and in the coming days, will probably pay with their lives. Or worse, their families will pay that price for them.

I'm grateful that my mother is already dead, that she does not have to see this. That she doesn't have to swallow down the bitter taste in her mouth, which is now filling my own.

Eventually, Professor Ahmadi grabs my arm and pulls me away. There's no hope for us here. Everyone is thrusting precious papers in the air, legal documents attesting to their right to leave the country. Everyone is lugging personal valuables and family treasures.

None of it matters.

"Should the worst happen, people will want to take everything, but in the end, they will be allowed nothing. Remember this, my sweet. Remember."

Now I fall in step behind Ahmadi as we awkwardly press our way through the incoming streams of traffic in order to return to his automobile.

"We will be married," he states as we are walking.

"I thought you were my father."

He halts so abruptly, I nearly stumble into him. "Sabera! Look around. Surely you see everything has changed. It's no longer safe for a young woman to be alone."

I want to argue with him. But I recall the look of that first Taliban fighter leering at me from across the street, anticipation already brightening his eyes.

The professor releases the handle of his suitcase long enough to grasp my shoulder.

"I have the connections and resources to get us across the border. We will have to travel by car, but it can be done. In return, Sabera, I will be your husband. You will follow my lead, you will do as I say, and you will accept me in each and every way. Do you understand?"

The grip of his hand tightens, strong and bruising for a man of his years, while beneath those thick brows, his own eyes hold a gleam.

I regard him for a full minute. I remember bursting pomegranate trees and the sound of my brother's laughter. I remember my parents and the look they shared every day of their marriage. I remember floating peacefully atop a deep, dark lake, my pale shirt spreading around me like butterfly wings, while his warm hand slipped into mine.

When I was a girl, I dreamed.

Now I nod once.

"I promised your father that I would keep you safe," Professor Ahmadi states curtly. "And I am a man of my word. I will accept the child as my own. I will provide for you both. Maybe it is not the marriage you expected, but I am an exceedingly brilliant man, Sabera. And it's clear to me you are an exceedingly clever girl. We might not do so poorly together after all."

He resumes forcing his way through the cresting human tide.

After a moment, I follow.

My father told me when the danger grew too great, I would need a man to save me.

My mother instructed me when the worst happened, never let anyone peer into my soul.

Use others. But never give too much of yourself away.

Perhaps they were both right in the end.

I have written this to you, Zahra, along with the other diary entries and assorted ramblings, because like any child who's lost a parent too soon, I know how uncertain the future is.

I have borne witness to so much death and tragedy.

And yet from the first instant I held you in my arms, I have also experienced the greatest love and deepest joy.

I would've liked to have watched you grow up, my sweet child, to experience the expanding years and significant life events I never had with my own mother. But maybe, much like my maadar jan, my days have always been numbered.

Now, Zahra, I will give you the same advice my parents gave me:

Trust in Isaad. He kept his word, claiming you from the moment of your birth, before falling hopelessly in love with your clever and curious mind.

He will never willingly let anyone harm you, including me.

Trust in yourself. You are descended from warriors. The men in our family foolishly believe that distinction belongs to them, but it is the women, going back generations, who have made the bravest decisions and fought the toughest battles.

Remember, my sweet girl:

All the love you've ever wanted, you have.

All the courage you've ever needed, you possess.

All the secrets of the universe you've hoped to learn, you hold in your amazing mind.

My darling Zahra...

Chin up.

CHAPTER 15

BY THE TIME DARYL DROPS me off at the Starbucks, I'm genuinely anxious, my white T-shirt glued to my skin in a combination of hopped-up nerves and blistering afternoon heat. I hadn't exaggerated to the detective earlier—I'm acutely aware that night is drawing closer and with it, my first care and feeding of snakes. If the trick is to face your fear, my fear needs to do a better job of acknowledging the moment and relinquishing its hold. Instead, I can feel my dread ratcheting up by the hour. I don't want to devolve into a quivering shell of humanity come dinnertime, but I might not have a choice in the matter.

I'm also uncertain about the conversation ahead. The cost of this meeting—two twin mattresses, pledged to Ashley the housing coordinator—is a promise I'm not sure how to keep. I genuinely do my best not to lie, but this might be one case where I promised more than I can deliver. It doesn't make me feel great about things.

I SPY THE Ahmadis' assigned caseworker, Staci Lynn, almost immediately. She sits near the back, as far away from a window as possible in the corner coffee shop. Currently she has her head down, studying something on her phone. Her dark hair cascades around her in a silky blue-black waterfall.

Then she looks up. At first glance, she's maybe late twenties, early thirties. Her white-collared shirt frames delicate features and alabaster skin, while her long hair serves as a veil, shifting to reveal a sliver of cheekbone here, a corner of mouth there. She turns toward me, and the strands sway back enough to reveal the entirety of her face.

Ashley had prepared me, so I manage not to flinch. It's still a startling sight. The scar begins at her left temple, pours down her cheek, neck, and jawline, then disappears beneath the collar of her shirt.

I had assumed thick, ropy markings. This, however, looks more like a slow melting, skin dissolving into skin, layer by painful layer as the acid did its gruesome work.

I approach the resettlement agency's social worker. "Staci? I'm Frankie Elkin. Thanks for coming. Can I get you a coffee or anything?"

She gestures at the steaming travel mug in front of her. I flush, feeling even more discombobulated. I need to get my head in the game. The situation regarding Sabera's disappearance seems to be evolving very quickly. If her daughter is also now in danger, I can't afford to be this far behind.

I head to the counter long enough to order coffee. Not knowing the system, I bog down the line, causing the addicts behind me to grow restless, including one dark-haired young man who shoots daggers at me.

Finally, I make it back to the table, where Staci has resumed scrolling through her phone.

"I need you to sit on my right," she states.

I pause from pulling out a chair to her left, make the shift.

"I don't have much of my outer ear." She pulls back her hair. Sure enough, where there would usually be a perfectly formed shell, she has what appears to be a diminutive flap of cartilage. "The external part of the ear, the pinna, helps funnel sound and amplify noise. In theory, I can still hear on my left side, but everything sounds muffled. It's better to have people address me on my right."

I nod. She lets her hair drop back in place. She has deep blue eyes, I realize. Pre-attack, she would've resembled a young Elizabeth Taylor. Post-attack, she remains stunning.

"Would you like to touch it?" she asks evenly.

I jerk back, not realizing how much I was leaning toward her. "I'm sorry—"

"I'm used to it. Children sometimes want to touch it. Their parents are horrified, but I don't mind. My scars have left me looking different. People are afraid of things that are different. The kids touch it. They feel that it's just skin, shiny and a little bumpy, but not that special in the end. They move on, let it go. Whereas their parents will continue to sneak glances every single time we meet. Personally, I prefer the children's approach."

"Ashley said you were a victim of an acid attack."

"On a public bus. An older woman walked up to me. Yelled something about sin and flesh and the workings of the devil, then threw acid on my face. I was sixteen."

I blink. "I'm guessing she's nutty as a fruitcake plus mad as a hatter?"

"Also totally off her rocker. She was found guilty, sent away to some institution. And I spent the next few years becoming a close personal acquaintance of my plastic surgeon." Staci gestures to her face. "This is six surgeries later. Clearly, he's a miracle worker."

"Obviously."

Finally, a faint smile. "Ashley says you want to know about Sabera Ahmadi. She's missing, possibly in danger."

"Not to mention just this morning, someone tried to kidnap her kid."

"Zahra? Is she okay?"

"For now."

"And Isaad?"

"No one knows. He took off yesterday. No one's seen him since. Look, I understand you're not supposed to talk about the families you serve, but you're the Ahmadis' caseworker, right? You're the one who's worked with them the most since they arrived in Tucson."

She shrugs. "I've assisted them with everything from opening their first bank account to teaching them how to ride the bus. Not to mention, I've purchased blouses for Sabera, blue jeans for Zahra, and socks for Isaad. So, yes, I suppose I do know them better than most."

"You could buy socks for Isaad?" I'm genuinely startled. "Doesn't that violate some cultural rule, a non-familial female handling garments for a male?"

"My role is considered professional. Given families arrive here with nothing but the clothes on their backs, the men are much less concerned about the source of their boxers than having the right garments for work."

"Well then, I've definitely come to the right person." I set down my coffee and regard her intently. "I really need your help.

Sabera, Isaad, Zahra really need your help. I understand there are expectations of privacy. But for their sake...Please talk to me. I'm not lying when I say their lives could depend on it."

Staci exhales deeply. I can see her compassion, a woman who was once victimized herself and now works on behalf of the world's most vulnerable. There are the rules of her job, then the spirit behind them—always put the family's needs first. I know what I believe the Ahmadis need most right now; I just have to hope Staci reaches the same conclusion.

Finally: "Given the circumstances...Ask what you want to ask. I'll see what I can answer."

I don't blink an eye before pouncing. "Have you ever caught Sabera drinking? I know she's not supposed to consume alcohol as a practicing Muslim, but that doesn't mean she doesn't."

Staci raises her travel mug. Takes a sip. I'm worried I've already entered a no-fly zone, when she murmurs, "Your question is too simple."

"Too simple? What do you mean?"

"The real issue, faced by all refugees—how well are they adapting to their new lives."

"Okay, how well is Sabera adapting to her new life?"

"And that's where things get complicated. As a caseworker, my primary goal is to protect my families. And I don't just mean from nosy outsiders." She gives me a look. "I mean from the employer who demands they work overtime without additional compensation. Or the landlord who tells them the broken air conditioner is their responsibility, or the bank that tacks on a dozen extra fees while saying that's standard.

"For many refugees, who've always lived with their extended families in a place where things have been done the same way for generations, America is less a land of opportunity than a shock to their souls. They're trying to learn a new city, a new culture, and a million new systems, from mass transportation to how to shop at a grocery store to how to file their taxes, et cetera. To say it's bewildering is an understatement. To hope it will all go well is naïve. There are pitfalls everywhere, even for a well-educated, urbanized couple such as Isaad and Sabera.

"The latest challenge for my Muslim refugees—I've built a network of employers at local resorts who appreciate their work ethic and are respectful of their religion, just in time to have hotel guests start attacking the females for wearing hijabs. Honestly, because life isn't already hard enough?" Staci rolls her eyes, thumps down her coffee.

"Here's the deal: when a family such as the Ahmadis arrive, Ashley the housing coordinator finds them their first apartment and gets them settled in. A volunteer such as Aliah helps teach them the local ropes while connecting them with the larger Afghan society. My job is to assist them with everything else. Get them enrolled in the proper ESL class at Pima. Guide them as they establish financial credentials. Walk them through employment options. For the men, it mostly boils down to construction/landscape work or driving for hire. Isaad definitely isn't a dirty-his-own-hands kind of guy and had the resources to buy a used car, so Uber Eats it is. For the females, there's some restaurant work, but mostly housekeeping at local establishments. Sabera didn't mind, not to mention she was accustomed to working outside the home. For both of them, given their English skills and advanced education, I felt there would be better opportunities ahead. At the moment, however…"

"This is not the end," I repeat what Aliah had told me during our first meeting. "It is the beginning."

"Exactly. Which brings us to the matter of childcare…"

Heavy sigh. "People have a tendency to assume refugees are taking away resources from the rest of us, but the truth is, most of our public-assist programs—section eight housing, Headstart preschool, et cetera—have too long of a waiting list to be of service. Ashley needs to secure an apartment for each family *right now*. I need to help them find childcare and secure a job *right now*. As a case agent, I may work with each family for over a year, but their federal monies run out in three months. Meaning in the first twelve weeks, I need to get them set up, employed, and stabilized. That's no mean feat, especially given everything there is for them to learn."

"That's why Isaad drives during the day while Sabera works as a housekeeper at night. So they can swap Zahra between them?"

"Best most families can do."

"Can't be easy on a marriage."

"Still easier than living in a refugee camp. Do you know why mothers sleep with their babies swaddled against their chests at night?"

I shake my head, pretty sure ignorance is bliss.

"Rats develop a taste for infants. There's more than one account of parents waking up to discover their newborn is now missing the ends of her fingers, or worse, the tip of his nose. Then there's the cockroaches that like to crawl into ear canals, and the daily knife fights that can break out over a bottle of water."

"Trauma," I murmur. "Ashley told me I shouldn't make any assumptions, because no matter what I thought I knew, my imagination would never be horrible enough."

Staci smiles faintly. "My experience has been horrific enough, and even I don't pretend to understand. I had one terrible moment of violence. Most of my families have been subject to ongoing chaos, brutality, and bloodshed for years. Let alone the constant anxiety of having no idea what's going to happen next, again for years."

"Is that why Sabera drinks?" I ask, because Staci is still avoiding that question. "To cope with her PTSD?"

Staci hesitates. "I think there is a great deal of stress in that household," she states, "and there are times when Sabera doesn't seem herself. But is it from alcohol? There can be many reasons someone seems... off."

"Pills, drugs?"

Shrug.

"Sleep deprivation?"

Another lift of the shoulders, but a little less exaggerated. I'm getting warmer, at least in her assessment of the situation. Though how can anybody, even a caseworker, know what's truly going on behind closed doors? I decide to move on for the moment.

"What about Isaad? Wouldn't he have PTSD, too?" I ask.

"Isaad's complicated. Absolutely brilliant, incredibly vain. He can't stand their apartment, resents being reduced to working as an Uber Eats driver, and already aspires to fulfill the American dream. But when not gnashing his teeth in frustration, he appears to be trying to do right by his wife and child. Angry and explosive, yes, but more bark than bite. He's the one more comfortable expressing his emotions, even the ugly ones, which can be a good thing."

"Sabera doesn't show her feelings?"

"Sabera is challenging. I've never seen her outwardly angry or anxious. She observes, listens, learns. But what she's thinking at any given time... I've spent hours in the car with her. Even given her some personal cooking lessons, which is my favorite way of coping. There are times I can tell she's enthralled. Other times when she's clearly exhausted. She never complains. Whenever I say, this is where we must go, this is what we must do, she does exactly as I say. She never shirks her responsibilities. But as for how well she's truly handling this level of change, I have no idea. Which, in my experience, is not a good thing. The more anxiety and fear that fester beneath the surface..." Staci's expression is genuinely concerned.

"They've been in Tucson a little over two months, right? Ten weeks?"

Staci nods.

"Meaning they have only two more weeks to be financially self-sufficient?"

"More or less. Given they have a young child, they qualify for some additional programs, which I'd just suggested they start applying for."

"Meaning their stress level must be ratcheting up."

"It's not an easy time."

"So Isaad gets explosive. She gets drunk." I'm still pushing, trying to get Staci to fill in the blanks or at least drop enough breadcrumbs that I can get there on my own.

Staci takes a sip of coffee, seems to debate her options. "One of my roles," she states abruptly, "is to help them line up a PCP and fill out the initial paperwork."

"Okay."

"Needless to say, our medical system is a mystery to most Americans, let alone outsiders. Then you add things like HIPAA and concepts of doctor–patient confidentiality, which don't exist in most parts of the world, and it quickly becomes overwhelming."

I nod gamely.

"Like many, Isaad and Sabera didn't know how to complete the forms. What do you mean you have to assign one emergency contact and grant your doctor permission to share information with them? Their culture is all about family, as in grandparents, aunts, uncles, cousins, parents, siblings. For them, it would be any of those people, all of those people. I had to explain that in this country, an emergency contact is generally your spouse, or an immediate family member. Also could be a close personal friend."

"Got it."

"I assumed they'd listed each other. But I didn't check. Their privacy matters." Staci takes a deep breath. "Which is why I was surprised when my phone rang in the middle of the night just two weeks later with an ER doc reaching out to me as the listed contact for Sabera Ahmadi."

"You were called? About Sabera?"

Staci studies me, waits a beat.

"Was it related to alcohol? She was that drunk, had passed out, become unruly, something…"

Still no answer. Because the caseworker can't comment on medical history, I realize. Why Sabera was in the ER falls under confidentiality. Though my mind is already buzzing with the possibilities. For now:

"Did you ask Sabera why she provided your name instead of Isaad's?"

"When it felt appropriate."

In other words, when Sabera sobered up. Or…There's something about the intensity of Staci's gaze. Like she's trying to sear specific information into my brain, except I'm too dense to get it. Something happened. Not alcohol or drugs? Meaning some other root cause? Either way, Sabera ended up in the ER, and Staci was contacted. Her caseworker. Not her husband.

I only realize I stated the last part out loud when Staci nods.

"I'd told Sabera that an emergency contact is generally a spouse, a family member, or a friend. According to her, based on those parameters, my name was the one that made sense."

"I know she doesn't have family here; Aliah said they died in Afghanistan. But that still leaves—" My voice breaks off. I think I get it, though I'm so startled I can barely finish the thought. "Are you saying, she doesn't have a spouse, either? She and Isaad...not married?"

"That's what she told me."

"They, what, lied to increase their chances of gaining refugee status and get out of the internment camp? But how is such a thing even possible? Aren't there a million background checks, requests for documentation, et cetera?"

"Absolutely." Staci leans forward. "Legal documentation is required, not to mention double, triple, quadruple checked. To make things even more interesting, I've watched them together. Isaad? The way he interacts with her, looks out for Zahra. That man considers them to be a family, even if Sabera doesn't."

"I don't get it."

"Sabera is challenging," Staci repeats. "Ten weeks later, I feel like I have some grasp of Isaad and his needs. Sabera, however, remains a complete mystery to me. Especially..."

She shrugs. The ER visit again. The clue she ethically can't reveal. But something significant happened. The question is, what?

When working cold cases, the reason I can generally make headway, versus, say, law enforcement, is that I'm an outsider, asking the right questions at the right time. That can get others talking in ways they wouldn't do with local authorities.

Medical matters, however, fall well beyond my purview. No doctor is going to talk to me. Maybe Sabera's husband, Isaad, if he ever reappears, though it's not clear he even knows everything.

Which leaves me with caseworker Staci and all the things she will and won't say.

I feel suddenly stupid, glancing up at her sharply.

"You're afraid." I utter it as a statement.

"Yes."

I study Staci a beat longer, as I fully take in her expression: "Are you afraid for her, or are you afraid of her?"

"Exactly."

I bow my head in defeat.

CHAPTER 16

Tonight's dinner is breaded cuts of thick pork chops, smothered in gravy and served with a mound of mashed potatoes topped with a golden pad of butter. Another ode to the kind of family dinners my family never had.

Daryl dives into his plate with gusto. I mostly cut my chop into tiny pieces, which I push around my plate. I'm acutely aware that dinnertime for humans will soon be followed by dinnertime for pythons. At least I did better at throwing Petunia's salad into her bowl this evening. Even managed to change out her water without screaming. But snakes...

A dozen babies.

One large big mama.

Why had I ever agreed to this? Except if memory serves, I never actually said yes. Bart just never accepted my sincere no.

Little shit.

Daryl is back to checking his phone.

"Booty call?" I finally press, mostly because I'm spoiling for a fight.

He stops chewing his food long enough to regard me intently. "Jealousy doesn't become you."

I scowl. My own mobile is tucked face up next to my plate, and not because I'm that anxious to get my next set of instructions from Bart.

"Oh, honey, just call him," Genni advises me. "Or her. You know we won't judge." Genni is looking particularly happy 1950s housewife in a crisp navy-blue dress with a white Peter Pan collar and an enormous star-shaped diamond brooch that both casts glittering rainbows upon the walls and threatens to poke out an eye. She's exchanged her red Lucille Ball wig for a blond Marilyn Monroe bombshell. They each have merits.

"I don't know what you're talking about," I reply stiffly.

She and Daryl roll their eyes.

"Twin mattresses," I declare, remembering my commitment to Ashley the housing coordinator. "I need to get my hands on a set. The cheaper the better, though they can't be in gross condition. Anybody have some ideas?"

"I don't do cheap," Genni begins, just in time for Daryl to say:

"Habitat for Humanity. They have a store in Tucson. Used furniture, appliances. Sometimes includes mattresses."

Genni stares at him. "Well, aren't you a fount of information?"

"Once furnished an apartment with less than twenty bucks. Learned some tricks."

He shovels in the last bite of mashed potatoes, neatly pats his lips with his black napkin, then pushes back from the table, phone already in hand.

"My evening awaits." He gives me a pointed look.

"Are you going dancing? Because if you see Roberta, I want

to know if her brother assigned more patrol cars to Nageenah's apartment complex. Whether or not Zahra is still there, the other tenants deserve that much."

Daryl doesn't respond to my blatant fishing.

"What did you two think of the kids?" I press. "You spent the most time with them."

"Good dancers," Daryl supplies.

"That's not helpful."

He shrugs. "Interesting music. Didn't know there was such a thing as Middle Eastern discotheque."

"Did Zahra say anything?"

"Not a word."

"Is it strange for such a young child to be so silent?"

"Works for me."

I roll my eyes. "You're not good at this game."

Second shrug. "The kids seem happy. I enjoyed their company." On that note, Daryl grabs his dirty plate and delivers it to the kitchen sink.

I sigh heavily, give up on my own dinner.

"That better not be a comment on my cooking," Genni informs me, gesturing to my barely touched food.

"No, it's a comment on what awaits."

"You are going to call him!"

"I'm not that kind of girl."

"Honey, we are *all* that kind of girl. Give me his number. I'll do it."

"Absolutely not!" I snatch my phone up before Genni can make good on her threat. Though deep down, I feel a piece of myself waver. Because the sex was that good? Or his company that comforting? In the middle of the night, he would roll over, wrap his arm around my waist, and pull me tighter against him.

The first time he did it, I stiffened in alarm. But as week turned into week...

It felt good to be held close and not because someone needed me, but because he wanted me.

I could've stayed. We both knew it.

And yet I couldn't have stayed. And we both knew that, too.

"I'm going to attempt to feed some snakes," I murmur. Just in time for my phone to chime with the first message from Bart.

Step one, remove a frozen rat from the freezer...

I sigh heavily and get to it.

I FILL A coffee cup with steaming hot water, then manage not to vomit while removing Marge's dinner, a rodent Popsicle, from its vacuum-sealed packaging.

It smells mostly like ice, which helps. As for how it looks once I've plopped it into the heated water... My nightmares are going to be particularly vivid tonight.

Petunia has returned from chowing down her salad and is now planted in the middle of the reptile wing corridor, staring at me.

"Any chance you'd like to feed the snakes?" I ask her. Then, remembering: "Oops. Apparently, they'd take that literally and turn you into dinner. Sorry. Though for the record, I hope you're really appreciating my company right now."

"Honey, Petunia has a lizard brain. You get that, right?" Genni has her entire six-foot-four self leaning against the kitchen counter. She's not even pretending to clear the rest of the dishes, just taking in the show.

"Start by delivering thawed rat to the one big snake or by

feeding crickets to the dozen baby snakes?" I ask Genni, since Petunia is no help.

"Have you tried extracting feeder crickets yet?"

"Aren't they in some box sitting beneath the ball pythons' terrarium? Just grab with tongs? Deliver one by one to waiting serpents?"

Genni tsks at my naïveté. "They're *shipped* in a box, honey. Then Bart dumps them in an aquarium for tending. Can't feed live crickets if the crickets don't stay alive."

I stare at her blankly. Boy Wonder never mentioned any of this, I'm certain.

"Crickets are fed cricket food. Which, between you and me, is ground-up crickets."

I make a slight gagging sound.

"Also, never give them water—they drown too easily. There's a pan of green gelatin cricket goo used instead."

ON CUE, MY phone chimes in rapid succession. Step four, reach into the feeder cricket terrarium and remove the first cardboard egg container...

I swear, then have to quickly read backward. Sure enough, there's an entire trade craft involved in feeder cricket extraction. Luring crickets into the hollow depressions in cut-up egg cartons, lifting the cardboard piece out carefully before plucking out the intended victim, then offering it to the waiting python baby...

By the time I'm done reading about live cricket distribution, feeding a single semi-thawed rat seems like a much easier proposition. Maybe.

I pick up the rodent-filled mug. Sigh heavily.

"You can do this," Genni assures me.

I shudder, squeeze my eyes shut. I don't want to do this, I really don't. And yet...

Some people make healthy life decisions. Some pay attention to their inner wants, needs, desires. And some of us...we just do what we have to do. Even if it hurts us later...

I step around Petunia, march one, two, three, four steps down the carpeted corridor.

And I suffer a strange sense of déjà vu.

Myself as a kid, returning home after school following one of my parents' blow-out fights, when my mother screamed she couldn't take one more minute of my father's drinking and he swore, begged, pleaded he would do better. Leading to a stilted breakfast where my father, who'd clearly spent the night sobering up with six pots of coffee, moved about the kitchen with relentless good intentions as he dished out overcooked eggs and prattled about the beautiful weather.

Except now it's eight hours later, which he's spent alone in a house that, no matter how hard my mother and I try, always has a hidden liter of Jack.

My footsteps slow as I approach the front door, my backpack growing heavier. My hand comes to rest on the door handle.

This is the moment. Twist the knob, push open the door, and...

Passed-out-drunk Dad is a given. Sober Dad...

Sober Dad is hope and heartache in equal measures, because it never lasts, and we all know it.

Which makes this moment right now, my small fingers curling around a smooth brass handle, a kind of limbo. Where I wish for the best, while assuring myself I can handle the worst.

Where I stand for endless minute rolling into minute because even when you promise yourself that you're strong enough…

It doesn't mean it won't hurt all over again.

I have loved my father my entire life. And to this day, memories of him hurt me, which is particularly awful, because my father never wanted to be that man. There wasn't a mean, violent, angry bone in his body. Just an illness that robbed his family of him all the same.

And soon enough, it became the curse he shared with his daughter. I've never been able to figure out which was worse during my own hard-drinking high school years: my mother's deep disappointment in my behavior or my father's self-conscious shame.

I wish they could see me now. I wish I could know them as the person I've become.

But life doesn't work like that. Moments come, moments go, and even the truly horrific ones, such as what Sabera Ahmadi experienced, are seared into our souls while journeying on. We're left in some kind of cosmic toaster oven, where the universe's memory is long gone, while we still struggle with the burn marks left on our psyche.

I'm not a young girl anymore.

And behind this door isn't the specter of my maybe drunk, maybe sober father.

The doubt, the dread, the terror, however, remain uniquely my own.

My phone chimes with additional texts from Bart. I don't bother to look. It's time to get this done.

Final deep breath, then I step into the darkened interior, my eyes requiring a moment to adjust to the gloom. On my right, the raised glass enclosure with its slithering mass of hungry baby snakes above, much smaller cricket cage below. Straight ahead, the even more impressively sized terrarium housing the coiled bulk of pale-yellow Marge, her head now rising into the air, forked tongue darting out to test the air.

Except Marge isn't eight feet away in the comfort of her custom home.

She's unspooling from a spot on the floor a mere three feet away.

I yelp.

I hurtle a half-thawed rat in her direction. Then, as she lunges for the dead rodent...

I get the hell out of there.

CHAPTER 17

BART AND I HAVE WORDS. Really, I have words, a long, incoherent stream of distraught babbling, while he listens. The end
result: Jamie, Bart's herper buddy, who shows up with a snake-
wrangling tool and empty pillowcase.

Jamie looks to be twenty to Bart's twelve. He also has the face
of an angel—fine patrician features, big blue eyes, and perfect
blond ringlets that brush against the top of his shoulders. Replace
his worn blue jeans and ripped black T-shirt with a pair of wings,
and his likeness graces many major cathedrals.

Genni lets Jamie into the house. I point emphatically at the
shuttered reptile room door. He doesn't seem to require an explanation, but saunters forward with his looped instrument. I yank
the door shut behind him, but not before catching a bunch of
kissing noises and coochy-coochy-coos. As far as I'm concerned,
he and Marge are welcome to live happily ever after, as long as I
never have to go into that room again.

When he appears just five minutes later, whistling away, I

stomp my foot and deliver more words. Less incoherent babbling, more pointed demands. He will go back inside. He will check the lid of Marge's terrarium six more times. And he can feed chirping crickets to the agitated pile of slithering baby pythons who seem really hungry and have just had an impromptu lesson on how to escape.

I have no idea how much help Bart originally asked Jamie to provide, but about thirty seconds into my tirade, Jamie steps meekly back into the snake room to get the hell away from the deranged human female. So be it.

I retreat to the living room with Petunia, where I impress upon her the importance of staying away from the pythons for her own safety.

By the time Jamie appears to say all the snakes are handled, Petunia and I are watching *The Simpsons* side by side, and there's nothing weird about it at all.

Daryl returns halfway through our second episode. Takes in the scene. Grunts.

"Heard we had an escapee."

"I've officially resigned my position."

"Petunia know that?"

"Don't be mean to my friend."

A second grunt.

"All's quiet at Nageenah's apartment."

I swivel around. "You've been there?"

"Got a system in place. Kids will be safe."

"Detective Marc calling in more uniformed patrol officers, or you and Roberta working your own magic?"

"Something like that."

I roll my eyes.

"Oh, mattresses will be delivered tomorrow. The crime scene apartment complex, right? On it."

"You found twin mattresses? You arranged for them to be delivered?" I'm genuinely shocked. And impressed. And touched.

Daryl shrugs his massive shoulders uncomfortably. "Been there. Tough enough for a guy like me. Definitely not good for a family."

"That's really kind of you, Daryl. What do I owe?"

He waves a hand. "Nah. You can do the next one." He pauses: "I'm assuming there will be a next one?"

"Thirty million people searching for a safe haven? Sounds like there's always a next one."

"People screw up people," he observes.

"There is that."

"Morning plan?"

I frown, absently stroking down one side of Petunia's protruding spines. I'd expected her skin to feel cold and rough, but it's surprisingly soft and warm, like petting worn leather. She closes her eyes, leaning into my touch with what seems to be appreciation.

"I don't know," I confess finally. "My main goal is to find Sabera before things get any worse. But where, how? Aliah swears that's her on the crime scene video. But then what? Sabera basically vanishes again, and now her husband—or not husband—has disappeared as well." I regard Daryl. "If you were on the run, or hiding from some kind of danger, where would you go?"

"Phone a friend."

"By all accounts, that would be Aliah, and she hasn't heard from Sabera. Or maybe Staci," I murmur, seeing how the caseworker had made emergency contact status. But I think the young woman would've said something this afternoon. Instead, she appeared genuinely worried while doing her best to tell me what she could.

"Previous address?" Daryl asked.

"Some military base in Texas, while before that is a refugee camp in Abu Dhabi, where the rats have developed a taste for newborn flesh."

Daryl shivers in revulsion.

"Totally agree," I assure him.

"Work associate?" he ponders next. "Place of employment?"

"She's only been employed for a matter of weeks. Seems a bit fast to make friends, especially working alone cleaning hotel rooms."

Daryl gives me a look. It takes me a moment; then I get it. "Tending hotel rooms. At a local resort. Where this time of year, there are probably plenty of empty rooms available for her to access. I'm an idiot."

Daryl doesn't bother to dispute. I swear Petunia nods.

"Well, now we have a plan for the morning. First thing, we hit Sabera's place of employment, do some exploring on our own, then engage management if we have to. But one way or another..."

"Find Sabera," Daryl states.

"Yep."

"Bring her home to her daughter."

"Absolutely."

"I like it," Daryl states, then turns and exits the room.

It's only after he leaves that I fully register he isn't wearing his dark suit jacket anymore. And on the right sleeve of his sharply pressed white dress shirt, there appears to be a small smear of red.

Almost like blood.

CHAPTER 18

WHEN I TOUCH BASE WITH Aliah in the morning, she still hasn't seen or heard anything from Isaad, meaning he's roughly twenty-four hours late to pick up his daughter. I can tell from the older woman's voice that she's growing increasingly concerned. She may not be Isaad's biggest fan, but not even she believes he'd willingly abandon his young daughter.

I press her on the subject of Sabera and Isaad's marriage—as in, do they even have one. Aliah is immediately dismissive. Of course they're married, they must be married, there's no way they couldn't be married. Then I mention Sabera's trip to the ER several weeks ago. That disturbs her a bit more. No, she didn't know. I can hear a hesitation in her voice. When I get more aggressive on the subject, however, she simply repeats that Sabera has never mentioned it. And, yes, Sabera is struggling, and maybe she had once succumbed to the lure of alcohol, but adaption was hard on everyone.

Aliah's steadfast faith in her friend is beginning to annoy me, especially as she clearly doesn't know her friend as well as she thinks she does. Though to be fair, apparently no one does.

The topic of Zahra is easier. Aliah and the little girl spent the evening watching Disney movies. Then Aliah got up this morning to discover Zahra memorizing every recipe in Aliah's extensive cookbook collection. Given the girl's interest, Aliah is now planning on bringing her to the deli, where they can prepare some of those dishes, starting with every child's favorite: firni. Aliah describes it as a light custard made with rose water, cardamom, and pistachios. Based on her description alone, I make a mental note to stop by later in the afternoon; the Afghan dessert sounds delicious and beautiful all at the same time.

Aliah provides me with the name of Sabera's employer, which at least is something.

Good news, the high-end resort is a mere ten minutes away from Bart's mansion. Basically, we head deeper into the Santa Catalina Mountains till we hit Ventana Canyon. While we're talking, I check out the establishment's website on my phone. It appears huge, with half a dozen sprawling buildings offering everything from luxury suites to fully furnished townhouses to separate apartments. Plus two eighteen-hole golf courses, three restaurants, and numerous swimming pools.

As hideouts go, it's perfect. Plenty of places for Sabera to hang low without anyone being the wiser. Aliah is instantly irritated she hadn't thought of it first.

I let her return to kid care; then I go in search of Daryl. I find him in the kitchen, wolfing down a thick stack of pancakes while poodle-skirt-clad Genni putters about the kitchen and Petunia basks in a sunbeam before the sliders.

When I pause to give Petunia a quick rub of her shoulders, Genni arches a brow.

"My, my, how times have changed."

"The enemy of your enemy is your friend," I inform her. "And both Petunia and I agree snakes are the enemy."

"I hear you, girl. I slept last night with a towel tucked beneath my door, and I stand by it."

I turn to Daryl. "Ready when you are."

He looks up mid-bite. "Breakfast is the most important meal of the day."

Genni starts fussing: "Sit, sit, I'll bring you a plate."

"I don't—"

But Genni is already pulling out a chair and dishing out flap-jacks swimming in butter and maple syrup. The first bite nearly makes me swoon.

"Did you grow up eating like this?" I want to know. "Because I come from the land of Pop-Tarts and Sugar Smacks."

"Crime against humanity," Genni declares. "But then, I come from the land of dumpster diving. Street kid. Foster child. Street kid again."

"I'm sorry."

A wave of her hand. "Life has a way of working out. Though you could argue I'm now overcompensating."

Daryl makes a sound that might be a guffaw. When both Genni and I stare at him, he quickly mumbles, "And thank God for that."

I study Genni. Daryl has been an excellent source of criminal thinking. I wonder what Genni can contribute from her life on the streets.

"Ever try to sneak into a hotel or crash for the night on the down-low?" I quiz. "Like maybe bribe the person at the front desk, or someone in housekeeping?"

"Honey, places I hung out didn't offer cleaning services."

"But the front desk?"

"Not if they wanted to keep their jobs. Management has opinions on these subjects, and many of the sketchiest motels still have cameras for exactly this reason."

"I'm guessing the Ventana Canyon Luxury Resort and Spa most definitely has eyes in the sky," I consider. "Not to mention, their staff's probably paid well enough to be tough to bribe."

"You want to identify a vacant room," Daryl provides, polishing off his last bite. "On the outer perimeter. Easier to get in and out without being seen."

"Is this in regards to the missing woman?" Daryl must've filled Genni in, because she immediately warms to the subject, taking up her customary lean against the kitchen island. "Does the resort offer washers and dryers for guests? I'd start there. No one questions someone walking around with a pile of laundry. Forget an invisibility cloak. Give a woman a toilet plunger and bucket of cleaning supplies and she immediately fades into the background."

"Excellent point." I build on that thought. "And given that Sabera worked the property, she probably knows where all the vacant rooms are. Though," I catch myself, "it also means she'd be recognizable to her former coworkers."

"Not if she comes and goes at night." Daryl again. "The resort offers entire townhouses with separate access. That would eliminate the risk of elevators, long hallways. She could pick her timing, then make her play."

"In that case, it's real simple," Genni adds. "Just look for the front door fixture missing a light bulb."

"Missing a light bulb?"

"First rule of law breaking, darling, it's best done in the dark. Sometimes, we'd throw rocks to break the bulbs, but shattered glass is its own kind of tell. Better just to unscrew the globe. Can take weeks, even months before someone notices."

"Huh." I switch my gaze from Genni to Daryl to Genni again. "You two are really good at this."

Daryl shrugs. "Lived a life."

Genni grins. "Misspent youth. The absolutely best kind."

"I had a misspent youth, as well," I insist, not wanting to be left out. Then I am forced to confess, "Unfortunately, I was too drunk to remember most of it."

I polish off the last of the pancakes, toss back the final swallow of coffee, and check in with Daryl, who nods.

Time to get to it. Search a luxury resort, locate Sabera Ahmadi camped out in a vacant unit, get her whatever kind of help she needs to return to her daughter and worried friend.

And then...

What do we want most in life? The things that ignite our wildest imagination or the things that ping our deepest longings?

You'd think a woman who lives her life as a rolling stone would go with the daring option each and every time. But lately I'm not so sure anymore. Maybe I want more than I think I want. Maybe the safe choice for me is the crazy option.

Who am I really, a woman who comes from nowhere and is willing to head anywhere?

I still don't have the answer.

So I push away from the table and go in search of a total stranger whose problems somehow seem easier to solve than my own.

CHAPTER 19

THE VENTANA CANYON LUXURY RESORT and Spa definitely takes the "luxury" part of its name seriously. Daryl and I depart Bart's already impressive estate to wind higher and deeper into the mountains. Basically, we exit his over-the-top wrought-iron gate to drive by even larger, more impressive entrances to private abodes, each doing their best to out-money their neighbors with their increasingly elaborately executed demands for others to keep out.

Based on real estate alone, money flows up in Tucson, and at a staggering rate.

Daryl and I are suitably awestruck as we finally roll between two towering, hand-carved granite formations that appear to both melt into the landscape and command high dollar at the next auction for modern art.

I wonder what this is like for the resort's refugee employees. Some of whom came from such rough circumstances that this must seem incredibly wasteful, while others, such as Sabera, who probably vacationed at the Afghan version of hot spots, must experience it as salt in the wound—oh, how the mighty have fallen.

Good news, Bart's crazy expensive black sedan blends right in as we cruise through the entrance gate/artistic statement. Immediately we behold a sprawling three-story complex, constructed of pink adobe cubes that make it appear to be at one with its mountainous backdrop. Based on the fact no one would ever choose this layout for their actual home, I'm willing to believe some top-notch architectural firm was paid an obscene amount of money for a Lego-like design Nageenah's toddler son could've managed.

Daryl doesn't speak so much as cluck his tongue. I get it.

The wide main road curves up to the front gates of the largest building—the main hotel/spa/resort structure. Four other vehicles are already queued up for pickup/drop-off under the misted portico manned by three red-jacketed valets wielding bottles of water. All the easier for us to bypass and continue deeper into the property as if we have every right to be there.

We pass a pro shop bordering the first eighteen-hole golf course, then an impressive but not massive building that strikes me as maybe a separate event space.

We roll by more ridiculously green fairways. The sheer amount of irrigation required to maintain so much lawn…Daryl is already shaking his head.

We curve around to the rear of the property. Here we discover a long expanse of townhouse buildings, constructed in batches of five, that appear to be carved out of the hillside itself. Then, finally, a squat mound of a building with multiple doorways, protruding decks, and a designated swimming pool. I'm guessing the longer-stay apartment option.

Daryl coasts our way to the end, then pulls into the last parking spot.

"Townhouses or apartment building," he states.

"Surprise me."

We both peer outside, where the thermostat has already topped ninety and we can watch the heat rise off the dark asphalt in iridescent waves.

"Ready or not," Daryl begins, as I declare, "Fuck me."

We both push open the doors and leave our lovely air-conditioning behind.

It takes a bit to clear the apartment/long-term rental building. First we can't access the locked gate, but instead must fuss around the beautiful manicured grounds with their mix of babbling water features, hard-core ancient saguaros (complete with personalized bios), and spicy mesquite trees while waiting for some golf-clad male or bouncy Lululemon female to return.

Daryl's intimidating bulk and swarthy appearance actually work to our advantage. People take in his sharply tailored black suit, then my grungy attire, and immediately assume he's a bodyguard and I'm eccentric new money. Given that makes me the power player in the couple, I'm all in.

Finally, we gain entrance. We roam a private pool complete with a waterfall and half a dozen cabana boys serving a parade of bored parents and hyper children. All the better for us to drift on past, slipping inside the building, down the lower-level hallway, then the second floor.

Unfortunately, nothing appears wrong with any of the units. Each door has its own light. Nor do any locks appear to be forced, though I'm guessing Sabera has the ability to digitize a key card for her personal use.

We exit the apartments, head for the larger townhouses. I've already sweated through my fancy microfiber hiking pants while

Daryl appears completely cool in his buttoned-up black suit. If I ever needed proof he wasn't human…

The townhouses all have a few steps leading up to a front stoop. Some are kitted out with colorful planters and bright furnishings. Others are completely barren. The rentals. We hit them first.

Not the first building, but end unit second complex. Barren porch. A certain feel of benign neglect. And, ding, ding, ding, a porch light missing its bulb.

Daryl and I exchange a look. We have a winner. Now what?

I'm contemplating throwing ourselves at Detective Marc's feet, when Daryl pulls out his cell phone. He attaches some electronic gizmo to his mobile, then holds up the other end to the key reader.

Red blinking lights flash to green blinking lights. Faint click.

We're in.

I stare at him.

"Bart's also lived a life," he states. Then he reaches out a hand, pushes open the door.

After that, I don't need him to explain the rest.

THE TOWNHOUSE IS three stories. Basic layout. Kitchen, living room, half bath on the lower level. Two bedrooms with private baths on the second floor. Crazy luxurious master suite top floor, complete with balcony and a view of the pink-washed canyon designed to make mere mortals weep.

There are closets and a pantry and a stacked washer and dryer. Nook to hide A. Cranny to disappear B.

We don't need to search any of that to know Sabera isn't currently present. The space is too gray, feels too empty.

Not to mention, we take our first step inside the shadowed unit and...

"Holy shit," Daryl says.

"Holy shit," I agree

And we know we've discovered Sabera's hidey-hole, even if she is long gone.

IN SOME WAYS, nothing is disturbed. The beds are meticulously made, the bathrooms shipshape, the furniture precisely placed.

But the walls, leading from the foyer into the dining room, wrapping around the primary seating area into the kitchen...

Sabera has covered the walls in script. Starting from the door-jamb and continuing in a near vomit of communication. Numbers. Letters. Equations. Words.

I was never a math kid. I'd like to blame the booze as I spent most of my high school years in no condition to learn. But those two things went hand in hand. I didn't just drink because I felt intimidated by general academics, my fellow peers, and high school culture. I genuinely struggled with general academics, my fellow peers, and high school culture, ergo it seemed a great idea to drink.

Now, confronted by this sheer mass of data, scrawled with a thick black Sharpie and covering nearly every visible vertical surface...

I have to suppress the urge to close my eyes and cover my head. It's overwhelming, bordering on horrifying.

Daryl is already shrinking to the side, as if the madness might be contagious. He heads to the relative safety of the kitchen, which is encircled in cabinets and thus saved from the worst of the hysteria.

I take a deep breath, blink several times as if to clear my sight, then do my best to follow the notations. If it's code, it's a lot of it, and I suck at cracking that sort of stuff. What speaks to me, however, is the feel of it. The forward slant of the hastily scrawled figures. The relentless top-to-bottom coverage, filling every available inch of space and then continuing on and on, up, down, around, and now as I follow it, beginning to progress up the stairs...

There's a feverishness to it all.

A desperation.

As if the person who did this was either manic or terrified. The question is, which?

The largest volume is in the dining room, where the expanse seems to be mostly filled with numbers, with random punctuations of symbols I don't recognize but am guessing are mathematical.

Slowly but surely, I start to make out phrases: *Two halves of one whole. A key that has no lock.*

And repeated the most, almost obsessively: *Chin up, chin up, chin up.*

In the heaviest section, there are more numbers than letters. But the sheer infrequency of the characters helps them pop out. It comes to me slowly but surely, as I pick out each consonant and vowel, then string them together.

Tell Zahra I love her.

I'm just lifting my arm to point when Daryl speaks up behind me. "You need to see this."

I twist around enough to spy Daryl in the kitchen. He jerks his chin toward a wad of fabric discarded in the stainless-steel sink.

Worse than the furiously covered walls, the fanatically mad scribbling...

The discarded white towels are covered in streaks of red. The one colorful item—a deep turquoise floral printed scarf, stiffened with gore—commands most of our attention, however. The infamous hijab Aliah gifted to her friend, now clearly soaked in blood. Maybe someone else's. Maybe Sabera's own.

Whatever happened to Sabera. Whatever is continuing to happen here...

My arm falls to my side. "Oh."

"Oh," he agrees.

He picks up his phone and gives Roberta a call.

CHAPTER 20

I DON'T THINK THE BLOOD IS Sabera's," Roberta murmurs thirty minutes later. She'd come tearing into the parking lot shortly after receiving Daryl's summons, a dramatic display of riotous brown curls and door-knocker silver earrings as she'd bolted out of her vehicle and up the front steps.

Unfortunately, she'd chosen to do the responsible thing and notify her brother, Detective Marc, on her way over. Which is to say, the three of us are now confined to the back patio where we are to touch nothing and talk to no one. Given it's nearly a hundred degrees outside, it feels like detention in an inner circle of hell. Which might have been what Detective Marc intended when he marched into the townhouse and discovered his three least favorite people once again two steps ahead of him. Or perhaps it was the fact I pointed that out specifically that tipped him over the edge.

"How do you know it's not her blood?" Daryl asks now. He's removed his black suit jacket in deference to the heat. I've already done my best to discreetly inspect his starched white dress shirt for bloodstains. So far, so good. He's also rolled up his cuffs to reveal forearms muddy with dark, swirling patterns of old ink. Tattoos, possibly jailhouse, given the blotchy quality. It's challenging to both listen to his words and read his body art, but I do my best.

"It's a lot of blood for starters. And only on the items in the sink. If Sabera was that grievously injured, how'd she not smear blood all over the rest of the place? Let alone have the strength to clean up before going all *Beautiful Mind* on the walls?"

I'm less convinced: "I checked the hijab while we were waiting," I mutter.

Roberta skewers me with a look. "You trying to justify my brother killing you?"

"Eh, guy's gotta save his strength. Has you to murder as well, right? Point is, the fabric has two sides. Unfortunately, it's the inside that seems more...saturated."

"Oh." Roberta's eyes widen slightly.

Daryl, on the other hand: "Head wounds are known for bleeding. Doesn't mean it's serious."

"Doesn't mean it's not."

"Listen." Roberta jerks her head toward the sliders, where we can hear voices grow louder as they approach. "Either way, this gives credence to Aliah's assumption—Sabera was at the scene of the double homicide, at least close enough to wear some of the evidence—"

"Or involved enough to create some of the evidence," I counter.

"Maybe she witnessed something she shouldn't have."

"Or did something she shouldn't have."

We're saved from further debate as the glass slider is yanked back and Detective Marc appears. I don't know what it is about cranky, glowering men, but my own mood immediately improves. Apparently for me, pissing off other people has an immediate therapeutic effect.

"When, where, why, how?" Detective Marc barks. "Start talking, and I mean now!"

I open my mouth just in time for Roberta to kick me in the shins. I'm so shocked, I shut up.

"I already explained to you," Roberta states calmly. "Frankie and Daryl came to the resort to interview Sabera's employer. As I'm sure you've also done."

Judging by the good detective's scowl, he has not.

"While driving through the property, it occurred to them that this would be a good location for Sabera to hide out, given her familiarity. A brief search for a vacant room that appeared recently disturbed led them to this unit."

"Which they accessed how?"

I remember Daryl's cell phone gadget and immediately fix my gaze on the flagstone patio.

"Door was ajar," Roberta states point blank.

Her older brother throws up his arms in disgust. "So help me God, Birdie, I've been able to tell when you were lying since you were three years old. Stop covering for him. You're a parole officer. You know better."

I just get a hand on Daryl's arm to keep him from lurching out of his chair in outrage.

Meanwhile, Roberta and her brother remain locked in a staring battle that most likely goes back decades. Neither appears willing to surrender anytime soon. As minute passes into minute, I sneak a glance at Daryl, expecting to see him gnashing his teeth at Detective Marc's accusations.

Instead, Daryl's gazing straight at Roberta, his look a mix of deep frustration and poignant longing. My own breath catches in my throat. But of course. Happily married Roberta had gone out of her way to state her relationship with Daryl was strictly professional, both in and out of the ballroom.

But Daryl, ostensibly unattached, still vested in his former PO's life Daryl...To judge by the expression on his face, he would die for her. Which then makes me wonder if he'd kill for her as well.

Daryl must feel the weight of my stare. He glances over, flushes hotly. I don't say a word. There are moments of discovery that demand comment and others you take with you to your grave. I understand completely which category this falls into.

"Clearly Sabera was here," I interrupt, tiring of the family drama. "Do you think she's already abandoned ship, or do we have some hope of her return?"

"I have no idea."

"Well, did you find any personal belongings, food in the fridge, toothpaste on the countertop? You know, basic living stuff?" My own voice is getting cranky. I'm hot, and this man has denied us AC.

"We don't even know Sabera Ahmadi was the one staying here. We have the crime scene unit scouring the apartment for evidence now. Which is what you do in an official police investigation—you rely on evidence."

I snort out loud. "Yeah, and how's that working for you?"

"Ms. Elkin, you know I can take you in for obstruction—"

Second snort. "Obstruction? I'm the only reason you've finally made progress. Or do official police investigations not worry about those kind of things?"

"Now, see here!" Detective Marc grows increasingly rankled, while beside me, Daryl relaxes. I pat his shoulder in support.

"Do you think the numbers and letters are code?" I prod. "Because they certainly look like some kind of riddle to me. I noticed random phrases here and there. *Two halves of one whole. Chin up.* Oh, and *a key that has no lock.* Hmm, haven't we heard that somewhere else recently? Also, did you catch the whole *'Tell Zahra I love her,'* cuz that sounds ominous. Oh, yes, and provides further support that Sabera was the one staying here. Well, how do you like that. I found some evidence after all."

Detective Marc makes a strangling sound. Roberta crosses her arms over her chest and openly smirks at her brother's discomfort.

"The scarf matches the one from the double homicide video and the description Aliah gave to us as belonging to Sabera," I continue. "Come on, what does it hurt to confirm one tiny little detail?"

Detective Marc glares at all of us, but finally nods once.

"So your point stands." I turn my attention to Roberta. "Based on the bloody scarf, Sabera was probably injured when she exited the crime scene. Meaning…"

"We don't know if she left the area before or after the men were killed," Detective Marc offers abruptly.

"What do you mean—"

"TOD not that precise. Based on the time stamp on the video, things were happening *around* then, but the precise sequence of things…Again, some more investigative work and, oh yes, *evidence*, would be required."

I frown. I can tell from looking at Roberta's and Daryl's faces they are equally troubled. "So to review: Sabera was in the same vicinity as the two murdered men. She was also injured in some fashion. That can't be just coincidence, right? Three people from the same country, in the same area, encountering violence."

"Hate crime?" Roberta speaks up. "Especially given the horrific nature of the killings?"

"Someone attacked her plus the two other men," Daryl tries on.

"But why would Sabera be there, in what you described as a dangerous section of town?" I want to know. "Especially three weeks *after* she disappeared. What happened in between?"

"Maybe she was attacked first," Roberta considers. "Was kidnapped or something like that? As well as the other two." She shrugs.

"And she ends up walking away while the men are pulverized by a hammer?" Detective Marc already sounds skeptical.

Roberta doesn't back down. "Fine. The two men were the kidnappers and someone killed them to rescue her." Her tone states, *Top that*.

Her detective brother has no problem: "Then where's her savior? She's the only one caught on camera."

Daryl re-enters the fray. "Bigger question, how'd she get from there to here? Warehouse district is a solid twenty miles from this resort. No way she walked it."

"Maybe she called Uber?" Roberta suggests.

"Or her husband." I glance at Detective Marc. "Do you have her phone?"

He shakes his head.

"Can you track it, get records of texts, voice mail messages, recent calls?"

"We're not idiots, thank you. Up until this point, however, we haven't had cause to subpoena records. Technically speaking, she's still not considered missing."

"But now that she's a possible witness, suspect—"

"Person of interest."

"In a double homicide. That must give you probable cause."

"I have more avenues of investigation open to me now than I did before," Marc agrees dryly.

I hesitate. "If Sabera was going to reach out to anyone, you would think it would be Isaad...Maybe the courier was a hint or alarm of some kind. A way for Sabera to send her husband a secret message. Certainly, based on the walls of this place alone, she's way into coded messages."

Detective Marc doesn't say anything, as there's nothing to say. Sabera was attacked along with the men in the warehouse. Sabera attacked the men in the warehouse. Sabera is covered in her own blood. Sabera is covered in someone else's blood. Sabera is in desperate need of medical attention. Sabera is a danger to herself and others.

Sabera is married/not married. A great mother/a distant mother. A devout Muslim/a closet drinker.

We have theories and more theories. What we need are answers.

"According to my conversation with Aliah this morning," I ponder out loud, "Isaad still hasn't reappeared. Is it possible he was the one staying here? He's a mathematician, right? Maybe all these notations..." But the moment I say it, I waver. The handwriting doesn't feel right. I'm no expert in these things, but there's a kind of looping flair to the script that seems distinctly feminine. I can tell from the others' expressions they think the same.

"Okay, so he's not the one who wrote the message, but what if he's the intended recipient? I mean, everything going on in there"—I wave my hand in the general direction of the townhouse—"certainly looks like some kind of riddle, and math geeks are good with codes. What if something terrible did happen to Sabera, something involving a hammer..."

Detective Marc rolls his eyes at my broad conjecture. I refuse to back down.

"She makes her way here, where she can tend her wounds, then leaves a message for her husband, telling him what happened in a way only he'd understand."

"Why all the secrecy?" Detective Marc asks bluntly. "If she already contacted him to pick her up, then he knows at least some of what happened. And if she's that grievously injured, he should be taking her to the hospital, not a stolen townhouse."

I scowl. Solid questions once again.

Daryl and Roberta give me disappointed expressions, as if I've somehow let them down.

My last-minute salvo: "Okay, try this on. Sabera was targeted, for some reason we have yet to determine. She gets away. Arrives here, by some means we have yet to determine—"

I can already feel Detective Marc's eye roll.

"Where she leaves a coded message for Isaad, warning him of the danger. Because she's not the only one at risk. Whatever happened involves him as well. Which would explain"—my voice picks up—"why he's now disappeared."

I feel pretty good about myself, right up until Detective Marc goes with the sarcastic hand clap. "Brilliant story. Except, oh yes, where the fuck is your evidence?"

I glare at him, then it occurs to me. "Cameras! Place this swanky must have one helluva security system. Access the tapes, fill in the timeline."

"Great idea. Why didn't I think of it first? Oh, wait, I did. Another pesky detail, the security system hasn't been working for the past few weeks. Some kind of electrical fritz, or so they believe."

My eyes widen. "Do you think she did that, too?" I begin.

"Sir." A uniformed officer with short cropped black hair materializes in the doorway. His light blue shirt includes a patch identifying him as Crime Scene Unit. "We've found something you should see."

The young Asian male focuses solely on Detective Marc. Of course the rest of us automatically take a step forward as well.

"Stay!" Detective Marc attempts, but is quickly overwhelmed when we all pointedly ignore his command and traipse into the house behind him.

The first blast of air-conditioning makes me giddy. The second gives me goose bumps as the frigid breeze hits my sweat-slick skin.

"I noticed another pattern in the script, west side wall, leading into the kitchen." The crime scene specialist points toward a sea of black notations. "This one is a bit harder to spot immediately, but if you extract each letter from the rows of numbers, then focus on just the lowercase entries—"

Which I now realize vary across the rows. Uppercase, uppercase, lowercase. Uppercase, lowercase, upper, upper, upper, lower, etc.

"It spells out another message. This one states…" The crime scene tech holds up a piece of paper where he'd been scratching notes.

beauty is power i am her sword

He gazes at Detective Marc expectantly.

Daryl recites, "'If Beauty is power, then a smile is its sword.' By John Ray, a seventeenth-century naturalist." In response to our shocked expressions, he self-consciously shrugs. "What? A lot of time to read in prison."

Beside him, Roberta has also perked up. "It's Zahra! Gotta be. Her name means beauty. I was talking to Aliah about it last night. So Zahra is power. And Sabera is her sword?"

"More like Sabera is Zahra's hammer," Detective Marc mutters darkly. "Honestly, can't anything about this case be normal?" He rubs his forehead. "Look, excusing the obvious…drama, homicide happens because of three things: money, power, love.

Anyone want to translate that to what the hell is happening here in Club Hypergraphia?"

"Hypergraphia means—" Daryl begins.

Roberta smacks him on the arm. "Hey, just because we didn't go to prison doesn't mean we're stupid."

I focus on the detective's question. He's right—every case I've ever worked has boiled down to one of those three driving forces.

Money, power, lust...er, love.

Involving a refugee who fled her home country with nothing but the clothes on her back, which suggests this can't be about money.

Involving a female Afghan trying to survive in a male-dominated world, which would argue she'd never be perceived as a source of power.

Leaving us with lust/love.

Involving a woman who told at least one person her husband isn't really her husband.

Now, that's an interesting thought. If only Sabera or her husband were available to pursue it.

I turn to the crime scene specialist. "Your name?"

"Chen. Jay Chen."

"Are you good at riddles, Jay Chen?"

He doesn't say yes, but neither does he demur. In other words, absolutely.

"A lock to a key for a key that has no lock," I recite. "That mean anything to you?"

He contemplates it for a moment. Shakes his head. "Should it?"

"We encountered it earlier. Any ideas on the subject would be appreciated. At least the second half, *a key that has no lock*, is repeated here. If you discover the first half, or what the hell any of it means, that would be helpful."

Chen has the good sense to glance in Detective Marc's direction. "Sure, why not?" the detective allows.

That much resolved:

"Are there any personal items left in this townhouse?" I speak up, because the good detective never answered that question.

"No."

"So most likely, Sabera is no longer staying here. Nor is she at the warehouse where two people were beaten to death with a hammer, nor is she at home. So what's next? Because hiding out here made sense, especially to lick her wounds. But now... Where would a strange woman in an even stranger land go next?"

Detective Marc is unconcerned. "One way or another, I think that'll become clear."

"How so?"

"Because in her own words, she's the sword. Sounds to me like I just need to follow the trail of dead bodies. Whatever's going on here"—he skewers me with a look—"clearly it's not over yet."

CHAPTER 21

THE RATS STARE AT US. We jolt awake during the night to discover them mere inches from our sleeping bodies, beady eyes fixed upon our noses, chins, ears. Even Isaad has taken to wrapping his head for bedtime. If he finds its hot and uncomfortable, he's wise enough not to utter a word.

Then there's the smell. Human sweat, raw sewage, soiled diapers. This "temporary" camp was meant to hold a couple thousand. Now swelled ten times past that point, it's like a septic wound, ready to burst.

Isaad announces my pregnancy the moment we arrive. I'm self-conscious, but quickly relent. A refugee camp is less a way station than a dumping ground for desperate humanity. There's screaming all night long. Innocent people caught in the grips of vicious nightmares. Young men caught up in explosive violence. Young women caught by callous predators.

As a pregnant female, I'm entitled to protective custody. Which is to say, Isaad and I are moved into a secured section within a larger gated compound, where we are closer to the police and new arrivals. Once upon a time, a family was entitled to their own little structure, but due to overcrowding, those standards have long since passed. We share the single-room unit with a family of six, one set of parents and four small children who greet our arrival with rounded shoulders and terrified eyes. A threadbare blanket hangs as a makeshift curtain down half the space in a pitiful attempt at privacy.

Our first night, after spending an entire day standing in line to receive a single ration of food, Isaad hands half to me. Then, after thirty seconds of staring at his own meager portion of cold rice drowned in greasy curry, he hands over his bowl to the father of the family.

"It is not for us," Isaad states gruffly. "We are Afghan, not Indian. This food will only hurt our stomachs."

The four children fall upon it gratefully, their parents gazing at us in quiet exhaustion.

And I think, not for the first time in the past few weeks, that there's more to my husband than meets the eye.

A woman can give her body. It's not so hard after all. The things men want, the demands they feel are so important. It costs us everything, but it costs us nothing, because a clever female, a strong female, can meet basic expectations, while keeping everything of value to herself.

In the beginning, it enraged Isaad. Our first night, when he made it clear he was my husband in every way possible. And I lay there, not thinking of lakes, or hot summer days, or those moments where once I could see an entire future in one man's eyes...

I thought of none of those things.

I felt nothing.

In the end, my "husband" rolled away in a huff of rage. We were on the road. Limited to sleeping awkwardly in a cheap hotel or cramped car. But as we grew closer to the border, still not having been blown up by an IED or shot by a Taliban soldier, Isaad's attentions grew more frequent, more urgent, more . . . creative.

Things of which I had no idea. Persistence that invited rather than commanded and was therefore even more threatening to my determination to remain aloof.

Which seemed to make him all the more determined on the subject.

By the time we arrived at the border, Isaad's resources had run dry. I volunteered the contents tucked inside the single volume I had plucked from my father's library—books may be priceless, but when making my selection I knew cash would matter most, hence my father's "safe book." Next up, having been allowed to cross into Pakistan and now desperate for entry into a designated camp, I produced my mother's necklace. It took a bit more haggling, as the officials had been bribed with many heirlooms by now, but fortunately, I'd picked the pendant with equal care. Ironically, the necklace was my mother's least favorite, as it featured stones from my uncles' mines. The impressive size and exquisite color of the watermelon tourmalines, however, made it an exceptional piece—and a final homage to a place and people that were no more.

We were finally granted entrance only to spend even more hours standing in line, where despite our more than generous offerings, uniformed guards stared at us in open disdain.

I waited for my husband to explode into a show of vanity and self-importance. But at each checkpoint, in front of bored officials and heavily armed police, he remained a study in devoted family man. He murmured reassuring words in my ear. He requested our safe passage. He begged for the life of my baby.

Day after day, line after line, obstacle after obstacle.

Professor Ahmadi, the once notorious Dokhtar Baaz, put his own future on the line to fight for my unborn child.

I learned perhaps there's more to life than pretty lakes and hot summer days after all.

The family sharing our cabin is kind. They have already been at this refugee camp for six months. They have relatives in Australia. They hope someone, anyone, might approve their paperwork sooner versus later so they can continue on to their loved ones.

They are Hazaras. In other words, as Shiites in Sunni-dominated Afghanistan, they have long been subject to discrimination. A return to the Taliban-controlled state would mean at best persecution, at worst, genocide. Unfortunately, their fate isn't much better in Pakistan, where they must face down glowering guards and distrustful neighbors. As if life behind coils of razor wire isn't hard enough.

After the first night of Isaad sharing his food, the woman, Malalai, appears with an offering of her own—adult diapers. She offers them first to me, and then, much to Isaad's consternation, to him.

It's not safe to use the latrines at night, she informs us. Forget the hungry rats and packs of feral dogs. The camp is filled with young men, lost, traumatized, inured to violence. Stabbings are daily, some the result of short-tempered exchanges. Some simply the last straw of troubled minds that can't take one second more *of the noise, the smell, the oppressive rain/heat/cold. The police are too few, the doctors and social workers nearly nonexistent.*

Keep my hair covered, she advises. Also, my head bowed and my gaze down. I may have escaped the Taliban, but that doesn't mean I'm safe. Women can change countries; we still can't change the minds of men.

Very quickly, we discover Isaad isn't wrong about the food. Afghan cuisine is a satisfying mix of sweet and sour, soft and crunchy, tangy and comforting. The endless curries served up here, however, rip through our intestines. By the third evening, both Isaad and I can only lie on our mats and moan, our one precious bottle of water not nearly enough to replace the fluids pouring out of our bodies.

Halfway through the night, Isaad staggers to his feet, determined to summon help. He collapses at the door. The husband, Rafiq, helps him back to bed. The couple have nothing to offer but their compassion.

When I awake again at first light, their five-year-old boy, Omid, is stealing our water bottle. I want to cry out in protest. But I don't have the strength, as he takes the bottle, tips it back, and pours the final few precious drops onto Isaad's parched lips.

"Sleep, Kaka, sleep," he whispers comfortingly. I would cry, but I don't have enough moisture left.

We survive. We learn. We adapt. Somewhere around the fourth week, I make my way through the camp to the communal showers for my designated slot, Isaad striding along beside me. At one time, I would've rolled my eyes at his puffed-up chest and self-important swagger. Now I'm grateful for his protective arm and beetled brow as mere mortals scatter before us.

Suddenly, a teenage boy lurches into our path. He isn't screaming as much as gasping, his hands clutched over his stomach, where I can see a splotch of red spreading rapidly across his tattered and dirty tunic.

Two older men come skittering to a stop behind him, one grabbing at the teen's arm, yanking him back. The boy staggers. The men burst into a frenzy of sharply delivered words. Isaad is already tucking me behind his imposing form. The men aren't Afghan. Maybe Bangladeshi or Sri Lankan or Burmese; the refugee camp is a virtual United Nations of homelessness.

More chatter, the second man now yanking at the boy as well.

The boy doesn't speak. He sways dangerously, his face leeching of color as more red seeps across his shirt.

The second man speaks up harshly, his intent clearly ominous as he prepares to drag the injured youth away. I don't know what else to do. I twist out from behind Isaad's looming form, wrap both my arms around the young boy, and pull him against me.

The sudden insertion of a clearly pregnant female shocks both of the men into silence.

I use the opportunity to hiss out forceful words of my own. The two men immediately raise placating hands before exchanging alarmed glances, then bolting away.

I can feel the boy shivering. Shock, pain, exhaustion. I whisper reassuring words as he collapses against me. I cradle his form as we sink to the ground, offering what comfort I can, as four other teens burst onto the scene, taking in me, the wounded boy, then Isaad's obviously enraged expression.

They begin to mutter in agitation, their language foreign to

Isaad and rapidly increasing his hostility. Quickly I cut them off with a slew of questions, followed by rapid-fire instructions. In the next few minutes, they mobilize, two returning with a thin brown blanket, the others helping lift their friend atop, then each grabbing a corner, the refugee version of a stretcher, as they heft up their friend's injured form and sprint in the direction of the makeshift medical clinic.

Bit by bit, the crowd returns to the demanding task of basic survival, till it is just me and Isaad. I'm covered in blood, while Isaad wears a look of confusion.

"What was that?" he asks.

"The boy was waiting in line for food. The men thought he'd taken their place. There was some kind of disagreement...The boy's friends came, but not in time to help."

"How do you know this?"

I hesitate, studying the man who is now my husband. I search his face for a long time. I must pick my next words very carefully.

"I listened to them."

"That is not Dari, nor Pashto, nor English." Isaad frowns at me. "How did you understand them?"

Then when I don't immediately answer: "Tell me, Sabera. Where are they from? What were they speaking?"

I am saved from having to confess that I have no idea, that all syllables in any language are nothing but bright, shiny notes, waiting for me to pluck them out of the air and string together in a song of my own making.

That I can do the same with numbers. And symbols and faces and names. For me, the entire universe is nothing more than an assortment of threads that I can weave together, rip apart, then form anew in any and all configurations. And most of the time, I can do it between drawing one breath and another.

It took me years to understand others don't experience the world the same way.

And it took my mother to make it clear that others must never know.

Life for a woman is hard enough.

A fresh commotion. Two dark-clad policemen appear, sending an immediate shiver of panic through the crowd. Then a tall man with unkempt curly brown hair and heavily whiskered cheeks strides up behind them. He wears stained blue surgical scrubs with a stethoscope dangling haphazardly around his neck.

"They said a woman understood him. You." His gaze locks on me, still seated on the ground with red streaks across my hands, my clothes, my face. "What's your name?"

Isaad takes an immediate step forward in aggravation. The two policemen muster accordingly.

The doctor raises a commanding hand, declares in a distinctly American accent, "Stop. You." His gaze once again zeros in on me. "Your name." It's not a question, but a command.

I murmur obediently. "Sabera Ahmadi."

"She is my wife—" Isaad begins. The doctor couldn't care less. His attention remains fixed on me and only me.

"Mrs. Ahmadi, the wounded boy that was just dragged into my clinic, you can understand him?"

"Yes."

"Then come with me. I need you, if that boy's to live."

The look my husband gives me...

Be still, I want to tell him. Everything will be all right. And it occurs to me for the first time that I've grown accustomed to his bristling eyebrows and hawkish nose and perpetually brooding features. I've come to appreciate the way in the middle of the night, when my dreams are especially bad, he will tuck my head against his shoulder, even if we never speak of it come morning.

My mouth opens. I grasp desperately for words of assurance. But just because I can understand nearly every language doesn't mean I always know what to say.

"Before the boy bleeds out!" the doctor barks.

The security men take a threatening step forward.

I shift away from my husband, toward the impatient physician.

His gaze homes in on my bulky figure. "And you're pregnant? Of course. Fuck it. All right, one life at a time in this hellhole."

Then a string of exasperated mutterings I understand better than he thinks as we head for the woefully understaffed, under-supplied medical clinic.

A young man I saved.

And who might well be the death of me yet.

Zahra, I'm sorry.

Zahra, I love you.

Zahra, forgive me for what happens next.

CHAPTER 22

DARYL ANNOUNCES WE NEED TO make a stop as we depart from the luxury resort, which has now been taken over by a sea of law enforcement vehicles and gawking bystanders. No doubt management is ripping out their hair at this turn of events. On the other hand, here's one family vacation people will be talking about for years.

I'm still lost in my own thoughts: Whose blood on the towels in the sink? Sabera's, the two dead men, Isaad's?

Too many possibilities. Too large a cast of characters. Not nearly enough information.

I'm distracted enough that it takes me a moment to realize Daryl has pulled into the dilapidated apartment complex from the first day, where in front of us looms a giant furniture-store delivery truck. Two guys with a dolly appear at the back of the vehicle, maneuvering a low-slung wooden dresser down the ramp. They roll it across the cracked asphalt, through the door of the unit I helped clean just the other day.

Ashley is hovering outside, her blond hair once again gathered in a messy topknot, as she shifts from foot to foot, looking torn between clapping wildly and bursting into tears. I know how she feels.

"You did all this?" I ask Daryl, taking in the new mattresses leaning against the side of the unit, as well as nightstands, sofa, coffee table, and standing lamps.

In response, a card materializes between his fingers in the front seat. He hands it over.

One side bears a brightly colored cartoon—Marge Simpson with her signature pile of blue hair and string of red pearls. On the back, a single sentence.

Marge says she's sorry.

The front illustration bears a hastily scrawled autograph across the bottom: Matt Groening.

I look up to meet Daryl's eyes in the rearview mirror. "Seriously?"

Daryl shrugs. "Bart is...Bart. And he really did feel bad about Marge escaping."

"Bad enough to furnish an entire apartment for a resettlement agency?"

"Gamers. Go big or go home."

We get out to inspect the move in progress.

Upon our approach, Ashley, the housing coordinator, throws her arms around my neck. "Oh my goodness, you did exactly as you promised."

I self-consciously wave my hand at Daryl. "It's really more his—"

Ashley flings herself at Daryl, who does his best not to stagger beneath a hundred pounds of pretty young thing.

"We got this employer, Boy Wonder, er Bart, er..."

Ashley gives him a giant squeeze. "God loves both of you!"

Daryl appears slightly terrified. "Just go with it," I direct him. He nods weakly.

Turns out, Bart had graciously provided furniture for not just the original apartment where I'd scrubbed at blood spatter, but for the infamous murder unit Ashley had already snagged for an incoming family. I'm not sure who picked the pieces, but someone did a great job. Nice-looking to be sure, but also sturdy and durable. Solid building blocks from which to create a new life.

There's still some setup at the crime scene unit to be done. Daryl sheds his jacket and we get to work, unrolling rugs, assembling beds, unloading kitchen supplies, with Ashley keeping up a steady chatter. I drift in and out of attention; busy work makes for the best thinking.

Sabera, Isaad, and their daughter, Zahra. Who what when why and how. An entire family, uprooted from their homeland, bounced around other countries and then sling-shotted here. We all believe we know their hopes and dreams. But do we? Can we?

Safety and security are basic needs. Once you move beyond that…Could Sabera really be doing all this because she desires freedom that badly? Did Isaad disappear because his need to control his wife ran that high? And what about little Zahra with her solemn face and crazy, eerie riddles?

A lock to a key for a key that has no lock. I can't wrap my head around it. Mostly, I'm haunted by the intent sound of Zahra's voice as she delivered that line. Memorized it? But from where?

Ashley, appearing at my shoulder.

"Umm…Frankie."

"No worries. Almost done." I billow out a thin blanket, tuck it around the twin-sized mattress.

"Frankie—"

Her insistent tone gets to me. I regard her directly, not bothering to keep the impatience from my face. She shifts uncomfortably.

"Nageenah just called. Two men are at the apartment asking questions about Sabera. Close-cropped hair, military posture. Nageenah is concerned. She said you'd know why."

My thoughts go immediately to the incident that happened yesterday, how the young boy had described the man looking for Zahra as similar to the guards from a refugee camp.

"Daryl," I call out.

"Already heard."

We don't bother with an explanation. Daryl grabs his jacket and we race for the car.

THE COMPLEX NAGEENAH shares with Sabera and her husband is only five minutes away. Three, when you have Daryl at the wheel. He careens to a halt in the parking lot with the sedan positioned to block the entrance/exit. In front of us is some kind of heavy-duty white SUV that appears outfitted for either a moon landing or deployment behind enemy lines. Military-grade indeed.

Just beyond the vehicle: two men in khaki cargo pants and polo shirts. One man is older, red-cheeked face, pale blue eyes. The other is younger with dark hair and an intense, burning gaze. Both sport standard buzz cuts and stand at rigid attention as they talk to Nageenah.

I notice another door cracked open down the way. The older brother and key witness, peering out at the scene. I try to judge from the boy's expression if he recognizes the men. But he doesn't appear frightened, just suspicious.

Daryl is already clambering out of the vehicle. I scramble to catch up.

"Try not to get blood on your shirt this time," I mutter, and am rewarded by a slight hitch in Daryl's step. So I wasn't imagining things last night. If only that felt more reassuring.

The two men turn at our approach. They don't seem particularly alarmed at seeing a hulking limo driver advance directly toward them, with a slightly built white woman scampering in his wake.

"You looking for the Ahmadis?" Daryl asks bluntly, posture definitely veering on the aggressive side.

"Sabera Ahmadi." The older white guy, whose wavy brown hair is shaved to Brillo pad thickness, does the honors. "You a friend of hers?"

I notice his companion retreats back a few steps and to our right. Classic flanking maneuver. Clearly, they're practicing some strategies of their own. Both take in Daryl's parking job, exchange glances. They widen their stances, hands hanging loosely at their sides. Battle positions, everyone.

I don't like what I'm seeing, but neither do I know what to do. There are too many players in this little drama, and I don't understand the roles or motivations of any of them.

Once again, I peer down the row of apartments. Four doors down, the young boy meets my questioning gaze, then slowly shakes his head.

So these men are not from yesterday. But working with, operating on behalf of...?

"There's been a recent incident," Daryl is saying. "Folks are a little on edge. Might be best if you just state your business."

"And you are?"

"Asked you first."

"Actually, I believe I asked you first."

The second man, starting to drift behind us. I plant myself squarely in front of him.

"Frankie Elkin," I announce loudly. "Working with the Tucson PD." I eye them up and down, then demand: "Rank and serial number."

I'm not actually sure what that means outside of movie scenes, but the older one finally cracks a smile. I haven't fooled him for a second, but amused is better than hostile, so at least we're getting somewhere.

"Sanders Kurtz. Retired captain, Army. This is Tim Westwig, retired first sergeant, Army. We're with No One Left Behind."

A business card materializes in his hand. Daryl takes it. We both eye the logo blankly.

"We're a private nonprofit dedicated to evacuating, resettling, and advocating on behalf of our Afghan and Iraqi interpreters," Westwig rattles off. "We have not forgotten bonds forged nor promises made."

I'm somewhat taken aback by the forcefulness of his tone. Behind him, Nageenah wears an expression that's harder to interpret. It's not distrust, per se. Maybe more like disillusionment. Then I clue in on the relevant piece of his statement.

"Wait a minute. Interpreters. You're trying to bring the Afghans who worked with the US military to the States?" I remember from news accounts how many people were dismayed by America's abrupt withdrawal from Afghanistan and the ensuing collapse of Kabul, which left many of the locals who served vulnerable to retribution.

"Yes, ma'am."

"It's been four years," Daryl begins in confusion.

I whack him on the arm. Timeline is not the relevant information here. "Sabera was a translator with the US Army?" I ask excitedly. Because that would make sense, given her language skills, not to mention possibly be relevant to what's happening now.

But the retired captain is shaking his head. "Not Mrs. Ahmadi."

"But then..." I'm terribly confused.

"We're here at Mrs. Ahmadi's request; she reached out to us about a month ago. She was aware her family supplied some assistance to the military efforts in Afghanistan. In particular, she was looking for information regarding her mother."

CHAPTER 23

"OUR MISSION," KURTZ IS EXPLAINING, "is to support local assets in Afghanistan and Iraq who qualify for the Special Immigrant Visa program, or SIV. Right after Kabul fell, we were able to evacuate eighty thousand Afghan personnel, but we abandoned another twenty-five to fifty thousand allies; an exact count is unknown as we lack a comprehensive list. To make matters more complicated, the principal applicant for the SIV, say the interpreter, is entitled to bring his family members as secondary applicants. Meaning that four years later, there are at least a quarter of a million eligible friendlies still left behind. Which is at least a quarter of a million people too high."

Kurtz pauses, studies Daryl and me as if to see if we're following his explanation. We nod as one. We're hearing him. Speaking for myself, however, I'm not sure what this means.

We've followed retired army captain Sanders Kurtz and former first sergeant Tim Westwig back to their offices, which are located in a newly opened commercial park. According to Kurtz,

No One Left Behind's main headquarters are in DC. He and Westwig have just opened up a satellite office in Tucson, however, and given the organization's close ties with the Davis-Monthan Air Force Base, a significant number of the approved SIV candidates are arriving there from Afghanistan.

The space is so recently constructed, it still has that new carpet smell, though Kurtz and Westwig have already made a go at interior decorating—the wall behind them is covered in framed photos, including shadow boxes containing folded American flags and half a dozen group photos of American men and women in uniform. Interspersed are other, more intimate snapshots of Kurtz with his arm around an Afghan male's shoulder; a trio of soldiers grinning around a campfire; Kurtz relaxing in the front of a heavily armored vehicle with a man whose features look startlingly similar to his own. Huge smiles split both their faces as they raise cold beers toward whoever's wielding the camera.

No doubt about it—war is a human enterprise. I wonder how many of the pictured men and women made it home again.

"As a company commander, I personally oversaw fourteen interpretors," Captain Kurtz continues. "Those Afghans risked their lives day in and day out. They worked seven days a week, rotating between time in the field and duties on base—assisting with interrogations, interacting with locals, and serving as go-betweens with the Afghan army. They faced all the same dangers we did— roadside bombings, snipers, enemy ambush, while serving in a civilian capacity. Which is to say, I watched unarmed men race toward burning vehicles to drag their US buddies to safety, let alone face down attacking assailants while radioing in enemy positions and coordinating air support. We had one incident of a US commander being grievously wounded; his Afghan translator grabbed his rifle and took out both of the advancing Taliban.

"These men trained with us. They served with us. And now, we're gone, and they're left behind to pay the price. These are guys who wouldn't even take a weekend leave, because returning home put their families' lives in jeopardy. They did what they did because they believed in our efforts and hoped for a better future for their country. *They* didn't let anyone down."

Again, Daryl and I nod as one.

I raise a tentative hand. "You said Afghan men. Does that mean all the interpreters were males?"

"In the field, yes." Westwig does the honors. "That's not to say there weren't plenty of skilled females. They generally served in different capacities, assisting with government ministries, enabling diplomatic efforts—"

"Admin," I intone.

"It's all necessary," Westwig counters.

"But your program never assisted Sabera Ahmadi? You said she came to you?"

"Yes, ma'am. Showed up right here at our office."

"Isn't that a little unusual?"

Kurtz speaks up. "We actively publicize our organization, particularly within the Afghan community. Time is not on our side. Last year, we evacuated four thousand eligible persons. We're very pleased to be able to bring that many individuals safely to the US. But if you think of the overall number of folks left behind, it remains just a drop in the bucket. Add that it takes three to five years to process a single SIV applicant and, well, our ability to reach enough people in a timely manner..." He leans forward. "Let me put it to you this way—the Iraq SIV program stopped accepting new applicants in 2014. Over ten years later, it's still actively working on processing the personnel still in the system.

Nothing quick or easy about government. Which, if you consider everything these people have at stake..."

He doesn't have to complete that sentence. We get it.

"So what did Sabera want to know?" I ask.

Again, Westwig and Kurtz exchange glances.

"Oh, come on," I huff out—God save me from self-important men. "You're operating as a private nonprofit, correct? That hardly grants client confidentiality. Let alone, in case you didn't realize, Sabera vanished three weeks ago, her husband is now in the wind, and oh, yeah, just yesterday someone tried to kidnap their daughter."

"What?" Kurtz and Westwig exchange startled glances.

"Exactly! The perpetrator had a British-adjacent accent. Ring any bells for you?"

Another exchanged look. At this point, I want to reach across the desk and knock their heads together. Daryl seems to sense my agitation. He places a large hand on my shoulder. When the big bruiser ex-con becomes the calming influence, you're definitely in trouble.

"Sabera knew her mother was working in intelligence," Kurtz relents. "On behalf of MI6, to be exact. And while No One Left Behind is comprised primarily of former US military connections, we partner with a fair number of Brits, given their own history in the country."

I have to raise my hand again. "Hang on. You're saying Sabera's mother was like a British spy? For real?"

Kurtz smiles. "Even as a child, Sabera recognized that when her mother went to the local markets, she was doing more than simply shopping for tea. Maryam Shinwari would pass a note here, pick up a slip of paper there. According to Sabera, she and her mother never spoke of it, but it was an open secret between them. Then, when her mother died in 2014—"

"How?"

"Cancer. Sad for any family, but particularly dramatic in the case of Maryam, as her father was a doctor of note in London—and wasn't involved in her treatment."

Kurtz lets that sink in.

"Sabera remembered overhearing her uncle demanding to know why Maryam's parents weren't doing more to help. Her father simply said that wasn't an option, though no one ever explained why. It made Sabera more interested in delving into her mother's background, including her mother's extracurricular market activities."

"Which I'm guessing proved to be enlightening?"

"Maryam's family emigrated from Afghanistan to England when she was a young girl," Westwig explains. "Father opened a medical practice, his brothers established various business dealings. Basically, the entire Tabrizi family made London their new home. Except one day, Maryam meets Saber Shinwari, who's a doctorate student at Oxford. They fall in love and Maryam returns to Kabul with her new husband, despite her family's disapproval.

"Then the Taliban seized control, and Maryam and her young son fled to London for safety. They spent five years living with her family, until the Taliban fell in 2001. After which time, Maryam declared she'd be returning to her husband in Kabul. Except her family strenuously objected. If she went, that was that—they were cutting all ties. Obviously, she made her decision and they made theirs. To the best of Sabera's knowledge, her mother never saw or spoke to her family again.

"But this is what the London Tabrizis didn't know—Maryam wasn't just returning to Afghanistan out of love, but out of duty.

While in the UK, she'd been recruited by MI6. They needed her to return to Kabul and go to work."

"So Sabera's mom is like a female James Bond?" Now I'm totally enthralled. I wonder what it meant to Sabera to learn her own mother was some kind of super spy. Isn't that what all children secretly fantasize about, that their parents aren't the tired, boring people they appear to be?

Westwig shrugs more philosophically. "According to our MI6 contacts, Maryam Shinwari's orders weren't exactly high risk— essentially, she was to resume her old life of mixing and mingling with the Afghan elite. Between her husband's respected position and his family's expansive commercial dealings, they routinely hobnobbed with high-ranking ministry officials, other wealthy businessmen, and society's movers and shakers. As you may know, Afghanistan's government had quite a reputation for corruption. MI6 wanted Maryam Shinwari to get the lay of the land—gather up intelligence on who was cozying up with whom, which government ministers were suddenly flush with cash, et cetera. Basically, who could be bought, who could be sold, and who could potentially be blackmailed."

I nod thoughtfully. I can see where that kind of insider information would be of interest to a spy agency, especially one with historical involvement in the country. "So what happened?"

Both men stare at me blankly.

I wave a hand to move their story along. "Sabera's mother got discovered? Someone else also noticed that she was passing notes in the market, her husband became angry, it all went to hell? Come on. What?"

"Maryam Shinwari contracted cancer," Westwig states slowly. "She became seriously ill. Then she died. That's what happened."

I frown, once more confused. "Then why would Sabera be approaching you all these years later? There must've been something more going on. What did she want?"

"The name of her mother's handler," Kurtz provides.

"Why?"

Both men exchange glances.

"Oh, come on, I thought we were over that!"

"Sabera implied she might have come across some valuable intel after her mother died," Kurtz concedes slowly. "She was willing to pass it along, but only to her mother's original contact."

"Valuable intel? After the old government is gone and the Taliban is once again in charge?" I'm not buying it. "What could a woman have possibly learned at a cocktail party a decade ago that would still have relevance now?"

Beside me, Daryl nods with matching skepticism.

Interestingly enough, both men shrug in agreement.

"We pushed," Westwig states. "Sabera demurred. She'd talk to her mother's handler and her mother's handler only. In the end, we agreed to at least ask around. If we could come up with a name from our own contacts, and that person felt like reaching out to Sabera, that would be on them. No harm, no foul. She agreed. We started making inquiries."

"And that's when things got more interesting," Kurtz interjects. "Sabera Ahmadi wasn't exactly telling the truth, the whole the truth, and nothing but the truth."

"Sabera's mother wasn't actually a spy? Or a spy for the British?"

"Oh, Maryam Shinwari checked out. What Sabera failed to mention is that she hadn't just observed her mother's activities, she'd gotten into the game herself."

"Sabera is also an MI6 agent?" I can barely contain myself.

Westwig shakes his head. "She didn't work for the Brits, but for us. Sabera approached the US embassy with her language skills. In turn, they recommended her to the US military. Though very quickly, the powers that be recognized she had an even more interesting and valuable skill. She was a natural-born cryptanalyst."

I blink my eyes several times: "A code breaker?"

"She created ciphers, cracked ciphers, invented new ciphers," Westwig explains. "The people we talked to said they'd never seen anything like it. She could remember almost anything, and seemingly recognize complex patterns in a single glance. Her skills quickly became the stuff of legend."

Daryl gives me a meaningful glance. Suddenly the condition of the townhouse walls made much more sense. Sabera wasn't just a linguist. She was a riddle master. Meaning...?

"Hang on a second," I interject. "If Sabera was working for the US military, why wasn't she evacuated when Kabul fell? Or on your radar screen now? You said you had no previous knowledge of her."

Westwig sighs heavily. Kurtz gives up the ghost.

"Which would be the second detail Sabera omitted. She had been working for the army's military intelligence corps. Until fourteen months later, a fellow cryptanalyst found an error in one of the messages she decoded. Further review revealed several more mistakes."

"She wasn't the wunderkind everyone supposed?"

Kurtz arches a brow. Waits.

My eyes go round as a second explanation comes to me: "They thought it was intentional. Like she was a double agent or something?"

"Let's go with 'or something.' The errors were random enough she could pass them off as slipups. But by then, doubt in her skills had turned into suspicion of her motives. She was officially dismissed. No one would tell me anything more on the subject. Then again, military intelligence never likes to admit when they've been less than intelligent."

Kurtz rolls his eyes, while Westwig nods in agreement.

I sit back, more flummoxed than ever. "So basically, Sabera's mother was a spy for MI6. Her daughter knew, but no one else. Then Sabera approaches the US military to offer her services in decoding. Except maybe she wasn't really there to help? She had another motive entirely? But what?"

Kurtz spreads his hands. "No one would comment."

"But maybe she was up to something," I try on. "Which earned her some enemies. Who may have then followed her to Tucson? Four years later?"

The men go from shrugging to open skepticism. Yeah, I can't exactly blame them for that.

"You said someone with a 'British-adjacent' accent was looking for Sabera," Westwig speaks up. "What did you mean by that?"

"That's the problem; we're not certain. The witness was a young boy. According to him, the man who tried to kidnap Zahra Ahmadi sounded like he had a British accent, except not exactly. I was thinking maybe Australian? Or maybe," now that I think about it more, "South African? Would a South African have a reason to be pursuing an Afghan refugee?" I inquire.

More exchanged looks.

"Some of the best mercs in the world," Westwig comments.

"And they've long been interested by Afghanistan," Kurtz comments. "Given the mining potential."

"Mining potential?"

"South Africa is one of the top mining countries. From diamonds to chromium, if it's in the ground, they can get it out. Which makes the South Africans very keen on Afghanistan, which is sitting atop some of the largest mineral-rich deposits in the world. Copper, iron, lithium, coal, gold, gemstones. You name it, they got it. And then there's the matter of rare earth elements—REEs."

"Which everyone wants," Westwig adds. "Especially to reduce dependence on the Chinese."

"But what does that have to do with Sabera Ahmadi?" I ask in total confusion.

"I don't know that it does." Westwig shrugs.

I feel ready to tear out my hair. Instead, I give up completely and rise to standing. Fascinating family legacy aside, learning Sabera's mother's past work isn't helping me with the present circumstance. After another second, Daryl pushes out of his own chair.

"One last question," I say as we turn toward the door. "Sabera's mother's MI6 handler. Did you find him?"

"We found her."

"Can I talk to her?"

"We can make you the same deal we made Sabera: we'll pass along your name to her. As for what happens after that..."

"Fair enough."

"You'll keep us posted on Sabera?" Kurtz requests.

"Sure. But I wouldn't get your hopes up. Sabera doesn't just create riddles, she's become one. And I'll be damned if I can decode what she's gonna do next."

CHAPTER 24

BY THE TIME DARYL AND I climb back into the car, I'm a hot, demoralized mess. It's only three P.M. and I can't believe everything that's happened. Good news, we discovered where Sabera has been hiding out. Bad news, she appears to be long gone, while leaving yet another puzzle behind.

First Zahra had supplied "a lock to a key for a key that has no lock." Now Sabera had added, "Beauty is power; I am her sword."

I'm a person who doesn't even like crossword puzzles. What am I supposed to do with brain teasers?

At least Daryl had been productive today, arranging for the delivery of furniture to Ashley the housing coordinator. Though what it means when outfitting a murder unit is the highlight of your day is beyond me.

"Daryl," I state.

He glances at me in the rearview mirror, my cue to speak.

"Walk through this with me. Something happened three weeks ago, causing Sabera Ahmadi to take off. She disappears until just the other day, when she reappears at a crime scene where two of her countrymen are brained to death. Do we think she's a witness, perpetrator, or possible fellow victim?"

He shrugs.

"Exactly. Okay, so what else do we got? She's been disappearing twice a week for a few hours each time. Going…somewhere. She's also most likely taken to drinking, also somewhere. Do we think those two things are related, unrelated, or something else?"

Shrug.

"Great, happy to know we're on the same page. Let's see…Oh yes, she's been networking with retired military officers to learn more about her mother's spying activities in Afghanistan. Also, she got involved in the intelligence game herself, until being forced to leave under less than favorable circumstances. Do we think she's a traitor, is working to her own end, or is representing yet another player in the geopolitical game? Maybe the South Africans?"

Third shrug.

"We agree! Okay, final puzzle piece: still-missing-in-action Isaad. What could've been delivered to him the other day to make him abandon his own child? A message from Sabera? A threat from someone else? A third totally different possibility that we haven't even considered yet?"

Fourth shrug.

"We're not doing very good at this game, Daryl."

Finally, a nod. I sigh heavily. My phone rings. Saved by the bell. I check the screen and feel some hope return. I put the phone on speaker.

"Hi, Aliah!" In the front seat, Daryl perks up. "Have you heard from Isaad?"

"Still nothing, I'm afraid. Zahra is okay. Are you with Daryl the dancer? She's been asking for him."

"Hi, Aliah!" Daryl booms from the front of the car. I've never heard him sound so enthusiastic.

"Ah, that is good. We would like to invite both of you to dinner."

I look up at Daryl, give him a questioning glance. Genni?

His crestfallen expression tells me enough.

"I don't think we can do dinner," I inform Aliah regretfully. "We have another commitment involving an iguana."

Long pause. I get it. What do you say to that? Then:

"I would like to invite you to come over," Aliah says, this time with just enough emphasis for me to catch on that what she really needs is to meet. "I'm at my restaurant. Perhaps you would like a snack?"

"We would love a snack," I fill in. Then, as another one of the day's developments occurs to me: "Hey, did you and Zahra make that pudding stuff?"

"We have made fresh firni, yes. Please, you should try."

Daryl hits the gas.

"We will be there in ten," I inform Aliah dryly. "Or five, given someone's appetite."

ALIAH ALREADY HAS a table waiting for us when we arrive. She has set out two square bowls filled with what looks like custard; half is a pretty pink, the other half a creamy white.

Daryl doesn't bother with words. He pulls out a chair, grabs a spoon, and digs in. Far from disapproving, Aliah beams with pride.

Zahra is nowhere to be seen. At my inquiring expression, Aliah nods her head toward the back. "She's in the kitchen, helping

Habibullah. She likes to measure and mix. We will make a good cook out of her, especially now that she's memorized every recipe I know, including the ones from my grandmother's grandmother."

Aliah takes a seat while I scoop up the first bite of the firni pudding. I nearly groan in ecstasy. It is at once thick and creamy, yet tastes light and airy, like a rose-kissed promise.

Aliah beams again. I like her concept of happiness. Except then her face falls as we come to the reason we are really here.

There is another customer in the store, a young man browsing the collection of candied nuts and dried fruits. Aliah waits for him to make his selections, then cashes him out. She locks the door behind him to ensure our privacy.

First things first: "Still no word from Sabera?"

Aliah's sad exhale says enough. "Did you learn more from the place where Sabera was hiding?" she asks.

I shake my head. Now we both sigh.

"I feel like I have been a bad friend," she begins. "I didn't know about the drinking. I was concerned, yes. There were things... But maybe I wasn't worried enough."

"You were worried enough to contact me." I eye her curiously. I still think there's more to this story than she's let on.

"It's not easy, what Sabera and Isaad have been through, are going through. The loss... it's hard to put into words."

I nod. We've covered this ground. Losing one's entire country, culture, family, way of life, is indeed daunting.

"There was an incident, maybe a few weeks after Sabera and Isaad first arrived. She showed up here, dressed in her work uniform. She was... flushed, agitated. I tried calming her, but when she looked at me, it was as if she couldn't see me. She just kept shaking her head. Finally, I got her to sit and brought her some tea.

Gradually, her breathing steadied, her eyes cleared. Eventually, she rose to standing. She gave me a hug, murmured something about having to get to work, and then left without another word.

"I assumed she was having some sort of spell, maybe a panic attack. I've experienced them myself. But now I wonder. Maybe it wasn't an emotional episode at all. Maybe it was due to alcohol. As one Muslim with another, it never occurred to me." Aliah finishes mournfully: "I've not been a good friend."

I consider Aliah, what she's saying, and what I still feel she's not saying. I also contemplate Staci's carefully guarded allusions that there's more going on with Sabera than meets the eye.

"When Sabera didn't return home from work three weeks ago, what did you immediately think?"

Aliah hesitates again.

"You were worried about her mental health," I prod. "Did you suspect self-harm?"

Aliah recoils. "No! Never! It is not done."

"In theory, neither is divorce. Or drinking. And yet..."

"No." She shakes head adamantly. "Never. Not that."

"But you suspected something." I eye her again. "First time you and I spoke, you implied Isaad might have something to do with Sabera's disappearance; you're clearly not a fan of his. But it's not really him you're concerned about, is it? Aliah, I need you to be honest with me."

Her gaze falters. She glances down at the table.

Daryl scrapes his empty bowl with his spoon. Without missing a beat, he reaches across the table and helps himself to mine. I don't stop him, my attention focused on Aliah.

She takes a deep breath. "That time Sabera seemed so disturbed...I stopped by her work at the end of her shift to check up on her. Except she wasn't there. Her boss said she called in sick, which I could understand, having seen her earlier. But when I went to her apartment, she wasn't there, either. Isaad thought she was working late. I didn't...I didn't correct him. Two days later, he called me, still looking for her. She had yet to return home or show up for work."

"Sabera disappeared once before? As in, this latest misadventure isn't the first time she's gone missing?" I give Aliah a pointed look. So I hadn't been wrong in my suspicions during our initial meetings—Aliah has definitely been less than truthful about this situation.

"It was only for a few days! Then she was back, something about taking care of a sick friend from work and she couldn't call as she'd run out of minutes on her phone. It happens. It does!"

I give Aliah another look. "You ever talk to her about it? Truly push the subject?"

"I thought eventually she might volunteer more information—"

"Such as the truth?"

Aliah flushes, appears genuinely remorseful. "After that... Sabera seemed more and more withdrawn. Jumpy. Anxious. Something was not right. I just didn't realize how wrong. I'm sorry. I thought I was being respectful, waiting for her to come to me. I wish now I'd pushed harder."

That would make two of us. "Aliah, do you remember the exact day this incident happened—Sabera coming here all rattled and distressed? The date?"

"I could look it up."

"Please do." There's a thought forming in the back of my mind. According to Staci, Sabera had once been admitted to the ER, leading to Staci getting a call instead of Isaad. I'm wondering if the hospital stay might have been Sabera's first disappearing act, especially given that Isaad wasn't summoned.

Maybe my theory's nothing, but maybe it's something, and at this point, I could use all the something I could get. For now, I switch gears. "Did Sabera ever talk about her mom?"

"All the time. She died when Sabera was a girl, but Sabera missed her very much. Her mother's name, Maryam, means beloved. Sabera would whisper it as a term of endearment. Clearly, they were very close."

"Did you know Sabera had reached out to an organization, No One Left Behind, to learn more about her mother's role as an MI6 agent?"

"*What?*" Aliah's eyes round. She appears genuinely stunned. "Her mother was a spy?"

"It's the real reason Sabera's mother returned to Kabul against her family's wishes. I mean, I'm sure she loved and missed her husband as well, but there was more going on than met the eye."

Aliah's mouth opens, no words emerge.

I continue with my newfound information. "Were you aware Sabera herself had worked briefly for the army's military intelligence unit in decoding?"

Aliah no longer appears dazed, but shaken. I imagine it's becoming clearer and clearer to her how little she knew the younger refugee.

"I did not." Aliah takes a deep breath in, releases it slowly. "But then, Sabera didn't speak much of her former life. That's not so uncommon. We may discuss missing a favorite food, or season, or smell in the air. The little details that skip across our memories. But our actual day-to-day lives... What was but is no more. Who we were but are no more. Most choose to leave it completely behind."

"Did she talk about other members of her family? Her father, siblings, cousins, anyone?"

"Her older brother, Farshid." A quick smile. "Sometimes, she would let stories slip. They would make her smile. And then, they would make her very sad. He died the day Kabul fell. Their father, too. That's all I know."

"I didn't think there was much fighting. Didn't the city just sort of . . . fold?"

"There was not an all-out battle if that's what you mean. The real war turned out to be suitcases of cash and secret handshakes behind closed doors. Many of the national police and security forces hadn't been paid in months, or even a year. Deals were made with frontline soldiers who had families to feed. Leaders were bought off who wanted to further fatten their wallets. After that, the Taliban simply had to appear, and mostly, it was over. But not everyone gave up their future so quietly. And some knew they would be targeted by the Taliban either way. Especially once it became clear evacuation was impossible, they made the decision to go down fighting. I lost some family, too."

"You still have . . . had . . . family in Kabul?"

"Of course. Only my mother and us two girls emigrated twenty-five years ago. Otherwise most of my family remains in Afghanistan. In the months leading up to Kabul falling, I could feel their tension when we'd video over WhatsApp. Then, after the city collapsed, for an entire week, nothing at all. It was one of the worst weeks of my life. Finally, an aunt reached out. The moment I heard her voice, I knew. My cousin's son, a known activist. The Taliban shot him dead in the street, then left his body as a warning for others. And now, all of my family lives under such a regime. I would bring each and every one of them here, if only it were possible."

Aliah gazes at me solemnly. "I can't help them, so I do what I can to help my fellow countrymen here. And I hope that back in

Kabul, someone will show equal kindness to my loved ones. Conditions there are bad, and only going to get worse."

She shrugs fatalistically. I wish I had hopeful words to offer, but we are both too experienced for platitudes.

"You said your cousin's son was killed because he was a known activist. Was that why Sabera's family died? Or maybe someone figured out her mother had been a spy?"

"Maryam had been dead for years by then. Sabera's father, however, was known for his progressive views on women's right to education. And being an academic of some note, he would've made for an easy target. Sabera's uncles, on the other hand, didn't sound like nice men at all. According to Sabera, they were corrupt, greedy bullies. Given their various business activities... Well, let's just say they were not well liked by their neighbors."

"Their business activities? Meaning...?"

"Their enterprises weren't just illegal but controversial. The practices had been outlawed by the government as the Taliban themselves were turning to such things for profit. But also, such businesses were extremely dangerous and exploitive of the locals. There's another term, not one we use in Afghanistan, but in other countries—blood diamonds."

I feel a cold fissure race along my spine. "Sabera's uncles were involved in illegal *mining*?"

She gives me a curious look. "Exactly."

"Aliah, start at the beginning, and tell me everything."

CHAPTER 25

I F ALIAH IS SURPRISED BY my sudden interest in illegal mining, she does her best to get over it as she collects her thoughts on the subject.

"Afghanistan has long been rich in gems and minerals—"

"Got that."

"Going back over two thousand years," she insists.

"So I've heard."

"But it lacks the necessary infrastructure for large-scale mining."

"I know that, too."

She skewers me with a look. I get her point, fall silent.

"Instead, the mining involves small sites, generally excavated by hand," she continues. "The local men will form cooperatives to lease the land from the owners, who can be anything from corrupt bureaucrats to wealthy landowners to corrupt, wealthy landowning bureaucrats."

"Sabera's uncles?" I guess.

"I believe so. Previously, the Taliban had utilized mines to fund their operations against the republic, so the government made it illegal. But of course, that didn't mean it stopped. In many remote villages, it's one of the only ways to earn a living. And precious gems can always be sold over the border in Pakistan, where there's a ready market.

"It has generated much talk in the Afghan community. Both from those who were frustrated by the former government outlawing mining—because how else were they going to feed their families?—to those who were angry and resentful of the wealthy few who actively engaged in continuing the illegal mines, mostly so they could profit at the locals' expense."

"Do the miners get paid?"

"A percentage of what they find. On a good day, that might mean the equivalent of one week's pay for a few hours' work. Like any kind of hunting, however, it can also mean weeks of absolutely nothing. But all of the time, it's extremely dangerous."

"High risk, high reward."

"There's no training, no safety equipment. The men learn as they go. They blast with homemade dynamite they make by mixing old gunpowder in plastic sleeves. They use ancient pneumatic jackhammers fueled by even more ancient petrol-run generators to work the seams, followed by pickaxes and hammers. Others will sort through the piles of rubble by hand, looking for the day's find—the most valuable being tourmaline with blue and green or green and pink coloring. You probably don't even know what tourmaline is."

"Never heard of it."

"Yet in my country, men die for it." Aliah shrugs, as if to say that is the way of the world. Maybe it is. "The work is very hot and difficult, but the men can't afford to spend money on safety equipment. They work dawn to dusk, blasting, jackhammering, squatting, sorting, no helmets, safety glasses, respirator masks. And they must work fast if they're going to find enough to make the day's haul, meaning they rarely shore up the walls.

"Many families in these towns have men missing limbs from blast injuries or suffering head injuries due to a tunnel collapse, or perpetually sick with a wracking cough. Then again, the work affords the opportunity for a man to support his family, which can be anywhere from twelve to twenty people. Even under the 'new' government, there were very few jobs that could do that. Now, I understand the Taliban has brought mining back. Made it legal and even encouraged some of the former national soldiers to operate artisanal mines in their backyards. The Taliban charge them a hefty tax, of course. But it has enabled some of the men who were in the Afghan National Security Forces to survive. At least for now."

"It is a hard life in your country," I state softly.

"Yes."

"But you, your fellow refugees, miss it."

"Home is always home, like family is always family. It doesn't have to be perfect for it to feel like the place we belong."

"Do you know what happened to Sabera's uncles?"

"I believe they were killed along with her father and brother when Kabul fell. Maybe by the Taliban, maybe by others settling an old score. These things happen."

I would like to say not in the US, but I've spent too much time in inner cities ravaged by gang violence to make such an argument.

"Do you know if her uncles worked with anyone from South Africa?"

Aliah appears genuinely bewildered by such a question.

"Any other information on Sabera's family?" I press.

"She didn't speak of home that often. She had not been in this country long, remember, and trying to figure out the here and now is hard enough, without pining for something you will never have again."

I nod. I want to definitively connect some dots—the attempted abductor of Zahra is unquestionably South African and absolutely connected to Sabera's family's illegal Afghan mines. Or even the attempted abductor is certainly a South African mercenary tied to Sabera's activities with the army's intelligence unit. But there's not enough information for either theory yet. Also, I'm not sure how knowing the answer to either supposition helps.

The why isn't nearly as important as the who and the where. And given Isaad has now disappeared as well as his wife, I feel we're losing ground on that front.

There's movement behind me. Based on Daryl's beaming smile, I know who's joined us even before I feel the slight tug on my ponytail.

I twist around in my seat to discover Zahra peering at me with her big gray eyes. Apparently, she's had a good day in the kitchen, because she's covered in sugar and flour and is wearing a small smile.

"Hiya," I say.

"Hiya," she repeats back.

That officially exhausts my small child vocabulary. Daryl has no such problem. He picks up his empty bowl and dramatically shows it off. "Best firni I ever had," he declares, then picks up what once was my dish. "Both bowls of it."

Zahra giggles. I scowl. I would've happily finished my pudding if someone hadn't stolen it.

Daryl remains unrepentant. "Did you make it all by yourself?" he asks Zahra.

She gives a quick shake of her head.

"Next time?"

A shy nod.

The girl wanders around the table to Aliah, then climbs aboard her lap. Aliah wraps her arms around her, resting her cheek atop the child's dark hair.

I feel a tug inside my chest. The way the four-year-old tucks in so trustingly. The way Aliah curls around her so protectively. The feeling of serenity emanating from them both.

I don't remember my mother ever holding me like that. But then, I don't have many memories of my mother. She was always out of the house working in order to compensate for my father's drinking. As a child, I resented her and idolized him, because that's what children do. Now, as an adult, I feel my own loss less and wonder about hers. Maybe she would've liked a moment with her daughter curled against her. Maybe she would've liked one minute to hold her child and feel at peace.

These are the things I wasn't smart enough to question when I was young, and now it's too late. My mother and father are buried side by side at a cemetery I never visit. And not so much due to their failings, but because I don't want to acknowledge my own.

Aliah's phone rings. She glances at the screen and immediately sits up, her gaze darting to me, then Daryl with intensity. I don't have to see the caller ID to know it's Isaad.

"Hello," she answers brightly, moving Zahra off her lap so she can rise to standing, put some distance between herself and the curious child. Zahra doesn't seem to notice, her attention on Daryl's empty pudding bowl, which she scrapes hopefully with her finger.

Daryl and I keep our focus on Aliah. She hasn't spoken another word, but her expression has gone from optimistic to puzzled. Abruptly, she pulls the phone from her ear, inspects the screen.

"Call dropped," she murmurs. Just in time for it to buzz again. She answers, starts to speak, stops. Her gaze is growing more and more concerned as the call apparently fails once more.

Now she's pacing the spice aisle, her movements jerkier. Zahra starts to take notice.

"More pudding?" Daryl booms out, startling all three of us. But this garners Zahra's attention as he hastily takes her hand and ushers her toward the rear kitchen.

Aliah's phone buzzes for the third time. "Isaad?" she whispers. Then louder, "Where? What? Isaad. Isaad, can you hear me?"

She holds the phone out between us. I can hear heavy breathing. A gurgling gasp. A long, shuddering sigh. Then...

"Isaad!" she demands.

This time the call remains connected. Only for the silence to go on and on.

"Isaad?" Aliah repeats.

But there's no answer.

I pluck the phone gently from Aliah's shaking fingers. Then I produce my own mobile to dial a whole new number.

"Detective," I say when he finally picks up. "I believe we have a situation..."

CHAPTER 26

D R. RICHARD DOES HIS BEST to save the boy's life, deter-
minedly packing gauze into the boy's gaping abdominal
wound, while another woman, a fellow refugee, inserts an IV.

Not knowing what else to do, I hold the unconscious boy's
hand, and then, thirty minutes later, when he starts to thrash, I
bathe his face and murmur the kind of nonsense I remember my
mother once murmuring to me. The other female glances at me
in approval. Her plain blue hijab and pale tunic are streaked in
blood. She doesn't seem to notice.

The boy is still gasping in agony when an ambulance finally
forces its way through the crowd to the med clinic. His eyes pop
open just as he's being loaded into the back, his dark gaze locking
feverishly onto me.

"Mama," he cries. "Stay with me! Please! Mama!"

I stand there frozen, his hand clutching mine. I have to let him
go. I can't let him go. He shouldn't be alone. This place is a sea of
orphans.

What have they done, the stupid politicians and military generals throwing away our lives as if they have no value?

What have I done?

Eventually, Dr. Richard untangles the boy's fingers from my wrist. A slam of the rear doors, and the ambulance lurches forward, weaving its way around the mass of still-waiting patients, pressed against chain-link fencing.

I don't know how long I stand there. Seeing nothing. Hearing nothing. Eventually, I register Dr. Richard before me, hands on his hips, expression unreadable. Does it hurt him, too, this calling where whatever he does will never be enough?

I wait to be dismissed. Instead, he offers me a job. And I say yes.

Dr. Richard, who's volunteered at refugee camps around the world, leads up the night shift from four to eleven p.m., bouncing around the woefully understaffed and ill-supplied clinic in a blur of curly brown hair and disapproving grunts as he pieces together human flesh with little more than Band-Aids and good intentions.

Also on duty are two nurses and four interpreters. Which is to say everyone does everything all the time. By the end of the first week, I know how to check vitals, provide oxygen, and assist with wound bandaging as adeptly as any trained medical assistant. I also learn how to wipe up blood, mop up vomit, and sterilize every available surface in ten seconds or less.

As the polyglot most in demand, my primary responsibility is to greet arriving patients through the small opening in the barred

door. At any hour, there are dozens of sick, injured, and desper-
ate individuals, all frantically waving their official papers. As the
night grows later, and the camp is cast into darkness, the crowds
grow thicker, the cases more urgent, the causes more violent.

I start with simple triage, recording everyone's name and
basic information on a whiteboard:

Green means urgent care—stomach bugs, feverish children,
broken bones. Address, treat, dismiss. Yellow is severely unwell
with irregular vital signs requiring a thorough exam—time we
rarely have. Admit for further analysis when we have a moment.
Red signifies a full-blown emergency—stabbings, heart attacks,
ruptured appendixes. Everyone drops everything to assist, much
like the young boy whose status I still don't know. Another rule
I have to learn. We exist in this moment. What happened before,
what will happen after, are not our chapters of the story. We must
focus on this and this only.

There are two exam rooms, one for the less critical, one for
the most. Though by nine p.m., the line between more or less
urgent is a matter of debate.

I've never been around the infirm before. From feverish chil-
dren to screaming young men to pain-wracked elderly. From
spurting arterial bleeds to bloated stomachs to rash-covered skin.
After the first week when Isaad huffs and puffs and demands to
know why I'm still going back, I don't know what to say, other
than someone has to. There's so much need. A bottomless well of
desperate families and single parents and abandoned children, all
trying to survive. If we don't help each other, who will?

There are concessions for the volunteers. I'm granted my fam-
ily's ration of food and water at the end of my shift, a precious
gift, given that normally Isaad or I would have to stand in line all

day for the same provisions, only to often end up with nothing. Isaad can't argue with guaranteed meals when so much about our existence is precarious. Far from relaxing, however, he takes up new responsibilities for our two-family shanty.

Isaad, once considered the most brilliant mathematical mind in Kabul, now tends to bookkeeping for local merchants, in return for another bowl of rice or a treasured piece of fruit. Even more interesting, the camp children have taken to following him around, led by Omid, who basks in Isaad's shadow. Isaad shows a surprising tolerance for his growing brood, even teaching basic arithmetic in the afternoon, using a stick to scratch equations in the dirt. Soon the whole place becomes accustomed to a glowering older man with his trailing pack of ducklings striding about camp on what always appears to be very important business.

By eleven p.m. he's back at the clinic to escort me home through the roaming packs of feral dogs, predatory men, and beady-eyed rats. But first, he engages in a nightly staring contest with Dr. Richard, before pointedly gesturing me to his side.

Dr. Richard doesn't engage; I understand. The clinic closes. Our moment ends. We move on to the next chapter. This is what it means to survive.

I both marvel at our adaptability and fear the consequences. When you have journeyed so far out of your comfort zone, spent so long living what surely must be someone else's life, can you ever return to the person you once thought you were?

Maybe this kind of slow erosion is as powerful as any traumatic break. You lose your home, then your country. You lose your loved ones, then yourself. You lose your heart, then your soul.

I lie awake deep into the night, my hands splayed around the rounded bulge of my unborn baby. I feel him or her kick inside me. I wonder if I will make it long enough to meet my future offspring.

And I wonder how my own child will ever truly know me when I don't even know myself anymore.

The crisis erupts two months later. The first young child presents with vomiting and diarrhea, followed quickly by dozens more adults and children, families lining up outside the clinic's chain-link perimeter well before our four p.m. opening. By the third day, it feels like half the camp is out with a stomach bug, including Malalai and Rafiq in our cabin, as well as their young son and Isaad's biggest admirer, Omid.

We administer water as they once did for us, Isaad trading for bone broth, a couple shriveled apples.

Cholera, Dr. Richard announces, his face dark with foreboding. We start handing out zinc and electrolyte tablets to the people still strong enough to stumble their way to the clinic. We quickly run out, however, as the first bodies start piling up.

By the end of the week, the clinic is a madhouse of moaning, cramping, dehydrated patients. Parents staggering in with two to three kids in their arms. Older children dragging their younger, more vulnerable brethren, from babies to grandparents. We can offer exam rooms only to the worst cases. The rest we medicate, emphasize the need for hydration, and send on their way.

It is not enough, and the strain starts to show on everyone's faces, especially after dark, when we begin our nightly run of code reds.

One evening, a young man is dragged through the back door, completely comatose. His friends have no idea; they found him that way. I lean over to check his pulse. His eyes fly open, and he screams so shrilly, I jump back, clattering into a stand of preciously sterilized instruments.

His shriek grows in volume, his eyes bulging in their sockets, while his entire body goes rigid. I sense violence, pain, and fear. An animal, about to break.

Dr. Richard shoves past me, syringe in hand. He stabs the patient deep into his deltoid and hits the plunger. The youth pants and stares, his expression wild and lost. Then, like a puppet whose strings have been cut, he collapses, his muscles going slack, his wailing now a whimper. His friends remain wide-eyed. I have yet to draw a breath.

"PTSD," Dr. Richard announces curtly. "Panic attack. Give him fifteen minutes for the drugs to fully take hold; then he can sleep it off at his campsite. We need the room."

The doctor drags me into the next room before he's even stopped talking. I'm startled to see that my cabin mates Malalai and Rafiq are back, once more holding Omid in their arms. If he looked pale and sickly before, he is limp and sunken now.

"No." The word is out before I can stop it. They're already talking, rattling off new symptoms, ongoing worries, every parent's deepest fears. I quickly translate for Dr. Richard, though I can tell he's accurately sized up the situation.

Another blur of recording vitals, documenting latest developments. We are out of IV fluids and electrolytes. Instead, I offer our next best solution—a clean rag soaked in salt water. Malalai presses a corner of the cloth against her son's blue-tinged lips. I want to tell her it'll be all right; charming little Omid will be up in no time at all to chase after Isaad and lord over the other ducklings. But the lies are too thick to emerge from my throat. I squeeze her hand, nod at Rafiq. Then there's another bang at our rear doors, red patient, incoming, and I have to scramble.

The first moment I see the badly beaten young man, my lungs cease to function. It can't be. It is. It can't be.

Farshid. My brother, my dear, dear brother…

Then he opens his dark eyes, and I recoil as if slapped. Not my brother, but Habib, our hotheaded cousin, who is close to Farshid in terms of age and features, but his exact opposite in everything else, including lacking all honor, loyalty, and kindness.

How did he survive? I thought all my uncles and cousins had perished. And why should Habib have survived when my brother was such a stronger, better man? The sheer unfairness…

I try to slip from the room unseen. I can't afford for any of my father's family to know I'm here.

Too late.

Through the swollen mess that is his heavily battered face, my cousin's gaze latches on to me. A second later, his entire expression changes from acute pain to sheer loathing. His bruised lips are already muttering a string of obscenities. Then, as his gaze slides down to my rounded belly… his cursing stops. His sly, triumphant grin begins.

And I go blank with terror.

He fell climbing a tree, Habib mumbles to the nurse. Or maybe he was trying to fix one of the broken overhead lights, or maybe there was a small disagreement between a couple of friends. Like always, he plays it fast and loose with the truth, just as his father, Fahima's husband, always did. Not that anyone here cares.

Last time I'd seen Habib, he was sitting at my father's table, impeccably garbed as befitting a wealthy, entitled male from a noted family. Now, he definitely appears worse for the wear. Then again, so do I.

I stand back as far as possible while Dr. Richard sets one broken arm, two broken wrists. He binds my cousin's ribs, inspects his swollen eye for signs of more significant orbital damage. Dr. Richard asks one of the nurses to administer fluids and painkillers; then when he remembers we are out of everything, he orders me to summon the ambulance instead. I've already been told the quickest any emergency vehicle can get here is at least two hours.

Dr. Richard shrugs. There's no choice then but to leave such a critical patient in one of our only exam rooms. A fox in the henhouse, I think as I keep my face carefully averted.

I return to the entrance, addressing families, passing along instructions. The clinic is full; we can't accept any others. Here's some aspirin, try to get your hands on some salt. Sleep, hydrate, rest. It's the best that can be done.

I peek in on Malalai and Rafiq long enough to see them rocking Omid, the salt-water rag tucked pitifully between his blue-tinged lips.

Then Dr. Richard is back, his curly hair a disheveled mop as he surveys the chaos around him. He glances at his watch, studies the ever-growing crowd of desperately sick and needy. That's it, he announces. Red patient must go. He instructs me to clean him up; then we'll move him outside till the ambulance arrives. It's not like there's any additional care we can offer, and others still require attention.

Orders issued, he returns to the melee of crying children and moaning adults. He has his war. I have mine.

So I return to the exam room to discover my cousin has regained consciousness and is staring at me in open hostility.

I wipe the blood from his brow.

"It's your fault they're dead. Did you not think we'd figure it out? You fucking bitch."

I dab at the bruise above his cheekbone.

"Two halves of one whole," Habib snorts in derision. "You and your brother and your whore of a mo—"

I clap my hand over his mouth to prevent further words. Habib's head thrashes beneath my palm. His nose is broken. It's clearly hard for him to breathe.

He twists his head far enough to escape my palm. "Where is it? You must know it's only a matter of time. Tell me everything, and maybe I can convince them to let you live."

My saliva-smeared hand is still clutching his chin. "They're dead. The Taliban are in charge. It's over now."

"Is that what you think?" A look of feral cunning crosses Habib's face. "Countries fall. Governments change. But greed never ends. Where did you hide it?"

"In the end, you will be allowed nothing." I shrug. "Were you able to get out with anything more than the clothes on your back? I thought not."

"I don't believe you! You were always smarter than anyone gave you credit for." Habib's gaze focuses on my bulging stomach. He smirks. "Though maybe not smart enough. You'll never be safe here. If I found you, so will the others. And they'll be much less patient with their demands. You want to live? You want to save your bastard child—"

I clamp my hand over his mouth again. My cousin squirms to escape. And suddenly...I just know. Habib does, too. I can see on his face the exact instant he realizes it's no longer his place to threaten me. That now, in these wretched circumstances, he's the one broken and vulnerable, and I'm the one who's powerful.

He stares at me defiantly as he begins to thrash more forcefully. I keep my palm slapped tight over his lips, using my index finger and thumb to pinch shut his already mangled nose. He screams, but the sound is trapped in his throat.

He's right. If my uncles have discovered what I did and if even one of them or my cousins is still alive...

I use my growing bulk to my advantage, pressing down hard against my cousin's struggling form. My hand is slimy, his will to live strong. But no matter how hard he tries to raise his hands to push me off, his injuries are too grievous, his body too weakened.

Habib's legs kick. His neck bulges with his effort to escape. But I don't let up. I push, I pinch. Push. Pinch. Push. Pinch.

When I was a girl, I dreamed...

Now I squeeze the final breath from my own cousin, my father's brother's son. Habib's body has just gone slack, his legs fallen silent, when I hear a noise directly behind me. I quickly release his chin, then whirl around to find Dr. Richard watching me.

I wait for him to speak first. To say he witnessed it all, to ask me what kind of monster I've become. But his expression is grimmer than that. And then, I know.

Little Omid is dead.

———

Later, I stumble out of the clinic. It's an hour before my official end of shift. My cousin's body had disappeared by the time I returned to the exam room. Then the white-clad men had appeared for Omid's tiny form...And I just couldn't take it one second more. Dr. Richard said I could leave and so I did.

Now I walk. Not feeling my legs or arms. Not smelling the fetid odors of human sweat and raw sewage. Not noticing the slinking dogs or leering men. A dark-clad male halts in front of me.

I stare at him.

"My good sister, you should not be walking alone."

I stare and stare and stare. Does he not know every woman in the world is alone, has always been alone, will always be alone? Does he not know, we expect it to be no other way?

Something in my expression spooks him. Maybe he can sense the rawness of my emotions, or the darkness of my deeds. He eases back into the periphery. I continue on, my bite-ravaged hand, scored by my cousin's desperate teeth, tucked behind me.

I walk all the way to the little cabin where Isaad sits on our mat, his expression nearly childlike in its pained bewilderment. I sit down next to my husband. I pull his head onto my lap. I let his tears soak into my robes as he starts to sob, then wail, then rage at the heavens. Why, God, why? He was just a little boy! When will life have meaning again? Why, God, why?

I stroke Isaad's hair, let him rail. My own eyes are dry, my grief contained, which is not how an Afghan mourns. Another sign I'm no longer the daughter, sister, countrywoman I used to be? Another sign I've become something so other, so alien, I'm no longer recognizable even to myself?

I think there are moments that cost you nothing and yet

demand everything. I think there are choices that allow you to survive and yet eventually cause you to perish. I think I never want to feel this way again, and yet I will never feel any other way.

I am lost I am broken I am numb.

And then...

My water breaks.

Zahra, on that dark night you arrived into the world.

And I knew, from the first moment that I held you, that I would do the same all over again.

CHAPTER 27

FOR THE SECOND TIME IN one day, I'm standing at a crime scene. Detective Marc has forbidden us from entering it. Based on the whispered details I've heard from the various law enforcement officers milling about, I'm grateful this time to stay on the outside of the perimeter tape.

The police were able to track Isaad's cell phone to an abandoned building near the double homicide from a few days ago. The entire area is a run-down collection of decrepit warehouses and vacant businesses—peeling signs hang haphazardly over broken windowpanes offering everything from auto body work to industrial cleaning. I'm not sure if this is where dreams go to die, or just never take off, but I understand better why Daryl refused to drive me here the first time I asked. Having finally made it to the infamous death-by-hammer location, I'd mostly like to go home now. Even if home involves runaway snakes.

Detective Marc needs someone to identify the body. The most logical person—Aliah. Of course, she has Zahra to consider and, given the recent spate of violent events, we all agreed leaving the youngster alone with the the deli cook wasn't a great idea. Daryl might not have served as a bodyguard for Wonder Boy Bart, but he's in full protective mode now as he assists Aliah from the rear of the black sedan. He's been driving her and Zahra around, waiting for Detective Marc's official summons. This must be the moment. Daryl hands Aliah off to Roberta, then returns to the driver's seat to continue with Project Distract the Four-Year-Old. I catch a brief glimpse of Zahra's curious little face; she seems more intrigued by her surroundings than alarmed. Then she and Daryl are off again. From crime scene to playground? I have no idea.

Roberta waits with Aliah until Detective Marc appears in the doorway of the dilapidated building and waves the older woman in. A brief whispered exchange between the two women. Roberta warning her about what she's about to see? Aliah appears stoic, head up, mouth set. I have a feeling this isn't the first time she's viewed a dead body.

She offers me a single nod of acknowledgment, then disappears into a house of unknown horrors.

So far, I've caught murmurs of maiming and burning. Torture most definitely, with many different possible means of death. I'm doing my best not to focus on the gruesome details, but given how much cops love to gossip, I'm having a harder and harder time. My pulse is pounding, and my vision keeps graying in and out as I struggle to stay rooted in the here and now.

Roberta, waiting beside me, eyes me strangely as I alternate between deep breathing exercises and compulsively checking the call screen on my phone.

That last dark, terrible night. He held things together, through the bullets and the blood. Now, back in a similar situation, I feel myself reaching for him almost reflexively.

It's merely association, I tell myself. Besides, I can't very well call up the man I just left in Seattle to say, hey, I know I told you it was time for me to move on, but now that things have gotten a little dicey, want to travel a thousand miles for a booty call? Pretty please?

I've always found my freedom liberating. Now, for the first time, it feels lonely.

I honestly don't know what to do with that.

Aliah is back. Roberta and I hover just beyond the yellow crime scene tape, doing a little dance till she spies us. We could be friends meeting up after the movie gets out. Except we're not.

Aliah appears paler, but still in control. It's only when she gets closer that I see that her hands are shaking.

Roberta and I don't say anything. We wait for her to find her words at her own pace. She takes a deep breath, then another.

She blurts out unexpectedly. "They burned his work!"

"What?" Neither Roberta nor I follow this statement.

"His little red notebook. The only thing he was able to save during his escape from Kabul. He started with an entire box of workbooks. His life's work, he said. Except it's not practical for any refugee to save personal possessions while walking and waiting for days on end at border crossings. He was forced to make choices. First he discarded his collection of theorems, papers on supporting proofs. Then he had to sort through each workbook, carefully tearing out the mathematical models he valued the most, then tucking them into a single volume—his little red notebook.

"He would bring it out from time to time, show it off. He would hold it, the way most might hold a baby. This is the mathematician he used to be. This is the man he once was. I have watched him shed genuine tears over that volume.

"And they burned it to ashes. On the floor right in front him. His hands..."

Aliah's voice has gone hoarse. "His fingers were black. Seared down to the bone and curled into claws. From trying to save it, salvage a single page. After everything he'd been through, that last little bit of himself. I never...I never thought Isaad was a nice man. But he was a brilliant man. And they used that to hurt him. What kind of people do that?" Her eyes grow darker, wilder. *"What is going on here?"*

But neither Roberta nor I have an answer.

"I NEED YOU to tell me exactly what he said when he called you," Detective Marc is requesting an hour later. Dusk has fallen, though not the temperatures. We are huddled inside Aliah's cheery little apartment. Like a reflex, she has produced jewel-toned bowls of dried fruits and nuts, Turkish delight candy, and hot tea.

Zahra was given a little plate of delicacies, then set up in Aliah's bedroom with an iPad blaring a kid's show that would hopefully drown out the very adult conversation going on in the living room.

I can't eat. Even Daryl is subdued, looking like the proverbial bull in a china shop with his enormous bulk and somber black suit. Roberta, however, adorned in glossy curls and silver bangles, is a perfectly framed treasure as she sips from her delicate blue-patterned teacup. Daryl's gaze keeps returning to her, a moth drawn to the flame.

My impression is that she has no idea. Her brother, Detective Marc, however, appears more astute on the subject. He's the only one who seems relaxed, cracking pistachios and tossing them back. Apparently, he's not one to let a gruesome homicide get in the way of his appetite.

"There was no speaking," Aliah reports now. "The call kept disconnecting. There, not there. There, not there. Then, finally . . . I could hear sounds, like moaning. But not words. I don't know." She raises her hands hopelessly. "I don't know anything more than that."

Detective Marc nods slowly. He doesn't seem surprised by her statement. He cracks another pistachio.

"Had you heard from Isaad before this?"

"No. I'd left many messages, but not received a call back."

"And in those messages, did you say you had Zahra? She was with you?"

"Of course. I told him she was safe but missed her father. He should come pick her up."

That nod again. With a sense of foreboding, I start to understand where this is going. Given Roberta's sudden sharp inhalation, she does, too.

Aliah's gaze bounces to both of us. "What? What is it?"

"His fingers," Roberta murmurs.

Her brother nods. "His fingers."

Aliah still appears confused, then . . . "His phone. How would he have worked the screen?" Her eyes widened. "Oh no!"

"I don't think Isaad was the one who called you," Detective Marc confirms. "And not just because of how badly damaged his hands were, but did you happen to notice his face? It was barely touched. We see that more and more. Perpetrators will inflict damage to other parts of the body, but leave the head alone—in case they need facial recognition to unlock the subject's phone."

Aliah's eyes close. "Oh no."

"What do you think they want?" Detective Marc asks her now.

"I have no idea. All of this..." She shakes her head. "I don't know."

His gaze flickers to me.

I can only shrug. "Honestly, still totally and completely confused. Though I did learn Sabera's mother was an MI6 spy back in the day, and she met with some former military officers to try to contact her mother's original handler."

"Huh?"

"Exactly. Sabera claims to have useful information to share, but given the Taliban takeover, what would be relevant, let alone valuable, now?"

Aliah seems equally bewildered on the subject, which I feel proves my point.

"I asked the officers from No One Left Behind to put me in touch with the MI6 handler if possible," I offer. "Sounds like a 'she'll find me when/if she wants to find me' sort of thing. I'll keep you posted." I mean this seriously. Jurisdictional issues, turf wars, are a detective's problem. I genuinely just want Sabera located safe and sound. Now more than ever.

"They accessed Isaad's phone," Daryl states.

"Mostly likely."

"Meaning they heard Aliah's voice mails and have her contact information. They could be headed here, even now."

"Why would they do that?" Detective Marc focuses his attention on Aliah.

She shakes her head again, clearly spooked.

"To get Zahra," Daryl states bluntly. "Isaad didn't give them what they wanted. They'll use Zahra next."

"But what do they *want*?" Detective Marc presses.

"A lock that has no key for a key that has no lock," I murmur. "When you discovered Isaad's body, was there anything on it? A note, coded message, hell, old-fashioned brass key? A private courier delivered something to him right before he took off. I've been trying to figure out what would be significant enough for him to leave his daughter behind and disappear."

"We found one item in his pocket," Detective Marc allows. He doesn't immediately elaborate. Roberta addresses the issue by reaching out and punching her brother's arm.

He gives her a look, downs two more pistachios, then picks up a piece of Turkish delight.

"A gathered band of long black hair," he finally gives up. "Like maybe a ponytail that someone had whacked off. I'm guessing it belonged to Sabera? Some kind of proof of life."

Roberta stares at her brother as if he's an idiot. "You mean a *lock* of hair?"

Detective Marc freezes with the candy halfway to his mouth. His eyes widen slightly.

I do the honors: "A lock that has no key... What do you wanna bet that token came with a note that Isaad read out loud, and a certain four-year-old overheard?"

"A lock that has no key," Detective Marc sighs heavily. "All right. I can buy that. Which, assuming it's Sabera's hair, makes her the key that has no lock?" He eyes us all expectantly.

"Of course." Roberta is on a roll now. "A key with no lock could definitely mean a cipher to crack a code, which given Sabera's skill set and feverish writings would make sense. Clearly, she has something others want, making her the key. Meaning whoever is doing the hunting needs Sabera to get their heart's desire. And based on what we've seen thus far, they're really, really intent on getting their heart's desire."

"If they had a lock of her hair, they had her," her brother interrupts.

"Maybe they did," I grant, then give Roberta and Daryl a look. "But as we debated while reviewing the bloody towels at Sabera's resort hideout—maybe one hammer later, they didn't."

Aliah appears horrified, Roberta impressed.

"They tried to squeeze her for this mystery information," Detective Marc fills in skeptically. "But somehow a twenty-three-year-old, slightly built female got the upper hand, killed both her captors, then made her escape?"

Roberta punches him again. "Give me a hammer right now and I'll show you how it can be done."

Wisely, her brother doesn't take her up on that offer.

"Tracks with everything we saw at the resort," Daryl agrees with me. "The bloody scarf—we wondered if she was the victim or the perpetrator. Maybe she was both. Kidnapped and assaulted, but able to escape. She couldn't very well return home, though—not with people looking for her."

"But she could reach out to her husband. Have you had a chance to subpoena Sabera's phone records yet?" I ask Detective Marc. "To see who she's called since she's gone missing?"

"You mean in the eight hours since we last spoke? Uh, no. Courts, not to mention due process, take a more leisurely approach to these things. However"—he skewers me with a look—"we could access Isaad Ahmadi's phone. As you imagine, there are dozens of calls from him to her, mostly short, just enough time to leave a message."

"Him trying to contact Sabera," Daryl grunts. "Get her to come home."

"Maybe." Detective Marc eyes us thoughtfully. "I've only had a moment to glance at the call logs—" His voice breaks off abruptly. "Shit, you might be right about something." He pulls out his cell phone, quickly scrolls through a few screens, nods slightly.

"All right." The detective's found what he was looking for. "It's not the number as much as the pattern. Sabera has been missing approximately three weeks, yes? Looking at that timeline, first couple of days, there's a flurry of calls from Isaad's phone to hers. Say, a husband desperately trying to reach his wife. But then the activity suddenly drops to two calls a day, almost like clockwork. You could argue, a routine check-in."

"He found Sabera." Roberta does the honors. "Knew she was safe enough."

"Until three days ago, when suddenly, the call activity spikes again, reaching a near frantic level during the thirty-six hours before Isaad receives the mystery package and takes off." Detective Marc glances. "One interpretation could be that within that timeframe, things went south—he could no longer reach Sabera. Hence his renewed intensity. Then the box arrives with her hair plus the mystery note, and off he goes to meet with whomever sent the message."

"She was discovered," Aliah breathes. "Sabera had hidden away to stay safe. But they found her, these men who want what she has. They took her. But then..." Aliah frowns. "She must not have given them what they needed? So they lured out Isaad instead? Because he might know something?"

"Or," Detective Marc considers out loud, "to up the stakes. If you can't make someone talk by hurting them, next best option is to hurt someone they love."

Aliah shivers, the rest of the room falling silent.

I'm frowning. I can both see and not see all of this. "It feels to me we're getting somewhere," I allow slowly. "First off, we can be pretty sure Sabera holds the secret to gaining something extremely valuable. Other people clearly know and somehow followed her to Tucson." I eye Aliah. "A city they didn't even know would be their future home?"

She shrugs.

I decide to let that go for now. "Let's just fast-forward to she was discovered. But she must've seen something first—or someone—that spooked her enough to go into hiding. Unfortunately, she was found out. The two men, who we know are from Afghanistan..."

Nods around the room.

"Tried to get the secret out of her. Failing that, they lured out Isaad. And then...somehow those two guys end up dead. Sabera not only walks away, but also makes it all the way back to the resort. While Isaad doesn't? He gets left behind to now be tortured by...other Afghan men, South African men, evil men? This...this is where it starts to fall apart for me again."

Detective Marc nods. "Yeah, that scenario gets messy fast. Unless there's a third party we have yet to identify. Which at this stage of the game, why not? It's gonna take some time to thoroughly analyze Isaad's call logs. He was a busy guy. Tons of calls, dozens of recurring numbers to reverse search, including ones in DC and Texas. Hadn't this family just gotten here? Because Isaad seems well networked for a newbie."

"They had only recently arrived in Tucson," Aliah corrects. "They have been in the US for nearly a year, the past eight months at a base in Texas. Which may explain many of the Texas numbers."

"There's another key time period to analyze as well." I gesture to Aliah. "Sabera disappeared once before, for three days, right?

I'd be curious who Isaad was calling then, and are there any cor-relations between those numbers and the ones he's been dialing for the past few weeks."

"Sabera vanished once before?" Detective Marc gives us a look.

"It was nothing." Aliah waves a hand. "She returned; all was well." Then as the detective continues to glower, she adds, "I will get you the dates."

"All right." I try to pull this together in my head. "Sabera is the key. Certain people with violent tendencies are clearly willing to do most anything to get their hands on her."

This earns me a round of nods. I warm to my subject.

"But just to be interesting, Sabera is also searching. Reach-ing out to retired military veterans with contacts in Afghanistan. Her two afternoons a week when she takes off on some unknown errand. Her absence after seeing you that afternoon, Aliah, when she came to your store all upset. If she's the one who's supposedly in the know, what's she looking for?"

Aliah appears genuinely bewildered.

"Could…could she have lost it?" Daryl starts. "Like had something but lost it after arriving in Tucson?"

"Like her mind," Roberta asks dryly, "because I feel like I'm about to lose mine."

"That's not a bad theory," I counter. "Sabera's agitated behav-ior, alleged drinking. There's something going on with her. Let alone the repeated emphasis on a past filled with trauma, trauma, trauma."

I shrug, not certain how to explain all the jumbled thoughts in my head. "There's still some kind of X factor we're missing. A third party who remains invisible. A connection to the past that's still hidden. Something real spooked Sabera three weeks ago. And now she's both looking and hiding. She's predator and prey. And both... both roles appear to be equally deadly."

I'm on to something. I can feel it. But the what remains just out of my grasp. Predator and prey, though. I'm stuck on that notion, and the full implications of it make me shiver.

"Now that Isaad is dead," Aliah asks hesitantly, "do you think Sabera will return? To keep her daughter safe?"

"I don't think her reappearing helps Zahra," I say honestly. "It'll probably make them both a target."

"Then we'll have to do it." Daryl rises to standing, expression set.

"Do what?"

"We'll guard Zahra."

"I can't order protective custody without more evidence of a direct threat," Detective Marc begins.

Aliah adds nervously, "I do not know that she will be safe here."

"We got this. You'll come with us, you and Zahra both. You'll be secure at the estate."

"Are we allowed to do that?" I ask in awe, because that would be perfect. Gated drive. State-of-the-art security system. Pet snakes. I certainly wouldn't attack anyone there.

"It's decided," Daryl states.

Detective Marc appears too surprised, Aliah too overwhelmed, to argue.

Just in time for Zahra to appear, iPad clutched in her tiny hands. She takes in the adults in the room, then wordlessly hands over the device to Aliah. Apparently, her show is over.

"Hey, Zahra, want to go on an adventure?" Daryl asks her.

"It includes an iguana. Her name is Petunia, and her skin is surprisingly warm," I tack on.

"I'm coming, too," Aliah adds soothingly.

The girl studies us. I wait for her to ask about her mother or her father. But in the end, she nods once, then returns down the hall.

It makes me wonder how much she might have overheard. And fear for what this little girl might have to survive next.

CHAPTER 28

B<small>Y THE TIME</small> A<small>LIAH FINISHES</small> packing up supplies and we make the drive back to the hills, it's past nine. Not having much experience with domestic life, I don't know how well Genni—let alone Petunia—will take us missing dinner. But Daryl must've phoned ahead, because Genni is waiting at the front door, all beaming smiles and red gingham cuteness as she greets our new guests. Tonight's fashion homage appears to be Mary Ann from *Gilligan's Island*, including a dark-haired wig with red-ribboned pigtails.

Aliah blinks several times, then manages to recover. Zahra simply stares up at Genni in awe.

Genni scoops up Zahra's pink backpack, slips it over her shoulder. "Hungry, hun? Of course you are. This hour is much too late for dinner, so I made you breakfast instead. What do you think, waffles with whipped cream and strawberries? Mmm-hmm, follow me, love. I got you covered."

Genni holds out a red-manicured hand. Zahra takes it and they're off, Genni's heels rat-a-tat-tatting across the tiled floor.

"Did that just happen?" Aliah murmurs at last.

"Yes," I assure her.

"He is a her? I know of these things, but have never..."

"She goes by the name Genni. And let me tell you, those waffles are going to be amazing."

While Daryl handles her suitcase, Aliah follows me to the kitchen, where Genni is mounding an impressive pile of homemade whipped cream atop a single waffle for Zahra's dining pleasure. The little girl looks both giddy and exhausted. She'll crash hard after all this. I know I will.

I'm halfway to the fridge to fetch Petunia's salad when Genni informs me she already took pity on the lizard. The "because someone had to" is implied.

I'm pretty sure I'm a complete fail as a reptile sitter, but am prepared to live with the shame.

Aliah and I dish up bowls of fresh-sliced strawberries, leaving our share of waffles to be devoured by Daryl. Genni fusses happily over the extra guests. She produces a toiletry bag and is soon brushing out Zahra's long, dark hair while the girl picks through a rainbow of colored ribbons.

The only life-form put out from the evening's unexpected turn appears to be Petunia, who has abandoned her usual spot in front of the glass slider in favor of a high perch on top of the curtain rod. Given the iguana did get fed, I'm not sure what she has to be so hostile about, but she keeps glancing down at us, flicking her tail and sticking out her eerily human-looking tongue.

"Don't be a brat," I finally inform her.

Zahra starts yawning minutes later. Daryl takes the hint to

scoop the last bite from his plate, then escorts Aliah and Zahra to their room. Genni is already bustling about, clearing dishes.

Petunia deigns to climb down the draperies. I toss her a strawberry as a peace offering. She gulps it off the floor, scuttles closer. I feed her a couple more, till her posture relaxes and we seem to be buddies again.

"Daryl said the little girl's father was found dead," Genni speaks up from the sink.

"Yeah. Tortured and killed. Not a good scene." All at once, I feel exhausted. I drop to the floor beside Petunia, stroke a line down her side. She's not exactly a purring kitten, but as pet therapy goes, she's not half bad.

"And the mother?"

"Still no word."

"But you think she's in danger, the girl as well."

"Let's just say wherever Sabera goes, violence seems to follow." I glance up at Genni. "Are you worried? Should we take them someplace else?"

Genni practically huffs at me. "Girl, I grew up dressing like this while living on the streets. You think I don't know how to defend myself? I might be a tall, gorgeous Amazon now, but I earned my scars along the way. I don't just sew my own clothes, I make sure they have plenty of pockets for rusty blades. You?"

"I killed a man." The words are out before I can stop them. I don't know why I'm talking about it, but it's too late to take the statement back now.

Genni comes around the massive kitchen island. She peers at me thoughtfully, then in a surprisingly graceful motion for a woman in two-inch Mary Janes, lowers herself to the tiled floor.

"Tell me about it."

"I didn't do it myself, per se. But I knew what would happen next, and I did it anyway. Led him into the clearing. I don't think he saw the bullet coming, but I did."

My hands are trembling again. Which makes me imagine Isaad Ahmadi's fingers, burnt black claws from scrabbling through the flames to save his precious notes.

He must've known he wasn't walking out of that warehouse alive. They lured him there with the lock of his wife's hair. Offered it up as some kind of exchange. Did he think he was saving Sabera? Did he love her that much?

A woman who'd once been his assistant, before becoming his bride—if indeed they were really married.

Aliah found him dominating, the proverbial controlling older husband. Sabera's neighbor, Nageenah, and the caseworker, Staci, thought the Ahmadis' relationship was more complicated. Then again, aren't all relationships?

I press the heels of my hands into my eye sockets, scrub at my own eyelids. When I lower my arms, Genni is regarding me with open sympathy.

"Honey, we all got our scars." She gestures down at her country chic ensemble. "And we all got our own kind of armor."

I get it. "Who worked here first, you or Daryl?"

"My charming self, of course."

"And you got this job...?"

"Bart Boy likes the bar scene, drag and otherwise. We bonded one night over our shared love of chicken-fried steak. Told him I made the best he'd ever have. And I was right. He offered me a permanent position before he even finished the dish. 'Course, I still have Thursday, Friday, and Saturday nights to strut my stuff. No girl wants to be too domesticated." She gives me a look. "Judging by how many times you check your phone, guessing you're struggling with some man trying to clip your wings?"

"They don't clip. That's the problem. Doesn't matter the person, place, or thing. Sooner or later I just have to go."

"It's not something you choose; it's someone you are." Genni nods. "People come in all types, honey. You just gotta be you."

"Sometimes being me sucks."

"Welcome to the club, my friend. Welcome to the club."

I regard her for a moment. "Have you met Roberta?" I ask her curiously.

"You mean Daryl's dance partner and unrequited love?" She arches a brow.

"You think Roberta knows?"

"Girl, I've watched them dance together. How any woman can be held like that and not know...Mmm-hmm."

"And her husband?"

"Nice enough. A little too vanilla for my tastes, but you know what they say about opposites attracting."

"She's the fire, he's the rock?"

"Or that's the lie they tell themselves to keep on keeping on."

"Do you think Daryl has a violent streak? I mean he's kinda got this whole reformed ex-con, gentle giant thing going on. But then again..."

"Still waters..." Genni agrees.

"I thought...I thought I saw blood on his shirt last night."

"Did you ask him about it?"

"No."

"Why not?"

"I don't know." It's a good question. "I mean, he definitely didn't cut himself shaving. Whatever else happened, maybe I didn't want to know."

"And now?"

"I think he would kill for her. Watching them together this afternoon. Daryl would kill for Roberta, no questions asked."

"Sounds damn sexy when you put it that way." Genni shivers delicately.

I trace a final line down Petunia's soft, leathery skin. "Lately, it feels to me like there's way too many people willing to kill for each other. Maybe we need some people desperate to live for each other instead. Because I'm honestly not sure how much more of this I can take."

CHAPTER 29

WAKE UP THE NEXT MORNING feeling completely disoriented.
The sun is streaming in through a crack in the curtains, and I
can hear a noise that is both mystifying and familiar. Children's
laughter. Coming from outside, along with the sound of splashing
water.

I lie beneath the lazy twirl of the ceiling fan and take a moment
to listen. More splashing. A girl's high-pitched squeal. The lower
murmur of accompanying adults. Zahra and company. Daryl, I'm
guessing, probably Aliah and maybe Roberta as well. All taking
advantage of Wonder Boy's toy-stocked swimming pool.

If I continue to stay right here, I can close my eyes and pretend
I'm really a guest at a luxurious resort. Maybe on vacation from
my high-stress job. And accompanied, naturally, by my sexy boy-
friend who's gone to fetch coffee. Soon he'll be back to rejoin me
in bed, where we'll wake up properly with the help of caffeinated
beverages and toe-curling sex. Afterward, I will lie with my head
on his chest while he strokes my hair.

He'll tell me he loves me and has never been so happy.

And I'll say...Please don't ever leave. Please come back even after I push you away. Please know me and understand me and forgive me, because I still don't know how to do any of those things for myself.

I don't realize I'm crying till I feel the first drop of moisture trail down my cheek. I swipe at it immediately, mortified to find myself so easily undone by pure fantasy. What is wrong with me these days?

Then I picture Vaughn and the look on his face as he drove me to the bus stop, unloaded my single bag, and handed it over to me. Understanding. Empathy. Acceptance.

I'm not sure which hurts more.

I roll onto my side and sob in earnest, ugly, messy tears I do my best to get out once and for all.

Then I sit up, wipe off my face, and prepare for the day ahead.

BREAKFAST THIS MORNING involves golden biscuits smothered in sausage gravy. Poolside play completed, Daryl is on his second helping, looking uncharacteristically casual in red swim trunks and a frayed V-neck T-shirt that shows off heavily muscled arms and an incredibly furry chest. Kind of like a bear dressed for a day at the beach.

Aliah is in her usual jeans and flowing top—apparently Daryl was in charge of pool duty. Zahra sits between them, smothering a split biscuit in strawberry jam—not her first, judging by the smears of sticky red adorning her smiling face.

I head straight for coffee, down the first few sips while standing.

Genni is frying up some eggs. She gives me a questioning look, but I shake my head, not ready for food just yet. Petunia, I noticed, is back to sunbathing in front of the glass sliders. She's keeping a wary look on the small human, but with Zahra safely occupied at the table, all is well for the moment.

"How did you sleep?" I ask Aliah at last, pulling out a chair.

"Like a baby. This place is amazing."

"And you, Zahra? Looks like you discovered the pool." I flash the girl a smile. Her still-wet purple swim shirt and trunks are creating a puddle on the kitchen floor. Far from being put out, Genni appears completely enthralled with her new pint-sized charge. If you like to cook and clean, I suppose a four-year-old would be a source of happiness.

Now Zahra nods in earnest, then shoves half a biscuit in her mouth, adding to the butter dotting her chin. This is the most childlike I've ever seen her. Like an honest to goodness preschooler. I wonder how many of these moments she's had, and given what's happened with her parents, how many more she'll have next.

Aliah has a fierce expression on her face as she watches the girl lick crumbs from her fingers. Whatever happens, I have no doubt she'll fight for Zahra's best interests. Which is good, because I don't have great feelings about how this case will end. The body count is getting very high, the threat of horrific violence too real.

Whatever's going on here, the people involved are playing for keeps.

I take another sip of steaming black coffee. Clear my throat. Then get to it.

"At this point," I begin, "we have more questions than answers."

I glance around the table. Receive several nods, a look of genuine small-child curiosity.

"There's only one person who can tell us what's truly going on."

More nods.

"I say we stop searching. Instead, we use what we know to get that person to come to us."

I don't directly address Sabera by name, given Zahra's presence, but the adults know who I'm talking about.

"Let's build a code, working off what we saw in the townhouse, and post it in the window of your deli, Aliah. A time and place to meet. See what happens next."

More interested expressions.

Zahra, who appears to be following the conversation perfectly despite my best attempts, provides a single, emphatic nod.

I'D TAKEN PHOTOS of Sabera's frantic scribbles covering the walls of her hideout in order to analyze them later for evidence of other riddles, clues, perhaps a nice simple statement: find me here. No such luck.

Now, I print out a few for samples, while Genni produces half an art studio from seemingly thin air. There are glitter pens, collections of neon-bright markers with crazy fruit scents, and sheet after sheet of stickers, not to mention construction paper in about every shade imaginable.

"What?" she asks as Daryl and I stare in amazement. "I got friends with kids. And let me tell you, I'm *definitely* the cool aunt."

I sort through the mad colored mess, feeling a little guilty when I settle upon a plain white poster board and a single black Sharpie.

Good news, Zahra quickly claims the rest. She and Genni start competing for who can draw the prettiest flower while Daryl, Aliah, and I scratch out various attempts at encoding a simple message.

We decide to follow Sabera's approach of embedding lower-case letters that combine to spell out key words. It's what she used to communicate about Zahra—"i am her sword"—so it seems fitting to repeat. Except we're trying to determine a meet place and time, which leaves us with how to share the right numbers in a jumble of digits, and oh, yeah, where to meet?

Sabera's apartment is too dangerous. Aliah's home and business feel similarly vulnerable. We could do the compound, but what if someone else sees the message and discovers Zahra hiding here? At the moment, this feels like our one safe place, and we're loathe to give it up.

"Dance studio," Daryl offers up abruptly. "Where Roberta and I meet for ballroom. It's part of a busy strip mall. Public. Plenty of people, plus the parking lot is well lit and heavily surveilled."

"In other words, lots of witnesses to deter any overt acts of violence."

"In theory."

Aliah looks up the address and determines it's part of a major bus line. She nods her agreement.

Setting a meet time for today seems too early—we're not sure when, how, if Sabera will see our poster. Tomorrow's a safer bet, except for the same issues—when, how, if Sabera gets our message.

"Daily," Daryl determines. "One of us will show up every evening at seven P.M. until she appears. Covers the most bases."

Aliah and I agree. We get busy with a fine collection of gibberish that includes the right mix of lowercase letters. I can't help myself; I include the phrase *CHIN UP* several times. It's what Sabera wrote the most, almost obsessively. I don't know what it means, but clearly it's significant to her. I want her to know that we heard. Whatever story she has to tell, we're ready to listen.

In the end, Aliah copies our notes onto the poster board in a beautiful, flowing script, with touches of embellishment.

"To make it more artistic," she provides. "It will be, after all, hanging in a business window."

Makes sense to me.

Our attempts have taken a solid hour, but stepping back and studying, the finished result seems worth it.

Zahra leaves her collection of glittery scribbles to check our work.

She climbs onto the chair in front of the poster, examines it for a full minute. I can practically see her eyes scanning across each line, copying each letter and word, filing them away in the great vault of her mind. Her face wears a nearly blank expression. The world's most adorable database, computing away.

In the end, she picks up the black Sharpie and before any of us think to stop her, she leans over the poster and adds a line. Then another and another. She builds a box in the lower corner of the poster, her movements slow and studied, the tip of her tongue pursed between her lips in concentration.

The box gets split into many little boxes, until she has created a five-by-five matrix. Then, she places a number in the middle of each square. Slow and focused again. She's not simply re-creating something she remembers; this is an image she's clearly practiced.

Directed by her father, or mother? Someone else?

When she's done, she moves to the next corner and laboriously builds a new box. Then creates a third at the top of the poster, dead center. Three five-by-five matrixes, arranged like points of a triangle, each bearing a different collection of numbers.

None of us says a word.

When she's done, she sets down the Sharpie, sits back in her chair, and nods once, as if satisfied.

"Zahra, did your father teach you that?" Aliah asks softly.

Zahra regards her with her too old, too serious gray eyes: "Two halves of one whole," she announces.

Then she dismounts from the chair and heads around the table for more glitter.

CHAPTER 30

AFTER MUCH STUDYING OF ZAHRA'S poster additions, we all agree they're clearly a puzzle of some kind. Mathematical puzzle, I further define, in an attempt to be smart.

Unfortunately, there's not a mathematician among us, so no matter how many ways we turn the squares, study the numbers, we got nothing. Daryl snaps a photo and attempts an image search. Still nada. He texts Roberta next.

She'll be right over.

But of course.

After that, the division of labor is simple. Daryl and Roberta will take over Zahra duty at the compound, with the stipulation Genni can borrow the youngster later to bake cookies. Aliah and I will return to her deli so she can make a living, while I hang up the poster and basically hang around for whatever might happen next.

First stop, fetching Aliah's vehicle so we have our own set of wheels.

Second, pulling into her business.

Third, taping our coded message onto the front-facing window, which takes hardly any time at all.

Turns out, so does waiting for whatever happens next.

I've barely put away the tape when the bell above the door dings, and in walks retired army captain Sanders Kurtz from No One Left Behind, bearing a plain manila envelope and a very intense look on his face.

ALIAH APPEARS IN a matter of moments, two tall glasses of doogh in hand. I pass, already knowing better. Kurtz, however, appears genuinely excited. He murmurs several phrases in what must be excellent Dari, judging by Aliah's charmed expression. She sets the drink in front of him, fussing with the place settings on the table. If I didn't know any better, I'd say she was flirting. Then again, I don't know any better.

"New restaurant?" Kurtz wants to know.

"Open eight months."

"Specialty?"

"Kabuli pulao."

Kurtz breaks into a broader smile. "My favorite! Two servings to go, please?"

Aliah nods, blushes, nods some more. She heads back to the kitchen. Kurtz takes a sip of his doogh, sighs happily. "You have no idea how much I've missed Afghan food since returning. At least Tucson has some options. Several of my military friends are completely out of luck."

"Do you miss Afghanistan?" I ask curiously.

He takes his time answering. "It's a beautiful country. Especially Kabul. You can wander through some of the most gorgeous historic gardens in the world, while staring out at white-capped peaks. Then there's the crazy crowded markets, bustling away in the shadows of ancient mosques. I could walk down the same streets every day and still discover something new. It is also, as you can imagine, a complicated country. Where hospitality and hostility have been ingrained in equal measures. Where the Hindu Kush are buried in snow, while the arid plains will bake every last drop of moisture from your body. I met some of the bravest and most loyal people I've ever known. And I encountered many whose sole goal was to kill me. So, yes, I miss Afghanistan, but maybe in the way you remember a particularly intense relationship. When it was good, it was really, really good. But when it was bad…"

I nod.

Kurtz sits back. "I'm assuming you still haven't located Sabera Ahmadi."

"You assume correctly."

"Zahra?"

"Safe. Sabera's husband, Isaad, however, is dead. After being tortured first."

"Jesus. When?"

"Last night."

"This is getting dangerous." Kurtz peers at me intently. "Don't you think it's time to leave the investigative work to the police?"

"No."

"It's not even your fight."

"It's always my fight."

Kurtz's eyes widen slightly. He doesn't seem to know what to do with me. Not the first time I've encountered such disbelief, won't be the last.

"I think," Kurtz says at last, "you may want to proceed with extreme caution. There's way more here than meets the eye."

He slides the manila envelope across the table to me. "I reached out to MI6 as promised. Then, when I walked into my office today, I discovered this sitting on my desk. I'm thinking it's their way of answering. Perhaps you'd like to pass the enclosed documents along to the proper local authorities. Given American confidentiality laws, this information is above their pay grade. God knows it's above mine."

He rises to standing just in time for Aliah to appear with his takeout order. Another exchange of charming grins on his part, coquettish giggles on hers, then he's headed out the door. At the last moment, however, he pauses, leaning back in.

"What's with the poster? Looks like a bunch of gibberish, framed by three magic squares?"

"Magic squares?" He has our immediate attention.

"We used to mess around with them in math class. You know—all the rows, columns, and diagonals must add up to the same total. Though"—he frowns—"these ones have repeating numbers, which any purist will tell you is cheating. So not the cleverest puzzles after all."

He disappears back out the door. Aliah and I don't have to say a word for her to immediately start texting Daryl while I rip open the manila envelope and pull out a sheaf of papers.

It takes me a second or two to understand what I'm seeing. And when I do, I feel sorry for Sabera and her family all over again.

CHAPTER 31

STACI AGREES TO MEET ME at the same coffee shop as before. The caseworker doesn't sound surprised to get my call. Understanding now what she was hinting at earlier, I suppose she isn't.

Once again she's seated near the back, her side-swept hair artfully shielding her acid-scarred face. She already has a mug of coffee steaming before her. I pause at the order counter long enough to pour myself a glass of water, then head over.

Staci watches me approach. Her expression is carefully composed. I don't blame her.

"I know," I state without preamble, "about Sabera's hospitalization—the seventy-two-hour psych hold."

Staci continues to study me.

"And I know the other piece of the puzzle. Sabera's pregnant. Were you ever going to say anything?"

"I couldn't."

I puff out an exasperated breath. "What a fucking mess."

Staci's turn to sigh. "Exactly."

———

I TAKE A seat, opening my messenger bag and withdrawing Kurtz's special delivery. I make a show of spreading out Sabera Ahmadi's medical records. I want Staci to see that whatever concerns she had about protecting her client's privacy don't matter anymore.

Staci's gaze flickers to the fanned pages. She doesn't bother asking where, why, when, or how. Most likely, she doesn't want to know.

"According to these reports, Sabera suffered some kind of mental breakdown while on a city bus. Started screaming hysterically, tearing at her hair, lashing out. The responding EMTs described her as 'speaking in tongues.' Except it wasn't gibberish, was it? It's just how a gifted polyglot might sound to people who are used to hearing only one language at a time."

Faintest nod.

"First thing the ER docs did was test her for drugs, which, in this day and age of bath salts and meth heads, makes sense. Except the tox screen came back negative. Even her blood alcohol level—zero. I wondered about that, given some of the things people have had to say. Sabera seemed stressed, distracted, tired. At times smelled of booze, maybe even slurred her words. But no drugs, no alcohol. Just a cocktail of various psych drugs and antidepressants.

"Because Sabera has had mental health issues in the past. Postpartum, to be specific. And once more, she has baby on board." I can't help myself. My tone isn't just intent, but borderline angry as I lean way forward. "Did she know? Was it planned? Did she talk to you about it?"

"She never said a word."

"And Isaad? Did he know?"

"I wish I had more answers. I don't."

"But you knew! You were the one who was called to the ER, so you knew about the baby! And then Sabera went missing, and *then* Isaad took off. Dear God, were you ever going to tell someone that there's a whole other life at stake?"

I sit back. I'm getting heated, which doesn't help anything. I'm just so frustrated. And tired. And frustrated!

I've read the illicit medical reports half a dozen times already. Maybe, if I review the documents thoroughly enough, they will make some sense. Maybe, if I dissect every word, the riddle that is Sabera Ahmadi will finally unravel. For now, I can only shake my head.

Staci takes a sip of coffee. The mug trembles in her hand. She's not nearly as unaffected as she pretends. That, as much as anything, helps me calm down. It can't be easy to be a caseworker. Taking on such an immediate and intimate role in the lives of total strangers, while having to remain separate at all times. God knows I couldn't do it. Obviously.

"Sabera suffered some kind of episode," Staci finally allows. "She was taken to the ER where she presented in a dissociative state. According to the psych consult performed by Dr. Cindy Porway, she appeared to be experiencing some kind of severe PTSD episode. Possibly a threat to herself and/or others. She recommended an involuntary psych hold."

Sabera's infamous missing days. Which apparently coincided with her distraught visit to Aliah's deli. So something had already gotten Sabera agitated; she went to see her friend, where she apparently recovered enough to board a bus for work...

And promptly went berserk.

"Did Sabera know she was pregnant before she was admitted to the ER?" I ask Staci.

"Sabera wasn't exactly talking when I first got there. Given her level of distress...let's just say the drug protocol was extremely thorough."

I roll my eyes. It leaves me with an interesting theory, however. As in maybe the inciting event in this terrible little saga had been Sabera discovering she was pregnant. The immediate news would account for her agitated state when she arrived at Aliah's deli.

"Look." Staci sets down her coffee. "Sabera authorized her doctor to speak with me. I'm not sure why me versus Isaad, but if she was ever going to get released, it had to be into someone's care, hence the call to me. When I first arrived, she was out cold from all the meds. When she finally came around, it was mostly to insist I never say a word about what had happened. I wasn't lying before. Part of my job is to respect privacy, both for the family and the individuals."

"You didn't find her need for secrecy suspicious?"

"Many cultures consider mental illness to be taboo."

"Sabera disappeared for three days. You're telling me Isaad never asked questions about that? Didn't reach out to you? Demand some kind of explanation?"

"Isaad called me repeatedly looking for her. He sounded worried, then frustrated, then very worried and frustrated."

"What did you tell him?"

Staci thins her lips, studies her coffee again. "Part of the psych hold is a more thorough evaluation of Sabera's mental and physical health. Dr. Porway had an entire list of considerations: Had there been any recent changes in Sabera's eating or sleeping habits? Signs of self-destructive behavior? Suspected alcohol or drug abuse? Maybe she was hoarding weapons or suddenly giving away personal treasures.

"Normally, this is the kind of information provided by a loved one. Except Sabera had put me on the spot. On the one hand, I'd just spent several intense weeks with this woman, trying to get her and her family settled into Tucson. I'd studied her background, helped her learn mass transit, taught her American social etiquette. On the other hand, these are questions involving intimate details of daily life. Had Sabera been acting strangely lately?" Staci shrugs. "If anything, compared to other refugees I've assisted, she seemed especially stoic. But maybe what I took to be mental fortitude was actually emotional disconnect. I didn't feel comfortable answering. Given that, I did my best to work those considerations into my conversations with Isaad—"

"How? Like he asked you if you'd heard anything from Sabera and you said, hey, how's that gun collection of hers coming? Or discover any more empty vodka bottles in the recycling bin? How did that not come off sounding suspicious?"

"Oh, I think it came off as very suspicious. And I think..." Staci hesitates. "At a certain point, I think Isaad not only knew what I was doing, but it wasn't the first time he'd been asked such inquiries. They've spent years living in uncertainty and fear, remember? Time involving Sabera losing her family and watching her country collapse. Of giving birth and then trying to raise a baby in squalid refugee camps known for their violence. Of course Sabera has a history of mental health struggles, postpartum, PTSD, and otherwise. Again, I don't know why she didn't list Isaad's name. Personally, I think he figured out exactly what was going on. And like me, he did his best to assist, while never acknowledging what he wasn't supposed to acknowledge."

I'm honestly not sure what to do with this. So Sabera disappeared once before for three days, but maybe for Isaad, that didn't count as a true vanishing act, given he connected the dots to a necessary medical intervention. Which could also explain why he didn't initially respond to Aliah's pestering when Sabera disappeared a second time around.

"From your point of view?" I ask Staci now. "When you heard Sabera never made it home from work a second time, did you assume she'd suffered another breakdown?"

"After the first twenty-four hours, I contacted local hospitals. I also reached out to Dr. Porway, who did some digging. One of the trickiest parts of a psych doctor's job is making the determination of whether a patient can be safely discharged or continues to be at risk for harm. Needless to say, she was very concerned about Sabera's well-being."

"Was it the news of Sabera's pregnancy that got her released the first time around? As a mother, surely she wouldn't harm her unborn child?"

"From what I understand, parenthood isn't the best indicator of success—women commit more murder-suicides involving their children than men do. A strong religious prohibition, however, can be very powerful. And the tenets of Islam clearly state that only God has the power to give and take away life. Suicide is not only murder, it goes against God's will and denies one entrance into heaven. Being a practicing Muslim was a major factor when contemplating Sabera's future."

"Did you agree? Seventy-two hours later she's all better and can go home?"

Staci hesitates. Once more, I can see the wheels turning in her head, what she wants to say, what she thinks she can say...

I lean forward, play my admittedly brutal trump card. "Isaad is dead."

"What?"

"His body was found yesterday. Badly mutilated. He was tortured, then killed."

"*What?*"

"Whatever's going on right now, it's not a simple matter of Sabera's mental health. The threat is real. The violence tangible. I don't know why, which is really pissing me off, but at this point, I consider finding Sabera a point of life or death. We help her—and her unborn child—survive this together, or they die alone.

"According to these medical reports," I continue relentlessly, "part of Sabera's discharge requirement was to enroll in therapy. Twice a week. From what I've heard, she had her neighbor, Nageenah, watch Zahra while she went to these appointments, under the guise of 'running errands.' Except Sabera only made it to three actual sessions. Then the therapist never saw her again. Though Nageenah claims Sabera kept disappearing two afternoons a week. Why? Where was she going, what was she doing? You need to tell me *everything*."

Staci appears visibly shaken.

"I don't know what I don't know," she starts.

"Join the club."

"Are she and Isaad married? He seems committed, she implied not. Clearly, it took the two of them together to get out of Afghanistan."

"I sense a but in all this."

Staci takes a deep breath. "The kind of severe PTSD episode Sabera experienced while on the city bus...it's generally triggered by some sort of external stimuli."

I wait.

"Say a sound. Why so many veterans can be set off by cars backfiring. Smell is also a very powerful association, say the scent of barbecue, which is apparently quite similar to human flesh."

I shudder.

"Or by sight," Staci concludes. "Seeing something reminiscent of the traumatic time. Or someone."

She pauses a beat. I go wide-eyed. I can almost nearly get this...

"Sabera would sometimes cry out while I was visiting her in the hospital. Nightmares. During them, she repeated one name, over and over again: Jamil."

"Jamil?"

"Later, when they started weaning her off the meds and she became more coherent, I asked her about it. She dismissed my questions immediately. Jamil was her brother, nothing more; she must have been dreaming about her childhood. But here's the thing—I've read Sabera's family history. Her brother's name was Farshid, not Jamil."

"Why would she lie?"

"Off the top of my head? I've also seen Zahra's birth certificate. Her middle name is Jamila."

"As in...daughter of Jamil?"

A single nod.

I feel my eyes go even wider. "Holy shit. Zahra...Jamil. Sabera...Jamil." Then, on the heels of that: "Why does Isaad feel like a committed married man, yet Sabera still fights it? The answer I'm guessing is Jamil. Okay then. Where the hell is Jamil?"

"There's no record of any Jamil in Sabera's background reports. Which brings me to the other thing she kept repeating during her hospitalization. 'I killed them. I killed them all.' And based on the tone of her voice, I don't think she was speaking figuratively. Sabera's final days in Kabul—something terrible happened."

Staci shrugs. "I don't think it's over yet."

CHAPTER 32

*F*ROM THE VERY BEGINNING, *I know something is wrong. Babies cry, babies wail. But there is no scream announcing my baby's entrance into the world. I catch a look on the volunteer nurse's face. She pats my shoulder.*

"You must have hope, my sister. These are tough times, but God's will shall prevail."

I hear a whimper then, followed by another. Dr. Richard sets you, Zahra, on my chest. He strokes your thin cheek; he tells me I have a daughter. But there's still too much silence.

You are so tiny, so fragile. A wisp of life born into a place rife with death. I've seen it myself working at the clinic. Malnourished mothers giving birth to malnourished babies who will now live in inhuman conditions while the rats gaze upon them in open hunger.

I bring your mouth to my breast. You do your best, and so do I. But we are both exhausted.

Isaad takes charge. He has through some miracle procured

extra bottles of water. You must drink, he tells me over and over. Your hydration is the baby's hydration. Drink, drink, drink.

Malalai is there to help with changing out soiled rags and swaddling up tight. She is a direct and efficient teacher. Do this, do that. Drink this, eat that. But our new little family continues to exist in a state of hush, as if we don't want anyone, not even fate, to know that we exist. Soon, in Malalai's eyes, I see the same shadow I saw on the nurse's face.

No one expects my baby to be long for this world.

Not even me.

I watch you all night long. You don't cry to wake me up, so I hold vigil instead. I try to catch the sound of your breathing and match it to my own. I drink a bottle of water, then bring you to my breast. I bundle you up, then guard against the rats. When it's cold, I hold you close. When it's hot, I fan your face. When it's wet, I cradle you away from the damp.

I can't let you go. I must watch, I must tend, I must count every breath because any minute, moment, second, your little chest might fall, and never rise again.

I hear the silence. But worse, I see the specter of death, actively stroking your sunken face while delighting in the hollowness of your belly. It is coming for all of us, but I know as deeply and surely as I've ever known anything, it wants you first.

Night after night after night. I stand guard. You, me, and the endless quiet.

As your whimpers grow fainter and my breasts turn red and hard.

Then, I start to hear all the sounds thrumming through the stillness.

The murmur of Jamil's voice, whispering in my ear, followed too soon by the crack of a rifle down a crowded street.

Farshid calling to me as we race through orchards bursting with bright red fruit. Two halves of one whole. As we should be, would be, could be for the rest of our lives, except we are not.

The rustle of paper as I flip through my mother's notes, reading entries I don't understand, piecing together puzzles I didn't know existed, poring over maps that hide secrets I never thought the world to have.

Two halves of one whole.

In the end you will be allowed nothing…

Nothing.

Nothing.

I gaze upon the baby swaddled upon my chest…

I must keep you safe. I must hold vigil. The silence wants you. I can hear it now, a buzz of gnashing teeth, so impossibly hungry. How had I never realized?

Then one afternoon, walking back from the latrine, my chest a hard wall of fire, my footsteps stumbling, I spy him, clear as day.

My cousin, Habib, standing across the way. Recovered and now openly smirking at me.

I start to run, knowing what he'll do a second before he knows it himself. I push, shove, bulldoze. The camp is so cramped, there are no clear walkways. I can already spy him moving out of the corner of my eye. His line is more direct, he's going to win, he's going to get to you first. Habib had threatened revenge, and no one knows as well as family how to inflict pain.

I careen forward, faster and faster.

But he's ahead of me. I can just catch sight of the flap of his shirt.

I won't make it in time.

I will not be able to beat him.

Your little chest rising, falling, never to rise again.

Babies should cry. Babies should wail.
I never deserved you in the first place.
And the silence tells me so.

"*What is wrong with her?*"

"*Off the top of my head, mastitis, postpartum depression, failure to thrive.*"

"*You must fix her.*"

"*Sure. I'll just order up a regimen of antidepressants, antipsychotics, and talk therapy. And while I'm at it, how about some fresh fruit, yogurt, and non-spoiled goat meat to make everyone happy?*"

"*You cannot let her suffer like this!*"

"*I have Prozac, Prozac, and more Prozac. It was never intended to be the be-all and end-all, yet in a place like this...*" *A drop in his tone.* "*I'm doing the best I can.*"

They are shadows to me. Figments of a dream scurrying along the edges of my mind. They want things, do things. I haven't the heart to tell them they're too late. I doomed myself years ago with small choices made, then larger ambitions attempted.

My baby. Where is my baby? The throbbing in my chest, growing, growing, growing.

Isaad is talking again: "*We must get out of here. For both their sakes.*"

A hollow laugh. "*You think I don't know that? I have no control over these things—*"

"*You are a doctor; you have contacts! You're more powerful than you think.*"

"*I can't—*"

"Please, I will give you anything. Money? I'm a mathematician. I have a notebook of original theorems, proofs. I'll hand them over to you. My life's work. It's worth something. In certain circles, it is priceless—"

"Don't insult me—"

"Please. I'm begging you. My wife. My daughter. I beg you…"

A hoarse, choking sound.

I see him again. Habib. My cousin is right there, standing behind them. I see his triumphant smile. He has a knife, raising it up high. "Did you not think we'd figure out what your bitch mother had done? What you did? Two halves of one whole. You'll pay, you will all pay—"

I scream. Am screaming. But they don't hear, don't see, don't move out of the way…

Zahra, I love you.

Zahra, I'm sorry.

Zahra, I love you.

Zahra, I'm so, so sorry.

"Shhh," the nurse tells me, a cool cloth upon my brow. *"Rest now. Shhh…"*

"Is she dead? My baby. Where is she—"

"Calm yourself, khwahar jan. Close your eyes, rest your body and mind so you can return to your family."

"I killed him. I killed them. I knew. I knew what would happen, but I did it anyway. For my mother. I remember exactly how they treated her. For her, I finished what she started."

"Shhh, my sister. Do not say such things."

"Two halves of one whole. I didn't know. Didn't realize

until it was too late. I loved him, too. If I had known, if I had known…" I'm choking, sobbing. Farshid, running through the orchard. Farshid, stating I will take care of you…Farshid, staring sightlessly at the sky, his face covered in blood. Why had I not pieced it together sooner? Me, the one who can stare into the fabric of the universe, knitting and unknitting at will.

And yet still so ignorant of the plain facts right in front of me.

My brother, trying stoically to save our family.

Myself, thinking I was so clever.

"Rest. Your daughter needs you."

"He will kill her." *Has killed her. Over and over again. I see it clearly. The blood on my hands. Her price to pay.*

"They would've given it all to the Taliban," I babble. "Untold riches, unbelievable power. I couldn't let them do it."

The nurse leans close, her voice a mere whisper in my ear. "I know what you did. And I heard what he said. God have mercy on both your souls."

I gaze upon her in wonder. "Are you real?"

"Yes, my sister."

"My baby still breathes?"

"Yes, my sister."

"I am alive?"

"Yes, khwahar jan. Rest now. Your husband is a good man…"

Then I'm floating on a lake, my hand tucked inside Jamil's. The sky is pure blue, the sun a bright promise. And now I am sure I'm dead, but I don't care anymore. I would stay here forever, float here forever, my fingers entwined with his…

"She is beautiful," *he tells me.*

I'm crying, my tears pouring down my cheeks into the gently lapping water.

"You have done well." He turns to look at me. I can see the hole in his head, where the bullet penetrated his bone-white skull, obliterated his brilliant brain. His blood, my tears, spreading out in the water around us.

"Two halves of one whole," he informs me.

I shake my head. "He is gone. You're gone. Everyone is gone."

"Are you so certain of that? What did you see that day? And what do you know?"

I'm confused and hurting. But gradually, as the water caresses my skin and Jamil's hand warms my own, I can picture my brother's blood-covered face as he lay sprawled on the ground. And I realize for the first time how much I didn't truly comprehend. Because that version of me didn't know how to take a pulse, or that head wounds bleed horrifically, or that even the most grievously wounded body can sometimes be healed again.

I was still a child. A well-intentioned one, but a naïve girl just the same.

"You have everything you need," Jamil says now. "You know everything you must know."

And I understand what he means, even as I dread what will happen next.

"What kind of fool falls in love when the world is burning?" Jamil whispers, so close it is his blood dripping down my cheeks. "What kind of fool doesn't?"

I awake with a start. The first thing I see is Isaad, kneeling on the floor beside me, his hair, his clothing in complete disarray. As my eyes open, so do his. For a moment, he looks as bewildered as I feel.

Then he grabs my hand, clutches it fiercely. "Praise be to Allah!"

He feels my forehead, touches my cheeks. "You have returned to us!"

"My brother is alive," I croak.

"What are you—"

"Farshid is alive. I must find him."

He gives me a look of deepest pity. "Like your cousin Habib? You have been screaming about him, jigaram. You point at shadows, warn us to look out. He is behind us. He'll kill us, you, Zahra. But no one's there. Whatever happened to Habib...I share your sorrow, my beloved, but he's gone. Whatever you think you see, it's merely the fever talking. Now it has broken, however, and your mind will be clear again."

I don't know how to respond because I swear Habib is standing in the room right now. As I stare, he smirks, plays with a knife. Except a blink of the eye later, he's gone and the shadows are just shadows, and I'm the one left disoriented. I should know the difference between what is real and what is a delusion. It's disorienting to hear that I do not.

Isaad pats my hand. "Dr. Richard says your condition sometimes happens to women after childbirth. You must rest, rebuild your strength. Our daughter needs you."

Which is when I realize there's a second person in the room. A tiny swaddled bundle nestled next to Isaad's bent knees.

Isaad follows my gaze. He picks you up, places you in my arms.

The sound of silence.

You staring into me. Me staring into you.

"She is beautiful," Jamil whispers. And once more, his blood mingles with my tears.

I love you. From the beginning to the end to the beginning again. Civilizations fail. Countries die. People pass. And yet a parent's love, hope, dreams…

I love you, Zahra.

And in that instant, I let you go.

Because my sins shouldn't be your punishment.

Someday, I hope you'll understand. As my mother taught me, so I will teach you:

You descend from warriors.

There are good men, amazing men, exceptional males out there, but too many…

They seek to erase us from existence. To force us to disappear within our own communities. To make us become invisible to even ourselves.

Never let them win.

Your voice has value. Your heart sings. Your mind glows. Your strength beckons.

I bow to you, one tired fighter to the next.

And I hope you will understand what I have to do next.

Two halves of one whole.

I finally understand. And there are things I must do.

I can only offer you this, a parent's lament to all the children out there:

I'm sorry.

I love you.

I'm sorry.

I love you.

CHAPTER 33

A LIAH IS SURROUNDED BY A sea of graph paper when I return. At
a glance, I can tell she has duplicated the five-by-five grids provided by Zahra, each sheet bearing a raft of scribbles in the margin.

"Do you know what magic squares are?" she asks upon my
entrance.

"Not a clue."

"Your handsome friend is correct; they are puzzles where the
sum of the digits across rows, down columns, and through diagonals are the same. From that regard, these are magic squares—the
numbers always add up to sixty. There's no way such repetition
can be by chance."

"What does that mean? Is the number sixty significant?"

"Maybe, but here's the problem, your friend is also correct—a
true magic square doesn't have any repeated numbers, and these
ones do. Which, apparently, classifies them as trivial. But given
everything that's going on, they don't feel so trivial to me."

I peer over her shoulder, studying the laborious process she's been going through adding up every single combination of numbers. She's right; there's no way this kind of perfectly synchronized addition can be by chance. But what does it mean?

I pick up a piece of graph paper, study the copied puzzle for a bit. If it's a code, by whom and for whom? And what does this five-by-five grid of numbers signify?

"Do we know how Zahra learned to draw this?" I ask.

"She says her mother learned them from her mother, a gift passed from generation to generation."

"Hand-me-down math puzzles?" The concept alone hurts my head.

"Two halves of one whole," Aliah repeats.

"Do you know what that means?"

"Not at all."

I take a seat. Study the assorted pages. "Was the grandmother a math professor?"

"Maryam was a fashion designer."

"That tracks," I mutter, given that nothing about this case makes sense. "But Sabera knows math, yes? She worked as an assistant for Isaad at the university?"

"Yes."

"Meaning, she'd understand these grids were wrong, er, trivial, as you say; they aren't constructed properly."

"I would assume she'd realize such a thing."

I frown. "You said the repeating digits shouldn't be there. What happens when you cull them out?"

"You are asking if the repeated numbers are significant on their own?"

"Sure."

Aliah shrugs. "I've analyzed them many times. As the saying goes, I got nothing."

I study the grids. All look Greek to me. For lack of anything smarter to do, I pull out my phone and Google magic squares. I learn that they date back to ancient China, have gained occult status, and can appear as symbols in works of art. As a matter of principle, they are constructed with non-repeated positive integers. There are, however, examples of famous "trivial" squares, including the four-by-four Sagrada Familia magic square whose rows and columns add up to the number thirty-three, the age of Jesus at the time of the Passion, but get there by repeating the numbers fourteen and ten. So famously trivial.

Basically, the more I read, the less I understand.

I'm also still struggling with the concept of the grids being a hand-me-down from Zahra's grandmother. Because Sabera's encryption skills weren't challenging enough? Except, of course, her mother was also an MI6 agent. Meaning maybe Sabera learned encoding from her?

Seriously, what were family dinnertime conversations like in that house?

I return to two halves of one whole. A key of some kind? Maybe we should halve the numbers inside the magic squares, except that results in messy fractions. Next, I try dividing out the total. If the magic sum is currently sixty, what happens if I make it thirty, and reconstruct the grids accordingly?

What I get from my awkward computations is that it's very difficult to create a magic square. Certainly, the only way I can get each row, column, and diagonal to total thirty is to repeat numbers again. I'd like to think it's because that's the only way it can be done, but it could also mean I'm not clever enough.

One thing I've learned in my years as an investigator: play to your strengths. The odds of me cracking this code and/or using it to locate Sabera are not high. Then again, the crime scene specialist from Sabera's townhouse hideaway, Jay Chen...He clearly enjoyed puzzles.

I give Detective Marc a call.

"What?" he growls.

I fill him in on Zahra's carefully replicated math puzzles. I do not mention our own attempt at a coded message inviting Sabera to a meeting; I'm not totally stupid.

"Fuck," he states.

"We're thinking the grids are magic squares. Which may or may not have something to do with two halves of one whole."

"Fuck."

"I was wondering if your crime scene expert, Jay Chen, might give them a look?"

Silence. Then: "Fine, send me a photo."

"Has he had any luck discovering more messages from the wall art?"

"He's running photos of the scripted mess through an encryption software."

"An encryption software? Huh, I wonder if I can find that as an app."

More silence.

"Any more breakthroughs from Isaad's cell phone, Sabera's cell phone? You had a term for it...wait, I remember! Any new evidence?"

"Are you trying to piss me off?"

"Generally I don't have to try." I change my tone to dead serious. "I am attempting to keep a little girl safe. Whatever happened to her parents, we both know she could be next."

Detective Marc sighs heavily. I don't think he's a bad guy. He's just a product of a system with limited thinking.

"Isaad Ahmadi's phone had half a dozen incoming calls from

a burner phone," he supplies. "All lasting less than thirty seconds, none leaving messages."

"You can't trace the burner?"

"Nope."

"What about triangulating the signal or whatever that is?"

"It's possible a few of those calls bounced off a tower near the warehouse district. Including the same evening as someone went whack-a-mole with the two male vics."

"So someone calling from the vicinity of the first crime scene," I muse. "Maybe the bad guys making contact with Isaad? Or Sabera having dispatched bad guys, calling Isaad for a ride out of there?"

"Whoever did the calling, it got Isaad there, and we all know how that ended." Slight pause. "For the record, the ME confirmed Isaad Ahmadi had blood on his clothes that matched the two Afghans discovered bludgeoned to death. She then tested the blood on their hands and clothing and got a match to Isaad. So definitely the three had some kind of altercation. How that ended with all of them dead, in two different locations, twenty-four hours apart, however, remains unclear."

"They lured Isaad to the warehouse. He got into a struggle with them, allowing Sabera time to flee. And then..."

And then I have the same problem Detective Marc has. Then someone should've won the fight. Isaad kills the men with a hammer, he and Sabera get away. Or the two men overwhelm Isaad, taking him prisoner to interrogate and torture for the next twenty-four hours.

Except the two men die the evening of Sabera's escape; Isaad isn't killed until the following day. Which is a particularly disturbing scenario.

Because Detective Marc is cooperating, I fill him in on my other breakthrough for the day.

"Sabera was hospitalized for seventy-two hours on a psych hold. Had some kind of nervous breakdown-slash-PTSD episode. Looking at her meds list, which includes Haldol...is she of sound mind is definitely worth questioning."

"Haldol as in the antipsychotic most often used for treating schizophrenia?"

"That's the one."

"Great."

"On the bright side, something bad is definitely happening. Sabera is definitely missing, Isaad was definitely murdered, some strange men definitely tried to grab Zahra. This isn't all in Sabera's head."

"On the bright side?"

"Trust me, I regretted the words the moment I said them. Current theory...we're in the middle of unfinished business. Most likely it involves Jamil, who may be Zahra's father and Sabera's first love and is supposedly dead, except you and I know that's not the same as actually dead. Then again, there's a big difference between international custody disputes and riddles involving hair locks and abducted human keys. Your thoughts?"

Detective Marc has a unique way to make sounds that aren't actually intelligible, and yet communicate just fine.

"New mathematical puzzles," I prompt him, returning to the beginning. "Maybe if Chen studied them..."

In response, I get: "What was the name of Sabera's psych doc?"

"Dr. Cindy Porway. Checking out her LinkedIn page, she looks really nice, like the kind of woman who would save stray dogs and give up her seat on a bus for the elderly. Maybe she'll take pity on us."

"I'll pay her a visit. Given the circumstances, she might talk."

"Ask her about Jamil."

"Sabera's first love and possible father of her child?"

"You do listen!"

A bunch of growly sounds again. So this is what Roberta grew up with. Interesting.

"I doubt Dr. Porway will confirm or deny anything," Detective Marc grits out, "but being a crack detective, I happen to have the ability to read facial expressions while cuing off of physical responses. I got this."

Detective Marc mutters a few words I don't have to catch in order to feel his love. He clicks off. I return to staring at numbered grids. By the time Aliah announces she's done for the day and we might as well return to the compound, I'm grateful.

I DON'T SEE the threat. Not even a hint of menace.

Aliah tidies up the kitchen, closes out the register. Her cook has already headed out. We exit onto the sidewalk; then she pauses to lock the glass door.

A squeal of tires directly behind us.

I'm just turning to see when the first blow knocks me on the side of my head. I fall to my knees. A second strike sends me face down onto the blistering pavement. I try to raise myself up but can't find my feet. My body is present. My mind refuses to function. I can only watch and see.

Two black-clad men. One grabbing Aliah from behind. The other yanking a dark hood over her face.

She kicks. Screams in her mother tongue. Breaks free long enough to attempt to flee.

"Fffuuu...Grab her!"

The second man snags her wrist. She smacks him across the

face. Then the first man seizes both her arms again, looping a zip tie around them.

Back vehicle door opens. The men toss Aliah in, then clamber after her as the white SUV rockets away.

I feel blood trickling from my temple.

I feel the sidewalk searing my cheek.

I feel...

Nothing at all as the world spins away.

CHAPTER 34

REALITY COMES AND GOES. PEOPLE screaming followed by
uniform-clad professionals. Police, EMTs. I try to hold the
moment. Things I need to say.

"Aliah," I attempt to croak out, but no sound emerges from
my throat.

Blinding lights. Speeding vehicles.

"Aliah," I whisper.

Fade to black.

I wake to voices. Daryl's, I think. He's moaning that he
should've been there, shouldn't have left us alone. He's demanding
answers, action, something.

Another man's placating tone. They were able to identify the
license plate on the SUV, trace the vehicle to a vacant lot where it
had been hastily abandoned. Crime scene techs working it already,
certain to have answers soon.

There's something important I need to say, but I don't remember what or why. Throbbing in my head, chest, arms. I roll to the side, vomit. Clamber of movement. People appear, some I know, some I don't. I stare at them all glassy-eyed.

Fade to black again.

Except it's not so dark. I'm in a liquor store, brightly lit. Paul stands across from me, gut shot, blood soaking through his shirt. He's smiling at me.

I throw my arms around him. He hugs me back.

"I'm sorry," I tell him, have been telling him, for years.

"Only the good die young," he informs me cheerfully.

"Wait, does that mean—"

"You're not dead yet, Frankie," he whispers in my ear. "You are loved, are worth loving. Try to catch up."

Then he's gone. I'm...nowhere at all. White on white on white, broken by a single man, who stands as tall in death as he did in life.

"Really screwed up this time, didn't you?" His tone is kind.

I reach out a hand, touch his shoulder. Warm and solid. I clutch his shoulder in wonder, with longing. Of all the mistakes I've made...

"How many bullets do you think you can outrace?" he asks me gently.

On cue, his chest starts to bleed. More blood pours out his back.

"Please," I try.

"Happiness isn't something you discover," he tells me. "It's something you make. Frankie, try to keep up."

Then he's gone, and an emaciated girl, arms lined with track marks, lounges on the floor. The first missing person I ever found, the first dead body I'd ever seen. Now she hums under her breath, while a young mother takes a seat beside her, skeletal legs still trailing lake grass. In another corner, a Haitian teen admires his bloody chest as a little girl in bunny slippers offers him her teddy bear.

Young and old. Children and parents. Lost, then found. By me. Except it was too late for each and every one of them.

"I'm sorry," I say, but no one pays me any attention.

They're too busy being dead.

Only I'm overwhelmed with the business of living.

Then, a presence behind me. I hear a voice I don't expect at all. His arms are strong and steady, as he pulls me back against his chest.

"It's okay to mourn," he murmurs. "It's okay to want. It's okay to be who you truly are."

There are so many things I want to say, but in the end, it takes only two words to say it all.

"I hurt."

"I know," he whispers.

"We know," the dead intone.

Then he's gone. They're all gone, everything is gone. An all too real person commands: "Frankie, wake up!"

I discover Detective Marc standing next to my hospital bed, hands on his hips, expression frustrated.

I realize two things at once:

I'm definitely still alive.

And I've seen one of the kidnappers before.

"IN ALIAH'S DELI. The day before?" I pause, trying to place my memories into some sort of timeline. My head hurts. I can't even figure out what today is. Trying for anything more sounds impossibly painful. Still: "He was browsing nuts and candy. Bought a few items. Firni pudding!" I pounce on the detail. "Ask Daryl. It's the afternoon we ate pudding."

"You're sure it's the same guy? A young Middle Eastern male. That's not exactly a precise description."

"Yes, but not just based on appearance. There's something..." God, my head hurts. I rub my temples while trying to sort through my chaotic impressions. "Movement. The way he held himself. A little too tight, too stiff. Initially I pegged him for former military. But then when he stepped toward the register, he had a rolling gait, like someone recovering from a grievous injury or terrible accident."

"And you saw him again yesterday?"

"The kidnapping happened yesterday?"

A nod.

"Aliah?" I can barely ask the question.

"No word."

"They took her as leverage."

Detective Marc doesn't refute it.

"To force Sabera to come to them? Or to..." I struggle with the next thought. "Torture her for information like they did with Isaad?"

There are so many more ways to hurt a woman, and don't we know it.

"The best way to help Aliah is to find her," Detective Marc corrals my racing thoughts. "So you recognized one of the kidnappers. He'd been in Aliah's store before. Scoping it out?"

I shrug. Wince at the stabbing pain. "Or following us." I suffer through another hazy memory. Thick black hair, light brown skin, twin dark eyes, fixed on me heatedly. "The coffee shop. Where I met with Staci, the caseworker from the resettlement agency. He was standing in line a few spots behind me. I think."

"Coffee shop, that's good. More places, more cameras, more images. I'll get some detectives right on it."

"Fffuuu," I whisper.

"What's that?"

"The other guy. He yelled something. 'Fffuu, grab her.' Fuck! Grab her? Frank, Grab her? I can hear it, but I can't understand it."

"The young male with the rolling gait, he said this?"

"No, the other man, to him. Maybe just cursing at him to grab Aliah. But maybe...a name, title of address? Fff something. I don't know." I rub my temples. A final detail comes to me: "There were at least three of them. Two to grab Aliah, one to drive the vehicle."

"That's excellent, Frankie. More than I expected."

"If those three belong with the two found hammered to death at the warehouse, that makes five. Five men, out to get Sabera for something she knows, has, is. Doesn't that seem like a lot of people involved in a treasure hunt?"

"Depends on the size of the treasure."

Even my semi-fried brain can grasp that.

"Zahra?" I ask.

"Still safe with Daryl and Roberta. I offered to contact child services. My sister...let's just say she made a suggestion only a sibling can get away with."

"Threatened to remove your manly bits?"

"With a rusty knife," he assures me.

"I like your sister."

Dramatic eye roll, but he isn't fooling either of us. He and Roberta have a special relationship, the kind an only child like me can admire, but never truly understand.

"Dance studio meet-and-greet," I mutter.

Fresh eye roll. "Yes, Daryl confessed your master plan for

summoning Sabera Ahmadi. At which point Roberta threatened *him* with a rusty knife. But"—the detective shrugs—"we need Sabera. Trying to coerce her into locating us...not a terrible idea."

"The bad guys are moving very fast," I murmur. "We, on the other hand, are very slow. That's not a great recipe for success."

Detective Marc nods. I try to sip more water through my cup's straw but get only air. He takes the pink plastic recepticle from me and fills it up. He volunteers: "Chen is working on the new math puzzles. His first thought was also magic squares, but there's something about them being trivial...He has a theory. Going to consult a friend who's also a math nerd."

I know better than to nod by now. I'm very, very tired. I want to close my eyes and sleep forever. I want to dream of rainbows and unicorns, instead of a gathering of the dead.

"I also have IDs on the two murdered Afghan males. Rafiq Bahrami and Ahmad Bahrami. Cousins. Both fled Afghanistan after Kabul fell, being Hazaras, an ethnic group the Taliban has a tendency to cleanse."

"Connection to Sabera and her husband?" I croak.

"Working on it. Records post-Taliban takeover not being so accessible. Especially, you know, for the Tucson PD."

I get it, though it doesn't diminish my disappointment.

"Also," Marc continues, "have been spending quality time with cell phone records, his and hers. First time Sabera disappeared, Isaad made a dozen calls to a number in New York. Interestingly enough, soon after, Sabera started reaching out to that number as well. It's the main number of a major hospital."

My eyes round. "The baby..."

"The baby?"

"I didn't mention that Sabera's pregnant?"

"*What?*"

"Just learned. Honestly. Right before returning to Aliah's deli. Had received a manila envelope with Sabera's medical records—"

"You have the missing woman's actual medical records?" Detective Marc sounds irate. "In a clear violation of how many HIPAA laws?"

"I didn't steal them. Someone else did that. I was just given them...from a friend."

I glance painfully around the room, waving my hand in a gesture of searching. "My brown messenger bag. Must be somewhere. Has records. Was gonna share. Swear it."

Detective Marc huffs, then crosses to a closet, where, sure enough, my leather bag is hanging from a hook. He delivers it to me, but when I open the flap...Nothing. The manila folder is gone. I poke and prod some more. Basic items, including my emergency whistle, lip balm, discreet zippered pocket of cash...I empty everything out, not that it's much, then...

I gaze at the detective blankly. "I had it. I slipped the docs into my bag, after speaking with Sabera's caseworker, returned to Aliah's deli. I phoned you, then we closed up shop, stepped outside..."

Everything gets blurry after that.

"Would one of your officers have taken it?" I ask.

Marc bristles. "No. And not the EMTs, either. Some of the looky-loos had access to your purse while you were down, but if anything they would've gone for a wallet, not a plain envelope. Shit."

I don't know what to say. I still barely understand what happened.

"Okay," Detective Marc regroups. "Sabera is pregnant?"

"With a history of postpartum depression. Also was being treated for severe PTSD. The first time she vanished, she'd had some kind of breakdown, was put on a psych hold. Didn't I mention that?"

"That you bothered to share."

"This hospital number both Sabera and Isaad were calling... Maybe it's related to mental health services? Or the ob-gyn unit?"

Detective Marc sighs. "I'll follow up with Dr. Porway again. See if she was contacted by another doc, say one from New York, regarding Sabera's care. She didn't volunteer such information, but that's not a surprise. She may be the type to champion the poor, but she still isn't one to break doctor–client confidentiality."

"You talked to Dr. Porway?"

"Not all of us have been sleeping for the past twenty-four hours. Yes, I met with the good doc. Much like you suspected, when I mentioned the name Jamil, I got an immediate reaction. When I pushed, and identified him as Sabera's husband slash Zahra's father, I got an even stronger reaction. I'm guessing from Dr. Porway's expressions alone, we're on the right track. I have officers running down witnesses from Sabera's bus episode. With any luck, someone saw something—or someone—concrete, that'll move us forward."

"X factor," I croak.

"What's that?"

"If only we knew."

I expect another glare, but instead the detective regards me thoughtfully. "You know our other missing puzzle piece? Isaad Ahmadi's vehicle. As in, where is it? We know he drove it away from their apartment and then...?"

I hadn't considered the car at all, so, good question.

"Have had an APB out for it the past twenty-four hours. So

far, I can only tell you where it's not—the Ventana Canyon Resort, where Sabera was hiding out."

Which would've made some sense.

"Or the warehouse district, where the murdered men, and later, Isaad, were found."

My head is starting to pound harder. "Maybe Sabera is driving it around. Sleeping in it. That's why we haven't found her."

"Ever notice the city's nice wide boulevards and clear lines of sight? Not to mention the cameras at nearly every intersection, let alone banks, businesses, city buses? If the vehicle was in play, trust me, it would've been spotted by now."

I don't have an answer for that. Which is when my bruised brain finally gets his point. X factor. The good detective is agreeing with me. There's some person, place, or thing we still don't know.

Which at this stage of the game is irritating. And concerning. And dangerous.

God, I'm tired.

"All right. You've got a grade A concussion. Time for you to sleep, avoid bright lights, then sleep some more. And I mean it."

Detective Marc heads for the door. I ease back into the dubious comfort of the hospital bed, but my thoughts are way too jumbled to settle. Where is Aliah? What are they doing to her?

How long can she hold out?

Isaad might have had reason to protect the woman he considered his wife, but Aliah? She's only a friend, after all. A mentor of sorts, and now surrogate mother to Zahra, but still, what could she possibly know? Just because she called me in...

Showing a great deal of interest in a fellow countrywoman she'd known only a matter of weeks.

And now being held as bait, to draw out a woman who hadn't even shown up for her husband.

I feel a little click in the back of my mind, accompanied by a jolt of pain through my poor concussed brain.

I really have been an idiot.

I search the bedside table till I discover my cell phone, which someone has thoughtfully plugged in to charge.

"Daryl," I manage a moment later. "Come and get me. And bring that electronic key gizmo from the townhouse. We have work to do."

CHAPTER 35

A LIAH'S TRADITIONAL BOLT LOCK RENDERS Daryl's high-tech gadget useless. His lock-picking skills, however, quickly get the job done. As someone who leads a fringe lifestyle, generally populated by other shadowy sorts, I have no idea how people living in the straight and narrow accomplish anything.

"What are we looking for?" Daryl wants to know. He's back to being his dapper-clad self, a suit and tie being one of the best camouflages for a life of crime. He'd already given me the requisite lecture that I should be in bed. I'd given him my standard refusal to take it easy. We're both now over it.

"Something personal," I inform him. "Family photos, correspondence, Dear Diary, that sort of thing."

He gives me a look.

"Yeah, I know."

I've searched many places in my time. But generally, my ransacking involves the home and belongings of someone who's gone missing and, more important, that I've never met. This, on the other hand, feels intrusive, borderline icky.

Daryl shoulders the load like a true B & E professional. Given his past drug addiction, he probably is.

He starts in the living room, while I take the hallway. Given we're looking for personal images/correspondence, we bypass the kitchen. Not that cooking isn't important to Aliah, but I want knowledge of her family tree. More specifically, the members who still reside in Afghanistan. Doubt the kitchen can tell us that.

We identify five photos in the end, including one that shows Aliah standing in front of her business, probably the day it opened. Her beaming smile gives me a pang. I can tell from Daryl's expression, it hurts him, too.

First, we inspect a framed photo of her and two other women, one older, one younger. I'm guessing her mother and sister based on the resemblance. The photo appears fairly recent, so not what I need. In her office, we discover a larger group photo. Old and faded, the background nearly unrecognizable. Maybe taken in Afghanistan? Impossible to be sure. We liberate it from its frame to read the back, which is completely blank. Seriously, who takes a group photo, then doesn't scratch at least a few names, dates, location? I'm annoyed, but maybe because my head is still throbbing and everything about this is triggering.

Standing in the middle of Aliah's beautifully decorated living room with its rich colors and bright tapestries. Walking through her bedroom, which still carries a whiff of her perfume. Hell, passing the kitchen, which still exudes mint tea.

We know Aliah. And in the past few days, she has come to feel like not just an ally, but a friend.

And now...I keep remembering the reports of Isaad's charred hands and a shudder goes through me.

Are they torturing her right now? Does she even have whatever information they're looking for? Or is she enduring all that pain and misery with no end in sight?

It's been nearly twenty-four hours, and I've been unconscious for most of them.

I can't do that again.

Daryl finds three more older-looking photos; the backgrounds of the shots appear more spartan, the subjects younger and in dated outfits. My vision isn't the best, so I teach him the tricks I know. Instead of looking for a subjective family resemblance, study physical details that can't easily be altered—the space between a person's eyes, the shape of their mouth, the contour of their cheekbones.

"How do you know all this?" Daryl asks, scrutinizing each picture.

"Work mostly cold cases, remember? Often involves age-progressed images, especially when the missing was originally a child. Can't look for a seven-year-old face ten years later. Must fast-forward physical appearance accordingly."

Daryl shakes his head. "Sad work."

"It is and it isn't."

"You find dead people," he states bluntly.

"Their story still matters. Do you want to be the little kid who grows up hearing her mother ran away, or do you want to be the little kid who learns her mother never came home due to an accident that sent her vehicle to the bottom of a lake? Either way, I can't bring Mommy home. But the difference of that narrative for her daughter..."

Daryl nods. "All right, using your expertise...This older group photo. The women are all wearing head coverings, which makes it harder, but I think that's Aliah as a little girl, next to her mother and sister. Meaning the older couple in the middle—"

"Aliah's grandparents?" I ask.

"Yeah. With a layer of aunts and uncles, then cousins."

"Her cousin's son," I murmur. "She mentioned that he died when Kabul fell. How many cousins are we talking about?"

A pause as Daryl counts. "At least fourteen. And most are young, like Aliah. Meaning their parents could've still had more."

Big families. Nageenah had commented that Afghans lived in large families and all were welcome...

"Only Aliah's mother emigrated with her two daughters." I think about it, at least as much as I can through the pounding in my skull. "The family units on either side of Aliah's...can you take a close-up shot with your phone? Even among relatives, we gravitate toward the people we like best."

"You think these are the siblings closest to Aliah's mother; meaning also the cousins closest to Aliah and her sister?"

"Gotta start somewhere..."

Daryl snaps away with his phone. Sets down that picture, finishes scanning the room. "Hang on, another group shot."

He pulls it down from the top shelf. This one contains noticeably fewer people while definitely having been shot more recently. I glance at it, nod slowly. Family reunion at least one, if not two, decades later. Daryl sighs, practices his new facial identity skills.

"Okay, got the two siblings that were on either side of Aliah's mother in photo one, plus their now grown-up kids, many with older children of their own."

I'm trying to picture a family tree in my head. If Aliah is now in her fifties, her first cousins would also be around her age. Meaning their offspring would be the official next generation of older teens, young adults. University aged, such as Sabera.

Daryl rattles off the age-appropriate options. Of the ten second cousins, four are male. One probably too young, leaving us with three candidates.

He brings me the photo, points out the figures in question. Three young men, dressed in Western garb. Good-looking kids, no doubt about it. Thick, dark hair, broad shoulders, lean forms. I try to figure out which one of them screams activist, but honestly, they all look like hope to me. Now, apparently one of these young men is dead, while the other two live under a regime that hates them for their taste in wardrobe alone.

The sadness hits my concussed brain hard. The huge waste of it all. What is it about humans that we can't get out of our own way? There's a classic observation about crabs in a bucket—none of them can escape because anytime one of them makes progress climbing out, the other crabs pull it back down.

I think only humans can recognize such behavior in crustaceans, without catching the irony of our own self-destructive history.

"Names on the back?" I ask at last.

Daryl takes apart the frame. "Not big on notations," he confirms.

He snaps more photos of the young men; then we return to our rifling of Aliah's personal possessions. Pictures are good, but personal correspondence, a beautifully hand-scripted journal, containing real stories, motivations, understandings, would be even better.

We search every drawer, cabinet, and closet in the living room, home office, and master bedroom. No such luck. Which leaves us with...

Both Daryl and I stare at her personal computer.

"Email correspondence," he states.

"Fucking internet," I gripe. "Has ruined everything."

"Luddite?"

"Traditionalist."

He takes a seat. "Know her email address?"

"Yes, but I'm assuming her account is password protected. Isn't everything?"

"Give me a sec."

"You have another electronic gizmo? Or, are you secretly a master hacker?" I'm genuinely enthused for either possibility.

Daryl gives me a look. "No. However, most people can't remember all their passwords, meaning..." He gestures around the office. "Let's do some digging."

A documented code or master sheet of codes. I'm on it.

Except the room is starting to spin, and I'm just so damn tired, and is that a stapler in the drawer or a murder weapon? I don't know anymore.

Daryl: "Got it."

Me. "Huh?"

"Sticky note, under the keyboard. Works every time."

He logs in as Aliah. I collapse on the floor, where I can gaze up at the white ceiling and identify shapes in the floating clouds... Sheetrock...clouds. My mind drifts. I think of my father, his lopsided grin that was both welcoming and a sign that he was already three sheets to the wind. Compared to my mother's grim-faced expression as she returned late from her second, third, fourth job.

Did they love me? I want to think so, but even now, I recognize they were two adults very lost in their own problems. They loved me in their own ways, I think, which means, basically, when they managed to think of something outside of themselves.

Yet another trait I inherited.

"I'm in," Daryl says. "Now what?"

Which is a truly excellent question.

CHAPTER 36

WE DON'T KNOW ANY NAMES of extended family members?" I confirm with Daryl.

"Got nothing."

"Can you search email by date?"

"Yeah." He positions his hands above the keyboard, eyeing me expectantly.

"Date Kabul fell. The second time."

"August fifteenth, 2021," he rattles off immediately.

"Are you a closet genius, Daryl?"

"Nah. I read. I remember things."

"Bet you killed it in high school."

"You're assuming I was sober."

"Hey, drunk as a skunk was my strategy!"

"And now," he observes sagely, "here we are."

"Here we are," I agree, and that thought lightens my mood, because if anything, it proves two kids can do everything wrong, and yet by some miracle still end up okay in the end. Or at least good enough.

I rub my temples.

"Okay," Daryl calls out. "Whole stream of messages from that time period. Lots of them."

"We're looking for something personal," I advise. "Contact from a family member or friend still over in Kabul."

"What is it you're hoping to find?"

"A name. Aliah's cousin's son. Shot to death by the Taliban, body left in the street as a warning to others. I want to know his name."

"Why?"

"So I can learn from my mistakes," I inform him seriously. "Because I knew from the beginning there was more to Aliah's interest than met the eye, but I didn't push hard enough. I didn't ask the right questions, mostly because I didn't figure out what that line of interrogation should be until *after* she was taken. Not gonna lie, Daryl. I hate it when I'm dumb."

Daryl grunts.

I'm concussed enough to ask yet another question I've been dying to know: "So how long have you been in love with Roberta?"

No longer a grunt but a growl.

"Have you met her husband? Is he a decent fellow?"

Heartfelt sigh.

"You're never going to say anything, are you? They're good together, you don't want to rock the boat, even if you and Roberta could be great together?"

Deeper sigh.

"I'm sorry," I tell him honestly, then resume watching cloud patterns in the ceiling.

"Got something," he says at last. "Email dated a week later. From maybe a family member? 'Heart is very heavy. Sad, terrible, heartbreaking news: Kabul has fallen. Taliban has taken over. They are safe for now, but Jamil was shot and killed.'"

"Fuck me, I *knew* it!"

Daryl gazes down at me on the floor, arching a single brow in question.

"Would you like to know Zahra's middle name? Jamila. As in daughter of Jamil. What are the odds?"

Daryl's brow furrows. "I don't..."

"From the very beginning, Aliah was too interested in Sabera. Come on, they'd only known each other for a matter of weeks. For that matter, Sabera is merely one of how many female refugees Aliah's helped over the years? Why the passionate advocacy on Sabera's behalf? Why the immediate dislike of Isaad, whom even the neighbor, Nageenah, didn't think was that bad? When Sabera was hospitalized after her nervous breakdown, Jamil was the name she kept repeating. A great love that ended tragically."

"Sabera had a nervous breakdown?"

"First few weeks she was here."

"Seriously?"

"We're getting somewhere, Daryl. These cases, they're almost always about secrets, generally held by the people we thought we knew the best and could trust the most. Okay, so Aliah is related to Jamil. Now we need to learn everything else she decided not to tell us. Can you search her email for Jamil's name? Were they in direct contact?"

Daryl goes to work. I resume admiring swirling patterns.

"Umm, got something. From a university address—"

"I *knew* it!"

Daryl doesn't bother asking. "Messages go back a coupla

years. Intermittent at first, then a whole bunch leading up to August 2021."

I wait, while he skims through.

"Jamil is the son of her cousin?" he asks.

"I would assume so."

"That would make him a second cousin. Huh. These read more like notes from a favorite nephew. Hmm...first emails are pretty routine. Lots of exchanging of well wishes and give regards to. But then, going into 2020—Jamil's asking dating advice. 'Met someone special, brilliant, amazing. A fellow student, you'd like her so much, Auntie...'" Daryl skims again. "Now we're January 2021, US is starting to draw down troops...He's worried. Wait!"

Daryl stops short. "He's heartbroken! Broke up with dream girl. He discovered something...She was using him? Nothing was as it seemed..."

"Dream girl got a name yet?"

"Nope. Very few names. Maybe worried about being monitored?"

I have no idea.

Daryl returns to clicking, reading, clicking. "Dream girl is back!"

"But of course," I mutter.

"Realized she had her reasons, they're on the same side after all—"

"What side?"

"Sounds like revolution. Existing government too corrupt, concerns about stability once US military presence is gone—"

"No shit."

"Need more dramatic progress..." Daryl clicks away. Then: "Fuck me."

"What?" I sit up too fast, head promptly spinning. But the darkness of his tone...

Another moment as Daryl peers at the screen, eyes scanning. "Sabera! Jamil identifies his sweetheart as Sabera, but with no last name. And he's attached a photo!"

He turns the monitor. An image appears, a headshot of a shy young woman wearing a dark blue hijab. Sabera Ahmadi smiling into her lover's camera lens. There's something about her look that makes both Daryl and me catch our breath. Is there anything more innocent than young love? Is there anything more haunting?

"Why include a photo now?" I ask, though I already fear the answer.

"He's worried about a spy in their midst, danger mounts..." Daryl's voice fades out as he glances over at me. "Essentially, Jamil is writing, should the worst happen to him..."

"Such as being killed?"

"He wants Aliah to find Sabera. Get her to the States. It's of the utmost importance..." Daryl resumes reading. "The Taliban can't get their hands on her. Her family is *not* to be trusted—"

"Wait, her family?"

"That's what it says. 'Please, Auntie, do whatever it takes to keep Sabera safe.'"

Daryl stops reading. He moves to the next email, except there isn't one. That's it. A last note from a young man who clearly hadn't exaggerated the risk to himself and others. I glance at the date, do the math. Six days after writing this...

Jamil is dead. And his pregnant girlfriend—did Jamil know? There's no mention in his email to Aliah, but there are clearly plenty of details he's omitting. Maybe that's why he wanted Sabera to be protected from the Taliban. And yet I already think he's referencing something more professional than personal. Something relevant to them both being on the same side of the revolution.

Her encryption skills, gifts with codes? Or languages, or memory? A key that has no lock.

And one—Jamil, Isaad, and now Aliah?—found worth dying for?

I have Sanders Kurtz's email address. "Forward everything to him," I instruct Daryl.

Then, as his fingers clack away on the keyboard:

"Daryl, what do you think they're doing to her right now?"

He doesn't have to ask to know I'm talking about Aliah. Gracious, determined, sparkly-eyed Aliah.

Daryl sighs heavily, forwards more of Aliah's emails.

"There's one thing I still don't understand," he begins.

"One thing? I got dozens."

"Didn't you say—and Aliah agree—that refugee placement is random? So what are the odds that Sabera and her family ended up here in Tucson, basically on Aliah's doorstep? Sounds too good to be true."

"Placement is *supposed* to be random," I consider out loud. Then: "Didn't Detective Marc mention Isaad's call log included a bunch of DC numbers? And Aliah emphasized that while the Ahmadis were new to Tucson, in fact they'd already been in the US for nearly a year?"

Daryl peers down at me. "You think they have some sort of connection?"

"Honestly, I'm beginning to think they have all sorts of connections. Certainly plenty of people seem to know about Sabera and have a vested interest in her future."

"Who would have that kind of clout?" Daryl presses.

"Excellent question." Though I already have one, make that two, prospects in mind. My head is pounding harder, however, and there's little to be done given the late hour in the eastern time zone. Here, on the other hand:

"It's almost seven P.M.," I state.

"Ballroom studio meet-and-greet," Daryl agrees.

"Maybe we'll get lucky."

I appreciate our optimism.

Just then the office door drifts open, and the barrel of a gun appears.

CHAPTER 37

*H*ABIB TAKES TO FOLLOWING ME *everywhere. I see him when I exit the showers, when I walk from our shack to the medical clinic. Sometimes he looks perfectly groomed and composed, like he could be sitting at my parents' table. Other times he is a broken, bloody mess. Always, he is smirking. I will get you, he tells me with his eyes. I will have my revenge.*

Initially, I hunch my shoulders and scurry by. Don't look at the shadow that isn't there. But over time, I start hissing at him angrily, which then leads to curt orders to stop it, and then, quite naturally, entire exchanges. About his greedy, treacherous father. About how I was totally right to do what I did and they didn't deserve an ounce of that gold.

And then... Almost conversationally, look at us, Habib. Oh, did you ever imagine this would become our lives? From a grand home and full table to this, begging day after day for a bottle of water, a scrap of meat? If the rest of our family could see us now...

Did your family always hate my mother? I want to know. Was it because they thought she was too good for them, with her crisp British accent and chic Western clothes? Because my father knew she was too good for him; it's what he loved most about her.

And what was it my brother was doing those last few months? Did you ever follow him, Habib? Pry him with questions? I should've pushed harder, I confess, paid more attention. I regret that now. I regret so many things.

Do you know where he is, Habib?

But ghost Habib isn't much for talking. Ironic given living Habib rarely shut up.

One night, walking home from the clinic, I catch a glimpse of my mother, disappearing between two makeshift tents. She turns, flashes a smile before vanishing from sight. I have to force myself not to chase after her. Maybe I have become a Parizan, a woman who talks to angels. Or maybe I've been overinfluenced by my mother's love of ghost stories, especially involving Wadi Al-Salam, where the restless spirits of six million souls—kings, prophets, peasants— roam the tightly packed cemetery, spooking visitors and playing childish pranks. She loved to warn us of ghouls, blame mischievous jinn. A pot not left in its usual space—the jinn did it. The smell of tobacco lingering in the hall—oh, your grandfather's ghost is restless tonight.

She would regale my brother and me with stories of haunted houses and hungry demons till my father begged her to stop for the sake of his children sleeping through the night. But Farshid and I always returned for more. What youngster isn't secretly fascinated by death?

And so I talk to my dead cousin Habib, while waving at my beautiful mother's spirit and gazing upon my beloved Jamil's shimmering form.

So many mornings I wake to discover him lingering next to you, Zahra. Sitting cross-legged on the floor as he admires your slumbering form. Stroking your cheek while you cry. Beaming with pride the day you take your first step.

Like Habib, some days he's as smartly garbed as the first time I saw him, walking across the university lawn. Other times, his brains leak out of the hole in his skull. The first time that happened, I screamed hysterically, and you burst into tears. Which led to murmured conversations between Isaad and Dr. Richard, then more pills poured down my throat. I quickly learn to honor each of Jamil's forms. Shrieking in panic, I learn, gets me heavily medicated.

Talking to shadows, on the other hand…

"Look at her, Jamil. Our little girl is growing up!"

You remain a child of silence, Zahra. But I swear each time you peer in Jamil's direction, you smile.

Since the death of sweet young Omid, our little shack family has fallen apart. Rafiq has become grim from the loss of his beloved son, as well as the continued burden of ensuring the rest of his family's survival. Malalai gazes upon you, Zahra, with such longing it hurts. Who lives and who dies in this place? How are we to know? How can we possibly protect the ones we love?

Isaad is sweet and patient with you, Zahra. And yet as I chat about childhood days with Habib, or delight in your progress with Jamil, he grows positively thunderous.

"You must stop this insanity!"

"Shadows aren't real!"

"Good God, woman, are you trying to drive me crazy, too?"

I shake my head as he doles out more meds, then discreetly spit out each pill behind his back. It's not his fault he can't see what isn't there.

Dr. Richard eyes me with concern, but then he has many concerns, most of them much more pressing than my idle prattling. I ask him about the kind nurse who tended to me while I was sick. The one who claimed she overheard me talking with Habib.

He has no idea who I'm talking about, which is strange given our clinic's tiny staff.

"Maybe she was a ghost, too," I muse thoughtfully. "Oh, the number of souls who've died in this place. Thank goodness I can't see them all. Such a thing would surely drive a person mad."

"Sabera," he begins. "How are you sleeping at night? Eating, drinking? You know it's important to keep up your strength for Zahra's sake."

"Do you know how I know they're real?" I ask him seriously.

He slowly shakes his head.

"My brother, Farshid, is not among them. I see my cousin, my mother, my beloved."

Dr. Richard's eyes widen slightly.

"But never Farshid. Which proves what I should've known from the beginning—Farshid still lives."

"What did you think had happened to your brother?"

"He was shot. I saw his body, collapsed on the street outside our home, his face painted in blood. I took his gun from him. He never moved."

Dr. Richard shudders slightly.

"My father was not so lucky. Those men used machetes. My father was a literature professor. Did I ever tell you that? He liked to wear sweater vests and debate poetry. I could see his teeth through the gashes in his face. His left ear, totally gone. The tip of his nose...what kind of men cut off someone's nose?"

"Sabera—"

"Head wounds bleed. I didn't know it then, but I've seen

it working here. Meaning maybe Farshid wasn't as grievously wounded as I believed. He had been knocked unconscious, left for dead, but wasn't actually killed. It's possible."

Dr. Richard doesn't answer.

"You don't have to believe me," I allow at last. "I know Isaad doesn't. Just tell me: if Farshid didn't die that day, if by some miracle my brother lived, what would've happened to him?"

Dr. Richard pauses, seems to genuinely consider my question. We're outside, locking up the clinic for the evening. Even this time of night, the camp teems with activity. Though now most of it's furtive, and the low, muffled noises carry dark tones of warning—whimpers here, groans there, an occasional sharp scream.

I peer into the dimly lit space, hazy with smoke from campfires. I'm looking for my mother, who has a tendency to stay tucked at the edges of my vision. I haven't spied her for days. Do ghosts take vacations? Have other places to be, other souls to haunt? Or do they simply grow tired of walking among the living, roaming an endless buffet from which they can never eat?

I don't want to remain here one minute more as a living person; I certainly wouldn't choose this place to haunt once I'm dead.

"Your brother would've been taken to a hospital," Dr. Richard replies at last. "Upon recovery, he'd try to make it to the border, like you did. Meaning it's possible he's at another camp. You could post his name on the bulletin board out front. Maybe someone has news of him."

"And if he couldn't make it to the border? A young man already attacked by the Taliban once and identified as an enemy of the state?"

"Go underground? Hide out with other members of your family, or friends?"

I like this idea, the fantasy of it, but I can already see Jamil, standing behind Dr. Richard, shaking his head. In the corner of the room, Habib smirks. Yes, his expression tells me. Believe in fairy tales. I will enjoy watching your eventual disillusionment break you.

I understand the truth of that sentiment. "The Taliban don't kill everyone immediately," *I state. For having worked in the clinic for nearly a year, I haven't just seen things, I've heard things as well.*

A slight hesitation. Dr. Richard shakes his head.

"I've caught stories of torture camps," *I continue.* "Caves where they chain up men, women, and children for hours, days, months. Farshid could be someplace like that."

"If so, then surely you understand, Sabera—"

"He would find a way to live! Trust me. If there was someone who could survive, it would be Farshid! Is there a way to identify these camps? Learn where they are, get a list of prisoners?"

"I doubt the Taliban are that forthcoming—"

"Of course not! But they don't have to give out the information for it to be known. Satellite footage, drone activities, glowing red silhouettes captured on infrared."

"How do you know—"

"Governments are always watching. And spying and selling and wheeling and dealing." *My voice picks up. I don't mean to grow so angry, but the emotion, like so many these days, washes over me in a giant wave.* "We are nothing but pawns to them—you, me, everyone in this rodent-infested hell! What's that saying—the boys throw rocks in jest but the frog dies in earnest? They are the children; we are the frogs. Throughout all of human history. Again and again and again."

I feel a brush against my cheek. Jamil trying to sooth. Or maybe it is my mother, offering a rare moment of comfort.

I'm pacing. Outside this impossibly understaffed, under-resourced clinic, where sweet, innocent Omid died and I killed my own blood relative, and now I can feel Habib starting to stir, pushing away from the wall in genuine interest, preparing to enjoy the show.

"Why?" I demand to know. From Dr. Richard, from my encircling ghosts, from the universe in general. "Why, why, why!"

"Sabera." Dr. Richard touches my arm. "Take a deep breath; you need to breathe..."

"It's been over a year. My country, gone. My family, gone! And for what? Can you tell me? For what?"

I'm panting. Up is down, down is up. I don't know...I don't understand...

Isaad has appeared. He stands next to Dr. Richard as they confer in low tones. There will be more meds. There are always more meds.

The Prozac protocol. I have watched it play out at the clinic countless times. From raging nightmares to vacant stares to trembling anxiety, have a Prozac. And another and another. Take three, they're small.

I start to giggle, because they're not really that tiny, and I have a hard time swallowing them. Jamil strokes my cheek again as two white pills appear in the palm of my hand. Isaad hands me a bottle of water. I know the drill by now.

Toss it back, swallow it down.

Prepare for the numbness that takes nothing away, just stifles it under a too-heavy blanket.

"She needs real treatment," Dr. Richard is muttering. "I'm sorry, but this is all I got."

"We must get out of here."

"You and eight thousand other people."

"She's special." Isaad jabs a finger in my direction. "You can't tell me you haven't noticed."

A pause.

"How many languages does she speak?" Dr. Richard asks.

Habib shakes his head. He's returned to looking like a broken, bloody doll, while Jamil stands beside him, leaking gray matter onto the ground.

"Countless," Isaad states. "Or perhaps, more accurately, endless."

"I've seen her..." Dr. Richard shakes his head. "People come in. None of us know where they're from, what language or dialect they're speaking. Your wife, she listens. Sometimes for minutes, sometimes for what seems like hours. Then, just like that, she utters their mother tongue back to them. The look they get on their face, when they realize that finally, someone can understand them, give them voice. It's nothing short of miraculous."

"We must get out of here," Isaad repeats.

Silence. Habib dances a strange little jig that ends with his broken arm locked at an awkward angle till brain-splattered Jamil reaches over and snaps it back in place. I applaud their efforts, sway in a circle.

Farshid, possibly still alive.

Farshid, having been tortured, still being tortured, for an entire year.

Are there other frogs in the caves? I see dripping wet tunnels, lined with helpless green amphibians.

"I...I might have a possibility," Dr. Richard says abruptly.

"Anything!"

"I have some military contacts. I recently learned they're active in an organization that helps get former interpreters out of

Afghanistan and Iraq. I could reach out, see if there's any favors they might be able to call in."

"But we didn't assist—"

"Let's just say I might be able to call in a single favor."

"Praise be to Allah." Isaad clutches Dr. Richard's hand in gratitude.

"It's just a possibility—"

"It will work. I know it will. Because it must!" Isaad glows with his newfound conviction.

Habib scowls sourly.

And Jamil smiles softly.

Then the Prozac hits, and I sink into a sea of nothingness, where only my hope for the future remains, a flicker of light dancing behind my closed eyelids.

Farshid, my brother, still alive.

Farshid, my brother, trapped in the dark.

Farshid, my brother, I am coming for you.

Miraculously, Dr. Richard manages to arrange for our transfer a few months later—a refugee center in Abu Dhabi, with better conditions and more resources. Upon hearing the news, Malalai weeps tears of joy and sorrow, while Rafiq does his best to appear happy, then twists away to gnash his teeth. They have yet to be granted refugee status, and as month turns into month ...

Did they ever make it out? Or one day, were they unceremoniously sent back to Afghanistan, where they and their three children would be ground to dust beneath the Taliban's relentless heels?

Is it possible poor Omid was the lucky one, after all?

Abu Dhabi offers access to real medical services, versus a two-room shack staffed by mostly volunteers. The doctors and nurses cluck at my rudimentary diagnosis and one-note pharmaceutical regimen. They have questions about my ghosts, which they refer to as visual and auditory hallucinations. I don't bother to correct them. Postpartum depression with psychosis, they murmur, as they start adding meds here, taking away there.

With access to adequate sustenance, you start to sprout up, Zahra. Still a silent, serious-eyed toddler, but now one who motors about on increasingly steady legs. Your face fills out. Your gaze begins to brighten.

Isaad learns to sleep at night, while returning to math tutoring during the day.

And I...I stop talking to shadows and weeping over minor incidents I can't explain.

Next up, we're on a plane heading to the United States. Some place called Texas, where we spend months answering questions, getting shots, learning "the ropes" of American life.

Once a week I speak to an eagle-eyed psych doctor who asks me even more questions, and seems to know every time I dissemble. She drills me on my ghosts, sleep patterns, lack of concentration, and constant irritability. She updates my diagnosis to major depressive disorder, recurrent, with psychotic features, and attempts to teach me things like reality testing. The problem, she informs me, is that I'm too smart. My genius doesn't make me crazy, but it drives much more complex illusions—Habib, Jamil, my conviction my brother, Farshid, is still alive—while enabling me to rationalize the visions.

I nod, and she smiles indulgently. We both know I don't believe in her truths any more than she believes in mine.

After those appointments come endless interviews with many military types, plus a linguistics professor. This agitates Isaad, but the testing isn't anything I haven't handled before.

Number of languages I speak? Where did I learn, how did I learn?

I fall back upon my mother's instructions. I offer vague details that sound like I'm cooperating while sharing nothing. The psych doc, who observes from the sidelines, makes notes on a clipboard, while suppressing more smiles.

She knows that I'm holding back, but she never says a word. We are two brilliant female minds, carefully navigating the limited thinking of the male powers-that-be chirping around us.

More adjustments to my care. Better night's sleep as they exchange the Prozac for Lexapro, fewer nightmares with the addition of the Haldol.

We all three begin to relax: Isaad, you, me. As my entourage of dearly departed souls slowly fades away.

Isaad declares me "fully recovered."

I don't bother to correct him. Personally, I believe the spirits of the dead simply aren't as strong in America, where I suspect sensitive Jamil is too overwhelmed and arrogant Habib too intimidated.

But trust me when I say this, my beautiful Zahra. My mother had it right in the beginning:

Ghosts do exist.

They're just not always who we expect them to be.

CHAPTER 38

"WHO ARE YOU?" THE BRUNETTE demands to know. A striking older woman, she's dressed in head-to-toe black and speaks with a crisp British accent. I blink at her in open confusion. What just happened to her pistol? Because I swear she entered at gunpoint, except now...now...

I glance at Daryl, whose jaw has dropped. He appears stunned, if not completely mesmerized. What is it about gorgeous women that make men so stupid?

"You're not Aliah Gulbaz," the woman states.

"Neither are you, which is interesting, given you just walked into her apartment."

She gives me a charming smile that lets me know I haven't fooled her for a second. "I'm a friend."

"Really? What kind of friend enters another friend's apartment heavily armed?"

"One who notices two strangers being where two strangers shouldn't be. And this? By American standards, I hardly think this even counts as a weapon." A flick of her wrist and the snub-nosed firearm reappears in the palm of her hand. Second flick and it vanishes. Up her silk sleeve? She treats us to a playful look, then stomps her right black stiletto, which causes a slender silver dagger to materialize. Second stomp, it retracts again. I'll admit I'm impressed, if not a little terrified.

Daryl finally joins the party, making a show of puffing out his broad chest. "Okay, *friend*, what's Aliah's favorite tea?"

Slight flare of the woman's nostrils. "Mint," she deduces.

"Snack?"

"Pistachios. Maybe pears. No, I'm going with pistachios again. I count at least four shells on the rug in the family room."

"All right, all right." I hold up a hand. This has gone on long enough. I turn to Daryl. "She knows who we are, just like we know who she is."

"We do?"

"British accent. Knows how to pick a lock almost as skillfully as you do. Has a penchant for concealed weapons." I turn toward the woman. "Sabera Ahmadi has been looking for you."

"And so, I understand, have you. Lilla. No last name necessary. At your service."

"Don't you mean MI6's service?" I ask dryly.

That smile again. "Another world, another life. Nice to finally meet you, Frankie Elkin. Daryl D. Daniels." She nods in his direction. "Now, shall we chat?"

WE TAKE A seat in Aliah's family room, because it seems the most logical gathering point. I want to know how she found us here.

"Followed you, of course."

"How long have you been watching?"

"Only for a few days."

"Few *days*?" Then as the implication of that sinks in: "Wait, did you see the men grab Aliah?"

"As a matter of fact—"

"But you didn't intervene?"

"I was too far away, poppet."

"I'm not your poppet—"

"I did give chase. Unfortunately, I'm new to these streets, and they, clearly, are not. I lost them at the third intersection. I managed to snap a few photos that might have value, however. I have others working on that now."

"I thought your spy days were another lifetime ago," I remark sullenly.

"Old habits die hard."

"Do you know where Aliah is?" Daryl again.

"No."

"Do you know what they want with her?" he presses.

"Same as everyone else, I'm guessing. They want Sabera Ahmadi. She is the key, after all."

"The key to what?" I ask, having had it with riddles by now.

"Apparently, to untold riches. Or at least that's what she told me, two weeks ago."

"I FOUND SABERA easily enough. It helps, of course, that I trained the woman who trained her."

"Her mother."

"Exactly. Spy craft 101—often the best place to hide is right under the enemy's nose. So I started with the resort where Sabera had been working." Lilla grants us a sparkling smile. Apparently, we were a little late on that one, but still get an A for effort. "Sabera had quite the story to tell. Discovering her mother's work, taking up the charge."

"Captain Kurtz said her mother's assignment was simply to socialize with the movers and shakers in Kabul, gathering intel on private relationships and personal finances along the way."

"The most interesting tidbits can be gleaned from the most innocuous of sources."

"Okay. But whatever secrets Maryam was passing along, that would've been at least ten years and an entire regime ago. How could any of her mother's duties still be relevant?"

"Excellent question. Maryam was working on something when she first became ill. She was following a trail of rumors. Government ministers buying up a string of mines."

"For illegal mining!" I feel like I finally know something.

But Lilla is already shaking her head. "The properties could've once held gems, minerals, rare earth elements. Except these were old worksites. Basically, already depleted."

"Why would they want exhausted mines?" Daryl asks.

"Indeed. These are men of wealth and access. Why purchase used-up properties? That was the question Maryam was investigating, but never got answered. She was diagnosed with breast cancer instead."

"You didn't offer to get her out?" I ask quietly. "Bring her to London for treatment, after all she'd done for your government?"

"I offered. But she considered Kabul her home. And she didn't want to leave her family. In the end, poppet, there are very few things we have control over. Maryam couldn't beat the illness killing her. She could, however, choose where she would spend her final days. And she was not the kind of woman you could sway once she made up her mind." Lilla's expression softens. "It was one of the many things I quite admired about her."

Daryl and I exchange troubled glances. So far, this conversation isn't helping us.

"You said Sabera decided to continue her mother's work," I prod, trying to get us back on track.

"Maryam kept extensive notes, including avenues she'd only recently begun to investigate. She encoded everything, but Sabera had no problem deducing the key."

"A magic square!" I attempt to skip ahead, only to once again miss the mark.

"I have no idea what that is. Maryam was a noted designer and fashionista. In particular, she had a great love for vintage dress patterns. Quite perfect, if you think about it—dimensions make for an excellent cipher, while what man would ever consider utilizing McCall's as an encryption key? Sabera figured out the system on her own. That, as much as anything, convinced me to take her seriously." Lilla pauses. Daryl and I nod dutifully.

"According to Sabera, her mother had hidden a series of coordinates, the latitude and longitude of the mines in question. But even before Sabera engaged the services of a fellow student, a geology major, to investigate the sites, Sabera had her doubts."

"A geology student?"

"Jamil helped her track down the first abandoned property. As suspected, the mine was exhausted of natural resources. Except it wasn't."

Jamil of Sabera's dreams. Jamil, whose name is forever incorporated into Zahra's. I recognize the sadness of that, young love that never stood a chance. Forget countries, culture, religion. In the end, we are all the same, wanting to love and be loved, and wanting to believe such sentiments can last forever.

If only for Zahra's sake it had.

"What do you mean the mine wasn't exhausted?" Daryl is asking.

"The tunnels were filled with bars of gold. You want to know what two decades of corruption, kickbacks, and bribery looks like? Apparently, an entire cavern filled to the brim with precious metals."

"Like the Nazis." Daryl sounds impressed.

Lilla merely shrugs. "No doubt, the powers-that-be knew their days of looting and pillaging were numbered. Moving physical resources out of a country, however, takes time. Hence the need for clandestine storage. What could be better than a series of abandoned mines? One savvy bureaucrat started selling the options, and every rich uncle, cousin, brother came clambering for their own unit. Lifestyle of the megawealthy and totally crooked. Which no doubt made them very pissed off about what happened next."

"Sabera's mother, then Sabera discovering their secret stash?" I ask.

Lilla smiles. "Oh, Sabera didn't just trace the bounty— she looted from the looters. With the assistance of a group of like-minded student revolutionaries. Upon discovering the ill-gotten gains, she guaranteed the ministers could never profit from their illegal activities. Including, I might add, stealing from her own uncles, who no doubt had been planning on bribing the Taliban regime, but suddenly found themselves high and dry instead."

"Sabera stole it all?" Daryl asks in awe.

"Indeed. Mines were emptied out, all coordinates were wiped clean from physical records, and, well…untold illegal fortunes seemingly disappeared overnight. Amazing how cranky that makes some people."

I blink my eyes. Beside me Daryl appears equally impressed.

"There was a minor wrinkle. American forces noticed some of the activity in a remote area. Inquiries were made. Fortunately, Sabera was working for US intelligence at the time. She managed to intercept the messages and muddle up the translation in order to buy time."

"That's what got her dismissed," I murmur. "We heard about that."

"Pity, but such things happen. And I can't blame her for wanting to keep her secret a secret. As someone who spent entirely too much time in Kabul, let me tell you, the walls' ears have ears and no story would make the rounds faster than one of discovering hidden stashes of untold wealth. Natural-born intelligence officer, that one. I would've recruited Sabera the moment her mother died, had I known."

"So Sabera's mother stumbles upon a system utilized by corrupt officials to store their ill-gotten gains. Sabera learns of it and takes it one step further—she thieves from the thieves. But how does that help her? She clearly doesn't have any money now."

"Kabul fell. More abruptly than anyone saw coming. Well, more quickly than the Americans saw coming. There were those of us in the intelligence community..." Lilla sniffs delicately.

"And the stashes of wealth?"

"Ostensibly, still there."

"In Afghanistan?"

"According to Sabera, yes. To make it more interesting, she and her partner in crime, Jamil, were the only ones who knew the entirety of the relocation, and Jamil died the day Kabul fell. Meaning Sabera, and Sabera alone, has that information now."

"She is the key," I murmur.

"Exactly. A walking and talking map for X marks the spot.

Except what is a young Afghan female going to do with loot that requires extraction in a Taliban-run country?"

I don't have to think about it: "Wheel and deal. Exchange what she can't use for something she wants even more."

"Brilliant!" This time Lilla does clap her hands. "Have you ever contemplated spy work?"

"No need. My current job is dangerous enough."

Lilla leans forward. Her expression has turned serious. "The one thing Sabera wants most in this world—her brother. She'd thought Farshid had died when the Taliban seized Kabul, but she now believes Farshid is being held in a torture camp somewhere inside of Afghanistan."

"A torture camp?" Daryl begins.

"The international community has known about them for decades," Lilla supplies briskly. "Including, I might add, that none of the prisoners last very long, certainly not four years."

Daryl and I gaze at her wide-eyed. Torture camps. Just when you thought a regime known for its horrific violence couldn't get any more horrific or violent . . .

"I did some research of my own, starting with Sabera herself," Lilla begins.

"Her medical records," I murmur. "You unearthed news of her hospitalization, mental health issues. You're the one who left the file for Captain Kurtz."

Lilla stills for a second, then another smile splits her face. She seems pleasantly surprised I connected the dots between the records and her handiwork.

"Pity, but Sabera and pregnancy don't exactly get along," she murmurs.

"You think this is all some kind of psychotic episode?"

"Possible. By the time I arrived in the States, it appeared Sabera had already left the apartment she shared with her family. When I tracked her down to the resort townhouse, however…" Lilla frowns. "My first thought—she looks so much like her mother. I'd seen photos, but still…Something about how she holds herself, the angle of her head. I hadn't expected the way it would hit me. I wanted to say yes to everything she asked, very silly in my line of work."

"Did she say why she was at the townhouse—what had made her go into hiding?"

"I'd assumed a spat with the hubby. Glowering old codger. Not really my concern. I was more focused on what Sabera had to say about her mother. That there's more to the string of abandoned mines than Sabera had first deduced. Something about her mother planting a code within a code. Sabera was willing to hand all of it over to me, including the current location of the plundered wealth, in return for rescuing her brother. Which, even she understood, might prove a smidge difficult for an international intelligence agency, the Taliban being, well, the Taliban and all."

"I see the issue," I agree, while Daryl nods beside me. "You agreed?"

"To bringing Farshid back from the dead? Why, poppet, thank you for having such faith in me. Trust me, nothing would make me happier than assisting Maryam's son. Realistically, however…" Lilla arches a brow. "Sabera, however, is definitely her mother's daughter. Just to sweeten the pot, she mentioned she believes the other still-secret mining locations involve large stashes of rare earth elements. Which, as you seem to know…"

"Every government in the world wants."

"Including my own. Not that Britain would be in position to harvest such materials given relations with the current regime.

On the other hand, ensuring the Taliban—and the Chinese, who are meddling everywhere!—do *not* have access to REEs would be considered quite valuable as well. According to Sabera, the trick to locating these massive sites of a massively important resource just happens to include Farshid. Only her brother knows how to unlock the code to the second half of her mother's riddle. Something about her mother always referring to them as—"

"Two halves of one whole," I fill in.

"Clever if you think about it." Lilla sits back, sighs heavily. "And pure Maryam. God, that woman was brilliant. The gears churning inside that one pillbox-hat-topped head…"

A thought occurs to me: "You said you tracked down Sabera once you arrived here. Does that mean you were following her as well? Do you know how she ended up in the warehouse district? Who killed the two Afghan men?"

Lilla sits up. "Dead men?"

"The ones who kidnapped her," I begin, while Daryl states, "The two Afghans bludgeoned to death with a hammer."

"Homicide by hammer? Ooh, I heard about that on the news. Wait, that had something to do with Sabera?" Lilla appears genuinely surprised.

"Sabera was caught on video near that scene. And afterward, we found a bloody scarf in the townhouse where she'd been hiding. It would seem she was somehow involved."

"Do you think she killed them?" Lilla sounds delighted.

"Do you think she killed them?" I try out.

"A former university student and current maid? I sincerely doubt it. Sabera's gift is with patterns, which makes her a brilliant linguist, mathematician, and encryption analyst. Natural-born double murderer, not so much so."

"What about her husband?" Daryl presses.

"A professor who specializes in math so esoteric most couldn't even recognize it as an equation? No."

"What do you think happened?" I venture. "You were 'looking into things' around this time."

"It's possible I'd returned to the townhouse a few times," Lilla allows. "If I had to guess, I'd ask the handsome fellow she kept meeting."

"Handsome fellow?"

"Yank. Middle-aged. Curly brown hair, beard. Rather scruffy, but all in all, I wouldn't kick him out of bed."

Daryl blinks, as if that's more of a description than he required.

"Does handsome fellow have a name?" I want to know.

"Not that I heard."

"Take any more photos that 'others' are now analyzing?"

"You sound like you don't trust me."

"I don't."

"And yet, I'm not the one with all the secrets. Look: I don't know what was going on between Sabera and Isaad. Why she moved out—"

"Isaad was killed. Tortured to death. Also warehouse district. His body was discovered just two days ago."

Lilla stills. Her gaze darts back and forth between Daryl and me. The shrewdness is back. Sabera's mother apparently isn't the only spy who tried to hide behind glamour. "Their daughter?" Lilla asks.

"You don't need to worry about Zahra," Daryl states gruffly.

"The danger is real," I emphasize. "Sabera may have mental health issues, but this threat is genuine. Just ask the two Afghans bludgeoned to death, or Isaad, who died with his hands burnt into blackened claws, or Aliah, who's been snatched from in front of her business. Whoever else is involved, they're playing for keeps."

Lilla doesn't speak right away. "If there's one thing I learned from Maryam," she drawls at last, "that family knows how to keep a secret. The entire family. Many, many secrets. Including..." She lifts her gaze until she's staring straight at us. "For kicks, I did look into Sabera's brother, Farshid. I couldn't find any record of him following August 2021. If you'd asked me, I would've said the reports were true and he died when Kabul fell. Except then I swear I saw him with my own eyes."

"You saw Sabera's brother, Farshid? Wait, what?"

"Just yesterday. When Aliah was abducted by those men. Someone who certainly looks a great deal like Farshid Shinwari, though in much rougher physical condition, was one of them." She shudders delicately. "Poor boy. If that's what the torture camps did to his body, God only knows what they've done to his mind."

CHAPTER 39

DUSK IS GATHERING AT THE edges of the city skyline by the time Daryl and I finally depart Aliah's apartment. Daryl had the forethought to text Roberta while we were talking to Lilla. Roberta made a heroic attempt to make it to the dance studio in case Sabera magically showed. Apparently, no such luck. Now Daryl is catching Roberta up on everything we learned from the British spy handler.

Which feels like both too much and not nearly enough information all at once.

Mostly, I have an itch between my shoulder blades. Lilla has been following us the past few days. Clearly Aliah's abductors have been watching as well. At least three men, one of them possibly Sabera's own brother.

What does that mean?

And where are they now?

I find myself staring compulsively at the view in the side mirror. Has that SUV been behind us the entire time? What about that nondescript white sedan or black pickup truck? I see danger everywhere, and the falling light and tinted windows aren't helping.

What's that saying? Just because you're paranoid doesn't mean they're not out to get you.

Daryl finally wraps up his call. He peers at me via the rearview mirror.

"Need anything?" he asks gruffly.

"New career."

"Your head?"

"Hurts like hell, but that might be more from the conversation we just had than the concussion I suffered."

"She talked a lot."

"And yet very little of it was useful."

"She talked a lot," Daryl repeats.

It takes me another second—blame the concussion—then I get it. What kind of career spy volunteers so much information? From Sabera's medical records to family legacy to this whole code within a code...In an intelligence officer's world, information is power. Why volunteer so much up front?

"Fuck."

Behind the steering wheel, Daryl nods in agreement.

"She's playing us."

Daryl nods. I swear again. Then: "But to what end? What do we know, what could we do, that would possibly have value to her?"

Except in this next instant, I get it. We might actually find Sabera Ahmadi. Personally, I feel Lilla's odds are higher, but I appreciate her optimism. And if we do find Sabera...

"She discredited her," I murmur. "The medical records. Sabera has a history of postpartum mental health episodes. And is now pregnant again, meaning God knows what. Maybe Lilla is trying to hedge her bets. If she can't reach some sort of agreement with Sabera to learn the location of the REEs, she needs to at least sow enough seeds of doubt so no one else is interested in what Sabera has to say. Though that doesn't explain her brother's possible return from the dead. Also if he's the one who kidnapped Aliah, what exactly are his intentions? Dear Lord, my head hurts! No spook double-talk necessary."

"Two halves of one whole," Daryl states.

"Yes, Sabera has alluded to that enough times, it must be real. The code, hidden gold, secret mines…" My voice lowers. "These are things worth killing for."

"Aliah," Daryl murmurs softly.

I sigh heavily in agreement, staring out the window at the darkening sky.

The white SUV behind us finally turns off. I breathe a little easier, till the truck behind it gains ground.

I don't have to say a word to Daryl for him to take a sudden left, then right, then left again. All vehicles disappear from our mirrors.

A few more defensive maneuvers and we're back on track. Unfollowed. Or so we hope.

I rub my temples. We can't continue on like this. And neither can Aliah.

I check a few things on my phone, sigh again.

"Daryl," I speak up at last. "I may have a plan, but I don't think you'll like it."

"Try me."

I walk him through it. I'm right, he doesn't like it.

But he also agrees we don't have any other choice.

THE COMPOUND IS ablaze with cheery lights when we finally pull through the gate. The outdoor torches light up the trunks of the soaring palms while bathing the barrel cacti and giant aloes in an amber glow.

I start taking inventory of everything I haven't paid attention to before—the number of decorative walkways around the giant mansion, the chest-high wrought-iron fence that extends out from the main house and wraps around the three freestanding bungalows as well as the pool. The sheer number of sliding glass doors and low-access windows…

A security fortress it is not, but maybe we can use that to our advantage.

We find Roberta, Genni, and Zahra gathered in the kitchen. Zahra is helping Genni frost animal-shaped cookies, while Roberta sits at the kitchen table amid a sea of graph paper. For a moment, she looks so reminiscent of the last time I saw Aliah, my heart catches in my chest. Please let us not be too late.

Roberta glances up excitedly at our entrance.

"I think I got it!" She holds up the grid sheet covered in scribbled numbers. "The moment Daryl mentioned Sabera's claim to know the location of hidden treasure, it got me thinking in term of coordinates. Check it out!"

She taps her notes. "Zahra drew three magic squares."

At the mention of her name, Zahra glances up. She flashes a shy smile at Daryl and me, then returns to studiously decorating the cookie in front of her. Which I now realize is shaped like an iguana. But of course.

Speaking of which, Petunia is staring at me pointedly from her perch in front of the glass sliders. I hastily cross to the refrigerator to grab her dinner.

"The top magic square," Roberta is explaining, "has the

largest numbers. I didn't notice that before—the two bottom squares all involve numbers smaller than twenty, while the top one goes higher. Made me wonder, why the difference? Factor in the repeated digits that make the square trivial, and those particular numbers written out in a row..."

Roberta beams. "Latitude and longitude. I'm certain of it. Afghanistan's latitude falls between thirty and thirty-eight degrees. Longitude sixty to nearly seventy-four. Separate the repeated digits in the top square and line them up in two rows of four units and ta-da—it's a GPS coordinate just outside of Kabul. I'm a genius!"

Color me impressed. I set Petunia's salad bowl down next to the sliders, as I don't want to miss the rest of the conversation. Petunia seems a little confused by this change in routine, but with a swish of her tail decides she can adapt.

From the kitchen island, Zahra giggles. She's clearly enraptured by the iguana, adding more blue and green candies to her heavily frosted cookie.

"Now, as for the lower two squares. Only four numbers repeat in each. I line them up and I get two thirty-something digits. Latitudes that fall within Afghan borders."

"But only latitude?" Daryl asks with a frown. In the next instant, he answers his own question. "Two halves of one whole. Ahh, got it."

Roberta nods emphatically. "I'm guessing the two bottom squares come from Sabera's mother. She taught Sabera the grids that provide the latitude of the two mineral sites she discovered. She gave Sabera's brother the grids—or some kind of other puzzle—that provides longtitude."

"But the top magic square provides both..." Like Daryl, it comes to me. "Because that's the code Sabera herself created, with the location of where she hid the looted gold. Okay, I get why Sabera would use a magic square as an encryption tool, but why would her mother, a fashion designer, utilize a math riddle?"

"For her daughter." Genni speaks up from the counter. "She needed her daughter to understand, and Sabera likes math, yes? She wanted to make sure Sabera got the message. Does the son like math, too?"

"No idea." I glance at Daryl and Roberta, realizing for the first time how little we know about Farshid, Sabera's brother and possibly Aliah's abductor. Which is a glaring oversight, given we're hoping to lure him through these front doors.

"Let's talk decoys," I begin.

Roberta's hand immediately thrusts into the air. "Dibs."

"Wait a minute," Daryl blusters, but Roberta's already dismissing his objection with a shake of her head.

"Gotta be me. One, Frankie is way too white to pass for..." Roberta cuts herself off, given Zahra's listening ears. "Whereas do you know how many times I've had people come up and chatter at me in some language I don't know? Just like I'm sure most Afghan refugees get addressed in Spanish. For some folks brown is brown."

"Can't be me," Genni concedes. "I'm a bit too...tall. While you"—she eyes Daryl's hulking form—"are entirely too male. Which leaves us with—"

"I am not too tall," Zahra speaks up. She regards us with her solemn gray eyes.

"You, my lovely, are too perfect to be anyone other than Zahra. And I think you are tall. Ginormous, in fact. A giant towering beast of a child with the best taste in cookies." Genni ends her spiel by popping a frosted bunny into Zahra's hand. Zahra obliging shoves it into her mouth, with a smear of hot pink icing across her lips.

"I'm not sure..." Daryl again.

"Yes you are. You just don't like it, that's different." Roberta is eyeing him sternly.

Genni and I quickly busy ourselves with random tasks, Daryl's discomfort too hard to take.

"Come on," Roberta murmurs softly. "We both know I can be selfish. And sometimes...maybe even cruel."

I grab the glass dish off the floor next to Petunia. Genni starts rinsing frosting bowls.

"But I never back down from a fight. You know that, Daryl. You know I got this."

"We're not even sure how many of them there are. Or how heavily armed, or well trained."

"Then I'm glad you have my back."

"I'll tell your brother."

"Then I'll have this conversation with him, as well. Still won't change anything."

"We don't even know if this will work. They might not be watching. They might not take the bait—" Daryl sounds increasingly desperate.

"They will. They have to. We're running out of time. Daryl, we got this. It's just a different kind of dance."

Daryl's shoulders come down. For a moment, he appears so crushed, so hopeless, I genuinely feel for the man. Despite Roberta's big words, what we're about to do is very dangerous.

Disguising Roberta as Sabera to lure known killers onto Bart's estate. Giving away our one safe location in order to ambush the abductors and demand they lead us to Aliah. Can you negotiate with men who think nothing of torturing someone to death? Can we possibly end up with Farshid himself and get him to tell us everything?

Can we save Sabera?

The last time I played for stakes this high, rain was coming down in sheets on a tropical island, gunfire had already erupted, and I'd just come face-to-face with a severed head. Before that night was through...

In the past, I've worried about my job's toll on me. I don't know how to compartmentalize; I don't have a trained detective's battle-hardened worldview. From the very beginning, I gravitated toward missing persons because I know I'm not cut out for murder and mayhem. Yet lately, too many of my cases have turned bloody, and I have the nightmares to prove it.

Now I'm forced to wonder if my job is not only a threat to me but also a danger for others. Who am I to decide who lives or dies in the hours to come? Because in my bones, I already know this to be true. We can plan, strategize, hope, dream, but given the body count thus far, this will end violently.

And here I am, pulling the strings.

A woman with no formal investigative training.

Who barely eked out a high school degree.

Who has spent most of her life drowning in a bottle.

Forget being self-destructive. Am I now actively damaging others, as any official law enforcement expert, including Detective Marc (let alone a certain sexy Boston investigator), would have claimed?

On the other hand, who else is there? A local Afghan woman has been missing for weeks. Her husband has been tortured to death, her child nearly kidnapped, and her closest friend abducted. The powers-that-be are already overworked and disengaged. Which leaves me and the other misfit toys—a dream team comprised of a recovering alcoholic, ex-con limo driver, ballroom dancing parole officer, and transgender cook.

Maybe it's a sad state of affairs that this is all who stands between Sabera and certain doom. Or maybe it speaks to the higher power of the universe that total strangers care that much.

I want to believe in the positive, but, mostly, as I look at the people around me, I wonder:

How many times can I cheat death?

And how many times can the people I befriend survive?

Because they haven't always. I carry that weight as well.

Genni starts packing up the cookie supplies. We have other preparations we need to make in the kitchen now.

As well as to the hallway, pool area, and heavily landscaped grounds. Even Petunia has a crucial role to play. And no, iguanas aren't bulletproof, adding to my sense of dread.

I have one last trick up my sleeve. Might be a long shot, but given the stakes, I'll take it.

And now...

Roberta pushes away from the table while Genni leads Zahra out of the kitchen.

We each know our roles.

A final quiet nod of acknowledgment to one another.

Then we start prepping for the night ahead.

Which for me, means a hushed phone call where I won't be overheard, and then a visit to the snake room.

CHAPTER 40

FOUR OF US PILE INTO Genni's vehicle, which turns out to be (naturally) a 1950s vintage Chevy truck in shades of soft white and mint green. Zahra is already cooing over the pretty pastel bench seat as Genni lifts her in. Roberta and I climb aboard more awkwardly, Roberta now sporting a dark blue scarf around her head, as well as a blousy white shirt and loose gray skirt. Given the ensemble came from Genni's closet, many safety pins are involved in keeping the wardrobe in place, but so far, so good.

We leave Daryl behind for the finishing touches. Again, we all have our assignments.

Genni's primary responsibility is Zahra. For the occasion, she has ditched her vintage costumes and sky-high heels. Instead, she's as demurely clad as I've ever seen her in sleek black trousers and a wraparound leopard-print top. There's an alertness to the way she moves, head on a swivel, feet poised for action.

I can see remnants of the street kid she used to be, constantly vigilant, never relaxing. I wonder how many rusty blades she's packing, and for Zahra's sake, I'm already grateful for each and every one.

Roberta has her disguise, Genni her ensemble. And I'm once again just me. I'm not a superhero and I know it.

Genni will drop Roberta and me off at the edge of the strip mall where Aliah's deli is located. We've chosen Genni and her truck because to the best of our knowledge, no one knows about her, making her the safest option for secreting us about.

She will depart with Zahra and head to a public place. We don't know where and we don't want to know. That way, should things go awry...

In what will hopefully be an excellent piece of theater, I will hastily escort a cowering and frightened Sabera-clad Roberta to the front of Aliah's deli, where Aliah's car is still parked. Our job is to look both rushed and terrified, while also taking enough time to attract notice of anyone who might be watching.

Next step, commandeer the car and drive to the warehouse district, where we know our evildoers like to operate.

More theater. Drive about here and there. Not too fast, not too slow, always looking, looking, looking, as if we actually know what we're doing and at any time might discover Farshid and company's lair.

With any luck, we will officially grab their attention. The moment we pick up the hint of a tail...

Rush back to the estate, bringing our shadow with us.

Where we will transition from warm-up act to the main event.

Is this plan terribly brilliant? No.

Can it totally, absolutely fail? Yep.

And yet... The police have made no progress locating Aliah or Sabera. We've been equally unsuccessful. Best results thus far have been others finding us, from Captain Kurtz to Lilla No Last Name.

At a certain point, might as well play to our strengths.

If we can pull the kidnappers away from Aliah, get even one of them to take the bait and follow us back to the estate where we're all set up to turn the tables and ambush them…We need a win and there's not much time left on the clock.

Genni gets us to the brightly lit strip mall. Nine P.M., still plenty of people strolling about, loading up groceries, grabbing takeout. So many ordinary people, going through just another day in the life.

The one thing I've never been able to do, no matter how hard I've tried.

Genni pulls over at the edge of the main parking lot. Zahra gives us all a questioning look. Roberta and I paste on our brightest smiles.

All good. Nothing to see here.

We slide out. They continue on.

And the show begins.

ROBERTA IS PARTICULARLY excellent as a nervous nelly. She cowers beside me, tucking beneath my left arm as if there's no way she could continue without my steadfast strength. I pull myself taller, champion of the downtrodden, as I scan the horizon and scowl fiercely at anyone who dares draw too close.

We traverse the entire length of the massive grocery. Pass a nutrition center, Mexican restaurant, mattress center, nail salon.

Turn the corner.

The storefronts are smaller here, the parking spaces less illuminated.

I can just make out Aliah's silver compact, parked where she left it two days ago. I feel a pang, fight it.

We're going to make this plan work. We're going to save Aliah. We're going to locate Sabera.

Failure is not an option.

Which bolsters my spirit right until the moment we slide into the front of Aliah's car. I start the engine and the point of a blade digs into the back of my neck.

Followed by a low, fierce voice growling from behind me: "What have you done with my daughter!"

Sabera Ahmadi materializes in the back seat. She definitely appears worse for the wear.

And based on expression alone, not that terribly sane.

CHAPTER 41

WHEN WE FIRST LAND IN *this city called Tucson, Isaad and I are struck by the towering mountains ringing the horizon. For one moment, it almost looks like home.*

Then, we disembark into a furnace blast of heat, unlike anything we've known. We stagger, take a second step, stagger again.

Your arms, Zahra, are wrapped tight around my neck. I use your weight to center me, focus my footsteps, which are shaky and uncertain. I don't want to be here. I don't know why, but ever since the caseworker showed up yesterday with our relocation instructions...

My skin feels too tight, my limbs twitchy, my mind agitated. I feel like there's something extremely important looming just beyond my grasp. I should know... What should I know?

Isaad, on the other hand, is in full swagger. He practically explodes out of the plane's hatch and vaults down the stairs. He's spent the entire night Googling everything there is to know about Tucson. Job opportunities, best neighborhoods for schools, the existing Afghan community. He's already decided we will do this, and go there, and try that.

The faint echo of musical chords chiming in my ears. A song I might have heard once, but it's been a long time now.

An older woman appears before us. A fellow Afghan, impeccably groomed with her stylishly short black hair, dark eyes, and beckoning smile.

"Manda Nabashin, Bakhair Amadin," she welcomes us. She introduces herself as Aliah. She's a volunteer, works with resettling families, has so many recommendations for us. Next to her stands a pretty blonde, America personified, with her freckled face and earnest gaze. She has secured an apartment for us, will take us to our new home.

Isaad immediately bombards her with questions about the school district and professional opportunities.

Aliah continues to stare at me and you, Zahra, with such quiet intensity, I wonder who she's lost.

A fresh prickle across my scalp. A shiver running up my spine.

The musical chords sounding louder. Beckoning. Come play with us, they whisper in my ear.

It comes to me. Patterns. The warp and weave of the world. A whirlwind of numbers, a cacophony of words. The shimmer of chaos right before I pluck apart the tumbling bits and string them together in an order of my own making.

It's been so long since I've peered into the abyss and seen the divine. Not since my days of Haldol and antidepressants.

I try to weave the pieces together now. A stranger's look of yearning as she gazes upon me for the first time. The feel of the searing desert air, baking my unprotected face. The fierce clutch of my child's arms, tight around my neck. Threads, tangling and untangling, knitting together, falling apart.

And for one moment…

The click eludes me. The universe resumes its random spinning, moving too fast for my medicated mind to follow.

"She's beautiful," the woman, Aliah, speaks at last. "How old?"

"Four," I manage.

The woman flashes another smile. "I think you will be very happy here."

Isaad and the chattering housing coordinator start moving forward while Aliah and I fall in step behind.

And you, Zahra, my child of silence, murmur a single word against the crook of my neck. You have intuited what my mind couldn't follow, like recognizing like.

You whisper, "Auntie."

And I know in that moment you are right.

At the first sight of our living quarters, Isaad is horrified. I'm indifferent. I drift through the dingy rooms capped with water-stained ceilings while you patter along beside me, holding my hand. I don't care where we stay. Mostly, I inspect each corner for signs of Habib's sulking spirit or Jamil's gentle presence. I inhale in the hallway, sniff the kitchen, hoping to catch a whiff of my mother's perfume.

I want my ghosts to be happy. Otherwise, I will have nothing of home left.

A cockroach scurries down a wall. Ashley apologizes profusely. Isaad comments the ones in Abu Dhabi were bigger. You giggle.

Finally, Aliah leads us to the modest sitting area, where she pours cups of fragrant saffron tea and sets out dishes filled with sweets, nuts, and fruit, welcoming us to our new home. Traditional Afghan hospitality. It has been so long...I feel my eyes begin to sting, while across from me, Isaad is clearly moved.

"Auntie," you whisper again.

I don't know that Aliah hears you, but she once more has that look on her face.

Isaad drills Ashley on rental contracts and how to contact the landlord and who is responsible for the grounds and, oh, yes, we will need a better air conditioner. I flip through a binder Aliah has prepared with information on local halal grocery stores, mosques, and medical centers, not to mention bus lines, language classes, community events.

I pause long enough for you to scan each and every page. I know your gift for memory already. Isaad suspects. He seems delighted rather than appalled, which is promising. As for your other talent, seeing what others cannot see, knowing what others cannot know...

Neither you nor I will ever speak of such things with him. It's our secret, such as the one I had with my mother. As she protected mine, so I will protect yours.

Then it is time for both women to depart.

The apartment immediately feels completely alien. Not a home, just a new and differently designed box. We have been in so many the past four years.

"We will make this work," Isaad declares boldly, his immense size already dominating the space.

I don't bother to correct him, as Habib has finally appeared, spinning his favorite knife upon his fingertip, while eyeing us both with his too-knowing gaze and triumphant grin.

I feel it again. A shimmer in the air, a clang of discordant notes. A pattern I should be able to recognize.

I'm left with a fresh shiver down my spine, while you gaze at me with open concern.

I do my best to summon a smile.

But I already think Tucson will prove a dangerous choice.

Isaad buys a car to deliver takeout food to people. I get a job cleaning rooms at a beautiful resort. Many of the other women are from Afghanistan. During breaks, their cheerful chatter in Dari and Pashto washes over me like a comforting stream. If I close my eyes and just listen, for a minute or two, I can believe I'm home.

I do my best to make friends, but I have journeyed too far from my country and myself, I can't remember how to act or what to say. Mostly, I sit in silence.

My twitchy feeling from our initial arrival refuses to relent. I have a constant itch between my shoulder blades, often whirling around for no reason. The other women begin to whisper, especially when Habib and Jamil start following me to work and I have to remind them again and again not to bleed on the carpet.

I come home exhausted, but fall asleep, only to suffer terrible nightmares.

I dream of blood and death and bullets. Of my father's mutilated face, of young Omid's blue-tinged lips. Of strangers whose names I recorded on a whiteboard only to watch them die hours later.

I take to once again watching you sleep, Zahra, holding vigil because I can feel the threat growing closer, a near constant pressure against the base of my skull.

When you wake up, we work on re-creating the matrices. Over and over. You have the memory; it's just a matter of teaching you a steady hand. It's very important you get them right. I don't have much time left.

One day, I catch Isaad counting out pills, checking to see if I'm still taking my Haldol. In his mind, my hallucinations have returned. I don't have the heart to tell him Habib, Jamil, my mother are more than mere figments of my imagination. They are my burden to bear as well as my only true comfort; I trust their senses better than my own.

He flushes and returns the bottle before getting to my stash of antidepressants. It's just as well. So many nights I've stared at the line of orange bottles and yearned to just open my mouth and pour, pour, pour.

Anything to dam the river of bloody dreams pouring through my sleep.

I hold myself tighter, determined to cling to my sanity through sheer force of will. I learn mass transit and strip malls and overly cold grocery stores with their prepackaged foods. I practice new social customs and American habits. I do not want to fail Isaad.

I don't want to fail you.

Then one day, riding home on the bus.

I see him. Right there in flesh and blood. My brother, Farshid, standing on the sidewalk. He's turned slightly away. But the hair, his profile, the set of his shoulders. He holds himself differently, too rigid, as if in terrible pain, and yet—

I clamber to my feet, shouting at the bus driver to stop.

Then as the other passengers start yelling at me to sit down, the man twists around. He finds my frozen form standing in the bus window. He stares straight at me.

Except it is not my brother, Farshid.

It's our cousin, Habib. The one I killed, thought I killed, tried to kill.

But now, very much alive.

And clearly coming to get me.

I don't remember starting to scream.

I mostly remember not being able to stop.

Once I got out of the hospital, it took several precious days more to get Isaad to believe me, to understand the full danger not just to me, but to you and him. We made the decision I should disappear, while Isaad takes the necessary steps to protect you. It only cost me one last secret, kept from the man I have grown to love. For if Isaad knew the other news the doctor had to tell me . . .

I think of my mother so often these days, and the terrible choices too many women are forced to make.

Isaad will keep you safe, Zahra. He was not the fire in my heart nor the husband of my choosing. And yet he has become my anchor, a pillar of strength even during moments of darkest despair.

My family awaits. I see them in my dreams. My mother and her fashionable ensembles. My father and his parting look as he heads out the door. My brother, teasing me as we race between dark green branches heavy with bright red fruit. Two halves of one whole.

We all belong to Allah. Into his graces we shall return again. There's no sorrow, just the comfort of his all-encompassing embrace.

I miss them more than I can say.

I love you more than I have words.

And now, my precious daughter, I will honor my mother one final time.

Chin up.

CHAPTER 42

"HABIB IS VERY CLEVER," SABERA is saying now. "He merely pretended to be a ghost so I would think that my family and I were safe. But no, he's been plotting all along. He will not rest till he has avenged himself and his family. He will do whatever it takes, regardless of the consequence. Just like Rafiq."

I glance over at Roberta to see if she's following any of this. She's lowered her headscarf to better hear Sabera's rasping voice. The woman is a mess, black eye, split lip, lacerated cheek. Her trembling hand, still clutching some kind of rusty steak knife, appears to have two broken fingers and one ripped-out fingernail. I feel ill just looking at such damage. I have no idea how she survived it.

We've almost convinced her we're the good guys. The fact we've been able to name drop everyone from Aliah to Nageenah to Captain Kurtz to spymaster Lilla is helping. We've also assured her that Zahra is safe, and we'll happily take her to her daughter, but first we need to rescue Aliah.

Which seems to be one development too many for Sabera's clearly stressed-out mind. Given the current conversation regarding ghosts who are not ghosts, I wonder about her mental state in general. How long has it been since she's taken her prescribed meds, because last I knew, suddenly quitting antidepressants let alone antipsychotics leads to very bad things.

Definitely, Sabera is highly agitated.

"Once you realized Habib was still alive, that's when you and Isaad made the plan for you to disappear?"

"I needed a place to hide. I should've been able to see it immediately, but the drugs... They dull my thinking. Eventually, I realized I could sneak into the vacant rooms and apartments at the resort where I work."

"So when you initially disappeared?"

"I never caught the bus. I backtracked to an empty unit instead."

"Did you tell your coworkers you were leaving Isaad?" I want to know.

"Divorce is shameful. I knew it would occupy their minds, distract them from revealing other details about me."

"What happened?" Roberta asks. "Because..." She gestures to Sabera's battered features.

"I was not careful enough." The words come out hoarsely. In the dim light, I can just make out a ring of bruises around her throat. "I kept looking for Habib, expecting Habib. I never saw Rafiq or his cousin till it was too late."

I've heard the name Rafiq before, as well as a reference to a cousin. It comes to me—Detective Marc, identifying the two dead men in the warehouse.

Roberta, on the other hand: "Who's Rafiq?"

"We shared a cabin with him and his family at the first refugee camp. His wife, Malalai, was very kind, helping us learn how to survive. And one of their sons, Omid, took a liking to Isaad, following him everywhere. Isaad taught him math. Can you imagine? One of the greatest mathematicians, famous for his arrogance, scratching basic sums in the dirt to occupy the camp children? He loved Omid, too." Her voice catches. Then, in a single breath:

"Omid died. Zahra was born. And Rafiq grew bitter that we had a child, while he and his wife lost theirs. We didn't know what happened to them. We transitioned to a different camp while they . . .

"They were never granted refugee status. Eventually, they were expelled back to Afghanistan, where, given they were Hazaras, the Taliban snatched them up. Rafiq told me his children died quickly. Malalai was not so lucky."

Sabera's gaze has taken on a distant, glassy look. Her tone is terrifyingly matter-of-fact. This is life. This is the world we live in. This is what can happen to any of us.

"But Rafiq got out alive? The Taliban let him go?" Roberta asks.

"He bartered for his freedom. Offered them untold riches, a cave filled with gold. He offered them to me."

Sabera returns her attention to us. "After the birth of my daughter, I was sick. Malalai tended me. I was too feverish to know. I thought she was an angel, sent to save me. I talked, said many things. I have no memory, but apparently I gave up not only my secrets but also my mother's. Malalai related these things to her husband. And eventually, he used this information to save his life. If they let him go, he would find the key and bring it to them."

"And they believed him?" I'm already skeptical.

"They might not have, except they had another prisoner at the time. A young male from a good family, also recently deported back to Afghanistan. My cousin Habib. He'd told them similar stories. They'd ignored him, but now with two men who seemed to know the same things about the same woman." Sabera shrugs. "A deal was struck."

Her gaze falls to her lap, where her right hand is still gripping the knife. She's no longer threatening us with the blade, nor does she let it go. Maybe at this point, being without a weapon no longer feels like an option.

"And Rafiq recruited his cousin for the cause? There are other men involved as well, yes? Including your brother, Farshid?" I ask gently, as that's the kidnapper Lilla identified.

Sabera shakes her head. "Farshid is dead."

"He's not here in Tucson?"

"No, I thought he was alive, wanted to believe he survived the fall of Kabul, especially as his spirit has never found me. But, no, fate was not that kind. The males in my family all look very similar, including my brother Farshid and our cousin Habib. Once before, in Dr. Richard's medical clinic, I thought I saw Farshid coming through the doors. But it was only Habib, bruised and battered and as cruel as ever. He threatened me and my unborn child. So I suffocated him to death with my bare hands. At least, I thought I did. But Dr. Richard arrived before I could be certain, and then Omid died and Zahra was born and now it's all a blur in my mind."

Sabera rubs her temple with her left hand, then winces in pain.

"I dream too much of blood," she murmurs. "It has changed me. Once I knew things, all sorts of things. Now I'm not certain of anything anymore.

"Jamil," she speaks her child's father's name. "I think his ghost is real, but maybe I've just needed him that much, to keep some piece of him with me. Does it matter? When I was a girl"—she sighs—"I dreamed."

"How many kidnappers are there?" Roberta asks, trying to regain focus. She looks at me, then stares pointedly at her watch. I get the message.

"I think five. But I don't know them all. Rafiq and his cousin threw me in the back of their vehicle and drove to the abandoned warehouse. Habib was there. And...and..." Another shrug. Roberta and I can fill in those blanks just by looking at her. "I didn't talk. I wouldn't talk. I already knew Habib would kill me. In many ways, it's only fair. I did kill him first."

"But you got away?"

"Isaad. Habib decided if I didn't care about my life, maybe I would care about his. He cut off my hair, put it in a box, and had it delivered."

"That was quite a riddle," I comment.

"I wrote it as a warning. Isaad would read it and know exactly what happened. He was to take Zahra and leave."

"He didn't."

"Isaad is a good man. Better than I deserved. He understood the warning, but he chose a different course. An ambush of sorts? I don't know the details. But he appeared earlier than they'd planned, before the other men had returned. Rafiq started yelling at him; Isaad replied with insults of his own.

"I was able to get loose from my bindings. I ran, assuming Isaad and...thinking my husband would be behind me. But no. I don't know what happened after that."

I catch the stutter. Isaad and...? I wait to see if she'll elaborate, but she doesn't.

I try a different tack. "Sabera, who were you calling in New York and in Washington, DC?"

She shakes her head, as if she doesn't understand the question, but just for a moment...a brief hardening of her gaze that comes and goes so quickly, I might be imagining it.

"You saw Isaad. You were there. At the scene of my husband's murder." Sabera turns her attention to Roberta. Clearly she'd been watching from somewhere close. I wonder how long she's been following us. And how she's been following us. A woman on the run who doesn't have a vehicle? Let alone, where has she been since fleeing the resort townhouse?

I feel increasingly unsettled. I've finally found my target, and yet...

"Did he suffer? Tell me. What did they do to my husband?"

"What matters is that Isaad died protecting you," Roberta offers gently. "He gave his life out of love."

"He and Jamil both died protecting me. If that's love, I don't want it anymore." Sabera raises her steak knife again, waving it in agitation.

"Sabera." I redirect her attention to me. "Remember what we told you in the beginning? They didn't stop with Isaad. They tried to kidnap Zahra as well."

Sabera blinks.

"When that failed, they grabbed Aliah instead."

"Do you know where they might have taken her?" Roberta asks. "The location they held you and the location of Isaad's body aren't the same. We have a sense of a general area, but not a place."

Sabera shakes her head. "Where's Zahra? I want my daughter."

"Zahra's fine. She's someplace safe and well protected."

"Take me." The thin serrated blade, waving again.

Roberta reaches out and slowly lowers it. "Do you truly believe being with you is someplace safe for Zahra? Given all that's happened?"

The distressed look on Sabera's face is answer enough.

"Habib...He came back even after I destroyed him. What more can I do?"

"It's okay." Roberta pats Sabera's arm. "We have a plan."

I add, "And the good news is, we no longer have to rely on a decoy."

CHAPTER 43

WE MAKE OUR WAY TO the warehouse district with Sabera sitting, plainly visible, in the passenger's seat. I have concerns about the young mother's volatile state of mind, but leaving her behind doesn't feel like an option, especially as it would leave her alone and vulnerable. We have enough of a mess without her disappearing a second time around.

So for now, we roll Sabera into our plan, assigning her the role of, well, Sabera. Meanwhile, Roberta is hunkered down in the back, our secret weapon, should we need her. Which leaves me as the driver.

It's been so long since I've operated a motor vehicle, I'm nearly more strung out over navigating late-night traffic than I am over actively seeking out known killers. During brief respites stopped at red lights, however, I continue a discreet inspection of Sabera Ahmadi.

Sitting in the front, the streetlights wash over her features in a continuous stream of illumination. She is definitely battered, the circle of bruises around her throat even more plainly visible.

But now there are other details I notice.

For starters, she smells just fine. As someone who's literally been passed out drunk in dark alleyways, I'm very familiar with the scent of vagrancy. Basically, a potent combination of sweat, sewage, and desperation.

For another thing, her hair, while jagged from being violently hacked short, doesn't appear oily or unkempt.

And her hands, now folded on her lap with the steak knife tucked between her fingers, are suspiciously clean. They've also gone from agitated trembling to perfectly poised.

From the back seat, Roberta whispers for me to make a right. I fumble with the blinker, turn down a street noticeably lacking in the lighting department. The avenue remains wide but is now even more rutted and potholed than the main Tucson drags.

We head deeper into the darkness, the buildings becoming larger and broader, but also more derelict. Definitely feels like we're in the right neighborhood.

X factor, I muse. What I'd mentioned to Detective Marc earlier.

Where has Sabera been hiding since bolting from her resort rabbit hole, especially as it seems to have included personal hygiene opportunities as well as access to transportation? And as long as I'm questioning her version of events:

Rafiq and his cousin weren't just killed during Sabera's escape. According to Roberta, their skulls were nearly pulverized. Sounds very personal to me. Which maybe reflects Isaad's emotional state after they kidnapped his wife?

Except how did he end up tortured and killed next? Sabera said she'd assumed Isaad and—stutter stop—were behind her when she fled. Who is stutter stop, and why not simply tell us?

MI6 handler Lilla had mentioned seeing Sabera meeting with a curly-haired, handsome Yank. If I were the betting type, I'd say curly-haired Yank equals X factor in my world, and stutter stop in Sabera's. But again, why the secrecy? Who is Sabera trying to protect, because from what I can tell, there aren't too many important people in her world left.

I don't like not knowing things I should know, especially as we roll by another hollow-eyed industrial space, a lone spotlight illuminating shattered windows and graffiti-covered walls.

Roberta delivers more directions. We cruise past where Sabera was originally held, then toward Isaad's site, a grand tour of crime scenes, complete with yards of yellow tape. Periodically we come across small clusters of individuals engaged in furtive exchanges. Not to mention huddled forms tucking into various doorways for a night's sleep.

Traffic is light. Periodically headlights appear behind me, but none have lingered.

It occurs to me the bare-bones lighting doesn't just help protect evildoers, it's also keeping them from seeing the bait.

I rustle around my pants pockets till I find my cell phone, then activate the screen and hand it over to Sabera.

"Pretend to be reading something on it," I direct. "While holding it close to your face."

She appears puzzled, then in the next instant, a single nod as she too realizes the issue.

I revisit our route, working a grid, from outer blocks to inner streets, then back out again.

Pass after pass. Headlights appearing in the rearview mirror, only to disappear again. All three of us growing increasingly anxious.

And then.

A pair of lights, nearly pinpricks in the distance, but

drawing quickly closer. Large vehicle. Maybe silver or white in color.

This is it. I can feel it. I glance over at Sabera to see if she thinks the same.

Her once glassy gaze is now perfectly clear, her shaky hands rock steady.

"X factor," I murmur.

"What's that?"

I clear my throat, declare more loudly, "Showtime."

We're off and running.

I HEAD IMMEDIATELY for the relative safety of the main avenue, having to step on the gas as our follower bears down. We can't afford to be run off the road, meaning I'm pretty quickly at speeds not safe for any driver, let alone one who barely remembers how to hold a steering wheel.

When we finally careen onto the wide, well-lit boulevard, making a hard left with wheels squealing, I'm the one who's a shaky mess, and I'm definitely not faking it.

This time of night, there are not a ton of cars on the road, but there are enough to provide a buffer. Also, we now have the relative protection of Tucson's traffic cams, not to mention possible police presence, to help keep violent impulses in check.

Our pursuer drops back, allowing a small sedan to get between us. Trying to convince us they've given up, are simply going to let their prey go free?

We're not that stupid.

Roberta continues providing instructions as we literally head for the hills, making the winding climb up to the compound. Habib and company remain one car behind. But with only a single vehicle between us, I'm confident they'll see me turn into the compound.

As planned, Daryl has left the massive wrought-iron gates wide open. We roll in, coming to a halt just opposite the main entrance's heavy, Spanish oak double doors. I have never appreciated their solid thickness and heavy-duty locks more.

Headlights whip past. Some stranger headed home to tuck in for the night, versus what we have planned.

A glow, growing larger. Passing by, but at a much slower speed than normal.

"Go."

Sabera and I pop out of Aliah's car. The property is aglow with all of Bart's fancy landscape lighting, illuminating palm trees, the circular fountain, and the main house in a wash of warmth and splendor.

I have my arm around Sabera's shoulders, careful not to grip too tight given all her injuries as we hustle across the broad cobblestone drive to the front portico. I make a show of fumbling with the door's overly ornate, overly complicated bronze lock, as we wait for it...

We don't see the vehicle, just catch the low purr of an engine as our tail finally eases through the front gate, headlights off. I force myself not to turn around as I push open the massive door and usher Sabera inside.

The SUV halts outside the pool of light. The sound of a door popping open before being carefully shut.

A presence not seen but now felt, watching from the dark.

I step inside, securing the dead bolt with an audible thunk behind me.

Fish hooked.

Now the real adventure begins.

I GUIDE SABERA carefully through the shadowy interior. Don't step there. Wait, circle around that, now head straight forward. We make our way to the kitchen, where the overhead lights are still on, though dimmed. Just enough visibility to call attention to the space, without making it look like we're obviously advertising. Sabera is growing increasingly confused.

"I don't understand. What are we to do?"

"Sit. Wait. See if our helpers get the job done first."

"Helpers?"

"It might be best if you didn't know. Basically, the biggest flaw with our 'bring the enemy to us' plan is that we lack some pretty important information about the enemy. How many? How heavily armed? How well trained? To hedge our bets, we, umm, decided to use the property and its residents to our greatest advantage."

If anything, Sabera appears more bewildered. She's still gripping her rusty steak knife. More power to her.

"Look, you said there were three other kidnappers, yes?"

She nods.

"Last time, they left two men to watch over their prisoner— you. With any luck, they'll follow the same approach. Meaning one man followed us to see where we were going, the two others stayed behind with Aliah. Though it's possible," I allow, "that two followed, one stayed. See, these are the things we can't predict."

Another nod.

"So Daryl—"

"Daryl?"

"Big guy, heart of a lion, soul of a lamb. You'll like him. He's already Zahra's favorite."

At the mention of Zahra's name, a spasm crosses Sabera's face. Longing, anxiety, despair. She's been separated from her daughter for how long now? And she still has only our word that Zahra's safe. I don't blame her for feeling distressed.

I return to the business at hand. "Daryl's thought was that if we couldn't predict the number of intruders, then the next best option is to control where they go. Given the size of this property, that's a tricky proposition. So many access points—you have no idea. Meaning they could come from multiple directions, dilute our own limited resources trying to stand guard on multiple fronts. So we set up strategic booby traps at various ingress points. And engaged some interesting assistants. If you hear screaming, don't worry, that's a good thing."

Now Sabera's eyes widen. "I don't understand. Even if some-one comes, how does that help? Habib is not going to simply give up. And he does nothing but lie."

I shrug. "It's possible we also have some ideas on unique forms of interrogation. Not to mention his vehicle could be a treasure trove of information, especially if it has GPS. Or worse comes to worst, we offer you in trade."

She blinks.

"I'm not saying we'd actually do that," I hasten to add. "But if we told Habib he was the intermediary to negotiate an exchange, Aliah for you, that might get the players out in the open. More times they're exposed, more opportunities we have to find them, and thus, Aliah."

"We? You, Roberta, this Daryl person?"

"Don't forget Genni. Zahra loves her, too. All six feet four inches."

Sabera shakes her head in general bewilderment.

"You're just going to have to trust us," I state softly. "We're here for you, your daughter, and Aliah. Whatever happens next, our goal is to save you."

It takes a moment; then she nods quietly. Satisfied that she's on board about as much as one can expect, I turn my attention to other matters.

I settle myself on the opposite side of the kitchen island, where I can lean forward and peer at her directly. "Rafiq and his cousin weren't just killed, their skulls were smashed to smithereens. The investigators are still picking up pieces."

She flinches.

"Would Isaad really be capable of doing such a thing?"

"I don't know what happened after I ran."

"You knew Rafiq was dead. Said so yourself."

"I heard it on the news. The two dead men, where they were discovered. I knew it was them."

I continue studying her. "You're very clean."

She blinks, doesn't say a word. But I can see it on her face, the realization she might have made a mistake and now must frantically think up an explanation.

"Where have you been staying the past two days? Not your former employers'; the police have been watching the resort."

"All hotels have empty rooms," she mutters. "Not so hard to find one."

"Yeah, it is. Without inside info on the bookings, access to a room key."

"I have a friend—"

"No you don't. You have one dear friend, Aliah, who is currently being held by killers thanks to you."

Another flinch.

I go for the kill shot: "What would Jamil think?"

Her head whips up. The look of raw distress across her face is almost enough to make me feel guilty. Then again, I'm sick of being lied to, especially by a woman I'm attempting to help.

She's just opened her mouth, possibly to say something honest, when a man's scream rips through the open intercoms, immediately followed by a string of cursing, then some muffled banging and thumping, as if someone had run into a wall, repeatedly.

"All right. Intruder one discovered the lone slightly ajar window and took advantage of it to enter the bathroom of the guest bedroom. Where he encountered a closed connecting door. Which he then, unfortunately for him, opened."

More cursing, a louder thud of something or someone falling. Hmm, this might work out even better than we thought.

"What... what is happening to him?"

"Other side of door: heat lamp and one very large and pissed-off Burmese python."

Definitely the sound of running feet. I'm glad I'm not the only one afraid of snakes. Though I managed this task. Shaking terribly, trying not to hyperventilate, I bravely donned the welding gloves, then used them to basically shoo a slumbering Marge into a pillowcase. Marge had not appreciated being disturbed, leading to one heavy, writhing load.

But she did like the heat lamp and settled into a strategic position outside the guest bath door. She slithered out of the pillowcase (I managed not to vomit), and true to what I'd read on the internet, coiled up in a massive pile to resume napping in the pool of provided heat. Until, of course, being disturbed a second time by someone crashing through the door. Based on my research, snakes really don't like that, and constrictors can move remarkably fast when provoked.

After handling Marge, the baby pythons were a breeze. They went into a small box, which Daryl hung up high in the hall outside the guest bedroom. At this stage, our intruder has two options. Take a right and head deeper into the house toward the private wing, or take a left and arrive at the vaulted marble foyer, towering living room, then kitchen. Again, big space, can't watch it all.

Daryl is currently stashed to the right, in Bart's bedroom, which has a retractable glass wall opening onto the pool area. Might look great in an architectural magazine, but a major point of weakness when it comes to thwarting a home invasion. No choice but to have a real person standing point.

Which brings us to the baby pythons.

Our goal: upon luring in the intruder(s), funnel them to a single location, where Sabera and I are already waiting, and will soon be joined by Roberta, who's currently in charge of perimeter sweep. At which point, Daryl should be able to rush in from behind, enabling us to ambush the wannabe kidnapper and do some pointed interrogation of our own.

Now, an entire series of short shrieks bursts through the intercom, along the lines of "Ah, ah, ah, ahhhh!" Kind of reminds me of someone juggling a hot potato.

Sabera stares at me again.

"Baby pythons," I whisper to her. "A dozen of them just rained down on our trespasser's head. Doesn't sound like he's a fan. Which is perfect. As now he'll retreat in the opposite direction, heading toward the kitchen."

"Aren't we in the kitchen?"

"Yes. At the moment, we're both bait. I didn't mention that?

But it's okay. Once the bedroom wing is out of play, Daryl can leave his post to advance from the rear, while Roberta will enter from the reptile wing, creating the perfect pincer maneuver. We just need to buy a little more time..."

The prowler is definitely proceeding in our direction, because I don't need the intercom system to hear what he says next.

His voice carries, loud and menacing, from the vaulted living room into the kitchen:

"American, I know you have my cousin. If so, you must realize I have come for her. Give her up now, and I promise not to kill you."

"Habib," Sabera whispers, her eyes dilating in fear.

I reach across the island, squeeze her hand hard. "Time, just a little more time," I reassure her.

Then, under my breath: "All right, Petunia. You're up."

CHAPTER 44

EDGE CLOSER TO THE OPENING into the living room. I can't help myself. Of all our traps, this one worries me the most. A snake as big as Marge, most people are going to jump and run from as fast as possible. Pythons as tiny as the babies, fling away and dance in the other direction. No reptiles harmed in the line of duty. But Petunia, if she does what she's capable of doing...

We hear it the moment the first trip wire is snagged.

Followed by what is definitely a curse in any language.

Odor hits next. Earthy and pulpy, with top notes of banana and orange. Second trip wire.

"Fu..."

A bucket of fresh apple peels joins the produce buffet dumping over Habib's head and shoulders. Iguanas have a highly developed sense of smell and are attracted to the scent of food, including most fruits and vegetables.

Sure enough, there's the clackety-clack as Petunia goes scurrying across the tiled floor in search of this late-night treat.

A low muffled moan of horror echoes through the space, followed by a sharp: "Let go let go let go," cursing cursing cursing. "Let go!"

I simultaneously beg Petunia to release whatever ankle, leg, or hand she has her teeth sunk into, while praying for Daryl to appear. Or Roberta. What's keeping them?

Then, the solid thwack of flesh hitting living flesh, three times in quick succession.

As if someone's trying to kick or punch a solidly built iguana away.

Now I want to kill Habib myself.

Clackety-clack, swish-swish. Petunia, beating a hasty retreat, hopefully with some prized piece of fruit or possibly a human finger in her mouth. I vote for a finger. Or a testicle.

I quickly withdraw. This is it.

I round the island to position myself with Sabera behind me, both of us tucked up against the granite counter for support.

Hoping for Daryl and Roberta to appear. And then...

Habib half stumbles into the kitchen, his shoulders covered in orange peels, his shoes dragging banana skin. Blood drips down his left hand, and there's a crazed look in his eyes.

But that doesn't keep him from smiling in triumph as he staggers to a halt in front of us.

And we get our first unpleasant surprise for the night.

Habib hasn't come alone.

He's dragged a bound and gagged Aliah, who appears absolutely terrified, behind him.

Now he jerks her in front of him, then in one fluid movement jabs a sinister-looking curved dagger against her throat. Long and slender, with a vicious edge, this isn't a discarded steak knife. This is the real deal.

Aliah makes more muffled noises behind her gag. Her eyes bore into ours, her initial fear starting to give way to rage. *Run*, I can see it in her face. Or maybe it's *kill the bastard*.

But we stand perfectly still as Habib presses the razor-sharp weapon against her skin and delicately carves a gleaming line of red.

His threat is clear enough. If he so much as sneezes, she's dead. Which leaves Sabera and me rooted in place, just as Daryl finally looms in the doorway, only to immediately draw up short.

For a minute, we stand in silence, a perfect tableau of pending doom.

Finally, Habib laughs harshly. "All right, cousin, this is it. The key. You will write down everything, or I will start slicing up your friend piece by bloody piece."

Come on, I mentally will Roberta to appear, or perhaps my Hail Mary backup plan.

But nothing.

We gambled.

We lost.

And now we face the consequence.

"I ... I NEED PAPER," Sabera manages finally. "A large sheet. To draw the map."

I don't know of any map, just magic squares, but I do recognize stall tactics when I hear them.

I leave her side, rounding the island to start scrabbling through kitchen drawers, making a show of searching for pen and paper. Honestly, I have no idea where Genni keeps her art supplies. Mostly I'm praying I'll come across something useful, except I'm so rattled, I can't fathom what that might be.

"What happened in the warehouse?" I ask now, trying to keep Habib talking. Distract him. Possibly open up a window of opportunity for Daryl to pounce. At the moment, there's no way he can ambush Habib without leading to Aliah's slit throat. "I mean two of your teammates, pulverized to death by a math professor? While his wife escapes? Not exactly a good showing on your part."

"I wasn't there! We'd left Rafiq and Ahmad in charge. They paid for their mistake."

The way he says the words...

I pause, glance up at him. "Isaad didn't kill them?"

"Isaad gave them a tap or two. My compatriots, on the other hand, when confronted by their failure..." Habib shrugs. "Rafiq and Ahmad were Hazaras. They should've known it would end badly."

I feel slightly ill, especially given the casualness of Habib's delivery. Just another day in the life of ethnic cleansing. I open a fresh drawer, discover whisks of every conceivable size. I know you're not supposed to bring a knife to a gun fight, but what about a whisk to a knife fight? My entire head hurts. From major concussion to this. I might black out after all.

Except I can't.

"Isaad was too slow. We caught him just a few blocks away." Another careless shrug. "I honor the man's courage. No matter what we did...he would not reveal your secrets, Sabera. Pity for him. They were not easy on him, as I have experienced myself."

There's an edge to his voice at the end. According to Sabera, the Taliban had tortured Habib first, before he sold her out in order to save his own skin. Now he's apparently grown comfortable with the business of death. Or perhaps just inured to violence.

"You would aid such people, Habib?" Sabera asks harshly. "They destroyed our country. Murdered our family."

"My father had a plan! You betrayed him. His blood is on your hands."

"And now my husband's blood is on your hands. Are we even? How many more lives must you destroy? You know they will only kill you in the end, just as they did Rafiq."

"Surely you know by now, dear cousin, that I don't die that easily."

"I had squeezed the final breath from your lungs!" Sabera cried.

"My last sight was your bitch-whore face looming over me. My next, the bright glare of a hospital room. It is not for me to question the will of God."

Sabera looks like she wants to scream in frustration. I hastily open a fourth drawer. Graters. Again, in a full range of sizes. What the hell does Genni do in this kitchen?

"The information I possess has no value. I explained this before. Two halves of one whole. You heard my mother say that our entire childhood. Without Farshid, I know only one piece. Deliver such useless results to your compatriots, and your fate will be even worse than Rafiq's."

"I don't care about mineral mines," Habib grits out. "I want the gold. The piles you stole from my father and his friends. I know you know where it is—you're the one who moved it."

"As you wish. I'll draw the map. You'll deliver it. Then you'll die." Sabera's turn for a careless shrug.

"Perhaps I'll take a page from your mother's book and keep half of the information to myself," Habib counters. "They will have to bring me along."

"Torture you for it, most likely. You still think you're so clever.

No." Sabera waves a dismissive hand. "You are as stupid as ever, cousin."

Habib hisses in a sharp breath.

I pause, momentarily stunned. What the hell is she doing, antagonizing the homicidal maniac? Then I get it. She's distracting the homicidal maniac, drawing him back into the tit-for-tat patterns of their childhood.

Even now, Habib gestures at her with his right hand, knife momentarily pulled away from Aliah's throat and directed at Sabera instead.

Daryl doesn't need a second invitation. With a roar, he explodes forward, catching Habib hard in the shoulder and spinning him around. Habib doesn't have a second to get his bearings before Daryl has both arms wrapped tightly around the man's torso in a massive bear hug, pinning Habib's arms in place as he squeezes.

Aliah stumbles back. I catch her elbow, pulling her behind the kitchen island with me. One of the drawers had kitchen shears. I grab them, snipping quickly at her bindings as Habib begins to gasp.

He butts his head back, catching Daryl in the face. The big man's nose gushes blood, but he merely grunts, continues crushing.

Habib tries to twist and kick his way out of it. His hand, down by his side, jabs at Daryl's leg with the wicked blade, but his movements are too constrained to inflict any real damage.

Sabera has moved forward. She's staring at her thrashing cousin with the most intense look on her face.

"This is for Isaad," she states clearly, then drives her steak knife into Habib's side, four times in quick succession, as fast and lethal as any prison shanking.

Habib looks at her wide-eyed. His body grows slack. He mumbles something, a whisper so low I can't make it out. It must not be a request for forgiveness, as in response, Sabera spits in his face.

And then...

Daryl slowly lowers the man's body to the kitchen floor. We're all breathing hard, clearly stunned.

This is it? We did it? We have Aliah, we have Sabera, now we can get Zahra and—

"Sorry," Daryl murmurs. "I thought I saw movement near the pool house, went to check it out." Then, frowning: "Where's Roberta?"

I gaze at him, and, in the next instant, realize our second unfortunate surprise of the evening. We assumed Aliah was being held somewhere else. But Aliah is right here. Meaning the other two captors didn't have to stay back. They must be here, too, somewhere on the grounds.

Which Roberta was going to quickly cover before making her own appearance. Except she hasn't appeared. Oh shit, oh shit, oh shit.

I'm just opening my mouth to warn Daryl...

The glass sliders explode. Another pump of a shotgun. Second explosion, this one taking out the chandelier overhead.

I fling my arms over my head as the ceiling rains down pebble-sized shards. Aliah collapses beside me. A scream from the other side of the island—Sabera.

I glance over to see Daryl, sprawled unconscious on the kitchen floor. There's blood everywhere.

I have one thought: Habib's knife. If I could just grab it for protection...

Then a dark-bearded man appears, blocking my view of Daryl as he leers at me from the end of the island.

He holds up Habib's curved dagger. He smiles.

In his black gaze, I see a dozen different kinds of hell.

And his gleeful anticipation of inflecting each and every one.

CHAPTER 45

Aliah is moaning. I sense her movement, hear the cascade of glass from her body as she attempts to hoist herself up on her arms.

The biggest noise, however, comes from the other side of the island. I can't see Sabera, only hear her sharp exhale, followed by a low moan, then a stream of guttural obscenities.

Beside me, Aliah stills, listening intently.

Our leering invader has drawn back. I don't know whether to be grateful or insulted by his lack of interest.

Sabera is the key. They came for her; they want her. Standing on the other side of the counter, closest to the blown-out sliders, she would've been struck by the force of the first shot transforming the tempered glass to a hail of pebbles. Second shot went high, however, a sign they still wanted her alive? Because otherwise she would've made for an easy target. Just like Daryl.

I can hear her. A mix of tiny screams and fierce hisses, as one of the attackers drags her to her feet. She's gotta be hurt, but she's clearly still fighting.

It pisses me off. How dare these insurgents come here—this home, this city, this country. I don't fucking care. They're evil, awful men, destroying entire countries, subjugating generations of women and children. The outrage provides enough adrenaline to drive me to my feet.

I'm immediately sorry.

Daryl. To my left. His face is a mask of red, his torso a glittering pincushion of glass and buckshot. So much blood, a growing pool surrounding his body. I can barely stand the sight.

And Roberta, who's still missing in action. What the hell did they do to Roberta?

My gaze lights upon Sabera, her arms wrenched behind her back as one of the men slides a knife around her ear, across her cheek, down her neck in a sickening imitation of a lover's touch.

She's shaking. Clearly terrified. And yet, the expression on her face…

She didn't break the first time they had her. She has no intention of breaking now.

Which should've clued me in, as the next moment, the first leering bearded man steps forward and drags me around the end of the island, placing his own vicious dagger against my throat.

My knees buckle. He hauls me back up. I attempt bravery, but mostly, I suffer an out-of-body experience:

Dear Death—been searching for you for a really long while. About time we get this right.

Sabera stills. It's harder to be stoic when someone else will pay the price.

I want to tell her it's okay. I've been running from a bullet for years now. It was bound to find me eventually. I assumed I'd suffer flashbacks of Paul, who took that bullet for me. Or scenes from Wyoming, or a certain Boston cop. As unfinished business goes, I could fill a warehouse.

But mostly I think of Seattle, of a brief interlude where I felt safe, seen, and heard. A gift, I realize now. Why do we never realize these things till it's too late?

Will he cry for me?

I honestly hope not. I've already been a big enough pain in the ass.

Before me, Sabera's expression hardens. I don't have to be a genius to understand the math. There's nothing we can do that won't result in our deaths. It's merely a question of how slow versus how fast.

Her gaze is faintly apologetic. I get that, too. She never intended for her actions to harm others. Welcome to my life.

I let my gaze fall to her belly, hope she gets the message. She's still fighting for two, and well, I'm only me.

The first razor slice down my cheek is so harsh and unexpected, I scream. The second, a matching cut, has me writhing and thrashing against my captor's impossibly strong grip.

I shriek, I can't help myself. But it's not so much a wail of pain as a roar of outrage. Son of a bitch. When I get my hands on him...

Then the blade's nipping at my throat, gouging, slicing, but I no longer fucking care.

There's something wrong with me. I've always known it. Where others would cower, lick their wounds, seek to pacify...

The more this fucker hurts me, the more I want him dead.

When he moves to carve a fresh hole in my shoulder, I smack

back my head as hard as I can, catching him in the nose. While Aliah rises to standing and pelts him with one, two, three objects in a row. Whisks. Or maybe graters, it's hard to tell.

He stumbles, momentarily outraged, while his partner shouts out at him in a language I don't understand, but I'm pretty sure translates to "get the fucking woman under control." In response, Aliah beans Sabera's captor with a colander, while Sabera starts cursing a long string of words I definitely get.

Clackety-clack-clack. Swish-swish.

One last play.

I slam my foot into my attacker's insole. Then, when he jerks his foot away reflexively, I jam my elbow into his gut. He doubles over, dragging the blade down my neck and torso. I'm so intent on my mission, I don't even notice.

I twist out of his grip and shove him to the floor, dropping a banana peel atop his face as I do so.

Petunia, God bless her...

Now the screaming is real. As it should be.

The motherfucker dares to try to stab my iguana. I stomp my foot on his wrist, three times for good measure. Then I snatch the knife from his nerveless fingers while Petunia takes a second snap at his nose.

I twist toward Sabera and her captor. I'm not human. I'm not real. Blood pours down my cheeks, neck, shoulder. I have a wickedly curved weapon in my hand and I want to drive it into the fucking horrible, awful piece of shit in front of me. Who tortured Sabera. Killed Isaad. Abducted Aliah.

Is this bloodlust? Because I feel nothing but a roaring in my ears.

The lone standing male has his hand wrapped around Sabera's short-cropped hair, jerking her head up, exposing her throat. The shotgun he used to blast their way in here dangles from a strap around his torso, but we are much too close quarters for that.

A woman possessed, I advance.

He glares at me, jabs his own knife into Sabera's throat.

I can see it plainly on her face. Do it. Strike even if it kills her. It doesn't matter, as long as he's dead.

Aliah advances around the island from the other side. The classic pincer movement after all.

He mutters something low. Neither Sabera nor Aliah seem deterred by what he has to say, so I disregard it as well.

He takes a step backward, dragging Sabera with him.

All I want to do is hurt, maim, kill. I want to thrust this blade deep into this man's chest. I want to feel his blood, hot and red, on my hands. I want to hear the gurgle of his dying breath.

Where have these thoughts come from?

Who have I become?

But all I can picture is my room of pain, the dozens of ghosts roaming my collective psyche, betrayed by strangers, killed by those they loved. Each and every one innocent in their own right. And still...

Sabera is murmuring words I don't know.

Aliah, shrieking in their language.

Me, advancing advancing advancing. I can kill him. I know I can. He'll slash Sabera's throat first, but still...

Another step, another step.

I'm not sane. I'm pretty sure I'll never be sane again.

As Sabera's gaze bores into mine:

"Do it!" she orders.

And then, as I rush forward in a blaze of glory—

"Stop!"

I just have time to look up. As my single phone call, my backup plan to all of our backup plans, Captain Kurtz materializes out of the darkness and clubs my target over the head.

Totally terrifying, absolutely evil Taliban soldier folds to the ground, Sabera extracting herself just in time.

I can't help myself. I stab my newfound weapon in Kurtz's direction.

"Some fucking cavalry you turned out to be. Could you have cut it any closer?"

Just in time for a second man to join him. Same facial structure but with curly brown hair. X factor/stutter-stop man. I knew it! I want to feel triumphant. But the world is starting to gray around the edges.

I feel my knife clatter to the floor. Then I'm crumpling to my knees, where I have an up-close-and-personal view of Daryl's blood-pooled body.

I don't cry anymore.

I just wrap my arms around my knees and pray for none of this to be real.

Until a new voice breaks the silence.

"Well, well, well. Leave it to you Yanks to get this party started without me."

Lilla No Last Name steps through the shattered sliders.

Petunia, quite wisely, scurries away.

CHAPTER 46

Movement from behind the British spymaster as Roberta stumbles her way through the shattered sliders, crunching pebbled glass as she goes. Her hair is in disarray. There's blood on her temple and marks on her wrists consistent with restraints.

She spares a quick nod of thanks to Lilla, whom I'm guessing liberated Roberta after she was most likely ambushed and tied up by the insurgents during her perimeter sweep. Ironically, she looks in better shape than the rest of us. Which is immediately confirmed when her gaze lands on Daryl's still form.

With a cry, Roberta vaults to his side. "Daryl, what have you done, you dumb lug!"

"Let me, I'm a doctor." The curly-haired man, who looks too similar to Kurtz to be anyone other than the retired army captain's brother. He spares me a quick glance while heading toward Daryl.

"You're injured—"

"I'll be fine."

"Sabera," he barks out, already kneeling next to Daryl's head. "First aid kit. Towels, disinfectant, gauze. Bring me whatever you can find."

Sabera spins in the direction of the kitchen, her face an angry display of small cuts and glittery glass shards. Aliah is also in motion, rifling cabinets and drawers just as I'd been doing moments before.

Meanwhile Kurtz deftly binds the wrists and ankles of both intruders, then drags them into a sitting position next to the kitchen table. The lower face of the man who attacked me is a study of gore. There's too much blood to be able to determine if he still has his nose, or how much of it. As he gazes at me with fresh hatred, I make a show of delicately stroking my own pert snout.

Lilla wanders over to Habib's body, squatting down low and inspecting his red-soaked abdomen.

"Your work?"

I jerk my head in Sabera's direction.

"Well played."

"Sabera," the doctor barks again.

She comes flying over, bearing towels, a sharp knife, and a whiskey bottle. Deposits her load, awaits his next instruction.

They've done this before, obviously. Many times.

"You know him," I state the obvious.

"I volunteered at Dr. Richard's clinic at the first refugee camp."

"Dr. Richard. But of course. Any chance, Dr. Richard, you now work at a hospital in New York?"

"Yes." His hands are dancing all over Daryl's body, taking vitals, inspecting injuries. Roberta appears in a state of shock, Daryl's head cradled on her lap, as the doctor leans over and rips open Daryl's jacket, then takes the knife from Sabera and slices down the front of his shirt, pinging buttons as he goes.

"Sandy," he commands his brother.

"Here."

"Plenty of damage, but here's the main issue: penetrating wound, lower left side. I'm going to dig out the obvious buckshot. Sabera, you will pack. Then, Sandy, you apply pressure. As much as you can. Ready. One, two, three."

They move in startling synchronicity.

Daryl groans once but thankfully doesn't regain consciousness. Dr. Richard moves up to his head, inspects the big man's neck, feels around the back of his head.

He gazes up at Roberta, his face merely an inch from hers.

"Your...?"

"Friend."

"Good news. Your friend is gonna have one helluva headache from smashing his head against a hard-tiled floor. And definitely requires a surgeon's touch. But a lotta this looks worse than it is. Little rest, plenty of fluids, he should recover."

Roberta chokes back a sob, sniffs out. "Okay."

Dr. Richard turns his attention to me. I shake my head. He turns next to Sabera. "Your face..."

"I've got her," Lilla interrupts. "As you say, better than it looks. Whereas..."

I've forgotten about Aliah. She's standing at the other end of the long island, and for the first time, I realize that she's swaying on her feet. Her hand is pressed to her side. When she pulls it back, it's covered in blood.

Dr. Richard wastes no time as I scramble to assist. Together we ease Aliah to the floor. I expect to see buckshot or glass, but instead, when he pulls up her blouse, we discover a crude bandage covering a previous injury that's resumed bleeding. Dr. Richard peels off the tape. I gag slightly and have to look away.

A symbol of some kind has been carved into her flesh, ugly, brutal, and already bright red with infection.

Dr. Richard, who clearly understands its significance, murmurs, "I'm sorry."

I take her hand, squeezing her fingers with my own. She trembles but keeps her chin up. She didn't give them the satisfaction of breaking before; she's not going to do it now.

I glance over at Lilla and Sabera, who seem to be doing okay.

"There, there, poppet." Lilla is cupping Sabera's face between her palms as she searches for further wounds to tend. The cut on Sabera's cheek has reopened, blood trickling down. Lilla brushes it away with her thumb. "The worst is past. Now we just need Zahra, and all will be well. You do have the child someplace safe, yes?"

She gazes at me expectantly.

I'm not ready to make nice, however.

"You." I start with Kurtz, who's now wrapping long rolls of gauze around Daryl's torso to hold the makeshift bandages in place. "You and the good doctor here, obviously you're brothers?"

A grunt of acknowledgment.

"He works in New York. And you... The main headquarters for No One Left Behind are in DC. You two are the ones who orchestrated everything."

This earns me a look from Kurtz. "Define 'everything.'"

"You got Sabera and her family moved to Tucson."

"Technically, the United Nations made it happen, by virtue of granting them refugee status. But once they finally arrived in the States, I possibly requested a few favors—in a strictly personal, not professional capacity, I assure you. What can I say, I've always been a sucker for my little brother's lost causes."

Dr. Richard rolls his eyes.

"Why Tucson?" I want to know.

"Aliah started it. She'd already been working official channels at the resettlement agency. Claimed she was family, so could assist with the Ahmadis' transition. Add to that, my organization was genuinely looking to open a satellite office here, meaning there'd be two of us to look after Sabera and her family."

"Because she is the key. And you worried something like this might happen?"

"Hope for the best, plan for the worst."

I scowl. "And you couldn't just tell me all this from the very beginning?"

Kurtz gives me a look. "Some mystery woman who shows up out of the blue? Barely has basic background info and almost zero digital footprint? Honestly, I figured you for CIA."

I blink, which flicks blood in my eye and makes it sting. I can't decide if I should be insulted or honored.

I'm still trying to piece this together in my head, which is no mean feat after the past twenty-four hours. "So...you two rescued Sabera when she was kidnapped the first time. Isaad contacted you, and all of you went to save her?"

"Isaad reached out to me," Dr. Richard corrects. "After Sabera spotted Habib in Tucson, he knew there'd be trouble. I'd just flown in to figure out options when Sabera was kidnapped. Once Isaad received the 'ransom' note, ostensibly from the kidnappers but created by Sabera with encoded instructions...Isaad chose to go on the offensive. Isaad would distract her abductors; I'd get Sabera out of there. It nearly worked. Until it didn't."

He keeps his gaze fixed on Aliah's wound, which he's deftly bandaging. "I had to help Sabera out of the warehouse. Once she was steadier on her feet, I sent her in the direction of the car, then returned for Isaad. But it was already too late. Rafiq and his cousin had attacked, Isaad grabbing a hammer. They were in the thick of things, Isaad yelling for me to go, he'd catch up.

"I never saw him again."

"You picked up Sabera," I fill in. "Several blocks away, as no traffic cameras caught a glimpse."

"She was keeping out of sight in the back seat. We returned to the resort long enough for her to get cleaned up, tend her injuries. But it was no longer safe. I ended up reaching out to a buddy of mine. We've been crashing at his place."

"Hang on." I might be slow, but I'm not totally stupid. "Any chance this buddy has a South African accent?"

Now Dr. Richard does look up, his expression clearly annoyed. "Exactly! And he wasn't trying to kidnap Zahra. He was trying to bring her to Sabera. But, no, that became a bungled mess and then..."

"Sabera couldn't leave town." I finally get it. "Without Zahra, she was stuck."

"Brava." Lilla claps her hands. "And now that we're all caught up...Where is the solemn-faced munchkin? Because this place is about to become very crowded."

I scowl. This is the second time she's pushed for Zahra. And I don't like feeling rushed. Especially as I still have doubts about so many things. Up to and including everything.

"Police and ambulance will be here shortly," Roberta speaks up. She has her cell phone out. "Daryl and Aliah need immediate medical attention. And as for them...Well, better someone else's problem than ours."

She stares at the two trussed-up Taliban fighters. I would like them to be someone else's problem as well. My gaze automatically goes to Lilla, as our official international woman of mystery.

She's staring at Sabera with a strange look on her face. Almost like regret.

Sabera raises a hand, rubs her forehead. Once, twice, harder.

I start to get a very bad feeling about things, just as Dr. Richard clambers to his feet, looking equally concerned.

"Sabera?" he asks sharply.

Her head comes up. She looks at him, almost surprised. Her mouth, opening, closing, opening.

A sudden wrenching gasp, as if she can't get enough air, will never get enough air...

She pitches forward at Lilla's feet.

"Sabera!" Dr. Richard is there, rolling her over, feeling for a pulse. "She's not breathing. What did you do?" Then, shouting straight at Lilla, "*What did you do!*"

He's already starting chest compressions, while the rest of us stare at Lilla in shock. He's right. Lilla did something, had to be...I catch a glimpse of a large, surprisingly ornate piece of jewelry on her finger. A woman who carries a pistol up her sleeve and a dagger in her shoes. Why not also a poisoned ring on her finger?

Kurtz is now on his feet, homing in.

Just in time for Lilla's snub-nosed gun to make an appearance.

"I wouldn't get any closer if I were you."

"You didn't have to do this!" I can't even...Sabera. We found her. We saved her. And now *this*?

"She is the key," Lilla states softly. "Come now, poppet. They're never going to stop looking for her. The first time they succeeded, it cost Sabera her husband. And next time? Who do you think they'll hurt then?"

Zahra. I almost get it. But I can't accept it.

"You killed her!" Dr. Richard is raging. He's still working chest compressions, but his movements are growing weaker. Sabera's eyes. Fixed. Dilated.

I think I'm going to be ill.

"There's a cost to secrets," Lilla murmurs, almost apologetically. "Even her mother understood, some things are best never to be discovered. I'd hoped Maryam had taken it all with her to the grave. I'm sorrier than you can imagine to realize she didn't."

"You'll pay for this," Kurtz rages. "We all saw you—"

"Do what? When? Where? I was assisting with her injuries. She took a turn for the worse. Terribly sorry. Such things happen."

I can't...I can't...

"She was pregnant. You killed both of them."

Lilla pauses with one foot through the destroyed sliders. "Oh, poppet, don't believe everything you read."

Then she's gone, slipping back into the shadows.

While sirens split the distance.

Daryl begins to moan.

And Dr. Richard gently gathers up Sabera's lifeless body and cradles it against his chest.

"I'm sorry, brother," Kurtz offers softly.

I have to turn away.

I can't take any more of his pain.

I can't take any more of my own.

I ease over to Aliah's side. We sit together and wait for this nightmare to end.

CHAPTER 47

THE NEXT FEW HOURS PASS in a blur. Police, EMTs, Detective Marc. Me scrambling to check on Petunia, who, fortunately, seems no worse for the wear. I coax her into her room, strawberries all the way, as first responders and spiky lizards don't mix.

Marge gets to stay in the guest bedroom, basking in her new, larger digs with the door firmly shut. I manage to wrestle up eight out of twelve baby pythons. Having done my research beforehand, I set up heat lamps to attract the remaining four. Which may or may not work. But then Bart isn't exactly the type to complain about a stray snake slithering across his bed. What we've done to his house, on the other hand...

Speaking of which, Bart must've finally checked the video feeds from his home cameras, which earns me an immediate call.

I'm not in the mood to explain things I don't have the words to explain. Just, "Everyone's okay. All good. Well, not Daryl."

More irate chatter.

I provide a rough assessment of Daryl's condition, which hospital. Bart demands to know name of doctor, surgeon, pretty much the entire board of directors. Way above my pay grade. He clicks off, I'm guessing to rustle up the trauma surgeon of his choice. What is it Daryl had said? Bart takes care of his own.

Please let that be the case.

Dr. Richard asks to ride in the ambulance with Sabera's body. Dead, apparently, is not dead, until the authorized official makes it so. I don't want to know. I can't even...

Daryl is rushed away, as well as Aliah.

EMTs gaze at me with concern. I keep waving them off, shaking my head. I catch a brief glimpse of myself in a hall mirror. Twin tracks of gore down both sides of my face. I give my attacker points for symmetry. I look like a clown crying rivers of blood.

Then there's the puncture wound on my neck, my shoulder.

I don't pause, I don't consider.

My outside matches my inside; I'm wounded all over.

Furtive calls from Genni. Given the hour, Zahra is sound asleep in the front of Genni's truck, which Genni is apparently driving around aimlessly, waiting for the all clear.

It makes me testy with Detective Marc, who's in a foul mood of his own, till we're nearly shouting at each other. What the fuck happened?

Ask his sister.

Are we seriously that stupid?

Ask his sister.

He stops speaking to me sooner versus later. I don't complain.

Two uniformed officers lead our intruders away, already looking way out of their league. I'm guessing it won't last for long. FBI, CIA, DOD, hell, some organization with initials bigger than TPD is bound to take over.

It's not my problem. None of this is my problem. I'm here to locate Sabera Ahmadi.

Who just died on my watch.

I roam the compound over and over again, the drying blood on my face making my cheeks itch.

Finally, I sit outside Petunia's room, just a girl and her iguana, while we wait for all the assorted experts to get the hell out.

Finally, as the last official departs...

Genni returns with Zahra, easing the slumbering girl out of the front of her truck, cradling her in her arms. A four-year-old child who's now lost her mother and her father, not to mention the damage done to Aliah, whom she trusted, and Daryl, whom she adored.

I feel like a total failure, fraud, failure all over again. I feel...

I can't do this. I shouldn't have done this. Who am I trying to fool?

"Now what?" Genni asks.

And I realize our next problem.

LILLA ASKED POINTEDLY for Zahra twice. Zahra, who remembers everything, including her grandmother's cryptic matrices and her mother's more recent riddle.

Sabera may be gone, but Zahra...

Lilla knows about Zahra. Lilla, who's been here.

And other members of the Habib–Taliban cabal? I have no idea.

But Zahra, beautiful, sweet, precious Zahra.

I'm exhausted, concussed, traumatized, but in a curious sort of way, the most alert I've ever been. Zahra's not safe. Not here, not anywhere.

I just watched Zahra's mother die right in front of my eyes, a woman who wouldn't break for anything. I'll be damned if I can't at least protect her daughter.

With Zahra passed out between us on the massive U-shaped couch, Genni and I debate options. Zahra is vulnerable here. Zahra is vulnerable anywhere. What to do, where to go?

It's Genni who comes up with the answer.

Where do people never search?

The place they believe they've already looked.

With that, we're off and running again.

FOR ZAHRA'S SAKE as much as my own, I shower first. The cuts on my face sting, bleed more, not to mention the knife wounds to my throat, my shoulder. Afterward, Genni inspects the damage.

"You probably need stitches," she announces. We both know that's not going to happen, so she makes judicious use of butterfly closures instead. She has a steady, adept hand. I wonder how many of her own wounds she's tended over the years. Is there anyone who goes through life without accruing a patchwork of scars?

Given my specialty is supposedly human nature, I search through Zahra's backpack. Sure enough, the bottom of a side pouch, a single house key...

This is it.

"You shouldn't stay here," I advise Genni. "Someone might still come looking."

"Honey, I don't run, I don't hide. Rusty blades, remember? Let 'em try."

I want to share her bravado. Mostly I feel eviscerated. Generally my searches end in identifying the dead. Only two have resulted in finding the living. But this, discovering the living to watch her die...

I can't do this ever again.

Zahra, sweet, exhausted, gray-eyed child.

Genni loads her back up in her vehicle. She drives us to our destination, stands watch as I work the key, pop open the front door.

A final wave.

I can tell Genni's trying to hold strong. It's easier to fight for yourself than to fear for others.

We can't linger, however, which might risk drawing attention.

Genni departs as quickly as she arrived.

And I carry Zahra's disoriented, half-conscious form over the threshold of her family's apartment. Full circle. At least tomorrow, the girl will wake up in her own bed, even if it's to a world that will never be the same again.

I will have to tell her about her mother. Her father. Aliah. Daryl. How do I find those words? Good news, four-year-old kid who remembers everything. You're still alive. Everyone you love, however...

And where do we go from here?

I don't have the answers. My cheeks hurt.

I tuck Zahra into bed. Her eyes open wide, peer deep into mine. She doesn't ask about anything or anyone. Her hand reaches out. Very lightly, she touches the bandages on my face.

And I swear, in that moment, she knows everything.

Zahra closes her eyes, rolls onto her side, curls into a ball.

I gently close her bedroom door, then take up position on the sofa.

All I want to do is sleep. Close my eyes, let the world, and all my failings, drift away. Instead, I will myself to stay awake. I must stand guard. It's the least Zahra deserves.

Just in time for the front door to burst open.

Spymaster Lilla strides brazenly into the Ahmadis' apartment. And she is not alone.

IT TAKES ME at least a minute. If not two or three. Because I'm not an international woman of mystery, and in my world, people who die generally stay dead.

But now:

Lilla, Sabera, and Dr. Richard.

I say what first pops into my head. "Thank God. And I fucking hate all of you!"

Lilla positively beams. Sabera and Dr. Richard at least appear chagrined.

I don't have the patience.

"I took a dagger for you and am doing everything in my power to protect your child. Start talking, and don't stop till I'm fully satisfied."

"Habib found me," Sabera begins apologetically. "And if he knows, others know."

"The key is still alive and now resides in Tucson." I'm almost this smart.

"They won't stop," Lilla agrees seriously. "This would be the beginning, not the end."

"Unless you're dead. And in fact, there are witnesses to your death."

Sabera shrugs uncomfortably. Dr. Richard has a hand on her shoulder. "Not our first choice," he provides. "But given the options..."

"And your brother?"

"You know how you keep a secret a secret? By keeping it a secret."

I want to punch someone. But on the other hand, I was just wishing if only Sabera could still be alive.

"I don't get it," I manage finally. "All the smoke and mirrors; I'm not cut out for this spy shit. Are you pregnant or not?" I finally ask.

"Isaad's memory will live on," Sabera answers, which I think means yes.

"Are you crazy or not?"

"My struggles are genuine. When I first saw Habib standing alive on the sidewalk here, I so wanted to believe that was another hallucination versus the ghost in my head. But Dr. Richard and Dr. Porway have been working together on my care. I have challenges. With the proper regimen, however, I do better than I've possibly let on."

"Because it's easier for people to think you're crazy? Let them doubt or underestimate you. Which is why you released her medical records?" I stare at Lilla, then scowl at Dr. Richard. "But also took them back."

"Covering all bases," Dr. Richard says, while Lilla states:

"Warring on all fronts."

"You people are terrible," I inform them. Then, because their actions were not without merit: "What now?"

"I'm dead," Sabera states. "I must stay dead."

"Fair enough."

"I've arranged transport for Sabera and Zahra to the UK," Lilla inserts smoothly. "We returned here merely to gather some belongings, then determine how best to grab the child in the morning."

I roll my eyes.

"Sabera and Zahra will be safe with me," Lilla continues unabashedly.

"A last favor to your friend."

"Something like that."

"You really loved Maryam."

"Something like that."

"And Farshid?" I have to ask, my gaze going to Sabera. "I'm still confused. Is your brother alive or dead, because you only know half of the rare earth elements puzzle. Correct?"

Lilla answers that question as well. "I have searched for the past four years. To the best of my knowledge, Farshid died during the fall of Kabul."

"But you implied you saw him grabbing Aliah!"

"Think of it as high art," Lilla provides. "Direction. Misdirection. Followed by direction. Misdirection. Resulting in..."

"No one knowing what the hell to believe."

"Now you're getting it."

I had previously vowed never to work for a serial killer again. Now I add spy to the list.

"But half a set of coordinates is still better than no coordinates," Dr. Richard continues. "The Taliban would love to have even that much, and of course, no one wants them to have a head start on locating such a valuable resource. The British government has incentive to keep Sabera safe."

I gaze from Sabera to Dr. Richard to Sabera again. He stands close to her, clearly protective. And perhaps she leans slightly into him, but...Another place, another time, I think. Which must echo Dr. Richard's own thoughts, as he flushes.

"I'm sorry for your troubles," Sabera says.

"You didn't ask for me to get involved," I allow grudgingly. "And it's not a terrible thing to be so loved. All Isaad and Aliah wanted was for you to be safe. You've made their wishes come true."

Sabera acknowledges my words with a slight nod.

"What do I tell Aliah?" I ask, though I'm pretty sure I know the answer.

"You cannot," Sabera begins.

Lilla all but flashes her pistol again.

"All right, all right, got it. Aliah, Daryl, Genni. They will raise a glass in your honor each year, I'm sure."

Sabera appears miserable again. She crosses to a small side table, opens the top drawer, and pulls out a batch of ragged-looking notebook pages, each folded into thirds and meticulously tied together with a ribbon. "I would like you to have this," she states abruptly, thrusting the bundle at me.

I take it reluctantly.

"I've been documenting," she begins, "moments of my life before the Taliban came. Letters to Zahra, trying to explain what happened and how much I love her, should the worst happen. It is not the greatest reward to bestow upon someone who has sacrificed so much on my behalf, but perhaps it will help you understand my journey. The choices I made. The true gift you have given me."

I'm honestly dumbstruck. "I can't take this. These writings are for your daughter—"

"Thanks to you, she will have me. I think she would agree that is a much better result."

My hands start to shake. Tears sting my eyes. I clutch the tied pages close to my chest, honestly too choked up to murmur a reply.

I've never...I can't...

I wonder if my own mother had ever thought of doing such a thing, and I wish that she had. Because there's nothing I would like more, now that she's gone, than to hear her speaking to me, even if it were only words on a page.

"We are in agreement?" Lilla arches a brow.

"I saw nothing. I know nothing," I acknowledge. "That's my story and I'm sticking to it."

"Always liked you, poppet."

"Always terrified of you, Lilla No Last Name."

That earns me a grin.

"And now?" she states crisply.

I can take a hint. I rise slowly off the sofa, nearly staggering from exhaustion.

"Tell Zahra she's my favorite four-year-old." I don't have to ask that she remember me, or Daryl or Genni. We all know she will. I just hope someday those memories will make her smile.

Dr. Richard has a vehicle tucked just around the corner.

Another awkward round of farewells.

Then we leave Sabera, Zahra, and their new handler to the business of disappearing.

Dr. Richard drives me back to the compound.

He doesn't speak the entire way, and neither do I.

EPILOGUE

I N THE WEEKS THAT COME, Genni and I hunker down. She arranges for the glass sliders to be replaced, then embarks on the mother of all deep cleanings, from scrubbing floors to shampooing rugs to dry cleaning drapes. Petunia and I learn to move out of her way or risk getting vacuumed.

It takes both Genni and me to get Marge out of the guest room, as the enormous Burmese python is both peeved at us and genuinely happy with her new digs. Finding the remaining baby balls proves much easier.

Out of sheer guilt, I finally engage in the care and feeding of snakes. I'm not a herper. No matter how many times I gird my loins and head into the reptile wing, it doesn't get easier; I'm still not convinced any snake is beautiful or has exquisite markings.

Petunia, on the other hand, has become one of my favorite roommates. Thus far, she's resisted biting or clawing me, which puts her ahead of Piper the feral cat. And she's definitely less frightening than Wolfie, the ginormous wolf spider who liked to creep around my cabin at night, snacking on unwary geckos. I do still miss my shy ghost-crab neighbor, Crabby, who brought me flowers.

While Daryl requires more time to recover from a belly full of buckshot, Aliah is released after twenty-four hours. She doesn't offer any more information about the marking on her abdomen. She's fine, she tells us when we try to coax her into staying at the compound so we can fuss over her in person. She just wants to go home.

I stop by in the afternoons and brew her green tea. After a bit of research, I splurge on an extremely nice saffron tea as a special treat. I seem to be operating mostly from a place of guilt these days, but at least I'm operating.

Aliah, of course, drills me about Zahra—where is she, what happened, what do I mean she's already gone? I can't even look at her as I mumble some cockamamie story about Dr. Richard having contacted Sabera's family in London and their immediate desire to take in their long-lost granddaughter. Dr. Richard personally flew her over. Zahra'll be safer there than here, etc., etc.

Aliah isn't happy. *She's* Zahra's family, too, except, of course, no one knows that.

Lilla, continuing her role as a behind-the-scenes master manipulator, organizes an immediate "burial" for Sabera. Following a brief tussle with the ME's office, as per Islamic custom, a body is to be buried as quickly as possible. Captain Kurtz arranges for Isaad's remains to be interred beside her. The gravesites provide comfort to Aliah, and I join her several times to pay my respects to Isaad, a man I never met but who clearly loved his family deeply.

The wounds on my face graduate from butterfly Band-Aids to long, thin scabs that Genni swears give me a rakish charm. I find myself fingering the raised welts in the middle of the night, when my nightmares are too vivid and my fears too real.

I stare at my phone a lot. Waiting for it to ring. Knowing full well I could call. Long, drawn-out debates with myself, the universe in general.

I failed, but not really.

I should move on, but I don't know where.

Maybe it's time to give this gig a rest. What else would I do?

As long as Bart's away, I don't have to make any decisions. While I might've taken this job primarily to enable me to search for Sabera Ahmadi, pet sitting remains my responsibility.

The house feels off without Daryl's oversized presence. When he goes from the hospital to some chi-chi rehab center coordinated by Boy Wonder, Genni and I take to staying up later and later, sharing stories of her days on the street, my own misspent youth. We laugh a lot, marvel at the fickleness of a universe that allowed us to survive, when we probably shouldn't have. One night we do mani pedis. Another she gives me a total makeover, complete with the Mary Ann pigtail wig. I look pretty good.

She offers to take me to her favorite bars, but I'm not strong enough to be around booze right now, and I know it. Instead, Genni makes us elaborate mocktails with dried strawberries and fresh basil or sliced apples and cinnamon sticks in sparkly water. Some of them are pretty good.

Then one morning I get up, step out onto the patio, and there's Bart, lounging in the middle of the pool on the inflatable unicorn.

Just like that, my time is up.

HOW DO YOU discover little-known, generally unreported, often totally overlooked missing persons cases? How do you not.

There are entire websites now dedicated to calling attention to the vanished at-risk, minority, and socially marginalized members of our society, from small children on up. The numbers make for staggering and somber reading.

Then there are community forums and various chat rooms where neighbors, loved ones, family friends beg for assistance.

Bart asks me to stay for Daryl's homecoming in a week, so I use that time to start reading and reviewing. I tell myself if nothing catches my attention, that'll be a sign. But as is often the case, dozens of profiles immediately tug at my heart.

A fourteen-year-old boy here, a seven-year-old girl there, a young mother, a struggling college student. Black, Hispanic, Indigenous. Missing weeks, months, years.

There's a whole world out there many will never know, and most will choose never to see.

I start to get that hum in the back of my mind, that jittery feeling in my limbs. Memphis, Austin, no, maybe Oakland. I've never been good at turning a blind eye. Maybe it comes from years of living on the fringes myself, or spending well over a decade sitting in church basements with fellow addicts where even when we look nothing at all alike, we know we are exactly the same.

Some people go through life thinking, why should that be my problem? I guess I'm more likely to think why not?

I show Petunia photos of smiling children and selfie-snapping teens. I read to her stats on various cities and communities.

By the third evening, she blows me off to watch *The Simpsons* with Bart. I take the hint.

I spend my last full day in the kitchen with Genni, cooking up a banquet of Daryl's favorite foods. Aliah joins us with a feast of Afghan treats from her store, including firni pudding. I don't care if Daryl's the one who's spent weeks recovering from a grievous injury. I grab a bowl of the rose-petal custard first.

Roberta shows up with both her husband and Detective Marc in tow, bearing a platter of tamales and jars of homemade salsa. Her husband proves to be much smaller than I would've pictured, perhaps even slightly nerdy. And yet there's a quiet steadiness to him that's immediately compelling.

Daryl might match Roberta quick step by quick step through a mad, passionate tango, but Luca is clearly her port in the storm. I get that.

By the time the guest of honor arrives, the kitchen smells unbelievable, and even Petunia, sitting on Bart's lap, is practically vibrating from the pent-up energy.

Then Daryl. Moving a little slower. Definitely a tad weaker. And yet still absolutely, positively Daryl.

Roberta bursts into tears. Her husband pats her back while her brother rolls his eyes.

A round of genuinely heartfelt hugs, then Daryl being Daryl says, "Let's eat!"

LATER, PEOPLE ASK me where I'm going next. Roberta votes for the Austin case. Genni's always wanted to visit Memphis. Detective Marc tells me to get a real job.

Bart merely nods a lot.

Daryl never stops eating.

Aliah loads me up with bundles of tea. I think life is pretty good.

In the morning, I will wake up, head to the bus depot, and, probably based on the first bus I see, make my final decision.

By the time we wrap for the evening, I'm humming to myself as I head to my bungalow for my last night of unparalleled luxury.

I'm just stepping through the door when my phone rings. After staring at it so many times, the sound startles me.

I glance at the screen. It's not from the area code I was expecting, and yet as his name flashes across my screen, I find myself smiling.

"Hey," I answer softly, cradling the phone against my shoulder. "It's so good to hear from you."

And just like that, I know where I'm going next.

ACKNOWLEDGMENTS

Dear Reader,

As most of you know, I'm an avid traveler. From hanging out with penguins in Antarctica to swimming with sea turtles in Palmyra to hiking with wallabies in Australia, I love to see it all! Exploring the world enables me to refill the creative well, while also introducing me to incredible people doing amazing things. Which oftentimes inspires my next thriller!

Case in point: in March 2023 I spent a week playing with gray whales in Baja California's Magdalena Bay (highly recommend!). On board the Lindblad vessel, I met Dana Narter and Ed Baruch from Tucson, Arizona, who volunteer with the Jewish Family & Children's Services of Southern Arizona to assist with resettling Afghan refugees.

The more they described the challenges facing their latest family—from how to navigate American mass transit to incorrect Social Security cards messing up school enrollment to the sheer enormity of adapting to an entirely new country while still mourning the life you used to live, but is no more...

I knew I had my next Frankie Elkin project.

So, bearing in mind that all mistakes are mine and mine alone, first up, I offer my complete and utter gratitude to Dana Narter and Ed Baruch, who personally took me around Tucson while also introducing me to an entire world of resettlement agencies and refugee communities I had no idea even existed. Being a fiction writer, I have dramatized many details. But so many of the issues encountered by Sabera and her family in this novel are sadly quite real.

Along the same vein, I never could've written Sabera and Isaad's story without the assistance of so many Afghan refugees courageously sharing their (often harrowing) experiences with me. This is by far some of the hardest research I've ever done, and I'm a writer who loves to learn. But whereas in the past, most of my pre-book work involved speaking with experts about a specific, well-defined process—how to track a person using GPS coordinates, how to survive in the wilderness, how to train as a sniper—this was a study in the human experience. I ended interviews often inspired and amazed by the resilience of the people involved. And several times, I ended in tears, overwhelmed by the sheer enormity of their loss.

I appreciate everyone who shared their stories with me, many of whom prefer to remain nameless. I respect your wishes and cherish our time together.

Several key people, however, were particularly involved in helping me understand Afghanistan and the refugee experience. I am enormously grateful to:

Shamsadin Zamani, former civil prosecutor from the Herat province of Afghanistan and recent arrival in the United States, who spoke candidly of having to rebuild a life for his family in a new country that doesn't recognize his education or expertise. Afghan hospitality is the stuff of legend, and Shams is no exception. He not only invited me into his home to meet his family but personally prepared a feast of authentic dishes to share. That afternoon is one I will never forget, given the great food, lively camaraderie, and inspiring reminder that even people from entirely different corners of the world still hope for exactly the same thing—a better future for our children.

Also in the incredibly kind and gracious category: Kosh Sadat, former brigadier general in the Afghan special forces, and now officially a United States citizen! Congratulations, Kosh! Kosh tirelessly answered so many of my questions on language, names, and culture (do Afghans believe in ghosts, how do Afghans mourn, what is an example of a traditional greeting). He did his best to educate me on a country that remains a complex mix of different languages, cultures, and terrains. Kosh is an excellent teacher. I could still be a better student. Any detail you love, that's all Kosh. All the glaring mistakes, however, are purely mine. Next up, Ritiek Rafi—a leader in the Afghan community in Tucson, as well as a real estate agent who now works with many refugee families making their first home purchase in the US. Ritiek shared her experience fleeing Afghanistan the first time the Taliban took over. Her personal and professional success since then is nothing short of inspiring. Also, Ritiek, thank you for the incredible lunch at Kabul Corner. Mantou has become one of my new favorite dishes, and much like Daryl and Frankie, I still dream of firni pudding.

(Just gotta add, trying out Afghan food has been one of the most delicious research projects ever! Coming in a close second—sampling Haitian cuisine for Frankie's first adventure, *Before She Disappeared*. Yum.)

Finally, a shout-out to a fellow thriller writer and absolutely amazing man, Del Roll. Del is a retired army officer *and* retired CIA operations officer who served multiple tours in Afghanistan. Not only did he share his experiences to aid another novelist, but he shared his contacts, too. Many readers ask me if authors are a competitive, backstabbing group of archrivals. Umm, no. Just ask Del.

To better understand the resettlement process, I interviewed three amazing and committed individuals who have dedicated years of their lives to jumping through hoops, scouring the bottom of the bucket, and then working a minor miracle to finally get the job done. My deepest appreciation and admiration to Jeniffer Acevedo Castro, former community engagement coordinator at Jewish Family & Children's Services of Southern Arizona, who walked me through the resettlement process, soup to nuts; to Nathan Fenoglio, who opened my eyes to the very real housing crunch in Tucson and elsewhere; and finally to Brooke Benge, Lutheran Social Services, SW, whose poignant explanation of each little step and every giant challenge involved in establishing an entirely new life in an entirely new country left me reeling for days.

Again, all mistakes are mine and mine alone.

So, refugee camps. This was definitely one of the most difficult subjects I've ever investigated. I read some genuinely heartbreaking first-person accounts written by doctors who volunteered at various migrant facilities. I also interviewed a volunteer who spent time at the Moria Refugee Camp, Lesbos, a place where conditions grew so grim, Pope Francis infamously likened it to a concentration camp. The volunteer spoke in honor of all the brave residents of Lesbos. The camp burned down in 2020, in yet another tragic turn. I'd never heard of Moria; now I will never forget.

If reading about refugee camps made for some dark days, then learning about No One Left Behind brought me the light. This very real nonprofit continues to work tirelessly to evacuate deserving interpreters and other eligible SIV applicants from Afghanistan. Thank you, Andrew Sullivan, chief advocacy officer of No One Left Behind, for explaining your mission as well as your challenges. In the case of this novel, all dramatic license is mine and mine alone (and yes, I took some). Readers, you should definitely check out the real deal at www.nooneleft.org.

My deep appreciation to Sara Walker, MD, psychiatrist, for providing a basic overview of PTSD, postpartum depression, and psychosis, even when I wasn't smart enough to use those terms or have any idea what might actually be wrong with my character, just definitely something. She went above and beyond, providing treatment options for not only here in the States, but also what might be done at an underresourced refugee camp. Again, it's highly possible if not downright probable that I exercised dramatic license with the details. What's the point of writing fiction if you can't have a little fun?

Which brings us to more fun! Math puzzles! Thank you, Michelle Capozzoli, PhD, University of New Hampshire, Department of Mathematics and Statistics. Michelle likes to drag me up mountains. In return, I torture her with book problems, including, hey, could you devise a code a four-year-old would be able to re-create but an adult wouldn't easily be able to decipher? Thank heavens Michelle is very good at what she does. And here's to the next hiking adventure!

Another wonderful partner in crime, Timothy W. Psaledakis, who this time around provided care and feeding instructions for iguanas and snakes. He also lobbied hard on Petunia's behalf—iguanas make amazing pets. I had one that used to sit on my lap, and my personal favorite, oh yes, they absolutely love it if you rub their shoulders. Let's just say Frankie's not the only one who had to overcome her fear of reptiles during the making of this novel. See prior notes regarding dramatic license. Tim thoughtfully provided expert advice. And then there's what I did with it.

As many of you know, it's become my tradition to auction off character naming rights in honor of local charities. I and the Conway Area Humane Society are very grateful to Mark Porway, who won on behalf of his wife, Cindy Porway. Also, to Andrew Orsini, who used his winning bid to recognize Lilla (No Last Name), per her request. Hope you enjoy your fictional adventures.

And of course, the annual winner of the Kill a Friend, Maim a Buddy Sweepstakes at www.LisaGardner.com. Many will enter, but only one will die. Competition was fierce as always. So a huge congratulations to Daniel Manly, who nominated Staci Lynn for literary immortality, a woman he describes as having a big heart and who is always looking to help others. After that, I couldn't bring myself to kill her, so I made her an incredibly compassionate, and, yes, slightly maimed caseworker. Hope you love the novel, Staci, and I wish you and Daniel an amazing future.

Finally, under the care and feeding of authors Betsy Eliot and Lori Lotti, thank you for letting me turn ladies' weekend into a let's plot Lisa's next novel extravaganza. I couldn't bring back everyone from the dead that you wanted, but it wasn't for lack of trying. Also, to Glenda Davis, Andrea Masters, and Elaine Stockbridge for our fabulous dominoes nights. Which also often led to yet more book assistance. Clearly it takes a village.

In that spirit, I must thank Grace for the final sentence in Chapter 1. I still don't think that qualifies as having written the entire book, given, you know, the number of sentences in a full-length novel. But it is a damn good sentence. You win. This time.

As for what happens next...

I'm once again off to see the world. First Patagonia, followed shortly thereafter by a trip through the Panama Canal. What will I see? Who will I meet? And which will become the basis of my next thriller? Dear Reader, stay tuned.

ABOUT THE AUTHOR

Lisa Gardner, a #1 *New York Times* bestselling thriller novelist, began her career in food service, but after catching her hair on fire numerous times, she took the hint and focused on writing instead. A self-described research junkie, she has transformed her interest in police procedure and criminal minds into a streak of internationally acclaimed novels, published across thirty countries. Her novel *The Neighbor* won Best Hardcover Novel from the International Thriller Writers. She has also been honored for her work with animal rescue and at-risk children. An avid hiker, gardener, and cribbage player, Lisa lives with her family in New England.

Bringing a book from manuscript to what you are reading is a team effort, and Penguin Random House would like to thank everyone at Century who helped to publish *Kiss Her Goodbye*.

PUBLISHER
Selina Walker

EDITORIAL
Conor Hodges
Charlotte Osment
Mary Karayel

DESIGN
Jason Smith

PRODUCTION
Helen Wynn-Smith

INVENTORY
Lizzy Moyes

UK SALES
Alice Gomer
Emily Harvey
Kirsten Greenwood
Jade Unwin
Phoenix Curland

INTERNATIONAL SALES
Anna Curvis
Barbora Sabolova

PUBLICITY
Rachel Kennedy

MARKETING
Lucy Hall

AUDIO
James Keyte
Meredith Benson
Nile Faure-Bryan